Praise for Moira Forsyth

Waiting for Lindsay

'Forsyth writes with warmth and sensitivity, exploring the ways in which an ordinary family is changed by tragedy.'
The Times

'An enthralling read.'
Family Circle

'Haunting and evocative.'
The Yorkshire Post

'Haunting.'
Inverness Courier

'Washes out the dark nooks and crannies of loss and love.'
Highland News

'An evocative, atmospheric read.'
The Press and Journal

Moira Forsyth is an author and editor. She has two grown-up children and lives in the Highlands of Scotland.

Also by Moira Forsyth

Waiting for Lindsay
David's Sisters
Tell Me Where You Are

The Treacle Well

Moira Forsyth

SANDSTONEPRESS
HIGHLAND | SCOTLAND

First published in Great Britain
And the United States of America by
Sandstone Press Ltd
Dochcarty Road
Dingwall
Ross-shire
IV15 9UG
Scotland.

www.sandstonepress.com

The publisher acknowledges support from Creative Scotland
towards publication of this volume.

ISBN: 978-1-910124-27-7
ISBNe: 978-1-910124-28-4

Jacket design by Antigone Konstantinidou, London
Typeset by Iolaire Typesetting, Newtonmore.
Printed and bound by Totem, Poland

For Linda

Acknowledgements

I am grateful to Dorothy Christie and Sheila Barclay, my thoughtful readers, and to Candia McWilliam for perceptive comments and support. Thanks as always to RLD for editing, encouragement and having faith.

Contents

	Going Backwards	1
I	The Treacle Well	5
II	Into the Forest	97
III	The Crack in the World	137
IV	Good Wives	189
V	The Golden Key	323
	Into the Future	398

Going Backwards

2012

Esther dreamed she was going backwards, time was going backwards. Back and back, faster the further she went, through her own unfurling life.

Leaves leap from the ground, reattach themselves to trees, soften and colour, blaze briefly, turn green, then begin to curl up, tighter and tighter, into bud. The sun falls and rises, comes and goes behind scudding clouds. Buildings vanish and older, more complicated structures, then simpler ones, take their place. The sea recedes, the snow softly, softly floats up into a leaden sky.

Once, she was a person who always moved forward, anticipating the future. She did it on the back of the comfortable dolphin sleep, eight hours a night, and only less when she had to get up early to catch a train or deliver husband or child to the station or airport, or a waiting bus for a school expedition.

That was in the days when she had trains to catch, the days when she had a husband and the children were still at home. Of course you move forward when you are always looking ahead, when the only things you care about are burning now, or lie in wait.

She had grown up in a family of five with grandparents, parents, uncles and aunts. Then there was Jack, and they made their own family, with children, cats and dogs, and people coming and going all the time. She was always at the centre of something. Now she was alone, walled by quiet. The remaining animal was a cat so elderly she rarely moved from her chair in the kitchen.

Pressing the button that lit up the face of the alarm clock, she saw it was ten to four, a bad time: too early to get up, too late for any worthwhile rest to be had.

It was cold in the bedroom; the temperature had dropped in the night. Her arm, moving from the clock to the radio lying on the other side of the bed, Jack's side, was chilled, and when she had righted the radio, still hissing faintly, and turned up the sound a little, the arm brought back under the covers seemed to spread its coldness to the rest of her.

The voice coming from the radio more intelligibly now was telling her about a project for women in Afghanistan, something about education. There was comfort in this remote, calm voice, relaying information which could make no difference to her life or cause her grief, conjuring mild interest only. She closed her eyes, the cold arm thawing by her side. Her feet were very cold too, but if she got up to fill a hot water bottle, she would be wide awake with no more hope of sleep. She wouldn't sleep anyway if she went on being cold. She lay still, the dilemma floating in her head. Despite the cold, she began to doze.

The shrilling of the telephone jerked her awake and she started up, heart hammering. In her blind haste she knocked the telephone off the bedside table, her groping hand unable to trace the noise, still calling her in the dark. By the time she had put on the lamp and fumbled under the bed where the phone had slid over polished floorboards, the ringing had stopped and the answerphone cut in, her own detached voice giving way to a *beep* as the caller hung up without leaving a message.

She was shaking with shock and cold. Tracing the call, she found it was a number she did not know. A mistake, that was all. The clock told her it was still only half past four. Rising with a sigh, she pulled on her dressing gown. At least she could get warm, even if there was no point in trying for sleep.

Even in the kitchen the chill of an icy February night had penetrated. She put water in the kettle and set it on the hot plate of the Rayburn, holding her hands over it for a moment to heat them. The cat looked up, blinked, then tucked her head down again, curling her tail over her eyes.

February.

Margaret had given her a calendar with a seasonal recipe for each month. It was still at January with Scotch Broth, a soup for winter days. As she waited for the kettle, she turned it over to the next month. Lamb hotpot with dumplings and curly kale. This was not a calendar for people on a diet. She was tempted to look at July, but suspected summer pudding or strawberry trifle.

February.

She hung the calendar on its hook again. 'It's over a year,' she told the cat. She had got through a whole year, the first year that everyone told her would be the worst. Everyone except Margaret who said the second year after being divorced was terrible, it all became real and permanent then, and she assumed widowhood would be like that too.

'Well, thanks,' Esther had said, 'You're not cheering me up.'

'No.' Margaret was frank. 'I know. But it's better to be warned, don't you think?'

All through the past year, she had done everything for the first time without Jack. Would doing it for the second time be worse?

She sat on the chair next to the cat's. Much worse, she realised, with a yank of despair. Now it's real, it's forever and the whole

3

world will expect me not to mind so much. They will expect me to get on with it, I've had my year of mourning, the sympathy, the flowers, the invitations, help with the garden and the house. I need to get out of deepest black and change to grey or purple or whatever it was they used to do in Victorian times. The year is up.

I've survived it, and that's what matters, isn't it?

The familiarity of the kitchen had begun to soothe her. My house, she thought, surprised all over again that this was how it was. My kitchen, my home. Here I am, the inheritor, with everything that means. It took an effort these days not to concentrate only on the year of grieving, the year she had just survived, but for once, her mind was travelling farther back.

When she made herself get into bed again for an hour or so, since daylight would be a long time coming (rain was spattering against the windows, a dreary day beginning), armed with a hot water bottle, she did drift towards sleep, and in that half dreaming state, encountered shadows, since she would not call them ghosts.

I

The Treacle Well

1958–1961

'Once upon a time there were three little sisters,'
the Dormouse began in a great hurry; 'and their
names were Elsie, Lacie, and Tillie; and they lived
at the bottom of a well – '

Alice's Adventures in Wonderland, Lewis Carroll

The New House

1958

i

One thing Janet knew. There would be no birthday party for the little one if it was left to her parents. Gordon would never think of such a thing and if Diana had thought of it, it would have been too much trouble. She did supply a bottle of whisky for the adults, seeing it no doubt as a celebration for them, rather than her baby. She still called Margaret 'the baby'. Another black mark: Margaret at twelve months was an individual, however timid and quiet.

There had been raised voices downstairs, a rare thing in this house. Janet was ashamed when she saw Esther's anxious face peering through the banisters. They were still living at Braeside, and although her parents had gone to bed long ago, she was aware of their presence. The house in Aberdeen was almost ready; she and Harry would be moving in three weeks.

'Why is Daddy shouting?'

'He's not, it's all right. Go back to bed.'

'*He is, Mummy!*' Esther looked disapproving. 'You was as well.'

'Were,' said Janet. 'You *were.*'

Esther looked confused, as well she might.

'Never mind, come on, I'll tuck you in.'

Louise was sitting up in bed drawing on a toy blackboard on her lap with pink chalk. The chalk had also transferred itself to the sheet and Louise's hands and face. Patiently, Janet cleaned her up, removed the tempting toys to her own bedroom, and tucked both children in again.

'Are we having the party?' Esther asked.

'Yes, tomorrow afternoon.'

'Good.'

'Jelly?' Louise asked.

'And ice cream. And cake.'

'Hurray!' they cried.

'Hush. Go to sleep.' She kissed them and stood up.

'I need a drink of water.'

Louise always pushed her mother a step too far; Esther could have told her not to bother. Janet was in any case distracted by a cry from the next bedroom, where Margaret was in a cot beside her parents' bed.

'Goodnight,' she said, and left the room.

'Leave the door open!' Louise shouted. Janet left a crack.

'More!'

'*Goodnight.*' She was on her way to Margaret, since there was little chance Diana would come bounding up the stairs.

Living at Braeside had of course saved rent while they bought and renovated their own house in Aberdeen, but the addition of her brother Gordon and his wife with their baby had made even this house seem crowded. Gordon had said, 'If Mum and Dad can put us up for a night or two, Margaret will get to know her cousins. And you know the folks will go to bed at sunset – they always do. We can spend a bit of time together, have a drink – you know what Mum's like.'

Now she knew why he had been so keen. He and Diana. She pushed the bedroom door open but it was jammed against one of several cases. The room was full of Diana, her clothes sprawled on the bed, the little dressing table crowded with jars of cream, lipsticks and a gold compact, a hairbrush fluffy with blonde hair, pink powder spilled on the polished wood – a mess. Janet manoeuvred herself round to the cot where Margaret stood clutching the wooden rail with one hand, a limp cloth rabbit hugged in the other. She was coughing, mouth wide open. As soon as she saw Janet she went quiet and her face, red with crying, became solemn and wary, as she waited to see what would happen next.

Janet picked her up. 'Oh,' she said, 'you're soaking. Let's get you changed. That'll help, eh?'

Margaret was used to being looked after by different people. She lay passively on the towel Janet spread on the bathroom floor while she was cleaned up, dried, and pinned into a fresh nappy. Janet talked softly all the time, but the child's steady gaze was unnerving. She was very hot; the red face, Janet thought, was not just because she'd been crying.

In the little-used farmhouse sitting-room, the rest of the adults had calmed down and were drinking Diana's whisky. When Janet joined them she said, 'Margaret was crying.'

Diana looked up but did not move from the big sofa where she leaned next to Gordon, shoes kicked off and legs in sheer nylons tucked up beneath her. 'Is she all right?'

'She is now. I changed her.'

'Oh God, another nappy.'

Janet wondered what difference this made to Diana. Since she and Gordon had arrived, she had not washed one. They were left in a bucket of water in the back porch until Janet or her mother dealt with them. Janet was going to have a washing machine in their new house; she could hardly wait.

'Do you want a drink?' Harry asked. She would not touch the whisky. 'I'll get you a sherry.'

'Just a wee one. Somebody needs to keep their wits about them, with three of them upstairs.'

Diana made a face. 'Oh, don't. I feel awful landing on you like this. I tell you what – let's go out somewhere on Sunday – maybe a nice hotel for lunch? Our treat.'

'What nice hotel?' Gordon asked. 'This isn't London, Di.'

'With the girls?' Janet could not imagine it.

'Or let me do the cooking? How about that?'

Gordon laughed. 'They haven't tried your cooking, or you wouldn't dare suggest it.'

Diana laughed too. She was never insulted, whatever anyone said. There had been some hard words earlier tonight, but Diana remained placid throughout; if she offended anyone, she had no idea of it till she was told.

'A picnic,' Diana said. 'What about that? Then there's no actual cooking and you'll get a rest, Janet.'

'In April?'

Diana laughed. 'Oh well, maybe not!'

Janet caught her husband's eye. He wouldn't say anything: *it's not my business*, he had told her last night in bed, as they talked about Gordon and Diana and the problem of Margaret. *He's your brother.* Yet he had almost lost his temper with Gordon today.

Margaret was delicate, an old-fashioned infant, pale and fragile, not at all like their own robust little girls with their polished rosy skin and dimples in their knees.

Harry brought her sherry, chestnut brown in its tiny glass. Its sweet warmth cheered her and she leaned back in the leather chair while he perched on its arm with his usual appearance of being about to fly off and do something more energetic. He was thinking about work, even in the midst of all this family drama, as well as the delays and difficulties with the new house. Could they really afford it, even with the change in his status in the firm?

'Look,' Gordon said, 'I don't want you to get the wrong end of the stick.' He moved away from Diana and leaned forward to address his sister and Harry. 'We'll take Margaret back to Ghana with us, of course we will. But she was never well in the heat and Diana's been fretting about her all the time. Until this contract's finished I can't look for a job in the UK. It pays well, it'll set us up when we come back.'

That, Harry thought, is what's really on his mind. He liked his brother-in-law but had no illusions. On the golf course, as someone to have a drink with or talk business, he was fine. But he loved his job and he was more interested in money than any of the rest of his family.

Gordon's explanation – or justification – was met with silence. There had been little sign of Diana even caring for her child, let alone fretting.

Diana, finding silence uncomfortable, said hurriedly,

'Heavens, it was just an idea. We'll have plenty of people to take care of her, you don't have to worry. I've had a lovely girl as our nanny since Margaret was three months. Pity we couldn't have taken her with us to the new job, but Gordon's going to be working a hundred miles away and we thought we should move house up country. She would have come with us, she adores Margaret, but she didn't want to leave her parents. I think she's keeping them, I think it's her wages they live on. Terrible, the poverty there,' she added, refilling her glass.

Before Janet or Harry could say anything, or refrain from

11

saying anything, before Gordon could manage to step in, the crying began again from upstairs.

'Oh dear, Gordy, will you go? I'm dead on my feet, honestly.'

'Tiddly, you mean,' Gordon said. He got up. The wailing was louder, more than the cry of a child in a strange bed, wanting her mother. If she knew enough to want her mother, Janet thought crossly.

'Ta.' Diana smiled at him, relaxing again. 'You're an angel.'

Gordon paused by the door. 'We should be raising a glass to you, Harry,' he said. 'The partnership.'

'Oh, that's old news.'

'Only a month,' Janet said. 'And it is wonderful – he's the youngest partner they've ever appointed at Mackie's.'

'I think you did mention that,' her brother teased. 'Maybe once or twice.' He winced. 'Listen to that bairn – she's not going to stop. I'd better go up.'

'It's a strange house and a strange bed, no wonder she hasn't settled,' Janet said as Gordon disappeared upstairs.

'So we really should go out – celebrate the great achievement,' Diana said.

Neither Janet nor Harry bothered to reply to this. Janet swallowed the last of her sherry, feeling the good effect of it wearing off already. Diana reached for her cigarettes, bored.

In a moment Gordon reappeared with Margaret, purple-faced but suddenly quiet in his arms. She gazed at the other adults, as if surprised to find herself among them, then, shy, buried her face in her father's shoulder.

'Oh Gordy, you shouldn't have brought her down. I've never known a nanny yet who thought that was a good idea. They're supposed to stay in bed when you put them there.'

Janet, who agreed with this in principle, said nothing.

'Put the fag out, Di,' Gordon said, 'at least while she's here. She was coughing.'

Obligingly, Margaret began to cough again, a harsh straining that went on and on, making her redder than ever.

'She's been coughing like that for ages – she's had a cold,' Diana said.

'It sounds worse now.'

Janet put her cool hands on Margaret's face, still turned away and wet with tears.

'She's awfully hot. I think she's running a temperature.'

'Should we check – have you a thermometer?'

'In the bathroom, if I haven't packed it away.'

She went to look. Gordon lowered himself onto the sofa with Margaret in his arms.

Diana sighed. 'Just what we need. What about calling a doctor?'

'It's Friday night,' Harry said. 'If you wait till morning you can take her down to the surgery.'

Margaret had begun to cough again, drawing in long gasping breaths.

'It sounds a real smoker's cough you've got, my precious,' Diana said, coughing a little herself and putting out her tongue to pick off a shred of tobacco. 'Must give it up. Bad example.'

'I don't think she's coughing because of the smoke,' Gordon said.

Janet had found a thermometer. 'Here we are – I'll pop it under her arm.'

She knew before she did it that the baby was running a high temperature, and she also knew what was likely to be wrong, having worried all week one of her own girls might pick it up. It was going round the whole area. One child had had to go into hospital because she was asthmatic. Louise was asthmatic.

13

'I think you should get her to a doctor in the morning, or call somebody out,' she said, holding up the thermometer and trying to read the mercury in the fading light. She bit her lip. 'I hope this is wrong – it's awfully high – 103.'

Diana did look worried now. 'What is it – do you know what's wrong with her?'

'I think it's whooping cough.'

Janet did the nursing. There were three weeks before the end of term, so the worst would be over by the time Caroline and Daniel came back for the school holidays. The move to the new house was postponed. Harry had had whooping cough, so he went to work; so had Gordon, who said he would go to London on his own to deal with the extension to the project he was working on in Ghana.

They had discussed vaccination. Diana thought Margaret had been immunised against whooping cough – Gordon wasn't sure – nobody knew. She had definitely had the vaccination for diphtheria and polio, they said. Janet sighed, and left them to argue, since it scarcely mattered now. Margaret was really ill, struggling to breathe. Diana began to panic. Her anxiety transferred itself to the child who cried even more when her mother held her, jigging her up and down in her arms, fruitlessly 'shushing'. Diana was clearly relieved when Janet offered to nurse her instead, taking Margaret's cot into her own bedroom. In the mornings, leaving her in bed to catch up on the sleep she had missed, Harry had breakfast along with his father-in-law and the men who had been up since milking and had already done a couple of hours' work. He sat in his suit and tie with the farm workers in their shirt sleeves and braces and nicky tams, their boots at the back door, and felt awkward, a fool in the midst of their easy banter.

In the office he was himself again, the junior partner, useful and competent. On his way home, he called at the house in Harrowden Place, so that he could walk round the empty rooms on his own and imagine his family there. It was a big house, too big perhaps, but he thought their family might grow, and he needed something to reflect his new status, the life they were going to move into, once they were in the city.

In the kitchen, the range had been cleaned; the plumber said he saw no reason they shouldn't go on using it, if they wanted to fire it up. Next to it sat a new gas cooker, since Janet had no intention of relying on a coal fired range for cooking – her idea was they'd get rid of it as soon as they could afford to refit the kitchen altogether. The longed-for washing machine sat in the scullery so that the rollers could be swung round over the deep sink to squeeze the clothes through. It was looking fine, the house, but they would still have a lot of work to do when they moved in, every room to decorate.

Upstairs was light and airy, the bedrooms square with sash windows. They all had fireplaces, but they could stuff paper up the chimneys to keep the draught out. The chimneys were all good and a bedroom fire would be needed now and then. It might be hard to heat the whole place in winter. He stood in the room that was to be decorated with flowered wallpaper for Esther and Louise, and found himself thinking it would hold three single beds if it had to, or the little box room next to it could become a nursery.

He saw it coming, that Margaret would stay with them, at least until Gordon managed to get a job back in this country. He also realised Janet was afraid to ask him directly, in case he turned the idea down flat. As if he would – there was nothing he would deny his wife. She wanted so little, content in their marriage, the

15

children, her pride in his achievements. Gordon was well paid and generous; he would make sure it cost them nothing. There was a precedent; that was what made him sure he was right.

Caroline and Daniel had stayed with his parents-in-law since their mother's death nearly fifteen years ago. When Bess died Gordon had turned to his mother to look after his nine-month-old twins. Now it seemed his second wife couldn't look after her own child.

Harry glanced at his watch. The Inverurie bus was due in fifteen minutes on the Deeside road. He should leave now to catch it. Soon, when they had settled in after the move, he would decide whether they could afford a car.

He had stopped worrying about whooping cough. Under Janet's care, Margaret was getting better, and there was no sign of their own two coming down with it. He locked the door of his new house carefully behind him and set off in the direction of the bus stop, swinging his briefcase. It was all about to begin: their family life, the good and solid future he had been planning and working for, perhaps since the day he had met Janet, during the war that already seemed to belong to another age.

ii

'You're doing a grand job, at any rate,' Celia Livingstone said, watching her three youngest grandchildren as they trooped across the yard on their way to the garden, Esther and Louise holding Margaret's hands. They were accompanied by the old dog that was past being much use to Andrew, but still looked for work. Today she was herding wee girls, Janet thought, amused at the way the collie circled, tail waving.

'Margaret's no bother.' She glanced at her mother. 'But – '

They were sitting with cups of tea on the bench by the kitchen door. It was early October, still mild, though the breeze carried a breath of autumn. Janet leaned on the rough stone wall of the house and lifted her face to the afternoon sun, closing her eyes. She had taken the girls out on the bus to Braeside Farm and the effort of managing the three of them – Louise so lively and disobedient, Margaret so whiny and still, at eighteen months, babyish – had left her feeling resentful.

'It's a pity Harry couldna come with you,' her mother said.

'Oh, he's busy, he goes to the office on Saturday mornings and he's in the middle of painting our bedroom. I thought it might be a good idea to take the bairns out of his way.'

Something in her tone alerted Celia. 'You're managing fine, though?'

'I suppose so.' How much to say? She was not in the habit of confiding in her mother and did not have Gordon's thick skin. 'I still feel Gordon and Diana should be looking after their own daughter.'

'No doubt,' Celia said, 'but until he's back from that foreign place, I dinna see what's to be done. I'm sure it's nae suitable for bairns. They keep moving and it widna be guid for her, being shifted about – they need to be settled in one place at that age.'

Janet wanted to remark that there *were* people in Ghana bringing up children successfully, but there was no point. Her mother did not understand Gordon's life or the place he lived in. The photographs he sent were impossibly exotic – the heat-baked landscape; the huts; the barely clothed native children crowding round Diana in her white dress; the women dignified but remote with their headdresses and robes – it was all too distant to be real.

'It's just – well, if I've got Margaret I can't really think about having any more children myself. Three's enough. And I don't see why I should have to give that up.'

'Were you wanting another bairn? What does Harry say?'

'I'd like to be able to think about it.'

'You're young yet. But I dinna see what the problem is. Was Harry wanting a boy?'

'Mother, you sound as if all that matters is what Harry wants! What about me?'

'We canna be thinking about ourselves all the time. You've a fine life – a good husband and bonny bairns. And yon's a grand house – I just hope you can afford it. Your father was worried about that, but as I said to him, I'm sure Harry kens what he's doing.' She patted her daughter's knee with a hand hardened by years of farming and gardening, housework and husbandry. 'Count your blessings, Janet, you're fine as you are.'

Janet bit her lip. As usual, a mistake to try to talk to her mother. Worse, she always put her finger on a sore place, as if she knew – though she could not know, it wasn't possible, those conversations in the dark in bed, the shadow that had fallen between Janet and Harry, the hurt in his voice when she said, *I can't think about another one. Not now,* and he answered only, *It's up to you.*

'Remember,' Celia added, 'I had to take on two of them – just babies – and I was a lot older than you.'

'Did you mind?' Janet could not help asking. 'Did you want Gordon to take them back when he married Diana?'

Celia sniffed. 'What do you think? They were better with us. That lassie didna ken one end of a bairn from the other. I was fair amazed she was expecting at all.'

An accident, was Janet's view of this. Diana had never shown any interest in having children. She had been the one to suggest boarding schools for Caroline and Daniel. Janet imagined Gordon saying in a few years' time, when she was definitely past wanting another child of her own, 'Right, we'd better get Margaret off to school now, like her brother and sister.'

No. She wasn't having that. If I'm looking after Margaret, there's no boarding school for her. Before she could ask her mother what *she* had felt about Caroline and Daniel going away to school, the dog barked in the distance.

'I'd better go and see what the girls are up to,' she said. 'Jess is a good nanny but you can't expect a dog to keep them out of mischief.'

Her mother chuckled: 'Your father always says she's the best working dog he's ever had.'

They rose together and Celia took their cups inside. Janet brushed crumbs from her skirt and headed towards the garden, calling for her girls.

Once Upon A Time

1960

i

Caroline was reading *Alice in Wonderland* again. They had reached the Mad Hatter's Tea Party. It was hot, so they were lying in the shade of the big apple tree, the tartan travelling rug spread out and a small table with a jug of Granny's raspberry wine, some old cups with blue flowers round the rim, and a plate of ginger biscuits. Esther leaned on Caroline, making her even hotter. Louise stretched out on the grass nearby, linking a daisy chain.

Once upon a time there were three little girls, Caroline read.

'That's us,' Louise interrupted, sitting up to look at Esther. 'You're Elsie, I'm Lacie, and she's Tilly.' She pointed at Margaret, asleep on Caroline's lap.

'E for Elsie and Esther . . . L for Lacie and Louise. Margaret can't be Tilly, she's an 'm',' said Caroline.

'Tilly is short for Matilda, I read it,' said Louise.

'Clever girl,' said Caroline, bending her head over Margaret and stroking her fine hair.

Esther said, 'I don't like Elsie. It sounds common. Margaret calls me Essie, that's better.'

'It sounds like a mouse,' said Louise. 'Elsie the mouse.' She tickled Margaret's face with the feathery tip of a grass stalk, so that she sneezed and woke.

'Well, the Dormouse is telling the story, isn't it?' Esther pointed out, 'so maybe it was telling about mice.'

She started to giggle, setting Louise off too. In a moment they were holding their stomachs, laughing and laughing and rolling down the grassy slope to the burn, Margaret staggering to her feet and trotting after them, wanting to join in without knowing what it was she was to join. The book was left lying open at the Mad Hatter's tea party, the pages fluttering in a tiny breeze. It didn't matter, since they knew the story through and through, and would go back to it at bedtime when the grown-ups were all downstairs, and they were left to themselves in the shady summer evening bedroom.

Caroline sighed and raised her face to the sun, closing her eyes but opening her mouth a little, as if tasting its warmth. Then she put a leaf in 'Alice' to keep the place, and closed the book. She got up to look for the little girls. They were at the burn again, she could hear splashing, so she supposed she'd better keep an eye on them. I wonder how long they'll be, she thought, shading her eyes and gazing down the slope. I wonder when I can stop being in charge. She had been quite keen in the morning, wanting to re-establish herself in some way. It was her home, after all, though the girls had often been here while she and Daniel were away at school. She sighed and rose to her feet, brushing leaves from her skirt. Then she set off down the garden to see where they had got to.

At the edge of the field, Esther was wading through the deep part of the burn, leading the way with Louise splashing behind but

21

not holding her skirt high enough so that the hem was already soaked. *La la la, I'm a Water Baby, la la lala* Louise carolled. Behind her, Margaret struggled to keep her balance. I'm too wobbly for walking on stones, she thought, resenting Louise for being between her and Esther.

'I'm not a sister,' she said loudly, as the thought came to her. They couldn't be three little sisters.

'It's all right,' Louise said, turning back for a moment, balancing on one leg and waving the other through the clear water, ankle deep. 'You're as good as. *Nearly* a sister.' She put the other foot down again and marched on after Esther who was a long way ahead, humming softly, as if she were on her own.

Margaret trusted Louise least of all when she was being kind. *Nearly a sister,* she thought. Is a cousin nearly a sister – or different from that? I *am* a cousin. 'Wait for me!' she called, beginning to hurry despite her fears. She wanted to be a sister; she didn't want to be left behind. A large pebble moved beneath her bare foot, she slid, faltered, and down she came, hard on her knees.

Caroline saw it happen but was too far off to scoop Margaret up in time; her yells pierced the air. She began to run down the slope, calling *it's all right, I'm coming!* Then, from nowhere, Daniel appeared and was in the burn, his great strides bringing him to the shrieking Margaret in five seconds, less. He had her, he held her, they were both soaked, his shirt absorbing the water from her frock, but his arms warm and firm around her.

Margaret hiccupped and sighed and laid her head on his chest. This was best, almost worth the sore knees and the wet frock and knickers – to have Daniel rescue her. Now she was glad she had been left behind. It was better being a cousin after all since it meant she was Daniel's sister. The others didn't have that; they didn't have a brother at all, even one so much older. *Half-brother*, Esther had corrected her last night, but who cared about that? Half was better than *not brother*, or *cousin*.

Caroline left them to it and went indoors. The sun was slipping from the garden now.

'Don't moon about,' Granny said. 'Go and shut up the hens for me. See if there's any more eggs while you're there and take a look for that broody one. I need to get her in a run by herself.'

Hens. This was not what she came home for. All through the summer term she had longed for this place, the big quiet house and her room at the top of it, the garden and the woods beyond, the silence. She forgot about the tractors at dawn, the cock crowing, the coming and going in the warm kitchen, the jobs they made you do, as if nobody could be left alone to just think. *Look after the wee ones, feed the hens, take in the washing, spread the pillow slips on the grass to bleach in the sun.*

She had wanted to get a job this year and make some money that would be her money, not from her father or grandfather. In a few months though, perhaps she and Daniel would get their mother's money that was going to come to them when they were of age. Did that mean eighteen? She hoped so. She and Daniel could do what they liked then, live where they liked. They had talked and talked about it, dreaming their future.

Granny always said, 'You dinna need a job – there's plenty to get on wi' here.' When Caroline protested that other people were paid for their summer jobs, it was all a joke and 'we'll see'. She must get hold of her father or Diana and make them understand she had to be independent.

'I wouldn't worry,' Daniel said. 'They give us plenty – we're lucky really.'

He didn't mind the work, but they had him out in the fields with the men. '*I* could drive a tractor,' she had said to Grandpa when she was fourteen. 'Let me do that too.' He had lifted her up with his hard rough hands and she found herself in the tractor seat, high, looking over the newly ploughed fields. He showed her what to do and she drove the tractor up the lane to the yard with him standing behind her; it throbbed and roared beneath her like a beast. Proud and terrified, she remembered how to bring it to a halt, but got down shaking when Grandpa reached over and cut the engine.

Somehow, though, that was the end of it, and she had always had to work in the garden or the kitchen. The nearest she got to the labour in the fields was taking the men's piece boxes and flasks out to them at twelve o'clock.

Soon she would be a student. Already school seemed a foreign land she had once visited. The dormitories and corridors and classrooms, the absurd rules, the teachers who had been so important only a few weeks ago: they had all vanished from her life. *I'll never go back there,* she thought, leaving for the last time, getting on the bus that was to take the girls who were not being collected to the station. She was met in Aberdeen by her Uncle Harry and the little girls. Daniel's term had not yet ended: he would be home in a few days, so she stayed on in Aberdeen with her cousins until he too was met at the station and he too had finished with school for ever.

Until just last year, when Aunt Janet or anyone else asked her about university and what she might do afterwards, she could not think so far ahead. All she was sure of was that she had a lovely time of being a student in front of her, a life so remote from future plans, or having a real job, she could not begin to see beyond it.

'What about teaching?' Janet used to ask, but that was because she was a thwarted teacher herself, Caroline thought, and had never had the chance to go to university. It was Gordon who had gone on to Higher Education while Janet learned shorthand and typing, since in her parents' view she was unlikely to need a career.

Caroline had never had any intention of teaching. Going back to school would seem unnatural; it was a world gladly left behind. All that was over. Yet it went on haunting her in dreams, through the summer. Nightly she would wake sweating, worrying about being late for class, or sitting an exam for which she had done no work. Perhaps it was just the results she was worried about and when they arrived, securing her place at University, the dreams would stop.

This last year she had at least had an answer for everyone when they asked: 'I've applied for medicine, like Daniel.' Then, in another couple of weeks the letter would come and they'd know if they had the places that were provisional on their predicted results. Soon, soon, they would both be sure.

His family had been amused by Daniel's certainty from early childhood that he was going to be a doctor, indulging him with a toy stethoscope and a white coat made to fit a seven-year-old. Later, as he passed exams and still planned to be a doctor, they were proud of him. You could see them all thinking about the day when they could say, *my nephew, my grandson, my son, my stepson – the doctor.* It was galling that the reaction to her decision had been so different. 'Are you sure, Caroline? It's a very lengthy degree,' Harry had said, and her father added, 'It's not easy for women, you know.' Worst of all, Janet said, 'You don't have to follow Daniel.'

She vented her fury on a cushion, that first time, throwing it at the wall when they had gone. Daniel laughed at her. 'Ignore them,' he said. 'It's up to you.'

He never asked her what had made her choose medicine and did not challenge her claim that it was a rational decision based on the subjects she excelled in, and advice from the one teacher in school she respected. 'You could study medicine with these grades, if you get what we're predicting, Caroline,' Miss Matthews had said.

'My brother's going to do medicine.'

'Is that any reason you shouldn't?'

No, no it wasn't. Suddenly she was set free; it was her decision, nothing to do with Daniel. Miss Matthews saw that.

Caroline closed the henhouse door on the soft crooning of the birds and trailed back to the house with two new eggs in a basket. The broody hen was nowhere to be seen. She felt like a broody hen herself, out of sorts, not wanting to be with the others. In the kitchen, Margaret was being put into dry pants and a pair of shorts that had been Louise's last summer, fastened tight with a safety pin. Esther was laying cutlery on the big table, concentrating hard on getting the spaces between just right. Louise was nowhere to be seen, but even at six she was better than Caroline had ever been at avoiding the duller duties.

Daniel was in the basket chair by the stove, a cat on his lap, his nose, as his grandmother said, in a book. He was in stocking feet, his boots lined up in the porch with his grandfather's and Eddie's.

'Just the twa?' Granny said, looking in the basket.

'It's all I could see, anyway.' She made for the stairs before she could be asked about the broody hen.

Upstairs the house was warm with a day's sunshine, and silent. She climbed to her attic room slowly, weary with boredom.

Sunlight lay across the landing but the top flight of stairs, uncarpeted, was in shadow, and almost cold without a window. Her own room felt stuffy, so she opened the window the full height of the bottom sash and knelt with her elbows on the sill, leaning out to the cooling air. A stirring of wind caught her hair and lifted her fringe. She was at the back of the house; below her was the slope of garden where they had been sitting and the burn and woods beyond. In the wood were the graves of sheepdogs that had belonged to the family years ago, when her grandfather was young: Mac and Bella and Jock. Caroline imagined herself walking in the wood, going deeper and deeper, till in her mind it became a magic forest where you could walk for days and, coming to the end at last, find yourself in another country. It wasn't really like that; you would probably reach the other side in twenty minutes of steady walking. Still, she liked to think of it, of being deep among trees, deep in the silence of the wood that was not a real silence, but a faint hiss of leaf upon leaf and a rustle of tiny creatures among twigs and dry debris.

Caroline! Come to your tea!

With a sigh, she heaved herself upright and pushed the sash down till only a couple of inches of evening air could come in.

I could go to Aberdeen, she thought suddenly, I could stay with Aunt Janet. There's more happening in a city, I wouldn't be so *bored*. And they wouldn't make me do all this stuff I can't be bothered with. I need a rest anyway, I need to have a *break* before I start all the hard work next term. It would be a fair swop: Granny gets the little girls and Daniel; Aunt Janet gets Caroline and doesn't have to look after children.

Just as suddenly, she changed her mind. She would be in Aberdeen soon enough, when term started and she didn't anyway want to go without Daniel. There must be somewhere else they

27

could go together, if her grandfather would spare him – even for a few days. Why shouldn't they have a holiday?

Daniel had been working out of doors with the men all day and deserved a rest, Granny said. The meal had been eaten and washed up and the children were in bed.

'You go up and read the wee ones their story,' she said. With a sigh, Caroline went up to the spare bedroom where all three girls were in the big bed waiting for her. Esther patted her side of the bed. 'Sit here,' she said.

'Look.' Margaret pushed the blankets off and tugged up her pyjama leg to show her bruised knee.

'Was that your tumble in the burn?'

'Big bump,' Margaret said with satisfaction.

'Come on.' Louise held out her book. 'She's being a baby now. Read mine first.'

Caroline read. Margaret tucked her thumb in her mouth and leaned on Esther, and Esther leaned on Caroline. Louise lay on the far side, listening and thinking, not leaning on anyone. Margaret's book was very short, mainly pictures, then they came to *Alice* again, and she read some more of that, for the other two.

'I can read it myself, you know,' Esther said.

'Of course you can.'

'I like the way you do the voices.'

Caroline did the voices of the playing card gardeners and the terrifying Queen – *Off with their heads!* – and the Cheshire cat. Then she shut the book at the end of the chapter and said, 'Time to go to sleep.'

'It's the Mock Turtle next,' Esther sighed, lying down.

'She reads it when you've gone downstairs,' Louise said.

Esther went red. 'Shut up.'

28

Caroline had begun to draw the curtains; she turned back to the bed. 'Shall I leave them open for a while?'

'Close them!' Louise yelled, flinging herself back on the pillow. 'Or I can't get to *sleep!*' Caroline could feel the heat of Esther's glare as far as the window.

'I'll leave them a little bit open,' she said, compromising.

'I'm glad you're here,' Esther said. 'It's lovely when you come back from school. Will you tell us about your school again tomorrow?'

Esther longed to go to boarding school. When there had been a discussion about who would look after Margaret when Gordon and Diana went abroad, and someone had suggested she could at least go away to school when she was older, Esther had offered to go instead. Margaret could stay at home with Louise, and then her parents wouldn't have to have an extra child most of the time. She had been much younger then, but she had never given up the idea: one day, she might go to boarding school too. When she wasn't reading *Alice* she was reading Enid Blyton. She had reached *In the Fifth at Malory Towers* again, and it was one of the little pile of books lying by her side of the bed.

'I don't know why you think it's so interesting. I was very glad to leave.'

'Oh well,' Esther said drowsily, 'you're nearly grown up now.'

Caroline kissed them all, Margaret already sleeping, and went downstairs. That's right, she thought, I am, and if I want to go away for a while, they can hardly *stop* me. Still, she would approach it carefully, since you never knew with Granny and Grandpa. They had not approved of boarding school; they did not believe people should leave home and never understood why anyone went 'gallivanting'.

It was when Gordon had remarried and planned to take his

new wife to Ghana where the next contract was, that he decided to send his children to boarding school. It was a narrow little world at the farm, secure and healthy when they were young, but not demanding enough for their secondary education.

'It's better if they're at school during the term and come to you in the holidays, except when we're home on leave of course,' he told his parents. 'We're going to keep a base in London.'

He felt better when he had made this decision and secured school places in Perthshire and Edinburgh. Doing this went at least some way to lessening the guilt he still felt about landing the children on his parents when they were babies. And yet, as Diana kept telling him, what else could he have done?

A year later, Diana was pregnant. She came home for the birth, which as it turned out was just as well: Margaret was premature and sickly for weeks. As soon as they could take her home from hospital, they brought her to Braeside, where Caroline and Daniel had been born, fourteen years ago. They let out their London house so that when they came home on leave, it was the farm they stayed at, until eventually, after she had whooping cough, Margaret stayed on in Aberdeen with Janet and Harry. To Caroline and Daniel, it was obvious their father no longer believed it was possible for him to bring up his own children. Nobody even mentioned it now; the arrangements were taken for granted. Gordon was looking for work somewhere in the UK, he said, but he often said so, and nothing had come of it so far.

In the kitchen a smell of warm laundry greeted Caroline; her grandmother was ironing.

'It's a' fine and dry the day,' she said. 'I'll get the lot ironed before Percy Thrower comes on the television.'

'Can I help?' Caroline said, knowing she was safe since only one person can iron at a time. She pulled out a kitchen chair and sat at the table that was scrubbed and clean, ready for the next meal.

Her grandmother glanced at the clock. 'Well, you can finish off for me if I dinna get done by half past eight.'

Caroline, thinking tactically for once, said, 'I'll do all of it, if you want to put your feet up.'

'Och, I'll put my feet up soon enough. You're nae great shakes at ironing, eh?'

'They show you at school, but nobody bothers much.'

'Well, you're done wi the school now.'

Here was her opening: what should she say?

'I was wondering if . . .'

Granny looked up from the iron, but her hand kept up its thump and glide across the board, smoothing the pillow cases.

'Oh aye?'

ii

A compromise had been reached. Caroline and Daniel won a week's grace in early September, before term began. They were going to Harry's partner's cottage in the Highlands, since he was climbing in the Alps this summer and it was empty. They travelled into Aberdeen on the bus, to catch a train for Inverness. Their grandfather could not be spared to drive all that way.

It was hot on the bus with the sun shining directly onto their faces, but outside a colder wind blew, flattening the barley in the fields as they passed.

'I wasn't sure you'd want to come.'

'So you said.' Daniel closed his eyes, leaning back. 'But maybe I fancied a change too.'

'Maybe you did.'

He opened his eyes and looked at her. Caroline sometimes thought, and thought it again now, *I would look like that if I'd been born a boy.* Daniel was beautiful, with his fine features and dark hair and eyes; she was less beautiful, though they were so alike. Janet said, when she moaned about it, 'You'll grow into your looks, Caroline, wait and see. You'll be bonnier at thirty than eighteen – not many women can say that.'

Janet was the source; Janet knew everything. Caroline sighed and leaned her head on Daniel's shoulder, and dozed.

Peter Macdonald was to meet them at Inverness Station and drive them west to the cottage near Ullapool. He was the crofter whose land was adjacent to George's place. But how would they know him?

He knew them, or at any rate knew they were the only young-sters, dark and thin and eighteen years old, getting off the train together. He came up to them as they walked off the platform to the station entrance, a little wizened man in a waxed jacket and flat cap.

'Aye,' he said, 'you're for George's place, then?'

'Are you Mr Macdonald?' Caroline asked. 'Hello.' She held out her hand and he took it in his hard grip. 'This is Daniel.'

'Aye,' said Mr Macdonald. 'How are ye the day?'

'Fine,' said Daniel, 'but starving – can we get something to eat soon?'

A grin split Peter Macdonald's face; his teeth, Caroline observed, had not seen a dentist for some time. 'Nae bother.'

He led them to a Land Rover smelling of animal feed and cigarette smoke, with a collie pacing about in the back. They squashed their cases in with Caroline on the back seat, while

Daniel sat up at the front with Peter Macdonald. The collie thrust its nose close to the grid between the back seats and the boot, and breathed on Caroline, its pink tongue hanging out.

'Down, you!' Peter shouted and the dog lay down, ears flat.

Once clear of Inverness, they were drawn on winding roads further and further from civilisation. Caroline leaned back and closed her eyes, sick of countryside, however majestic, not wanting to look at the hills. *We should have gone to London, stayed in a Youth Hostel or something there. Or with Diana's friends, Diana has friends in London. We should have gone to a city.*

Her thoughts drifting, she was aware of Daniel and Peter Macdonald talking, mostly Daniel, Peter confining himself to speeches of half a dozen words at a time. He smoked thin cigarettes he had rolled up ahead of the journey and kept in a little heap by the gear lever with his matches. Daniel was fascinated by his one-handed ignition of both match and cigarette. In concession to his passengers, he had rolled down a window, but all this meant for Caroline was that the smoke drifted behind him along with waves of cold air. I'll die of smoke inhalation, she thought, or maybe freeze.

By the time they reached Ullapool, Daniel was asleep and Caroline felt sick. She was thankful to stand outside in fresh air while Peter called at the Post Office before heading up the final stretch of road to the cottage.

She and Daniel walked along Quay Street, lined on one side by shops, on the other by the wall dividing town from water, and watched the ferry for the Western Isles departing.

'Why on earth did we come?' She stuck her hands in her anorak pockets and tucked her head down against the wind. It was colder here.

Daniel put an arm round her shoulders and hugged her. 'Just wait – we'll have a wee house all to ourselves and we can cook and eat anything we fancy. '

'Nobody to tell us what to do. Or not do.'

'How far is this place from Ullapool do you think – can we walk there?'

When Peter came out of the Post Office and beckoned them back to the vehicle, they asked him. The dog rose, briefly excited, then subsided at Peter's *Get down!*

'It's a couple of miles – but you could bike it.'

'We could if we had bikes.'

Peter laughed, a creaky sound, out of practice. 'Aye, that's right enough, but there's a pair of old bikes in my shed. Would you like the use of them?'

Daniel turned to look at Caroline. She nodded.

'Yeah – great, thanks.'

'Right you are – I'll bring them down with your milk in the morning.' At the far end of Quay Street he drew the Land Rover into a parking space and said, 'Would you fancy fish and chips to keep you going the night?'

They would. The rich smell made piquant by vinegar overpowered even Peter's rollups as they drove two miles further up a narrowing road. Caroline pushed a chip or two through the grid for the dog. Hungry and tired, she thought she had never tasted anything so good.

The cottage was a traditional Highland croft house: two rooms and a small bathroom downstairs, and a narrow staircase leading to two bedrooms with sloping ceilings. It was cool and dusty and had a smoky smell they later knew was from peats burned in the open fire.

'You'll need to keep your milk in the burn just up there,' Peter said. 'The kitchen gets warm in the mornings, but that's a fine cold place.'

There was no fridge, the small electric cooker needed cleaning, and the cupboards held a basic selection of dishes and pots. This much Caroline established, but did not care, since for a week it was theirs and it was perfect.

Peter left them with a roar of the Land Rover as he went on up the hill to his own place, the dog up and pacing about again as she recognised the familiar landscape.

'Right,' Caroline said. 'Beds. Food. Let's get sorted out.'

They found linen in a cupboard on the landing; there was a double bed in each room, both with creaking springs and sagging mattresses. Daniel sat on one and bounced.

'We'll hear each other turn over, won't we?'

Caroline laughed. 'They are pretty noisy.' She had cheered up; it was an adventure now.

They made cocoa with boiling water and squares of Cadbury's chocolate melted in the bottom of the mugs, and ate some of the fruitcake Janet had sent with them. By now it was dark and too late to bother lighting the fire, so they went to bed. They left the bedroom doors ajar, talking to each other across the short landing.

'It's very quiet, quieter than Braeside,' Caroline said, listening to the silence.

'So it is,' Daniel murmured, sounding sleepy.

He slept quickly and easily, while she would lie awake for hours. The bed smelled of something musty but sweet; Caroline pulled the blankets round her, curling up tight.

Daylight woke her early with sunlight through the thin curtains. The bed was warm as a nest. She stretched out, hearing it creak, listening for an answering creak from Daniel's room.

'Are you awake?'

'No.'

'I'm so cosy, are you?'

'Mm.'

'There's a spider's web in the corner with about a dozen poor dead flies. I don't think George does much cleaning in this cottage.'

'He just comes for hill walking – don't suppose he cares about the cobwebs.'

'You *are* awake. Go and put the kettle on. I wonder when Peter will bring the milk.'

'I'm awake *now*, thanks to you disturbing me. It's so early he's probably still milking the blooming cow.'

Caroline got up with a rush of energy and pulled the curtains back.

'Wow, we really are in the wilds. Nothing but hills.'

Pulling on a jersey and a pair of socks, she went downstairs in pyjamas to visit the bathroom and then inspect everything in sunny daylight. The sky was brilliantly blue, without a cloud. Caroline opened the front door and breathed in air that was already tinged with the warmth to come. We are going to have such a wonderful week, she told the hills and the stunted tree by the gate and the sheep on the rough ground beyond.

Peter Macdonald was as good as his word: at eight he came down in a truck, bringing them milk in an enamel jug with a lid, two old bicycles and a pump for the tyres that had gone soft with disuse. Daniel pumped them up while Caroline got breakfast ready.

'There's a record player and some LPs in the living room,' she told Daniel as they ate. 'Not *exactly* what we'd choose – I don't think George is an Elvis fan, or even The Shadows. More kailyard folk . . .'

36

'So that's the entertainment sorted out.'

'What will we do today?'

'Read?'

She ignored this. 'We'll go for a walk, will we, or take the bikes out?'

'I don't know if you've noticed, but every way you turn is a *hill*, Caro. I think we'll save the bikes for going into Ullapool when we run out of food.'

'Walking then.'

He grinned. 'Don't know why you bother asking me – you'll decide anyway.'

After school, and coming home, being just with Daniel was a relief. He demanded nothing; he expected nothing. She did not have to be anyone special with him, she had no image to maintain as she had done at school for so long it had become the person she was, away from home. Here, with Daniel, her other self, nothing was required but simply to *be*, day by day, and eat and sleep and read and talk. And walk, they would walk for miles.

They did.

'What will you *do* all day?' Janet had asked them when they decided to take up the offer of the cottage. 'I hope you won't be too bored.'

They were not bored. The days passed too quickly, the evenings stretched out with talking and they went to bed later and later.

'We could stay up all night,' Daniel said on the Thursday. 'It doesn't matter, there's nobody to make us get up next day.'

'Let's do it.'

They went outside at midnight and stood under the stars, dazzling in the black sky.

'You can see the stars like this at Braeside,' Daniel said when Caroline gave a little jump of pleasure on the doorstep.

'I know, but they look different. Brighter.'

They sat on the drystone wall and Daniel smoked, the scent of his French cigarette raw and sweet in the night air. Caroline did not smoke, but now and again he let her have a draw on his. Everyone else they knew smoked Players No 6; only Daniel was different.

Caroline went indoors and put a record on. Through the open door came the rhythm and reel of fiddle music, so infectious they began to dance and Daniel caught her in his arms and jigged away with her down the path to the gate and back across the rough grass in front of the cottage. They danced and danced till they were breathless, then collapsed on the lumpy chairs indoors, hot and thirsty, so that they drank two of the cans of beer they had brought, all the more delicious because a novelty. Theirs was not a drinking family and they were only just eighteen.

At two o'clock in the morning, Caroline said, 'I feel we've been up for hours and hours of the night.'

Daniel smiled. 'We can go to bed if we want to. It's not obligatory to stay up all night.'

'No, but it's giving in, isn't it?'

'Oh yes.'

'What will we do then?'

'Read?'

'Pfft. What about Scrabble?'

They were well matched; at home only Janet could sometimes beat them. One game to Daniel, the second to Caroline.

'Best of three?'

'Right.'

Third game to Daniel.

'Best of five? What time is it?'

Daniel checked his watch. 'Half past three. Fine, best of five.'

'Ok.' As she cleared the board and tumbled the tiles about again, Caroline said, 'Why did Dad give you a watch and me a ring? I never thought about it at the time, I was only fifteen, but now I think, do women not need watches too? And it's sort of wasted on you, you don't wear it half the time.'

'There's no clock here, have you noticed?' Daniel said. 'You're right, that's the only reason I'm wearing it. I don't think your ring would fit me, do you?'

'Idiot.' The tiles were ready. Caroline began picking hers and put them on her wooden stand.

'It was only because of Margaret,' Daniel said.

Caroline was sighing over all the vowels she had landed. 'What was?'

'The watch and ring. Sorry, darlings, I married a new woman and now we're having a baby, but never mind, I still love you, so here are expensive presents to prove it.'

'Dan! It wasn't like that.'

'Oh yes it was.'

They were kneeling by the fire, long gone out, but even now the night was mild. They had hardly needed it at all. Caroline sat back on her heels. 'Do you really think that? Did you mind him marrying Diana?'

'We talked about all that. No point now.'

'You don't mind Margaret.'

'Of course not, poor wee thing.'

'She adores you.'

'Esther adores you – we're quits.'

Caroline shook her head, smiling. 'Maybe.'

Daniel grinned. 'Louise adores Louise.'

'That's true too!'

'Are you ready? Winner begins.'

He placed his letters: HOUSE

Caroline considered, wondering how many of the vowels she could get rid of.

'Are we allowing place names?'

'Sure, why not?'

They had their own rules when they played alone. They even allowed the words they had made up as children, when there had been just two of them, living with Granny and Grandpa after Daddy went abroad. It was like that again in the cottage perhaps, Caroline thought, no grown-ups, nobody to make us go to bed or eat up our veg.

She placed her word:

O

HOUSE

I

O

. . . and they began again.

Game 4 to Caroline.

'Right, last one. Best of five.'

'I'm going to muddle the letters much better this time – I had so many vowels to begin with.'

'You overcame the obstacle though, made it through and triumphed.'

'I won by four points. It's not much of a triumph.'

They began again. Game 5 to Daniel.

'I'm getting tired,' Caroline said. She was cross with disappointment. It was only a stupid game. 'What time is it anyhow?'

'Sorry, watch has stopped. Do you want to go to bed?'

'Not till morning.'

In unison, they looked up at the window. Because the lamps were lit they could not tell how much light there was outside. Daniel rose and switched them off. A grey dawn showed beyond the window, changing the light indoors, shadowed and dim, but good enough to see each other, if not to read or play Scrabble. Caroline had had enough of Scrabble, anyway; she began to drop the tiles into their little cloth bag.

'It's morning,' Daniel said. 'I'm going to bed.'

'We made it then, we stayed up all night.'

It was not all it was cracked up to be, she thought, as she went slowly upstairs. Daniel was in bed first, and probably, given his facility for sleep, already unconscious. She looked into his room: he was lying on his side, eyes closed, the covers as high as his nose.

Caroline lay awake in the growing dawn, tired but no longer sleepy, having waited it out. If they slept all morning it was a waste of the day, so it had been a daft idea. She was regretting it now, not wanting a minute of the week lost or missed. It was Friday too, their last full day. Peter Macdonald was coming to take them through to Inverness tomorrow morning. They should really just get up again and have their day. And yet, she was growing warm and sleepy. Only an hour or two, she promised herself, then we'll get up.

When she woke at twelve, Daniel was in the doorway with a mug of tea.

'Thought you were never going to surface,' he said. 'Do you want this?'

'Oh – what time is it?'

'You know what,' he said, coming to sit on her bed while she struggled up and took the mug from him.

'What?'

'I'm going to buy you a watch for our next birthday.'

'I'll just pawn the ring. Get my own watch.' She turned her hand with the ring loose on the third finger. When it had first been given to her, it had been too big, and she had worn it on her middle finger. 'I suppose I do like it – a bit. They wouldn't let me wear it at school so I had to put it on a chain round my neck and tuck it inside my shirt.'

'My chain?'

'Yes, the one you gave me. So I had my two nearest family members entwined together!' She smiled, mocking. Daniel leaned forward and pulled the delicate chain out from under her pyjama top.

'Is it a good idea to wear it in bed?'

Caroline shrugged. 'I just do.'

'Get up then,' he said. 'Last day – we'll have something to eat, then do our walk and cook an amazing curry for dinner. OK?'

'Yes, good. I'm up.'

In adulthood, when she was so often solitary, Caroline sometimes thought of this week, this rare example of knowing you were happy at the time you were, not merely in retrospect. She often heard people say – *oh that was a lovely time, we were so happy then* – when they had had apparently no idea at the time how precious the hours and days were. But she knew, she knew every day, every minute, that the week in George's cottage was perfect happiness.

'Let's come back every year,' she said as they took their cases outside to wait for Peter.

Daniel shut the door behind them. 'Fine with me.'

'Yes?'

'Oh yes.' He looked across at the hills, then back at her. 'We might need it even more when we're older, and life's got. . . . I don't know. Complicated.'

'Will it be?' She had no imagination about the future; it did not exist except in dreams and they were fleeting. She only saw that one day she would be free to choose, as they had been free to choose these last seven days. There was something about Daniel's expression that made her uneasy. Did he see something she did not, but should have done?

'Dan – ' she began, but he had turned away, picking up his case. The Land Rover was coming down the track, the dog barking behind the driver.

'That's the end of your holiday, then,' Peter said, heaving the cases in. 'You'll be hard at the studying next.'

As they drove down the track to the main road, the cottage receding behind them, a stab of fear pierced Caroline. She turned her head, swivelling to see through the mucky back window the last of the cottage, the stunted tree by the gate, the gorse and the sheep. For a wild few seconds she had been afraid it was a vanishing dream, their whole week an illusion.

It was still there. They would come back.

Coming into Money

1960

When Janet took the dog out in the afternoon, Caroline and Daniel were alone. They were in the small living room at the back of the house, called the den, that was more often used than the sitting room at the front. It had the old sofa and chairs, and the fruitwood bookcase that had belonged to Harry's parents, on top of which sat a photograph of their parents, young and newly engaged. At either end were an ugly pewter tankard and a blue vase. Today the vase was filled with the last of the Michaelmas daisies – by now nothing else was blooming. Caroline stared at the window, watching rain wash over the glass, blurring the autumn-stripped back garden, grey and brown all the way to the wall and the gate into the lane. Daniel lay on the sofa and folded his hands across his chest like an effigy, gazing at the ceiling. A small spider hung from the light fitting, wavering. If he opened his mouth, it might suddenly extend its invisible thread by a few spider miles and drop right in. He kept his mouth shut. Caroline turned away from the window, leaning towards him, hands clasped on her knees.

'They can't do that, can they? It's our money.'

Daniel shrugged. 'I guess it's up to them, or they wouldn't. Cowie's wouldn't let them.'

'We should go and see them – Cowie's, I mean. Who is it dealing with this – what's his name?'

'I don't know – Cowie?'

'There's nobody with the actual firm's name any more – they all died years ago.'

'Why do they still call it Cowie's, then?'

'Oh, Dan, stop it. It's the reputation, that sort of thing. Everybody knows them.'

'I didn't. And what sort of reputation, eh, keeping people's money away from the rightful inheritors?'

'Is it Mr Douglas – he's friendly with Dad – I know he sees him when he's in Aberdeen. He's a solicitor. That would make sense, wouldn't it? Somebody Dad knows already.'

'Is that Bob Douglas?'

'It must have increased over the years, with the interest. I wonder how much it is now.'

'They have to tell us that, surely?'

'We'll ask.'

There was a pause, while they each imagined asking.

'Anyway,' Daniel said after a moment, 'we don't actually need it yet. We're housed and fed and Dad sends money. So, with the student grant, we have enough till we're earning and by then we'll be twenty-three – or is it twenty-four?'

'For a medic, you have terrible maths.'

'For a medic, you have no empathy.'

'What for?'

'Me being terrible at maths.'

Caroline smiled and gave him a nudge with an extended foot. 'Idiot.'

'Hey,' Daniel said, sitting up and swinging his legs to the floor, 'maybe the money was invested in a wild scheme in Borneo and it's all gone, but they haven't the nerve to tell us.'

'Borneo?'

45

'Well, some obscure country. A high-risk speculation.'

'You're living in an Agatha Christie novel,' Caroline said. 'It's in Unit Trusts or something dull like that.'

'What's that?'

'Unit Trusts? Honestly, you must know what they are.' But she didn't either, and hoped he would not ask.

'The trouble with being intellectual,' Daniel said, 'is that you don't know anything useful.'

'Are we intellectual?'

'We read Agatha Christie, don't we?'

Caroline was wondering if after all she should be studying English Literature instead of medicine. She hoped it would be better next year, once this awful stage was past. It was only determination not to let anyone see she cared that was getting her through Anatomy. She had nightmares about it. Daniel did too, though he made a point of being blasé in class and with other students, even with her.

If she hadn't been so adamant about doing medicine, she might change direction now. It couldn't help but be easier, English, just reading and analysing all those books, and writing about them. She read all the time, and so did Daniel. They had the biggest collection of books of anyone she knew. Janet had books of course: the house was full of them and they were all hers, not Harry's. Harry probably only read *Accountant's Monthly* or something. That and the *Press & Journal* and the *Sunday Times*. They had been in Harry's office yesterday, and waiting for him had been struck by the utter lack of anything to read in the reception area. It seemed a waste of the comfortable leather chairs. 'Far be it from me to recommend the dentist,' Daniel had said, 'but at least Mr Simpson has *Reader's Digest* and *Punch*.'

'I still don't understand why we can't get our own money *now*. We are grown up: we can drive and get married and join the army.'

'We've not done any of that yet,' Daniel pointed out.

'We could drive if we had our money. We could buy a car and live in a flat and be independent. But not, of course,' she added, 'join the army. Or get married.'

'I don't think they can hang onto it after we're twenty-one,' Daniel said. 'So let's not bother for now, eh?'

He did not want the responsibility of their mother's money, left to them in trust until they reached adulthood. They had – naively it appeared – assumed this meant eighteen. Harry had told them that in law and in the trustees' view it meant twenty-one. He and Grandpa and their father were the trustees, and Caroline, who had not let go, did not mean to let go as easily as Daniel, was wondering which of the other two she should approach.

'Leave it,' said Daniel, reading her mind. He picked up *To Kill a Mockingbird*. He was reading it the way Caroline, equally annoyingly, had read *Gone with the Wind*: in bed, at the dinner table, in the bath, on the bus. Books did not survive this treatment well. *Gone with the Wind* had food smears, pages rippled by steam, corners knocked. Caroline saw *To Kill a Mockingbird* going the same way.

'I'll read it when you've finished,' she said. 'It's obviously gripping.'

'Shut up,' he said. 'I'll never finish if you keep interrupting.'

The front door opened and they heard Janet come in with the dog. There was a skitter of claws on the polished floor, then the door closed and they heard them go past and into the kitchen.

Caroline got up. 'That's Janet back. I'm going to talk to her about the money.'

'Good luck,' Daniel said, not looking up from the book.

In the kitchen, Caroline felt less certain of what to say. Janet acknowledged her with a smile, but she was rubbing the Labrador dry with an old towel. She opened the door into the back porch and the dog went into his bed, settling down with a grunt.

'Would you hand me my book from the sideboard?' Janet asked. She often read while she worked at the sink, the book propped up behind the taps.

'Nobody in this house treats books very *well*,' Caroline said, handing her a battered copy of *Frenchman's Creek*. 'It's going to get all spattered if you read it in the kitchen.'

'It's old,' Janet said. 'I've had it for years.'

'Do you have to read it now?'

With a sigh, Janet put the book on the windowsill next to her pot of parsley. 'I liked *Jamaica Inn* better,' she said. 'What is it, did you want something?'

'You know Harry spoke to us about the money yesterday?'

'Yes.'

'It seems so unfair. Not being able to have it. It's our money.'

Janet had gone into the larder to rummage in the vegetable basket. She came out with carrots and potatoes.

'You'll need it later, when you've graduated. Best to wait till then.'

'That's what Harry said. But we think we should have it now, so we can get a flat and be independent. That would be easier for you, wouldn't it, if we didn't have to live here? Medical degrees take *years*.'

Surely this was what Janet really wanted: her house to herself again. She was standing with the carrots in her hands, as if deliberating the merits of the proposal. In the end, all she said was 'You've just begun. We'll see how you get on after the first year or so.'

'I might change my mind,' Caroline said.

'About what?' Janet put the carrots in the sink and ran cold water over them.

'Medicine.'

'Don't be silly, Caroline. You've been accepted into medicine – that's a great achievement. You can't just throw it away.'

'I wouldn't be throwing it away – I'd change to English or History or something instead.'

Janet abandoned the carrots. 'Oh, for goodness sake.'

'What?'

'After all the fuss you made! You were adamant, you said it wasn't just because Daniel had applied for medicine. You don't seem to realise how privileged you are. A degree isn't something you keep changing – you have to stick to it, once you've begun.'

'I don't want to *keep* changing. I just think it's maybe not the right career for me after all.'

'You thought it was last year, and the year before.'

'But how could I *know*?'

'How can you suddenly know you'd like something else better? What if you didn't?' Janet was out of her depth. 'I don't think you can do that anyway. Just change to another subject.' She softened, trying to understand. 'Look, is it because of . . . of the bodies in the Anatomy class? That won't last for ever – it will be quite different next year.'

'I'm getting through *that* all right.' Caroline opened a cupboard and got the biscuit tin out. 'I'm hungry – when's dinner?'

'Not for a while, but don't start eating biscuits. You could lay the table for me.'

Caroline banged the lid on the tin again and went out, eating a digestive. 'All right,' she said. 'In a minute.'

Janet cleaned the carrots and sliced them into a saucepan. She found Caroline difficult. How indignant she had been when they suggested the only reason she was going into medicine was to stay with Daniel, do the same as he did. But that *was* the reason; she just wouldn't admit it. Better for both of them if they'd gone into different disciplines, indeed, gone to different universities. Janet leaned against the sink, dropping potatoes into clean water, dismayed for a moment by how obvious this was, yet how little they had considered it.

'It's up to them,' Gordon had said. 'Aberdeen's an excellent medical school. Diana thinks it's fine for them to do the same degree.'

Diana! What on earth had it got to do with her? Janet and her mother had had the bringing up of Caroline and Daniel. As a stepmother, Diana wasn't even of the wicked variety, she was simply absent. Useless.

'Damn it,' she said aloud. She wiped her hands on her apron and propped *Frenchman's Creek* up behind the taps to read while she cleaned the potatoes.

Daniel was still reading, but looked up when Caroline came into the room.

'She's not even our mother and anyway it was Granny who brought us up.'

'So it wasn't a complete success, consulting Janet?'

'Move.' Caroline shoved his legs off the sofa and sat down next to him. Daniel laid his book down with a sigh. 'She thinks I should stick to being a doctor. Which is ironic, considering none of them thought I was up to it in the first place.'

'I thought you were asking her about the money?'

'I was. I got distracted.' They lay back on the sofa in companionable silence. 'It's quiet without the girls, isn't it?'

'You realise that's why they they're at Braeside and we're here – so Harry could talk to us about the money? He's just doing Dad's dirty work for him though.'

'I suppose so. He said they'd talked about it, him and Dad and Grandpa.'

Once, she had felt secure knowing the adults in the family would always look after them. Now she resented the idea of these three men deciding about their money, their future.

'I hate the way they think they're in charge of our lives. They're not.'

'Nope.'

Caroline kicked at the rug, flipping the corner of it over. 'We're adults. We should make our own decisions.'

Daniel said nothing for a moment, but eyed his book which had slipped to the floor. Caroline kicked the rug again, folding it over *To Kill a Mockingbird*.

'Caro, you don't have to be a doctor.'

'I know.'

'We can do different things from each other, it wouldn't matter.'

'I know *that*.'

Abruptly, she got up and went out. He heard her a moment later in the kitchen, clashing cutlery and plates.

Daniel stretched out on the sofa and let his hand trail along the floor, unfolding the rug and feeling for his book, but he did not start reading again. He laid it on his chest, opened flat at the page he had reached, and closed his eyes, thinking about Caroline, not about the money. He did not care about the money; it meant nothing. He didn't even care about living in a flat, though he could see the attraction of it, especially for Caroline, who seemed less free than he was, even at eighteen.

He could not remember wanting to do anything else. He had always planned to be a doctor. 'I see myself in one of those white coats with a stethoscope,' he had said to his grandmother, teasing, but she had taken him seriously. Yes, it would be a fine thing to be a doctor. A fine thing for *them*, he realised. He had heard his grandmother say so to Eileen one day when she called for her to go to the Women's Rural Institute, their weekly outing. 'Daniel's going in for a doctor,' she said. 'He's always been a clever boy.' He liked the idea of doing what he pleased and pleasing everyone else at the same time. He did not have Caroline's ability – or wish – to argue everything out, to be stubborn when it would be easier to give way.

He should be in his bedroom, studying, but he could not make himself move. They had lived in Harrowden Place since becoming students, and of course it was better to be in the city. Sometimes he missed Braeside and he knew his grandmother liked to have him there. He and Caroline would probably go there at Christmas. They could take the little girls with them for part of their holiday. He was fond of them, but had been known to forget Margaret was his half-sister, not his cousin and one of the Duthies. If he had not had Caroline, he might have missed his mother. But there was Caroline, his mirror self, and there had been Granny always, Eileen sometimes, Aunt Janet often. How many women do you need, he wondered? Is having your own mother important? Are mothers necessary? He closed his eyes, growing drowsy. The fire had been left to die down and cinders collapsed softly in the grate with a final lick of flame, but the big chintz sofa was warm and deep, and he was dreaming.

Celia Livingstone remembered Bess, but for her too, she had become a shadow, someone in photographs taken long ago, first in a snap sent by Gordon to let his parents see the girl he wanted to marry, then in their wedding photographs and only a year later, with her babies in her arms. Already she looked tired and ill and nine months later she was dead.

Bess, lacking family of her own, was living with her parents-in-law, since it was 1943 and Gordon was in the army, posted to France soon after the twins' birth. After she died, Celia brought in someone to help. Eileen was a retired district nurse, glad enough to live at the farm for a few months instead of with her cantankerous mother. She went on coming in until Caroline and Daniel went away to school. Now she was at Braeside once or twice a week, supposedly to help, but Janet told Harry it was just for a blether and her fly cup.

When Bess died, Gordon was first stunned, then helpless, and profoundly relieved his mother was taking charge. When the war ended, the habit of living at Braeside was established, so he looked first for work locally. Having completed his engineering qualifications, he thought he would eventually build a house on his parents' land and settle there. They hoped he would marry again. A few years later, bored and restless, wanting a change, he applied for a job in London. That was where he met Diana.

He will want his children back now, Celia thought. She and Andrew discussed it when the children were in bed, never in front of them. Gordon had married another English girl. 'Fit wey could he nae find a guid Scots quinie?' Andrew said. 'Well, it could have been a foreigner,' Celia retorted.

Just before he and Diana married, Gordon told his parents he would be working overseas for the next few years. The return of his children was postponed.

'You're doing such a wonderful job with them, Mum,' he said to Celia, when Diana was not in the room. 'Di's not used to children, and it's a bit daunting for her.'

'Oh aye,' said his mother. Gordon glanced away, embarrassed.

'We thought – I realise it's a lot for you and Dad, and if you retire soon – '

'Retirement?'

Gordon knew his father was thinking about it. They could lease the land to the Soutars at Easter Logie, keeping the house and an acre or two for themselves. Andrew was thinking of selling the whole farm, but Gordon and Harry thought the house worth hanging onto. 'Property will go up in value,' Gordon said.

Andrew had no interest in property for its own sake; he thought more of the impossibility of removing himself and his wife from their home of nearly fifty years and starting all over again in a new bungalow. 'I dare say we'll need the space anyway,' he conceded. 'With your bairns here.'

'They won't be here all the time. We thought we'd find schools for them, boarding school. Most people working abroad send their children to boarding school and in England it's the usual thing, Diana says.'

Later, in the kitchen with his mother, who had so far said nothing to this, he raised the matter again.

'We're planning to look at a few schools while I'm home on leave.'

'Will they be going to the same school?'

'Oh no. They're boarding schools, as I said.'

54

For a moment she was silent, but her scepticism, it seemed to him, thickened around them.

'Your father says they're like two halves of a mussel shell. If you try to get in atween them, they'll shut up tight.'

Taken aback, he said with a laugh, 'We'll just have to prise them apart.'

'Aye,' she said. 'We'll see.'

He would have to speak to his father again; he would make it all right with her.

She got up and went to fill the kettle, setting it on the range. When she opened the oven door the warm wheaten smell of scones wafted out. Diana appeared in her summer frock and red shoes, which she had discovered were unsuitable for teetering around the cobbled yard or down the garden paths, the packed earth softened by rain.

'What a *wonderful* smell!' she cried.

Celia watched her son as she slid the scones onto a grid to cool. He was gazing at his wife in what, had she thought of so fanciful a term, she would have called adoration. With a sigh, she went to find her husband.

He was at the edge of the corner field next to the vegetable garden, with Bonnie the old pony.

'Are you coming in for your fly, Father?'

'Aye, fairly.' He scratched the pony's back with a stick, letting it nuzzle him, then turned to follow her indoors. They'd have to call it afternoon tea now, their fly cup, since that was the usual thing in England, she said, but her husband, hearing the sardonic note in her voice, only laughed.

'They're putting the bairns to boarding school,' she told him as they crossed the yard together.

'Aye, so I hear.'

'English ideas,' she said.

'Well, we'll hae them home in the holidays,' he comforted her. He knew she would miss the children, but nothing would have made her admit that, even to him.

'Well,' she said, closing the subject, 'he can be the one to tell them they're being parted. I wouldna relish that myself.'

'Wake up!' Caroline hit Daniel with a cushion, hard enough to rouse him with a start.

'What?' He blinked and snatched at the book sliding off his chest. 'Hey – I was asleep.'

'I know. Dinner time.'

'Ok. Just a minute.'

'I'm going to work all evening. There's so much to get through before Christmas.'

'So you're sticking with it, are you?'

'I can't give up in the middle of Anatomy. It would look so feeble.' She took a poker to the fire. 'Look, it's gone out. We'll be in trouble.' She heaved a shovelful of coal onto the embers, smothering them. A smell of soot rose up.

'You've killed it now.'

'Oh well, I tried. Come on.'

Left alone again, Daniel sat on the edge of the sofa, watching the last specks of red glimmer in the hearth then vanish, defeated. He had been dreaming. What was it? He tried to catch at the mood of the dream, something rich and exciting, warm with promise, but it eluded him.

Something about his mother, he thought. Or maybe not. He got up and followed his sister.

The Ring

1960

Once Esther had the idea, she could not stop thinking about it. In the end she decided to walk down the lane behind the house and search on her own.

It was almost four when she went, so although there was a clear sky, last night's cold wind having swept the clouds away, it was already dusk. She had been trying to get out there all day, but the house was full of family and after what had happened it was difficult to move without being noticed. Because it was so late, she took a torch from a shelf in the porch.

She slipped out of the back door and down the garden path to the gate that opened onto the lane between the gardens of the houses in their street and those of the road behind. The walls were high most of the way along but many of the gardens had mature trees whose branches dipped over the tops. Their fallen leaves were packed on the rough stony path making it slippery on wet days. People used the lane as a short cut to reach the bus stops on Fountainhall Road. Today, late on a December afternoon, it was empty. Esther had not told Louise and Margaret she was going. They were too young to keep secrets.

She left the gate propped open with a stone, because the latch was hard to undo from the outside. Then she began walking with her head down, looking from side to side, sweeping the breadth of the path with the torch beam. She was sure there must be something. This was how Caroline would have come home, getting off the bus and walking up the lane to their back gate. She knew it so well the darkness wouldn't have bothered her, and she would have been able to slip into the house and upstairs without anyone knowing. The fact that she had not *come* home meant something had stopped her, but she would have left a sign, Esther was sure. She had had a dream about it. In the dream she was in the woods across from Granny's house and was searching there among leaves and pine needles. When she first woke she had a confused feeling that she must get out to Braeside, but after a few moments decided the dream was telling her simply to search and this was the obvious place to start. Here she would find a sign to show Caroline had been on her way home; it would be something everyone else had missed or had not realised was linked to her.

Then something gleamed in the wavering light of her torch. She had found it.

It was Caroline's gold ring, that is how tiny it was, and easily overlooked. It was an odd design: two parallel rings so slender they were little more than wires, linked by six bars a little broader, two each white, yellow and rose gold. Esther had seen her turn that ring, loose on the third finger of her right hand, round and round. She must have taken it off and dropped it for me to find, Esther thought, so that I would know she was nearly at our gate when she changed her mind, or something happened. She wiped it clean on her jersey and put it on her own finger to keep it safe. Caroline had long elegant hands, the knuckles flat; Esther's were much smaller and not so beautiful. One day, she hoped, she would have hands like Caroline's. She put the ring on the third finger of her left hand where it was much too big. She was only nine, but one day she would be married. How would it feel to have a ring there all the time? Her mother had never taken hers off, not once, since her wedding.

Esther closed her hand round the ring, holding it tight. She glanced about her before she left, but she knew there was no point in searching for anything else. Luck, or persistence, or something more mysterious, had helped her find the ring. She went in the back gate and ran up the garden to tell the others.

Esther knew she came from a good family. She had heard her mother say of someone else: *what can you expect, she's not from what I'd call a good family*. It was unusual, however, for them to go out *as* a family, grandparents, aunt and uncle and children. It could happen only when Gordon and Diana were back on leave, and in the holidays, when Caroline and Daniel were home from their boarding schools. It was unusual for their grandparents to go on outings of any kind, except annual events like the Dunecht Agricultural Show. Certainly they came into town, Grandpa for business and Granny for shopping, but rarely to go to the theatre, unless it was to hear Andy Stewart or Kenneth McKellar. The children would be taken to the pantomime in a week or so; to make two visits to the theatre in a month seemed glamorous and extravagant.

Esther and Louise associated the changing of the seasons and celebrations of all kinds, with clothes. In May they took off their long fawn or grey socks for the last time and threw away the elastic garters that had been so tight a few months ago, cutting into their legs just below the knee. The elastic had become grubby and chewed-looking, so that Janet said 'I don't know what you do with it', but legs grew every year and they had to have new garters anyway. They put on short white socks and brown sandals, and their legs felt bare and skippy. In September when those same legs, brown with running about outside in the garden or at Braeside, became goose-pimply, the long socks came out to be darned or replaced, and they went to buy new Clarks shoes for winter.

Christmas parties were like a change of season in an afternoon, and so were visits to the theatre. Party dresses were even thinner than summer frocks, party shoes silver and flimsy.

The day of the theatre outing was dreary with a north-east wind cutting round corners sharply enough to make you gasp, so they had stayed indoors all day, drawing at the table in the den, making paper dolls and designing clothes to fix on them with tabs over their shoulders and round their waists. They had had paper doll booklets bought for them some weeks ago when Margaret was ill, but these had been discarded, the tabs torn and the dolls themselves no longer crisp in pink underwear, upright on their cardboard stands. 'We can make our own,' Esther said. Margaret was allowed to colour in, her expertise with scissors and draughtsmanship too slight for anything else.

In the afternoon their grandparents arrived. Gordon and Diana had been Christmas shopping and they came in just before tea. There was a quick meal of scrambled eggs and toast, so that they could all get ready for the theatre in time.

Their grandmother wore her church and town coat, dove-grey, a grey hat with a curled purple feather tucked in the brim, and grey gloves and shoes. She also wore a pair of fox furs draped over her shoulders. Esther was mesmerised by the heads with their shiny black noses and gleaming eyes, even more by the little paws hanging down. As an adult she retained a clear memory of the two foxes, kindly keeping her grandmother warm, the russet blaze of their fur against her grandmother's grey wool coat. Then, she did not quite appreciate they had been killed for this purpose. When she was allowed to play with them they seemed alive, with distinct personalities.

Their grandfather was uncomfortable in suit and white shirt, his tie tightly knotted, his red farmer's face above it the face of a man who has been drafted into something he did not quite mean to join.

'Everyone's in their best clothes,' Esther said to her mother when they were shivering in vest and pants, ready to put on their party dresses.

'Is it a party?' Louise asked, hopeful.

Janet said they had better get dressed in the den, since the bedrooms were too cold. But first the chilly bathroom, to wash faces and hands. Louise ran downstairs, clutching her silver party shoes. They all had new dresses this year, with fluffy boleros to cover up bare arms in case the theatre was not warm enough. Louise eyed Esther's blue dress, wondering whether she would like it when she inherited it next year. It was unusual for her to have a new dress that had not come from Esther. They were early Christmas presents from Diana, and much more elaborate than usual. Janet, doing up buttons at the back, thought how poorly finished they were and wondered if they'd last more than a season. She inspected finger nails and brushed hair; Esther's was tied in a single plait down her back with a blue satin ribbon to match the dress. Then they were made to sit quietly while Janet got ready herself and Harry marshalled everyone in the hall, to make sure they left on time.

At the last moment there was a debate about who was going in which car.

'Why are we going to this play anyhow?' Louise whispered to Esther while this was going on.

'Auntie Diana knows the man who wrote it – he's famous.'

'Will we see him?'

'He wrote the play, he's not in it, so I don't know.' Esther thought about this. 'I think he'll come on and bow at the end.'

Louise giggled, making an exaggerated bow, thus drawing attention to herself, which up till now she had succeeded in not doing.

'Louise! What have you done to your face?' Her mother had noticed. 'Go up and wash that stuff off right now.'

Everyone turned to look at Louise's face blushing scarlet as the stolen lipstick – Diana's, to judge by the colour. Her eyelids were smoky green with something else taken from her aunt's make-up pouch, since her mother used nothing but a powder compact and lipstick. Before Louise could argue her father said,

'Och, leave her, Janet. It's too late now – we need to get a move on. If she wants to make an exhibition of herself, let her.'

Harry hated to be late for anything. Impatiently, he herded them into the two cars and they set off.

Eleven of them went to the theatre; ten came home.

The playwright did take a bow; Esther and Louise stifled giggles and everyone clapped. There was a lot of standing about after the play ended, the adults drinking champagne. They had sherry and whisky at home, and brandy at Christmas for the pudding and pies and butter. No-one had wine and none of the children, including Caroline and Daniel, had ever seen anyone open a bottle of champagne. Tiny amounts in slender glasses were given to the children. 'Nearly as nice as fizzy lemonade,' Louise conceded, gulping it down.

At first it was exciting, seeing the actors come into the bar dressed in ordinary, rather scruffy clothes, but still imbued with glamour. Then it became dull, just grownups talking. Esther felt cross and bored, stuck with Louise and Margaret and unable even to see her older cousins who had disappeared into the crowd.

There was just as much fuss getting back into the cars as there had been leaving the house. When they were home Janet made Horlicks while their grandmother filled hot water bottles. Diana was out in the porch behind the scullery with the back door open, smoking. Because so many people were staying in the house that night, Esther was to sleep in Louise and Margaret's room, leaving her own for Granny and Grandpa. Daniel was in the box room on a camp bed, leaving his room for Gordon and Diana. All this moving about and the extra people in the house made it seem quite festive, as if it were Christmas already.

It was Esther who noticed Caroline was not there.

'Has Caroline gone to bed?' she asked, taking her hot bottle from her grandmother and hugging it tight. Because they had been out all evening, the living room fire had died and the house felt cold.

'I dare say, after drinking champagne. You run up and put that bottle in her bed,' her grandmother said. 'She'll be cold if she's nae a bottle in wi' her.'

'Make mine next then.'

'Dinna you worry, it'll be ready. Time you were a' in bed.'

Esther ran upstairs. It was a good excuse to rap on Caroline's door and go in and sit on the bed and talk and smell her special scent, sweet and spicy, and feel the touch of Caroline's light fingers on her arm, and watch her flick her dark fringe from her eyes.

There was no reply to Esther's knock. She could tell the room was empty so she went in and put the bottle under the bed covers, before trying the bathroom instead, tapping on the door

63

and calling, 'Caro?'

'It's me,' came Daniel's voice, thick with tooth-brushing. 'I won't be long.'

'Where's Caroline?'

He opened the door and looked out, a smear of toothpaste at the corner of his mouth. He wiped it off with a towel and said, 'She's not in bed.'

This was not a question, but she did not notice.

'No, she's not. I can't find her.'

Daniel shoved the towel roughly onto the rail by the wash-basin. 'She must be downstairs then, mustn't she,' he said, going into the box room and shutting the door.

The house was quiet. Esther's father and Uncle Gordon were standing in the cold living room with whiskies; Diana had gone to bed and so had Grandpa who was so used to getting up at dawn to feed beasts he never sat up late. By the time they left the theatre he had had more than enough standing about talking. Only her mother and Granny were left in the kitchen.

'Here you are, Esther,' Granny said. 'You go on up and put out your light. Time we were a' in the Land of Nod.'

'I'll do the rest, Mum,' Janet said. 'You go up – the electric blanket's on in your bed.'

Esther said, 'I put the bottle in Caroline's bed, but she's not there.'

'Go on,' said her mother, 'and don't bother Caroline. It's late.'

No one listens, Esther thought, trailing crossly upstairs, her bottle making a hot patch on her stomach as she hugged it.

Esther lay awake listening to Louise's noisy breathing, a snuffling little girl's snore. In the spaces between she listened to the silence in the room next door, the silence that was not Caroline.

In the morning they paid attention; in the morning everyone knew that Caroline had not come home.

There was a general feeling at this point that it was the family's collective fault she was missing. She had gone to the ladies' cloakroom just before they left the theatre; they had all got into the cars and everyone in one car assumed she was in the other. At least, at the time, it was thought to be everyone. No-one questioned Daniel and he volunteered no information.

As the anxious day dragged by, it seemed more and more their fault. They had not even noticed she was not in the house last night. How could they have been so careless? By afternoon, Harry and Gordon were talking about calling the police.

The house had never been so full of people. Everyone stayed on, even the grandparents who had to make arrangements for milking, for the hens, for all the work of the farm that would have to go on without them for a few hours at least. There was no longer any question of Gordon and Diana leaving for London to fly back to Egypt next day. He was due to start managing a new contract the following week.

From the landing at the top of the stairs, the children heard Gordon talking to someone on the telephone in the hall below. There was only one telephone in the house, so there could be no private calls, but this meant it was often a source of interesting information.

The three of them sat on Caroline's not-slept-in bed, keeping close to each other, as if one of them might vanish if left on her own.

'Where's Daniel?' Margaret asked.

'Out with Daddy. I think they've gone to the theatre to ask about Caroline.'

'Where *is* Caroline?'

'We don't know, Tilly, but don't worry. They'll find her.'

'Is she lost?'

'Yes,' Louise said. 'She got lost in the middle of the night.'

'Let's think where she might be,' Esther said.

'At Granny's,' said Margaret, unable to picture Caroline anywhere apart from their own house or their grandparents'.

'No,' Esther said. 'She can't be. Granny's here. Where do you think, Louise?'

'*I* don't know,' Louise sighed heavily and lay down across the bottom of the bed, dangling her head near the floor where she could see Caroline's blue slippers under the bed.

Downstairs, the adults had become unsettlingly quiet.

Louise sat up suddenly, her face red from being upside down. 'Do you think a bad man has got her?'

Margaret started to cry. Esther put her arms round her.

'That's silly,' she scolded Louise but Margaret cried harder than ever. 'Maybe she went away with a nice pixie,' she said in a desperate attempt to stop this wailing. She looked at Louise and made a face, to show this was just for Margaret who was too little to understand, and still believed in fairies and pixies. This face was also meant to convey to Louise how stupid she had been to say anything about bad men. Louise made a face back, and resumed dangling over the side of the bed. She thought she had seen one of the teddies under there and wanted to have another look. Margaret sighed and laid her head on Esther's lap, and although this habit was supposed to have been thoroughly trained out of her, she tucked her thumb in her mouth. Louise came up triumphantly with the missing teddy but as neither Esther nor Margaret paid her any attention, she shivered, complaining of cold. 'I'm going downstairs,' she said, but did not move, did not go down to the warmer kitchen where the adults who were there sat at the table, not talking. Eventually, she leaned on Esther and cuddled the dusty teddy, sucking his ear.

When Esther read in her teenage years about what happened at Ayers Rock, she thought of herself and Louise and Margaret, the Elties, huddling together, bewildered and beginning to be frightened. Perhaps they were more afraid of being the one left behind than the one who vanished, led away by goodness knows what pied piper.

'Caroline was in the lane,' Esther announced, making her dramatic gesture, taking the ring from her finger and laying it on the kitchen table. 'This is her ring.'

They looked at the ring, then they looked at Esther.

'What?'

'Where did you get this?'

Her grandmother reached across the table and picked up the ring.

'Yes,' she said. 'There's not two like it. I said to Gordon when he bought it, it's an extravagant thing for a girl of fifteen. She'll have plenty rings in time, I told him, but – '

'What's extravagant?' Gordon asked, coming into the room. He looked more gaunt than usual, his hair on end because he had run his hands through it so many times, his long elegant hands like Caroline's. His face was greyish. Even in her triumph at bringing home the ring, Esther saw that.

'This ring,' Janet said, taking it from her mother's hand and giving it to her brother.

'It's Caroline's,' he said. 'It's hers. Where – '

'Esther found it in the back lane.'

The glory of being the one to find it palled in the face of all their questions. She was instructed to take them to the exact spot where she had picked it up, but once there, she was no longer sure. Her father spoke sharply to her and Esther burst into tears. She had thought it would prove Caroline had been here, that somehow it would help them to find her. Instead, all the grown-ups began talking at once, frighteningly unlike themselves, intense and angry. Someone pointed out Caroline might have lost the ring there any time. When was she last seen wearing it?

She always wore it. Esther was certain of that but no one was listening to her now. For years afterwards, she hated to think of that afternoon, memorable not for fear or anxiety but embarrassment, that unwelcome emotion, so close to shame. The only moment of quiet and pleasure in all of it was the instant of finding the ring. *She left it for me*, Esther had believed then, *she left it as a sign for me.* Questioned by her parents, she could not explain why she had gone into the lane, why she thought some sign of Caroline would be found there.

'Caroline must have said something to her,' she heard her mother say.

'You think she *planned* this – she intended not to come home last night?' Gordon sounded shocked.

'I don't know,' Janet sighed. 'I don't understand this at all.'

Before they could start questioning her again, Esther crept out of the kitchen and up the stairs to her own room. Below she could hear Louise and Margaret playing in the den, Louise being bossy. They seemed just as usual, as if they had forgotten for the moment that anything was wrong. She sat on her bed, feeling miserable. After a little while, there floated up from the open kitchen door the sounds of a meal being prepared, the squeaky larder door being opened and shut, running water in the sink, the clash of saucepans and the clatter of cutlery.

Esther found her book again and lay down on her bed with it, pulling the quilt round herself to keep warm.

Just after seven, it all came to an end.

So far, nothing had gone beyond the family except the visit to the theatre manager. When the evening staff came on again, he had said he would question them, in case anyone had seen Caroline leave. Harry and Gordon had agreed between themselves to wait until eight o'clock, then they would telephone the police. Daniel said, 'You don't need to, she'll be all right,' but they paid no attention. They don't even listen to Daniel, Esther realised, and he's nearly grown up.

They had eaten high tea at six and Louise and Margaret were in their bedroom; lying on her own bed reading *Alice Through the Looking Glass* again, Esther could hear Louise instructing her teddies.

Esther thought about what Daniel had said. If *he* thought she was all right, she must be. Caroline had left the ring as a message, for whoever found it. Esther was sure she was the one, Caroline had known she would look for it. That was what the dream meant. She wished she could have the ring, but her grandmother had put it in her purse.

She heard the front door open and close.

No one said, 'It's me'; there were no footsteps across the hall. Something fizzed suddenly in Esther's veins, as the champagne had done. She got up and went to the top of the stairs. With a sister's instinct, with her own instinct for trouble, Louise appeared and stood next to her.

Caroline was in the hall, wearing the same clothes she had worn the night before. She was carrying her sequinned evening bag and her coat was open. She was standing quite still, as if waiting for someone to come and find her. Esther's hands, gripping the banister, were hot and damp with sweat, sticking to the polished wood. Then someone came out of the kitchen below. She heard a gasp and her mother was there, reaching Caroline before the children looking down at her managed to move.

'Granny,' Esther whispered at her grandmother's elbow. 'Can I ask you something?'

Celia was pulling on her gloves, smoothing them, tugging the wrists up. Beside her was the suitcase which Grandpa was just about to put in the car. He had gone out to warm it up, but the front door was closed, to keep the heat in.

'Now then,' she said. 'We'll see you all at Christmas.'

'Granny, what about the ring?'

Her grandmother looked down at her, puzzled. The she remembered. 'Oh, michty, wi' a that commotion, I forgot it a-thegither.' She clicked open her handbag and rummaged in it for her purse. 'Here, Esther, hold this bag for me.'

Esther held the leather bag with its gold clip. At the corners, the leather was rubbed and greyish. Her grandmother had always had this bag; it smelled of the 4711 cologne that she put on her handkerchief, a few drops in the morning. Esther had watched her and pleaded for some for herself. On the previous day, she had gone around for hours, sniffing her wrist for that elusive scent. Yesterday. Only yesterday they had gone to the theatre and everything had been exciting but also safe. Now it was not exciting and it was not safe.

Celia held out the ring on her gloved hand. 'Here you are – be a good girl and give it to Caroline for me. I've nae time now, your Grandpa's in a fair rush to get back to Braeside.'

Made bold by the nearness of Granny and the temporary absence of everyone else, Esther said, 'Where did she go?'

Her grandmother's face was briefly bewildered, then she patted Esther's arm. 'Nowhere. Dinna you worry about it. She's home now.'

'She didn't drop the ring on her way home, did she?' Esther sighed.

'Nae doubt she dropped it some day on her way home,' her grandmother said. 'But goodness knows when. I'm surprised she didna miss it.'

The door opened with a bang and Grandpa called. 'Come on then, Celie, we'd better get hame afore the weather changes. I can smell the snow.'

'Run and tell your mother we're away,' Celia said, and Esther, clutching the ring, flew to the kitchen to fetch Janet.

In the goodbyes, she managed to uncurl her hand and show Louise the ring. Louise's eyes gleamed, but she said nothing until the goodbyes were over and they were on their own in front of the fire in the den.

'I asked Granny for it.'

'Are you going to give it back to Caroline?'

'Yes, of course. It's hers.'

They went upstairs to find Caroline, who had not come down to say goodbye. On the landing they heard voices from her bedroom. 'Daniel's there,' said Louise.

Esther tapped on the door: 'It's me and Lou, can we come in?'

They were sitting on Caroline's bed, talking. You could see they were talking about something private. Caroline was saying, 'That was one of the reasons, really,' but she stopped when Esther and Louise came into the room.

'What is it?' She didn't sound friendly. All idea of asking her where she had been, vanished. Esther held out her hand, and opened it slowly.

'I found your ring,' she said.

Caroline stared. Slowly, she took it from Esther's open palm and peered at it. 'Yes,' she said. 'It is. Where on earth did you find it?'

'In the lane of course,' Louise said. 'Where you left it.' Esther gave her a nudge, to shut her up. 'That's what you *said!*'

'I lost it,' Caroline admitted. 'I'd no idea where it was.'

Esther had to ask. 'When did you lose it?'

'A week ago. A while anyway.'

'Oh.'

'Thank you – how on earth did you spot it – you mean the back lane, don't you? I've not come that way for days.'

'I just had a feeling it would be there, that's all.'

Caroline slipped the ring over her finger. It was loose, anybody could see that.

'It must have come off when I took off my glove to open the back gate,' Caroline said. 'I bet that was it. You have to put your fingers through the hole to lift the latch on the other side. It's stiff and I couldn't get hold of it with gloves on.'

'Mystery solved,' Daniel said. He smiled at Esther.

Janet was coming upstairs. 'Where are you girls? Come and wash your hands for lunch.'

'Off you go,' Daniel said. 'We'll be down in a minute.'

In the bathroom, washing hands, Esther said, 'I gave Caroline back her ring. She was really pleased.'

'I'm sure she was,' Janet said, unimpressed. 'It's gold, that ring.'

Esther, going slowly downstairs while Louise argued with her mother about whether her hands were clean, paused at the bottom. She could hear, if she listened hard, the murmur of voices from Caroline's room. Was she really pleased to have the ring back? Esther wasn't sure. The mystery was deeper than ever.

In the afternoon fires were lit in both the den and the front sitting room.

'Are we going to have visitors?' Esther asked her mother.

'No.' Janet sighed. 'We want to talk to Daniel and Caroline tonight, so you three can play in the den.'

'Can we have our tea in it, in front of the fire?'

Louise always pushed a bit too far. Esther held her breath, but Janet smiled and said, 'We'll see.'

Louise bounced. 'Hurray!'

'What do you want to talk to them about?' Esther asked, but Janet brushed this aside, having conceded enough.

They all ate together in the kitchen, but the girls were allowed to take their bread and butter and a piece of cake into the den. They were glad enough to go; it had been an uncomfortable meal, full of awkward silences that in the end inhibited even Louise.

A little later, when the sounds in the kitchen had ceased, they heard voices in the hall, and the sitting room door closed firmly. Now there was no sound but the ticking in the hall of Granny Duthie's grandfather clock. A moment later, Janet came in to take their plates away.

'Now, we want peace and quiet, no interruptions.'

She went out, shutting the door. A moment later, the sitting room door was also closed again.

Margaret had been rearranging the furniture in the dolls' house. She looked up.

'What are they talking about?'

'Caroline,' Esther said. 'I think. Being away all night.'

'Is she getting a row?' Louise asked, surprised.

While the others played, Esther read, but the Five Find-Outers' adventure seemed less absorbing, silly. She raised her head, listening. There was nothing to hear. Nobody raised their voice. In an old house like this, with panelled wood doors, you could not hear from one room to another unless you opened them.

Louise looked up. 'What's wrong?'

'I don't know.'

'I'm going to open the door a bit – we might hear what they're saying.'

'Then *we'll* be in trouble.'

'Caroline *is* getting into trouble then.'

Louise opened the door as quietly as she could. Only last week, Harry had gone round with a can of WD40, spraying the hinges that squeaked, and this, thankfully, was one of them.

'What are you doing?' Margaret asked. Esther and Louise, guiltily huddled in the half-open doorway, said 'ssh!'

There was nothing to hear but voices, soft and indecipherable. Nobody shouted. Only children shouted and screamed, but that was because they hadn't yet learned that you mustn't. In their family, only Louise had ever done it. Even she knew you weren't supposed to.

Suddenly, the sitting room door flew open and Caroline yelled, 'You can't say things like that to us. We're *grown up*, for God's sake.'

Shocked, Esther and Louise leapt back and pushed the door to – but not quite shut. Hearts beating fast, they went on listening, unable not to.

Nothing but Harry, sounding reasonable and quiet, nothing and then –

'I wish we didn't have to stay here – I wish we could just *leave*. You're not my mother, you can't tell me what to do.'

Then the sitting room door banged and someone came rapidly across the hall and ran upstairs. Caroline, of course.

'She shouted,' Margaret whispered. 'She said *God.*'

Esther and Louise looked at each other. 'Better shut the door.' Louise shut it. 'We'll just wait. I don't think we should go and ask.'

'No.' Even Louise didn't want to do that.

It wasn't easy to sit and do the ordinary things they were doing before it happened. After a moment, Margaret, who had been fidgeting on the sofa, said, 'I need a pee, Essie, do you think it would be all right to go up to the bathroom?'

Esther shook herself back to the sensible everyday.

'Yes, I'll take you.'

'I'm coming too,' Louise said.

While Margaret was in the bathroom, Louise crept along the landing and listened at Caroline's door. When she came back she said, 'She's not crying or anything.'

'Of course not,' Esther said. 'Grown-ups don't cry.'

Louise looked doubtful, and Esther herself was no longer sure. Caroline hadn't sounded grown up at all.

Esther went into the bathroom to make sure Margaret had washed her hands. The clock on top of the bookcase on the landing told her it was nearly bedtime. In a moment, surely, their mother would come. But it was Daniel who was coming upstairs now, two at a time.

He ruffled Louise's hair as he went past and when Margaret appeared, picked her up for a moment, tickling her and making her squeal. 'What are you all looking so secretive about?' he asked.

'Nothing,' Esther said.

'Caroline's in her bedroom,' Louise told him.

He set Margaret down, smiling at them. 'Don't worry, it will all be ok. Promise.'

Then he went into Caroline's room, and that door was shut again too.

Louise shrugged. 'Oh well,' she said.

'Can I go and see Auntie Janet now?' Margaret asked, fretting.

So they went down, but Janet was still in the sitting room with Harry and when she came out, hearing their voices, she looked if not angry, then stiff, annoyed.

'What's wrong with Caroline?' Louise asked.

'Nothing,' Janet said. 'Bedtime. Do you want some milk first?'

In the morning, nobody said anything. Daniel and Caroline went out early, as they had a lecture at nine. After that, it was all the same as it had been before, so perhaps Daniel was right. Everything was fine.

Grandpa

1961

'Where does this go?' Esther asked. She was following her mother's instruction to make herself useful, by tidying the sideboard in the hall. It was her weekend to stay with Granny at Braeside, something they were taking turns to do since their grandfather's death in March, four weeks ago. She had carefully dusted the Japanese vases that she thought so beautiful. One had a crack but you couldn't see it if you turned that side to the wall.

Celia, coming in from the fish van with a parcel of haddock fillets, looked at the envelope Esther was holding.

'Put it in the top drawer of the bureau in the sitting room. It's the papers your mother needed to get your Granda's death certificate.'

'Oh, I'm sorry.'

'Na, na, dinna bother – I just didn't get round to putting it away.'

Esther took the envelope into the sitting room, rarely used and always a little cold, the fire lit only for Christmas and visitors. The last time had been the day of the funeral. The bureau drawer was stiff so she put the envelope down to make it easier to tug open with both brass handles. When she picked the envelope up she took hold of the wrong end and half a dozen documents slid out. Alarmed, she tried to stuff them back as her grandmother came in to the room.

'I'm sorry, Granny, I didn't mean to look – they all fell out.'

'You can fairly hae a look at them.' Her grandmother took the envelope from her and they both sat down on the slippery coldness of the hide sofa.

'Now, this is his birth certificate. He was born in 1893, and here's his father and mother's names. Andrew Livingstone, the same as your Grandpa, and Ellen Donald. And they had to put in his father's occupation.' She pointed.

'He was an innkeeper,' Esther read.

'He had the Dunecht Hotel,' her grandmother told her. 'He was forty by the time Grandpa was born, so he'd built up a good business. He had a coach and horses too, and ran a coach service to Aboyne and Banchory.' She turned to another paper. 'This is our marriage certificate.'

'It's a long time ago,' Esther said, reading it.

'Aye, that it is.'

'It says here Grandpa's occupation was 'grieve' – what's that?'

'He looked after the Pittcaithley Estate, that belonged to Sir Matthew Cummings.'

'But – ' Esther hesitated. 'He was a farmer.'

'In time, he was. My folks died when we were not long married, and there was a bit of money came to us, so we bought our first place then.'

Esther thought Braeside had always belonged to her grandfather's family. She was silent, adjusting to this different story.

'It's a hard life, whiles,' her grandmother said. 'But we never thought of anything else.'

Esther had heard her parents discussing the farm in the weeks since her grandfather's death. 'You won't leave here, though, will you? We'll still come and see you at Braeside?'

Her grandmother's hands, roughened by work, the veins standing out blue in thinning skin, smoothed the papers flat on her lap. Her ring was loose, worn to a thread of gold.

'We'll see,' she said. 'I canna farm it myself, I'm getting too old for that, and Eddie and Dod are getting on as well, they'll be looking to retire soon. If I have a few hens and my garden, that'll do me.'

'I could help you, I'm quite strong. I could come for the Easter holidays, that's soon, and then all the summer holidays. But I don't know if I could be a farmer. I'm going to the High School when I'm twelve. Mummy says I'll be a teacher, but actually, I'd rather be a farmer and live in the country like you.'

Granny said only, 'That's right, you stick in at the school.' She replaced the papers in their envelope. 'Now, put this away for me in the drawer, and we'll hae a fly cup. I've a bittie gingerbread left – or what about making a dropped scone?'

These early weeks of widowhood were bewildering. Gordon and Harry were taking charge of business correspondence, for she had never dealt with such matters in her life. She should have paid more attention when Andrew was alive. Still, these things were the least of it. It was the lack of him in the house and out of doors Celia felt most painfully. Though the men went on working as they had before, used to the routine of the farm, Celia still looked for her husband's tall stooped figure among them. The farm should have been given up a year ago, as Andrew had wanted to do. She had not gone against his view, but she had done nothing to hurry the business, so time had drifted on, with no change. Now these hard decisions had to be made alone for the first time in forty-five years – just as the Spring was coming in and there was so much to do. Yet when her son and son-in-law suggested changes she could not answer them. She had to ponder what Andrew would have said, and make the decision he would have made.

Having Esther in the house was no trouble; the bairn was quiet and well behaved, and liked to have a job to do. They lived harmoniously together, and it was a comfort to find the child already asleep in the big feather bed when she put the lights out and came through in her nightgown, to wind the clock and say her prayers. Esther was still a bairn, her hair in two thick plaits tied with ribbons, but she was already growing long-legged. In a year or so she would be much less fond of spending weekends with an old woman. She looked forward less to having Louise, not ready yet for the demands of Louise's constant chatter, her need to be doing something – usually disruptive – or her stream of questions, many of them unanswerable.

It was in church the children were least able to distract her. Always, there, she was conscious of Andrew's presence at her other side, upright in his suit, his Bible held between the work-worn hands, knuckles enlarged by arthritis. Esther sat quietly in his place, sang all the hymns in her clear, tuneful little voice, and sucked her pan-drop peacefully, day-dreaming through the sermon. Louise, however – Louise shuffled and fidgeted, sighed and kicked her shoes off, took the pan-drop out to see how small its smooth pebble had become, dropped it, dived for it, had it wrapped in Granny's hanky, and finally – thankfully – fell asleep, her hot head heavy on Celia's lap. Roused at the end of the sermon for the final hymn and the blessing, she was dazed, eyes unfocused, her rosy cheek imprinted with the shape of a coat button.

Outside, the dog, that had been lying in the shade of the churchyard wall, came up wagging his tail, and they walked back to Braeside. Now, there was no difference between the girls. Whether it was Esther, released from good behaviour, or Louise, revived, each of them would skip ahead of Granny and Eileen, racing the dog up the hill.

Margaret, of course, was still too young to be away from Janet on her own, even in this familiar house. She was a clingy child. Just as well she'd not had to grow up with her own mother, who had shown so little interest in her even as a baby. Diana had looked less blooming than usual at the funeral, despite her heavy make-up. Was she sickening for something? It certainly wasn't grief: she'd had no more attachment to her father-in-law than to any other member of Gordon's family. Margaret, trying to please her, excited rather than happy in her mother's rare presence, had been whiny and fretful until Diana and Gordon went to London. Now they were in Egypt, but Gordon planned to come home soon to deal with whatever arrangements were made about the farm.

Celia had never been critical of her son, but now Andrew had gone there was no one to whom she could say what she thought about Diana, so she said nothing. Still, there was no better mother than Janet; the girls were a credit to her and Margaret would be well looked after. She turned her attention to the scones, and got the baking bowl out.

'Can I spread them?' Esther asked.

Her grandmother handed her a dish of softened butter. 'There's rasp jam in the larder. You can get that out if you like.'

They had their tea in the kitchen, kept warm by the range on this cool April day. Andrew's old dog, never before allowed in the house, lay in front of it. His feathery tail swept the floor when Esther bent to give him a piece of scone.

'You're spoiling that dog.'

'So are you, Granny!'

'Aye, well, he's auld and done like me.'

Esther felt hot all over. '*You're* all right, aren't you Granny? You don't have a bad heart like Grandpa?'

'I'm fine lass. I've a sore heart, but that's a different matter and it'll nae kill me.'

Esther thought about this. 'So have I,' she discovered. 'It hurts, just here, when I think about Grandpa.' She pressed her chest with both hands.

Tomorrow afternoon Granny would put her on the bus so that Daddy could meet her in Aberdeen and take her home in the car. They had a new car, blue with slippery leather seats. She described it in detail to Granny. The name sounded like a person: *Morris Oxford*. She imagined Morris being mild and gentlemanly, with a moustache.

'It's big enough for all of us. It was a bit of a squash in the last one now me and Louise are bigger.'

'You'll be all right on the bus.'

'Oh yes.' She was the only one allowed to go on her own; Louise could not be trusted and Margaret was too little. Now that her father had a new car she was less sure about this privilege, and would have liked to be fetched in it.

She was in the shed helping her grandmother get the hens' mash ready when they heard across the yard the sound of the telephone ringing in the house. Her grandmother went to answer it, hurrying at the shrill sound.

She was gone a long time, so Esther went into the steading to look for kittens. She was hoping the tabby's would be born this weekend. She was certainly very fat now, trailing her belly close to the ground, mewing for attention then turning her back and walking away when you spoke to her. In the shadowy barn Esther found the cat making a nest for herself on some sacks, but still without kittens. Eventually, she realised she had been gone a long time, but when she went back to the shed where the eggs and hen food were stored, her grandmother was not there and the pails were still on the floor, filled with mash. Esther crossed the yard to the house. In the kitchen her grandmother was sitting at the table, doing nothing. This was so rare that for a moment she was nonplussed.

'Granny – will we feed the hens now?'

'That was your Uncle Gordon on the phone,' her grandmother said. Her face was different, grimmer, and Esther felt almost frightened. She waited, chewing the end of one plait, so that for some time afterwards she associated the news of Diana's illness with the taste of hair in her mouth.

'I thought she didna look herself,' Celia Livingston said, to herself and not to the child, whose presence she barely seemed to take in. 'What a mercy they're nae in some foreign place now. What's to be done, though – what's to be done?'

Had her husband still been there, she would not have said a word in front of the bairn, who stood looking at her, mystified. It was a sign of how the world had changed in a few weeks that she so far forgot herself as to say the dread word *cancer* to a little girl.

The following weekend was Louise's but she had been invited to a birthday party.

'We *said*, Louise,' Esther scolded her. 'We said one of us would keep Granny company now she doesn't have Grandpa. You promised, we all promised.'

'I know, but Granny won't mind,' Louise said, blithely indifferent to Esther's disapproval. 'Susan's invited the *whole class*. I can't be the only one who doesn't go to the party.'

'I think that's just selfish,' Esther said. She ran downstairs to her mother, and offered to go to Granny's this weekend instead of Louise.

'You don't have to,' Janet said. She had been touched by the girls' solicitude, but looked doubtful. 'Granny really won't mind.'

'I want to.'

'Are you sure? Is it not a bit dull for you on your own?'

'I'm not on my own. I'm with Granny. We do lots of things and it's not boring at all.'

'Well, if you're sure. I'll see what your father says.'

Esther was satisfied. This was a matter of form: one parent always made a show of consulting the other but experience told her that what one gave permission for, the other endorsed.

'Poor Margaret,' Louise sighed when Esther told her. 'She'll be all on her own.'

'You're only going to the stupid party for an afternoon,' Esther retorted. She thought for a moment. 'She could come with me. I'll ask Mummy.'

For a few seconds, Louise swithered, realising she might be the one left out of something. The party won.

However, Margaret was beginning ballet lessons that Saturday, filling her with a sense of her own importance for – Janet realised – the first time. Louise's bragging about the party had no effect; nor did the thought of not being able to go to her grandmother's with Esther.

Esther was glad to be going to Granny's; at home her parents were always talking about Diana, who was in hospital in London, and although their conversations ended abruptly when one of the children came into the room, Esther and Louise had at least gathered a good deal of information and caught some of their parents' foreboding. They had been told not to speak to Margaret about it and even Louise realised this was an order that must be obeyed.

Esther could hardly wait for the week to pass. At Braeside the kittens *must* have arrived. There was Granny's raspberry wine, sweet and sharp, to look forward to, and the creamy porridge she made for breakfast; there were the plants on the window sill it was Esther's job to water. There was Easter Logie to visit, the neighbouring farm; in their yard she could speak to Jessie the sheep, old and very grubby, who had started life as a pet lamb.

On Wednesday she came back from school miserable and feverish; on Thursday Janet kept her at home; by Friday they were certain she was incubating chickenpox, rife in the city. Her parents had another conversation behind closed doors. Was it better to quarantine her with Granny or keep her at home so that the others caught it too? Better to have chicken pox when you're young, Janet decided.

'Well, keep her here then. If she's going to be ill, you'll want her at home anyway, won't you?' Harry knew nothing about chickenpox, except it had made him scratch incessantly when he had it as an eight year old.

Janet said, 'What about this blessed party – and the ballet class? Should I keep the other two at home in case *they're* incubating it?'

They pictured, briefly, Louise's paroxysms of grief and fury should she be denied the birthday party.

'For goodness sake,' Harry said. 'It's not the plague. Let them go. Half of Aberdeen's got it already, according to you. We'd be as well spread it round the other half.'

By Saturday morning Esther was too miserable to argue

about staying at home, but she fretted about the kittens. 'Phone Granny up,' she begged. 'Find out if they're born yet – can I go *next* weekend?'

A week and a bottle of calamine lotion later, Harry drove a subdued Esther, still scratching scabs, out to Braeside for convalescence. It was going to be a long month: Louise was in bed now.

Celia, who would otherwise have had Eddie drown the unwanted kittens, had moved the cat and her family into the kitchen for Esther's sake and there was a fresh batch of pancakes waiting.

'I don't know,' Harry said when he got home again to Janet running up and downstairs after Louise, who did not take kindly to being ill. 'You're always saying your mother was such a disciplinarian with you and Gordon. Esther can do what she likes – cats on her bed and cream in her porridge!'

Janet laughed. 'I can assure you, she was never like that with us!'

'Any word from Gordon?' he asked.

'No. But I can't think about Diana if I've got three lots of chickenpox one after the other. '

Later, she was sorry she had said that, as if she did not care. Just as Margaret finally ran out of scabs to pick, Gordon called to tell them Diana was back in hospital, but the treatment was awful, she was very ill. He sounded depressed, even hopeless. Janet put down the phone feeling that it must be bleak for him, so far from home. Gordon had lived for many years away from home, Harry reminded her. 'It's different now,' she said. She meant, death makes a difference. They knew Diana would not get better.

She had coughed all the way through her father-in-law's funeral. They had told her off for smoking too much. She had had bronchitis in the winter, and blamed that for her cough, for feeling unwell, not going to the doctor until it was too late. Perhaps it was always too late; she had probably had lung cancer for months. When Janet thought of Diana she saw her with blonde hair and red-tipped nails, pastel twin sets and pretty dresses – *oh, that bonny white one with the scarlet poppies.* She could hear her loud laugh and see her raising a glass of gin and tonic, stacked with ice. Now she imagined Diana in hospital, diminished, desperately trying to stay pretty, stay herself. She was ten years younger than Janet, and it seemed impossible someone so vivacious could die.

In the end, Harry said, 'You'd better go and see them. You could stay a week or so anyway. Your mother will come and give me a hand.'

Nervously, Janet planned a journey to London on her own.

'I'll pay the fare,' Gordon said, his voice warm with gratitude. 'If the family can spare you – '

'They can,' she said. He was her brother after all – and who else would be close enough for this second terrible loss?

On the unfamiliar sleeper, finding it, despite her anxiety, a novelty worth experiencing, Janet lay awake, rocked by the train's rhythm, thinking of the two of them as children at Braeside, then during the war, when she was so afraid for him, as their parents were. In wartime, she had travelled these long distances by train in uniform, but never alone, and sitting up all day or all night. She must have had more confidence then. Something happened to you when you married and had children; you were reduced from the person you'd been at eighteen and nineteen, though so much had been added to you. Drowsily, she puzzled it out, missing her children already, and Harry. She was not afraid of what lay ahead, wanting only to give Gordon comfort. She had not been with Bess when she died, since she had been posted to

Exeter all that year, her leave periods short and far between. She had not realised anyway how quickly death was going to come.

This time, there was no mistaking it.

London was warmer than Aberdeen. Janet realised that Spring, which had come in reluctantly at home and lingered on, still cold with night frosts, was long past here. Gordon took her first to his and Diana's London flat in a nineteen-thirties block: handsome, even grand, but compared to home, bleak. When she saw through their open bedroom doorway, Diana's dressing table scattered with pots of cream and bottles of scent, she wondered, feeling uncomfortable at the thought, how soon Gordon might have to clear it all away. He did not speak as if that was the case; his thoughts seemed to be all of improvement, remission.

'The sooner I have her back home the better – the hospital's getting her down,' he told Janet as he hailed a taxi to take them there.

Diana was in a side ward on her own. Even before she saw her face with its orange lipstick gaudy on pale skin, the loss of weight, she would have known how ill Diana was, for Gordon told her he was allowed to stay for long periods, beyond visiting hours. This time, since Janet was here, he did not stay. 'I need to catch up with some work,' he said.

Diana seemed pleased to see her. Janet put a clean nightdress in the locker and changed the flowers wilting in the vase. Diana watched her moving about the room.

'You're a darling,' she said. 'You make everything so comfy.' She opened the top of the tin of scented talcum powder Janet had brought and sniffed. 'Lovely, thank you. All the hospital stuff stinks of disinfectant. Bring my *Mitsouko*, will you, next time? It's on the dressing table.'

'Is there anything else you need?'

'Sit down, darling, do let me look at you, all fresh from bonnie Scotland.'

Janet sat down, reminding herself Diana was ill and she should try to be nice to her. For a moment it was very quiet in the room, though the noise of the hospital went on around them, seeming further away than it could possibly be.

A nurse came in and looked at Diana. 'I'll come back and do your blood pressure and temp soon,' she said. When she had gone, Diana raised her eyes.

'Why are they bothering? Even if my blood pressure's sky high, it doesn't really matter now, does it?'

'Well – '

Diana put a thin hand with apricot-polished nails on Janet's arm. 'You know I won't get through this.'

'Wait till the treatment's finished, then you'll see.'

Diana made a mocking face. She raised her hand and the diamonds in her engagement ring – loose and slipping – winked in the light; she looked at it with something close to satisfaction. 'One thing about this place – you lie about doing nothing so it's terribly good for your hands. My lovely long nails . . .'

Your nails are fine, Janet thought, but oh, that's all. Helping Diana to sit up, she thought how brittle she was, the beautiful elasticity of her skin gone, her bones themselves fragile-seeming, all of her growing fleshless, becoming a husk of the lovely woman she had been. Her blonde hair, coarse and dry, showed an inch of darker roots already.

She made the pillows more comfortable and helped Diana lean back into their nest. She wondered if the talcum powder or Guerlain eau de toilette could make any difference, for she no longer smelled like Diana, of flowery scent or shampoo or expensive soap. The smell of sweat and sour sickness instead – Janet tried not to breathe it in, tried not to mind, since Diana, if she knew, must mind so much.

'Margaret sends her love,' she said. 'She's too little to understand, but she made you a card.' She took it from her bag and put it into Diana's hands.

Diana looked at the childish drawing for a long moment. 'Sweet,' she said. 'That's nice.' Her head went back on the pillow and she looked, all at once, exhausted. 'Useless mother, wasn't I?'

'We love Margaret,' Janet said, 'and she's happy with us.' Now that there was no possibility Diana would ever take Margaret away from her, she could be more generous than her thoughts had been, these last five years.

Diana turned her head on the pillow to gaze at Janet. She bit her lip, thinking, making up her mind.

'Is something wrong – do you –?'

'No – I need to tell you. Tell you something.'

Janet's heart sank. 'You don't have to tell me anything,' she said.

'Oh, I think I do. You don't like me much, but I bet I can trust you. You and Gordy. But you're not to say anything to him, promise me?'

'Anything about what?' Don't give me a secret, she thought, don't give me something I can't say to my brother or my husband. She did not know how to stop her though, this fading woman, insisting on her lipstick, her rings flashing in the harsh hospital light, putting on her brave face.

So Diana told her.

Outside, it had begun to rain and Janet had not brought an umbrella. She stood in the shelter of the hospital entrance way and shivered, for all the air was so mild. I didn't misunderstand, she thought, I know what she said. But is it true? She might be delusory, it can happen.

She knew it was true, knew as if she had always known it. Not heeding the rain, she began to walk away from the hospital, but not towards the underground station or the taxi rank according to Gordon's instructions. She hardly knew what she was doing, she just wanted to walk. After a few minutes the rain stopped and the clouds cleared a little.

She had been in London for a few months towards the end of the war, but it had seemed friendlier then, and anyway, that was years ago. Now she found herself taken back to that time. She had wandered into an area still not rebuilt and was confronted by the ragged sides of bombed houses, abandoned homes exposed: fireplaces intact or leaning out, plasterwork crumbling; scraps of wallpaper still with some colour on sheltered areas; and through it all, the persistence of vegetation growing tall as the first floors and even some rooftops. Suddenly this dereliction seemed unbearable. She turned quickly to make her way back to the busier place she had left, hoping to find a taxi, unable to face the underground, the difficulty of getting on the right train, going in the right direction. All that was too much, with the burden she was carrying.

In the end, Daniel and Caroline did not go to the funeral. Diana had become much worse soon after Janet got home, the treatment was stopped, and in a week she was dead. Janet and Harry were still discussing whether she should go back to London, when Gordon called to tell them. They began talking instead about who should go to the funeral. It would be another long and expensive train journey on the sleeper. Was Mother fit to have all the girls, could she come into Aberdeen to stay with them? What about the work on the farm – surely they could manage without her for a few days? Time it was sold, Janet said, admitting this for the first time. And what about Daniel and Caroline?

'They're adults, they can decide for themselves,' Harry said.

Janet thought about Gordon, managing alone. 'I need to speak to him,' she said.

She tried to discuss this with Daniel and Caroline. What did they want to do? Daniel said he would go to London if his father wanted him to. Caroline said she would go if Daniel was going.

Gordon's voice on the end of the phone line was harsh and strained. He wanted other people to decide, and in the end Janet, talking it over with Harry again, began to think there was no point in Caroline and Daniel leaving their studies at this important time. They could go to London and stay with their father later – that would be more sensible.

'What do you think?' she asked them.

'We'll be in the middle of exams,' Caroline said. 'How long would we have to be away?'

'Does Dad want us to go?' Daniel asked.

'I don't think he knows what he wants.'

'Oh well,' Caroline said, 'we can always go to London in the summer. I quite fancy that – do you, Dan?'

'I think you're right,' Janet said. 'These exams are important.'

Caroline made a face at Daniel behind Janet's back. It was a standing joke with her, how important Janet thought education was. Daniel said it was because she hadn't had the chance of enough of it herself.

When Caroline had disappeared upstairs – to work, she claimed – Janet said,

'Daniel, do you know about blood, blood groups? Have you learned about that?'

'We did that in biology at school,' he said. 'Why?'

'Can you tell . . .?' She was so hesitant, his attention was caught. 'You always have a blood group that's the same as one of your parents, don't you?'

'It's a bit more complicated than that,' he said, and tried to explain. 'Why do you want to know?'

To his surprise, she reddened, uncomfortable. 'Oh, it's just something I read in the paper,' she said. 'Right, I'd better go and collect Margaret.'

Daniel sat on in the den when she had left, and wondered. He was so unused to Janet lying, he could scarcely believe she had. You always knew exactly where you were with Janet, and though you might not like where you were, it was at least clear. Now he was not so sure.

When Janet came in again with Margaret, she was worrying about something else altogether. Margaret was hot and miserable, running a temperature. 'I can't leave her if she's not better,' she said to Harry.

'Couldn't Caroline keep an eye on her?' he asked.

'She's got too much work to do,' Janet said, her tone sharper than they had ever heard her use to their father. 'Anyway, Margaret's my responsibility.'

Harry himself, hearing something in her voice that was not just anxiety, looked surprised, but since the children were in the room with them, and Daniel too, he did not answer.

Margaret did not have any illness the doctor could diagnose, but her temperature went on falling a little during the day then rising sharply at night, so Janet kept her home from school. Margaret slept a lot. In the end, Harry went to London alone, but it was not satisfactory. Janet felt she had let her brother down. She should have made his children go to London with Harry. Yet she could scarcely expect them to care very much about a father who had left them with his parents, sent them to boarding school, remarried and gone away again, and who even now rarely saw them. He had been obsessed with his wife, not his children. As for Margaret, Janet went on caring for her, doing her best.

'Tell Gordon to come up and stay with us a while,' she told her husband, packing his case for him, sponging a mark from the black tie so rarely worn. 'Tell him to come home. Oh dear.'

When he had gone, she was left to worry on her own about Gordon, about letting him down, about whether Daniel and Caroline should have gone to the funeral – but most of all, cripplingly, about what Diana had told her. Soon, she must decide whether to tell Harry – *when* to tell him. They had no secrets and she did not want any now.

On the day of the funeral, Margaret was well enough to go back to school, and went eagerly. She was going to be a teacher, she told Janet. 'I love my school,' she said.

Margaret had not yet been told her mother was dead, only that she was ill. Janet had no idea how to tackle this with a six-year-old. Today she must tell her; today she must deal with this. For one thing, Louise could not be relied on and was already being self-consciously mysterious in front of Margaret. Still, she was apprehensive as she set off for the school at quarter to three.

Margaret ran across the playground, holding out a picture she had drawn in class. *This is me, look, Auntie Janet, this is me and this is you and this is my Mummy Diana and my Daddy and this is our cat.* It was a very crowded picture but the cat at any rate was large and recognisable.

'Clever girl, that's very good.'

94

They did not have a cat, but Margaret had heard enough about the kittens at Braeside to long for one.

'We'll get one of Granny's kittens, will we?' Janet said, thinking perhaps it would help to distract her, while also wondering how much she would understand about her rarely seen and barely known mother. Margaret held Janet's hand, the picture clutched in her other one, and skipped beside her all the way up the road, her little satchel bouncing on her back.

They would have half an hour before Louise and Esther were home; school finished earlier for the Infants' classes. Margaret would have her glass of milk and biscuit at the kitchen table and draw more cats, and Janet would explain that she would not see her mother again.

A month after the funeral Gordon came north for a fortnight's leave. It was June. Summer had come in a rush of warmth, and the trees were lavish in their green finery. The car moved in and out of sunshine on the North Deeside Road as he and Harry drove to Braeside to help his mother arrange what should be done about the farm.

He and Harry agreed: she should keep the house and an acre or so and lease the rest of the land to Bert Soutar at Easter Logie, who would also buy the remaining stock. It was, after all, their inheritance, and though he had no wife now and could not imagine having one again, Gordon thought of his children, and how the property might, in ways he could not yet see, be part of their future. He had not lived in it since he was a young man in his first engineering job and he had no feeling for it beyond a faint nostalgia, but it was a good house and arable land was valuable. Harry was right: the world was changing, and they should hold on to what would last, and increase in worth as the years went on. On the road out of the city they talked it over, in complete agreement.

For Gordon it was a relief to discuss it in this calm, reasonable way with Harry, and come to good business decisions. Everything else was temporary and unreliable. Everything else, for him, was inarticulate with pain.

II

Into the Forest
1964

Not long afterwards, there was once more great dearth throughout the land, and the children heard their mother saying at night to their father: 'Everything is eaten again, we have one half loaf left, and that is the end. The children must go, we will take them farther into the wood, so that they will not find their way out again; there is no other means of saving ourselves!' The man's heart was heavy, and he thought: 'It would be better for you to share the last mouthful with your children.' The woman, however, would listen to nothing that he had to say, but scolded and reproached him.

Hansel and Gretel, The Brothers Grimm

The Typhoid Summer

1964

They were always being told to wash their hands. That was the boring part. The best thing was having a much longer summer holiday.

One morning early in June when Janet came into the girls' bedrooms to open the curtains, instead of saying 'Time to get up' she said, 'Last day of school today.'

'What day is it?' Margaret sat up. 'Thursday – today is Thursday. Why is it the last day?'

'It's because of the typhoid epidemic. On the wireless they're saying they've decided to close the schools early.' Janet sighed, as if it might not be wholly good news. 'You're all to get letters home today.'

Louise started bouncing on the bed. 'No more school!' Then an idea struck her and she stopped, anxious.

'We'll go back in August, they won't keep them closed?'

'It will all be over by then,' Janet said. 'I hope.'

Louise was going up to the High School in August, to be with Esther. Margaret's feelings about this were divided between resentment at being left behind in Primary and relief at not having to leave Miss Gardiner, the best teacher in the Universe. Margaret was much taken up with the idea of the Universe. Daniel had told her theirs was not the only world – there were others out there on planets they didn't even know about.

'Have they got typhoid in other places too?' she asked Janet as she started to get dressed in the school skirt and blouse left on the chair where they'd been neatly folded the previous night.

'Just Aberdeen,' Janet said, picking up socks from the floor. There was another one under the bed. So that was where they all got to.

'Uncle Harry said it's an epidemic. What's that?' Margaret asked.

'It means a lot of people have the same disease, and it's spreading.'

'Could it spread over the whole world?'

'That won't happen,' Janet said firmly. 'Not if you wash your hands properly.'

'So – everyone in the world has to wash their hands or they'll get it?' Louise asked.

Janet, growing exasperated – mainly at the thought of the three of them home from school until August – snapped a brusque reply and went downstairs with a pile of washing.

How often should they wash their hands? After touching animals, Louise said, but how was this possible – Margaret was always hauling the cat about.

'Animals don't get typhoid,' Esther decided.

'How do you know?'

'Oh don't be silly, Louise, it's a human disease and they think people got it because they ate corned beef.'

'I ate corned beef!' Margaret exclaimed.

'When?'

Margaret could not remember. Surely she would have typhoid by now if it had been the *poisoned* corned beef?

In the kitchen Harry was reading the *Press & Journal*. 'Three more down with it,' he said. 'They've opened up an isolation ward at Woodend.'

'Daniel, you're not working anywhere near this, are you?' Janet asked. He had appeared in trousers and shirt, barefoot.

'Near what? I don't have any socks.'

'The typhoid patients, Janet means,' Harry said.

'No, they're all in isolation and none of them at Foresterhill, where we are. It's ok.'

'How serious is this?' Janet asked, calling through from the scullery where she had filled the washing machine and was attaching its hoses to the scullery taps.

'Well, quite serious, I don't think our consultant on the ward will like it if I turn up with no socks.'

'You know fine what I meant – the typhoid epidemic.'

'Who knows?' Daniel put two slices of bread into the toaster then filled a bowl with corn flakes, scattering the overspill across the table. 'There's been a bit of a panic, but I think they'll contain it now.'

'It was the corned beef, then?'

'Yeah, seems like it.'

'I never liked corned beef,' Caroline declared, coming in to make herself instant coffee and cut a grapefruit in half.

'I ate corned beef!' Margaret insisted.

'No, you didn't,' Janet said. 'There's nothing wrong with it usually. Though I must say, I think it will be a while before anyone in Aberdeen buys it again.'

As Harry folded the paper and rose from the table, Daniel said, 'I've booked driving lessons.'

'What?' Janet closed the scullery door behind her and the rumble of the washing machine faded.

'Thought it was about time.'

'We're going to get a car. Dan will learn first, then me, but that means he can teach me so we won't have to spend so much on my lessons.' Caroline dug carefully round her half grapefruit with a sharp knife. The toaster popped and the kettle started to whistle. Unperturbed, Daniel and Caroline carried on with breakfast. Harry and Janet looked at each other.

'Well,' Harry said, 'it's your money. But cars depreciate in value very quickly.'

'That's right,' Caroline said. 'It's our money.'

When Harry opened the front door, sunshine streamed across the parquet and glinted on the stained glass of the inner door.

'Another lovely day,' he said.

'Harry – '

'I know you're worried about this business of Bess's money,' he said, 'but we can't stop them having it. They're over twenty-one, and adults. They have the right to spend it if they want to.'

'Not on cars, surely. I thought they'd keep it for when they've graduated and have to live on their own or move away and work in other hospitals. That would be good for them. Sometimes I wish we'd encouraged them to go away to university.'

'They went away to school.'

'I know, and I felt bad about that.'

'It wasn't your decision, Janet, and it wasn't mine. It was up to their father. It was Gordon who sent them, and he paid for it. Nothing to do with us. And neither is the money, really.'

'You and Dad were trustees too.'

'Our duties have been discharged – I've no further responsibility.'

'It's a worry, though.'

He kissed her. 'I know. But they're sensible – Daniel certainly is. Don't fret. Think how miserable it must be to be one of those families with typhoid.'

'Och, you're as bad as Mother, making me count my blessings!' But she smiled and kissed him back and let him go to work, closing the door on the morning sunshine that was already lighting up the rooms at the front of the house.

Louise and Margaret spent some time speculating on what kind of car Daniel might buy.

'He should get a sports car,' Louise said.

'As long as we get a ride in it.'

'One at a time, in a sports car – they only have two seats in front and no back seats.'

'That's no use,' Margaret said. 'I hope he gets a big car, then we can all go in it.'

They put this to Daniel when he was home from the hospital that night.

'I'm going to get a Mustang,' he said, teasing them.

'That sounds like an animal,' Louise objected. 'It's not a real car.'

'It's an animal, but it's also a car.'

They looked doubtful. Daniel, relenting, said, 'It's American. Actually, I'll just have to buy whatever I can afford. Maybe a Triumph Herald.'

They liked the sound of that. 'Why do cars have two names?' Margaret asked. 'Like people.'

Esther, appearing in the doorway, said, 'I thought our Morris Oxford sounded like a person. Austin Cambridge was the other one – his friend. Austin and Morris, two nice old gentlemen.'

'Triumph Herald sounds younger,' Margaret said. 'He could be their nephew.'

'And Mustang is their dog,' Louise added.

'I give up,' Daniel said, laughing. 'I can see the car's name is more important than anything else about it.'

Harry knew the owner of J&S Pirie, the Ford dealership in the city. 'I'll ask him to look something out for you, when Daniel passes his test,' he said.

'Let's hope I'm not one of those people who takes forty goes . . .' Daniel said, grinning. 'Thanks, Harry.'

He had no interest in cars. It was Caroline who had come up with the idea of buying one, but he admitted it would be useful.

'Car first,' she said. 'Then a flat.'

'I thought it was the flat you were most bothered about – living on our own?' Daniel said.

They were in the den. It was late and everyone else was in bed. Except when they were studying in their rooms, this was the time they were most likely to be alone. Sometimes they had friends back in the evening and the den was theirs, the girls kept out. But it was not like having your own place.

'We have to break them in to the idea,' she said.

'You're so devious. Is it necessary? As Harry said, we're adults, we can please ourselves.'

Caroline shrugged. 'Yes, but they'll resist it. Don't you think?'

'If you say so.'

'We'll just rent, eh? No sense in going to all the bother of buying somewhere for a couple of years. After that – who knows where we'll be? I don't want to do my clinical training in Aberdeen as well.'

'So you keep saying,' he teased.

'Oh shut up. Neither do you.'

For a moment they contemplated a life somewhere else, a different hospital, a different city, other experiences unimaginable beyond their bare outline. Perhaps, Daniel thought, we've lived too sheltered a life, protected by family, but limited by them too.

'You're right,' he said. 'The world lies before us, in all its glory.'

'Is that a poem?' she asked, suspicious.

'Could be. You know, the trouble is you look so ungrateful, rebelling against a kind and loving family. What we really need is some cruelty or neglect. Unreasonable parental behaviour.'

'Well, we do have our father.'

He would not answer that. There was nothing more to be said about it. Caroline picked up the crumpled *Evening Express* from the floor and turned to the 'To Let' section of the Classified Ads.

'This probably isn't the best time to look,' Daniel suggested. 'In the middle of an epidemic.'

'No one else will be looking, so there'll be no competition if we find a nice place.'

He laughed. 'You're a very determined woman.'

Esther had her hair cut at last: the long plaits had gone. Caroline had encouraged her – think how easy it will be, no more tugs, and hair washing will be so quick! You look lovely, she said, when Esther came home feeling strange with her giddily weightless head. Glowing, she cared only for Caroline's approval. When her mother said 'That fringe is too heavy', Esther tossed her new bob and said, 'it's *with it*, Mum.' Janet, picking up a basket of washing to hang outside while the sun shone, said only 'With what, exactly?'

For a while, Esther kept the plaits tied with navy school ribbons in a dressing table drawer, wrapped in tissue paper. But they were like conkers fallen from the living tree; they lost their russet gloss. Finding them there a few months later, she threw them out. Only Margaret minded – she had planned to make them into a wig. Her own fair hair was fine; it would never grow long and thick like Esther's.

When Esther went to Braeside for a week of that surprisingly long and tedious summer of the typhoid epidemic, Granny admired the new grown-up Esther.

'My, my, you're a young lady now. You winna be chasing after kittens in the hay bales these holidays.'

There were no kittens this year; the old cat had died. She had a growth, Granny said, and Esther did not want to know more. Her last remaining kittens were roaming tomcats now and rarely came indoors. Both Granny and the dog seemed older and stiffer but the hens still pecked busily about the wild ground behind the fence at the back. Early in the evenings she listened to their soft crooning as she sat on the doorstep shelling peas or hulling straw-berries for their six o'clock high tea. The garden was as productive as ever, and the weather had blazed into heat the moment Esther stepped from Harry's car and sniffed the different country air, heady with the perfume of summer.

Granny kept to the old mealtimes and pattern, having the main dinner in the middle of the day. At home, when Daniel and Caroline had come to stay with them in term time, as students, Janet had moved theirs to early evening. After Granny's mince and tatties or fish pie, Esther was too stuffed to do anything but lie on her full stomach and read. It was hot so she lay in the shade of the big apple tree on a tartan travelling rug with a bowl of strawberries by her side, and read her way through her library books. When they were done, she began on Granny's papers. She read the *Weekly News* and the *People's Friend* from cover to cover,

106

and the old *Reader's Digests*. She liked *Increase your Wordpower*, and would test Granny on the new words she had learned.

When her mother telephoned to arrange to collect her, she said, 'Can I stay another week?' Surprised, but pleased (she worried about her mother), Janet agreed. 'Do you want Louise out with you?'

'She won't want to come – she just likes to play with her friends.'

'What about Margaret? It would be good for her.'

Margaret was more biddable but at nine would not read as much as Esther wanted to. She also liked to have Granny to herself, but she could hear the hopeful note in her mother's voice. 'Oh well. All right.'

'That's a good girl – she likes your company and it will leave me a bit freer.'

Esther spent her last day without Margaret reading and reading. 'You'll wear your eyes out,' Granny said.

'I'll take Gyp for a walk soon,' Esther promised.

She went up the quiet road behind Granny's house, the fields on the other side once grazed by their own cattle, but now leased to Easter Logie. The rent earned Celia an income to supplement her pension, and Gordon and Harry managed the business side of the property for her. Janet worried about how her mother would cope as the years went on. At present, Celia kept the place with only Eileen's help and Eddie coming in to dig the garden. Eileen was getting on too, and overweight. Esther heard her panting as she trundled upstairs to put ironing away, or heaved herself onto a precarious chair to dust the tops of doors. Why? Esther decided this was not something she would ever bother doing when she had her own house.

She and Gyp walked slowly, Esther to make the most of the

day, Gyp because he was old and it was hot. She pretended Gyp was Black Bob, the dog in the *Weekly News* serial, who was so clever, frequently saving his master from danger, but Gyp, quiet and steady, did nothing to help this game along. It had all to be in her own head.

The clover in the verges sent up a warm smell of honey, and the grasses were as high as Esther's hand, trailing along their feathery tops, now and then pulling one up so that it came free from its sheath with a sweet white stalk you could suck till the juice was gone and it was stringy in your mouth. Now and again she slipped off her sandals and carried them in her hand by the straps, so that she could feel the hot tar beneath her feet. It was burning, melting in places, so she had to put the sandals on again. At the top of the hill, they looked across to Easter Logie Farmhouse, but didn't turn up the lane towards it. Instead, Esther walked slowly along the edge of a barley field. It was too early for the ears to have folded over but the crop was high and turning gold. Gyp went through the barley and she could see his white-tipped tail weaving among the stalks. 'Come out,' she said, but half-heartedly. It was a little cooler in there for him. Soon they reached the gate and went through, Esther closing it carefully behind them. They came down the brae through a copse of birch and rowan and at last it was shady enough for Gyp.

'Let's have a rest,' Esther said, and they both sank gratefully onto dry leaves, to sit listening to birdsong high above their heads and the scutter of foraging birds and other tiny creatures in the undergrowth around them. Gyp stopped panting and closed his jaw with a gulp, sinking his head onto his forepaws. As she lay propped against a tree trunk, there suddenly came to Esther a memory of searching among dry leaves in the lane for Caroline's ring. Did Caroline still wear that ring? She did not think so. Of course, as a student doctor, she couldn't wear jewellery when she was with patients.

Where had Caroline gone that night? How queer, Esther thought, nobody mentions it and I don't even know if she was made to tell. *I bet Daniel knows.* She wondered if he and Caroline were home yet; they had gone to London to spend some time with their father. *Will she wear the ring when she sees him?* Esther did not think so. For a few minutes she was in a fret to be at home, so that she could slip into Caroline's room and look in the wooden casket with its inlaid pattern of gold flowers, where she kept her jewellery: her mother's rings and pearls, and a heap of cheap silver chains and earrings which were what she usually wore. Diana's huge collection of clip-on earrings and coloured beads, gaudy and dated now, had been relegated to the dressing-up box, along with their mother's dance dresses from when she was young and had no children to keep her at home. Diana's diamond engagement ring had been put aside for Margaret in a blue velvet box in Janet's dressing table drawer.

Esther closed her eyes, to think better. When she opened them, dazed, she realised she had been sleeping. Alert to the change in her breathing, Gyp opened his eyes too and raised his head.

'Right,' she said. 'Let's go back. I want some raspberry wine and a scone.'

When Margaret came, she brought several of her dolls. On the Monday the weather changed and it rained steadily so Esther, beginning to be at a loose end, set up a school for the dolls in one of the attic rooms. It had been Daniel's, was still Daniel's when he came to Braeside, but that was rarely now, and almost all his things had migrated to Harrowden Place. Margaret had chosen this room to play in: Daniel's teddy was still on the bed, and became another pupil at the school, the only boy. Granny gave them a slate to be the blackboard, with a small broken piece for chalk. Esther cut up paper and stitched notebooks for the class; Margaret found a short garden cane to be the teacher's pointer.

Esther, sneaking off after a while to Caroline's attic room next door, lay on the stripped mattress with her book, *Jane Eyre,* her mother's old copy found in Granny's bookcase. She was deep in the horrors of Lowood School when Margaret appeared in the doorway, bored with the game when Esther was no longer there.

'It's playtime,' she said, 'my children are all in the playground. Are you coming back to be the French teacher again?'

Esther, with a year of learning French at the High School behind her, had been showing this new knowledge off to the dolls. Now she couldn't be bothered. She just wanted to read.

'In a minute,' she said. 'Let me finish this chapter.'

Margaret perched on the edge of the bed, then got up and wandered round the room. 'Caroline had this room,' she said, 'didn't she?'

'Mm.'

Margaret opened the wardrobe door but all that remained were a pair of black lace-up shoes, very dusty, and a grey cardigan and skirt, also from Caroline's school uniform. She closed the wardrobe door and tried the dressing table next. She studied her reflection for a few minutes, tucking her hair behind her ears to see if that suited her better. It didn't. She thought her ears stuck out too much. With a sigh, checking that Esther was still reading, she opened the drawers. Nothing in the top one, nothing in the middle one, nothing but a white button in the bottom one and an old jersey. She shut the drawers quietly, not to disturb Esther. She was still hopeful about the French teacher, if she didn't annoy her. *Bonjour Madame,* she whispered. *Comeintally voo?* Then she caught sight of a box behind the tilted mirror, a wooden box like the one Caroline had in Aberdeen for her beads and rings, but much smaller. She drew it towards her and opened it.

'Look!' she cried to Esther. 'There's a ring in here!'

Silence.

'What?' Esther asked, surfacing. 'What did you say?'

'There's a ring in this box. It's Caroline's. Do you think she knows it's here?'

It was the gold ring Esther had found in the woods. She took it from Margaret and without thinking, slipped it on her own middle finger. It was not as loose as it had been three and a half years ago when she was ten, when Caroline had disappeared for a whole night.

'I don't know. I think she must have put it there. I knew she wasn't wearing it any more.'

'Is it the ring you found?'

Esther was surprised Margaret remembered. 'Yes,' she said.

'There's a bit of paper too – maybe it's a secret letter,' Margaret said, taking the paper from the box and unfolding it. She was the Enid Blyton reader now, and was entranced by secrets: drawers, passages, rooms and worlds. 'Oh, no, it looks like a poem.'

'It's not a letter,' Esther said, taking it from her, 'or a poem, though it does look like one.'

It was a list, in Caroline's much younger handwriting, her school writing, neat and rounded.

For Esther, my ring
For Louise, my mother's crystal earrings
For Margaret, my mother's pearls
For Daniel, everything else

'It's a will, or a bit of a will,' Esther discovered, and a thrill of shocked pleasure ran through her. *For Esther, my ring.*

'What's a will?'

'It's what you write down to tell everyone who is going to have your things when you die.'

'Is Caroline going to die?'

'No, silly. Well, not for years and years.' She sat down on the edge of the bed and let Margaret take the piece of paper from her. Side by side, they read it again.

'I'm going to make a will,' Margaret decided. 'I don't want Louise to have my dolls.'

'I doubt if she wants them.'

'But she wouldn't look after them. I'll leave them to you, Essie.'

Esther did not answer her. After a moment, growing restless, Margaret said,

'Shall we give it to her, the ring? And the letter? The will.'

Esther thought about this. 'No,' she said at last. 'I don't think so. This is still her room, really, and we shouldn't be looking in her things. She might not want other people to know the ring's here. Your Daddy gave it to her.'

'He never gave me a ring,' Margaret said, jealous.

'You're not old enough.'

'I'm going to get Caroline's pearls, though. What are they like?'

Esther got up and put the ring back in the box. Then she folded the paper again and laid it on top, closing the lid.

What should she do?

In the end, going downstairs with Margaret because the rain had stopped and it was time to pull pea pods for their dinner, she made up her mind to speak to her mother, and see what she

112

thought. Perhaps she didn't need to do anything at all. Except Margaret had begun to covet the pearls, without being able to remember what they looked like, and she could see it wasn't a secret any more.

The Car

1964

Catching up with her friends at home, Esther forgot about the ring, but Margaret did not. At the dinner table, she announced to Louise, 'You're going to get Auntie Bess's crystal earrings.'

'What?'

'Caroline's going to leave them to you in her will.'

'Oh good,' Louise said. 'What about Auntie Bess's emerald ring? I like that.'

'What on earth are you talking about?' Janet asked.

Esther told her. Janet was amused but less interested than Esther had expected.

'Not exactly a legal document, then,' Harry said. 'No witnesses?'

Esther shrugged, not being sure what he meant. 'It was only a bit of paper.'

'No, it's true,' Margaret insisted. 'Can we go and look at the earrings and the pearls?'

'Certainly not.' Janet turned to Esther. 'When was this bit of paper left at Granny's?'

'Oh, I think she wrote it ages ago – her writing's different now, not so neat.'

114

'Practising to be a doctor,' Harry said, making a joke wasted on the children.

'Well,' Janet said, 'you'd no business reading it in the first place – you wouldn't read anybody else's letters, would you? So I suggest you forget all about it.'

'Am I not getting the pearls then?' Margaret persisted.

'For one thing, there is no guarantee Caroline will not outlive the lot of you!'

Margaret fretted about this for days afterwards, imagining her life somehow shortened, indeed likely to come to an end any time.

One night she crept into Esther's bed late, and whispered, 'Are we really going to die before Caroline?'

Esther, who was reading *Villette* with some disappointment, finding it nowhere near as interesting as *Jane Eyre*, closed the book and put her arm round Margaret. 'Silly Tilly,' she said. 'Honestly, none of us is going to die for years and years and years until we're really old women.'

This, for Margaret, was almost as unimaginable, but more reassuring.

'I'm going to ask Caroline anyway,' she said, 'when they come back from London.'

'Don't say we looked in her box,' Esther warned.

'No, I won't, I promise.'

'You'd better go back to your own room. It's boiling with two people in the bed.'

Reluctantly, Margaret slipped away, and a few minutes later Esther heard her singing to herself, the bedroom door wide open to let what air there was drift through the open window and across the room to the landing. It was the hottest week of the summer so far.

A little later her mother came upstairs and looked in, saying, 'Time you had your light out, isn't it? Dad and I are coming to bed now.'

'I'm too hot to sleep.'

Janet sat on the edge of the bed, looking to see what she was reading. 'Do you like it?'

'Not really. Well, it's not like *Jane Eyre.* '

'Esther, the ring you found – it was the ring Uncle Gordon gave Caroline?'

'Yes, with the different coloured gold.'

'The ring you found after that night we went to the theatre.'

'Yes.'

Janet straightened the top sheet. Esther had pushed the blankets and quilt to the bottom of the bed. 'Are you all right like this?'

'Yes. Still too hot.'

As Janet rose to open her window a little further, Esther said, 'Mummy, where did Caroline go that night? Nobody ever told us.'

Janet paused, then drew the curtain across the window again. 'Oh, she just went to stay with a friend,' she said. 'Now, try to sleep.'

Esther lay awake thinking that was the stupidest thing anybody ever said – *try to go to sleep.* As if you could! Sleep came or it didn't. She had often tried to catch that instant when unconsciousness took over, when you fell from dozing into the other world of dreams, but had never managed to do it.

Stayed with a friend. It didn't even *sound* true. Did that mean her mother knew where Caroline had gone, or not? Was she not telling, or did nobody know?

Daniel knew. That was certain. He would be home on

Saturday, him and Caroline. The house would feel different, full again, and soon she would be back at school. Everyone had stopped worrying about typhoid.

Daniel passed his driving test in August. A week or so later, Harry's friend found them a used Ford Anglia with low mileage.

'What colour is it?' Caroline asked.

'I've no idea.' It had not occurred to Harry to ask, but he caught his wife's expression as she and Caroline exchanged glances in a rare moment of common understanding.

'Not white,' Janet said. 'It'll never look clean, especially in the winter.'

'Oh God, no.' This was not what Caroline had in mind. Nor was a Ford Anglia – she thought them ugly. Still, there were bound to be other cars.

In a friendly meeting over a couple of pints in Ma Cameron's, Daniel bought a Mini from a friend, but this turned out to be a mistake. It was corroded with rust and quite soon Daniel put his foot through the floor. Fortunately, as Harry pointed out, the car hadn't managed to take him past the house next door when this happened. 'At least it was cheap,' Daniel said when they sent it to the scrapyard and were obliged to buy a blue Ford Anglia from Harry's friend instead.

Caroline lost interest in learning to drive once Daniel could. 'Book lessons first,' he said. 'I don't want to take you out till you can drive a *bit*.'

At Braeside, on Grandpa's land, he took her out once or twice, and so did Harry. Then exams loomed, and the weeks passed in a blur, intense with work. They both let it drift after that, with no lessons booked.

*

In October, Caroline heard about a flat from one of her friends, and by the end of the first week in November they had moved in. This was more successful than the Mini. It was tiny, with three rooms and a lavatory at the turn of the stairs. They had baths at Harrowden Place or in the Student Union which provided utilitarian bathrooms with deep porcelain baths. Caroline liked to lie a long time in one of those, in scalding water, topping it up now and then, emerging beetroot-faced but feeling clean and relaxed. It was far better there than Harrowden Place where someone was always banging on the door or trying to shout things to you through it, engaging you in a conversation you did not want to have.

It was what they noticed most sharply on their first night in the flat: the silence.

'We can have friends back now,' Caroline said, 'without having to *check* with anyone. We can have parties.' She sounded more certain than she felt, at this moment. The silence seemed a presence in itself. The tenement block was in a busy street, but the traffic did not matter, hardly impinged. What mattered was that nobody talked to you, nobody gave you instructions, made requests, *interrupted*.

'Do you mind having the wee bedroom?'

'I told you. No, it's fine,' Daniel said.

They sat on the lumpy sofa in their rented living room, ate chips from paper parcels fragrant with vinegar and drank beer. For almost half an hour, neither of them talked.

Daniel finished first and leaned back with a deep sigh.

'I never realised we were so quiet,' he said.

'That's what I was thinking!'

'Will I put a record on?'

'In a minute.'

They sat on in the stillness they had created, content.

'It's funny without Daniel and Caroline,' Esther said.

'I keep expecting them to come in,' her mother agreed.

'Louise says she's going to have her own room at last. Is she going into Caroline's?'

'I thought we'd use it as a spare room. High time I had one, considering the size of this house.'

'You can break it to Louise, then!' Esther said, laughing.

'Margaret says she wants Daniel's little room but we'll redecorate it first.'

'Really? Oh well, that solves it then.'

Esther, having had her own room for so long, gave no further thought to it, and changed the subject. Margaret, thinking of it so much, was only worried Louise would take a fancy for Daniel's room, and insist on having it herself.

Later, when the girls were in bed, Janet said to Harry, 'Margaret's very quiet. The girls are missing their cousins.'

'Our cuckoos have flown the nest, after all,' he said, smiling at her. 'Are you?'

'Missing them? I hope the flat is warm enough, with just that wee gas fire,' was all she said.

'They should have bought one, it's just money down the drain, paying rent,' Harry said, still annoyed at having his advice ignored.

'I dare say they'll get fed up with that place,' Janet said. 'It's not up to much.'

She had done everything she could. She had insisted on cleaning it before they moved in and they had finally done so equipped with home baking and a chicken casserole. She had checked the scanty inventory and bought them Pyrex dishes, a set of good knives and an ironing board and iron. They had not expressed more than dutiful gratitude for any of this, and she realised they felt much as she did. Everyone had done their best, and now it was over. The years of being responsible for Caroline and Daniel were finished.

At least, that was how it seemed then, as Harry and Janet sat on their own in the den. It was cosier than the sitting room, and they seemed to feel they had to reclaim it, before Esther wanted it to have her friends round, and Louise started complaining there was nowhere for her. Margaret said nothing, about the den or about the absence of her brother and sister in the house. She didn't feel well. It was the feeling she had when her temperature was going up. She didn't want to miss school, so she wouldn't tell Janet just yet.

The Accident

1964

When Caroline began to wake up there was a hazy moment suffused with the dream she was rising from, evaporating so fast there was only the essence of it left when memory took over. Then there came that dead weight again and nausea rising in her throat. All day she would feel as if she had been punched. She was dazed, winded, as if recovering from a blow to the chest.

In the darkness of the December morning, she was conscious of her heart thumping: was she feeling it or hearing it? She could not decide. The more you thought about it, the worse it got. Not just the painful heart.

Rain rattled against the window panes and a bluster of wind shook the lilac tree, its branch tips brushing the side of the house, bending with a gale that had come with the thaw. They both had leave not to go in to Marischal College or the hospital, with the agreement that this concession would be reviewed in two weeks. For a few days she could go on lying in bed till there was at least some daylight and it was easier to make herself get up. She had been trying to work here, but she missed their little flat, the rickety folding table in the window; the view of the narrow street; women in headscarves tied turban-fashion over their curlers, hurrying along with shopping bags; men in flat caps going to work early in the morning; the schoolchildren in twos and threes, calling to each other.

Daniel sat in his old room at the oak table he had always used in the Harrowden Place house and stared at open books, a half-filled notebook. He was not working either; he was doing nothing but stare at the same pages, not seeing them.

In a week, the world had changed.

A man Harry did business with had come to dinner with his wife last Saturday night. He was the genial sort who brought sweets for the children and had a brief conversation with Caroline and Daniel, heartily acknowledging their adulthood in a way that emphasised their youth. He said, 'You're looking well on it anyway' when Caroline responded to his version of the usual enquiry – *How do you like medicine? You must be nearly finished now?* She had said, rashly, it seemed, 'Yes, it's great, I'm enjoying it – only a year to go till we graduate.' They had only called in on their way to the party to collect a pair of gold sandals Caroline had left in the wardrobe here.

The temperature had been falling all week and when they arrived they peeled off scarves and opened their coats in the newly warm hall.

'So, the new central heating is working then!' Caroline said. She was both amused and resentful that this had been done almost as soon as she and Daniel had left.

'I wish we'd done it years ago,' Janet sighed. 'What a difference it makes.'

'Anyway, the flat is easy to heat up,' Caroline said.

They were in the kitchen, where Janet was putting slices of melon on plates. She began slicing between flesh and skin, concentrating.

'Well,' Caroline said, 'we just came in to say hello and to collect my shoes and the records Dan left behind. We're heading out to Bridge of Don to collect Alison on the way to a party.'

Janet looked up. 'Is that the chain Daniel gave you for your 18th birthday? It suits you.'

Caroline fingered it, light and delicate on her neck. 'Yes.'

Janet's attention was on the melon again. 'Sorry dear, I need to get on.'

She's fussed, thought Caroline, she doesn't really like dinner parties. She went into the hall, where their scarves and Daniel's fur-lined gloves, the birthday present she had given him in anticipation of winter, were piled in a heap on the hallstand. Daniel came out of the sitting room.

'Time we got going,' he said.

'What time is it?'

'Eight o'clock.'

'Oh help, come on then.'

They snatched up their things and made for the door, calling goodbye as they went, leaving Harry and Janet and their guests to beef casserole and lemon meringue pie.

Janet, taking plates of melon slices through to the dining room, saw that Daniel's gloves had fallen onto the floor, unnoticed. By the time she had put the plates on the table and come back to open the front door, their car had gone. She shut it again quickly, to keep the heat in.

'I think it might snow,' she said to Harry and their guests when she went to tell them dinner was ready. 'It's terribly cold outside.'

As they got into the car, Caroline thought how happy she was, how relieved they were off on their own, and did not have to go back to Harrowden Place when the party was over, and creep in trying not to wake anyone else.

'Even with the central heating,' she said to Daniel, 'I wouldn't go back now, would you?'

He laughed. 'I fancied a bit of that lemon meringue pie though!'

'I wish we'd not stayed so long – we're going to be late for collecting Alison now. I said to her just after eight o'clock and we've got to get out to the Bridge of Don.'

'Ok,' he said, 'we're on our way now.'

When the terrible thing happens and you are thrown into the outside world with no say in what will happen next, when you are so frightened you can hardly breathe – where do you turn? Who is there?

Harry of course. Their father was in London, Grandpa was dead, Granny too old and anyway out at Braeside. Besides, Harry is the person who will know what to do. Harry will take care of everything. Harry will make it all right.

This time, he could not. Caroline and Daniel knew that, even as he took over. He drove them home from the police station, spoke to the police and arranged for the car to be taken away when they had finished examining it. He dealt with the insurers through his own insurance broker. He took them back to Harrowden Place and contacted the university. He provided all the reassurance he could. They were so grateful they made no objection to returning to his house for a few days *till this is sorted out*. Janet and Esther went to the flat to fetch their clothes and books and they were re-installed in their old rooms, still unchanged.

It was as if they were invalids and could do nothing for themselves. Caroline lay awake in the dark morning thinking about this, and about what happiness was, a thing she felt she could be objective about, now it had gone. It was talking about happiness that made it vanish, perhaps. It seemed they'd had no trouble at all in their lives, till this.

If *she* felt like this, what about Daniel? It was the first time she had not known exactly what he was thinking. That separation from him was the worst of it, beyond even the terror of not knowing what might come of this. *They won't prosecute,* Harry said, *it wasn't Daniel's fault. It seems the fellow was blind drunk but they have to investigate because he died. It will be fine, wait and see.*

That was crazy! How was it ever going to be *fine* again? *I'm going mad,* she thought, lying in the dark, listening to the sounds of the family getting up, the girls thudding up and downstairs, water running in the bathroom, bedroom doors banging, dishes clattering in the kitchen, the kettle whistling, while she didn't think she could ever eat breakfast again. Then Harry's deeper voice in the hall – *get a move on, you'll be late* – because he was giving Esther and Louise a lift to the High School.

She was a mad person still lying in bed while all this ordinary life went on outside her door. How could they do that, how could they be so cheerful and normal when her life was ruined and Daniel's life was ruined and –

'Pull yourself together,' Janet had said last night. It was like a slap in the face.

'*What?*'

'It's much worse for Daniel, a horrible thing to happen to him,' Janet said. 'But it wasn't his fault, and he will get over it. You should be helping him to do that, not dramatizing it like this.'

When Caroline had left the room, slamming the living room door behind her, she heard, faintly, Harry's doubtful voice, 'Maybe you're being a bit hard on her – it was an awful shock for them both. A terrible thing to happen.'

Caroline paused. She was not so angry and upset she did not want to hear what Janet said.

'I'm not denying that,' Janet agreed. 'But if she's going to be a doctor, she'll have to learn to rein herself in a bit. She's no help to Daniel like this.'

Furious, Caroline ran upstairs and flung open Daniel's door. It was already ajar; he was lying on his back on his bed, eyes open, staring at the ceiling.

'Honestly – she doesn't understand a thing.'

Daniel turned his head in her direction, and she pulled up, frightened. It was as if he had gone blind – knew where the voice came from, but could not see the speaker. Could not see her.

'Dan?'

'Sorry. What?' He began to sit up.

'Nothing. Just Janet. It doesn't matter.'

'Right.' He lay down again.

Caroline perched on the side of the bed. 'Have you been working?'

'Not really.'

'It's nearly Christmas anyway – we've got time to catch up.'

He did not answer. She put her hand on his stockinged foot. 'You're cold.'

'My feet are always cold.'

She rubbed his toes between her palms, warming them. He lay still for a moment, putting up with this, then he said, 'It's not just that I can't concentrate.'

'Oh, I can't either.'

'It doesn't seem to have anything to do with me any more.'

She let go of his foot. 'What do you mean?'

He turned his head towards her and in the dim afternoon light she saw the shadow of his lashes on his cheeks, the hollows of his eyes, the tight line of his mouth, that had always been curved for humour, on the verge of being amused. *What are you smiling at?* Diana used to ask him, *you always look as if you've got a joke you're not sharing.*

Caroline thought of the dead man, of Diana, dead too, of something lost from them, a life that could not be recovered. She blinked back tears – *pull yourself together.*

'Caro,' Daniel said, putting his hand on her arm. He did see her, he still saw her. 'Don't cry.'

'I'm sorry. '

'You don't need to be.'

'It'll be all right, Harry says.' She dashed the tears away. 'Do you want a cup of tea or something?'

'Yeah. I'll come downstairs. It is cold up here – and I'm sick of being cold.'

'I'll put the kettle on.'

When she had gone, he went on sitting on the edge of the bed, his cold feet on the floor. He had been cold since last Saturday night, since the accident. He closed his eyes, seeing it again, the whirl of snow in the headlamps, the black shape rearing up in front of the car in the dark, the *whack* of the body on the bonnet, then flung in the air like a flying scarecrow, brakes screaming, Caroline screaming, the skid of the car on the wet road and onto the verge, into the hedge and coming to a halt, the engine cutting, silence. Eerie silence and a smell of snow and blood, his own blood, the taste of it metallic in his mouth, the cut lip, but no pain. No pain at all, then.

He opened his eyes. He was shaking. The room was familiar as his own flesh: the embossed cream wallpaper, the dark red carpet, the Lloyd Loom chair with its blue cushion flattened by Margaret's cat sleeping there. He looked at his table by the window, the books open: the central nervous system, the beautiful tracking of nerves and muscles throughout the body, the heart, the pumping of blood to and from the magic heart, the intricate diagrams he had come to love, the work he had thought would be his whole life.

Downstairs in the hall, the telephone was ringing but he did not hear it, it did not reach him. Then Caroline came running upstairs, calling him, and the door was thrown open.

'It's the police – Harry says you've to come. Come down Dan – they want to speak to you.'

'Sorry, Dad,' Daniel said. 'You don't get a say in it.'

'You're an adult, of course,' his father began, his high colour intensifying on his cheekbones. His outdoor, weather-beaten face, too long exposed to Mediterranean or African sunlight, had become impassive, brick red, the eyes small and dark like Janet's but dull, without her fierce alertness.

Daniel's face was equally unreadable: oblique, almost sly. Was that what humour turned to when there was no fun left and it was all serious, terrible? From the top of the stairs Esther watched them, keeping absolutely still. She was just behind the top of the Christmas tree, so perhaps invisible to them if they should look round, but she was taking no chances. It was the biggest tree they had ever had, obtained from someone Harry knew in the Forestry Commission. Esther, on the landing, was level with the fairy, which had slipped a little and leaned sideways. If they moved into the sitting room, whose doorway they blocked, she would no longer see Gordon and Daniel, but might still hear what they said. Hearing raised voices she had come out of her bedroom but had not really meant to eavesdrop; now she could not advertise her presence without being accused of it. At this moment, she could not anyway have torn herself away, so she waited, holding her breath.

'You never had a say,' Daniel said. 'Not when it comes to something like this.'

'You've been well funded through this degree, you've wanted for nothing, the pair of you. You wouldn't have had to touch your mother's money if you hadn't been so determined to live in a squalid flat and buy that bloody car. It's sheer madness to throw away your career like this.'

'I'm mad then.' Daniel shrugged. 'Makes no difference. I've made up my mind.'

'Don't be stupid.' Gordon had raised his voice and but Daniel was lowering his. Esther could barely hear him as he replied.

'I owe you nothing. There's nothing good come out of this *thing* – but I have learned that.'

'What on earth are you talking about?'

Gordon's roar brought Janet hurrying from the kitchen. 'What is it? What's wrong?'

Esther had instinctively moved back when her mother appeared. If she pretended to come out of her room now, she would seem to be there just because of the shouting. Something about her mother made her hesitate. Two tiny worry lines were drawn between her eyebrows and there was a tension as if she had been pulled tight. Esther saw her mother was upset and her heart jolted. She bit her lip in case she started to cry. It was awful when they shouted – awful because it was so rare. Something tugged at memory – Gordon shouting, her father's voice hard and angry, her mother placating them. It was the same now.

'He's not thinking straight,' Gordon said, sounding weary

rather than angry. 'Tell her Daniel, tell her what you think you're going to do.'

'Think!' Daniel sounded amused for the first time, but not the old amusement. 'I'm not just *thinking* – I'm going to do it.'

'*What?*'

Daniel turned to his aunt. 'I'm leaving, Janet.'

Janet frowned, the little lines deepening. 'Leaving what? Here? Well, it's up to you, if you'd really rather be in the flat.'

'No, medicine. He's giving up his degree.'

'No!'

'He should take a year out, if he must,' Gordon went on. 'I think it's a mistake, myself. Work's the best thing.'

'But that's what you mean, isn't it, Daniel?' Janet asked. 'Caroline said you felt you couldn't go back just yet.'

'No. I'm leaving altogether. Medicine, our flat, Aberdeen.' He paused, considering. 'Probably Scotland too.'

'No!' Esther had never known her mother look or sound so bewildered. She always knew what to do, what to say. I wish they'd stop, she thought miserably, I wish they knew I was here.

They moved into the sitting room and, just before her mother closed the door, she heard Gordon say, his voice rough, 'All right, you don't think you owe *me* anything – but what about your grandparents – and Janet? And Harry? I don't know what you'd have done without him. '

Esther got up painfully: her legs had gone to sleep and the tingling was agony. She stamped her feet and shook her legs one after the other, willing them back to normal.

'What's going on?'

It was Margaret, standing in her bedroom doorway. She must have heard the shouting, but had stayed where she was until there was silence.

Esther rubbed her calves. 'Pins and needles.'

'No, Daddy – what was it about?'

'Daniel says he's going away – giving up being a doctor. Leaving Aberdeen – I don't know if he will though, I'm sure he won't do that.'

You always had to reassure Margaret. Yet there might be some things you could not reassure her about. The accident had been bad enough, but they had shielded her from the worst; they had *all* done that. It's not just me and Louise, Esther pondered as she went into Margaret's room with her. We don't tell her things because the grown-ups don't. Think of Diana dying. But Diana had become an almost mythical figure, the beautiful dead mother and aunt. Margaret had been very young then, hardly able to understand, Janet had said.

Margaret was crying so Esther sat on the bed hugging her, telling her it would be all right – though perhaps it would not.

The thought occurred to Esther that Caroline might go too, and she shivered. Despite the central heating it was not very warm upstairs, and with the door ajar, a cold air seemed to come in from the landing. Still, Margaret was hot for once. She often seemed such a cold, puny little thing. Esther got a clean handkerchief from the chest of drawers. It was one of the pack Eileen gave them every year – the same square flat parcel, promising disappointment. This Christmas's handkerchiefs had forget-me-nots embroidered in the corner. Even Margaret had graduated from hankies with nursery rhyme figures printed on them. She patted Margaret's eyes. 'Here, Tilly, you take the hanky.'

'I don't want Daniel to go away.' Margaret brightened suddenly. 'Caroline won't let him.'

'No.'

'Well then.'

Esther could not think of anything that had ever divided Daniel from Caroline. If he were going, she would go too, or it would be with her blessing.

'Let's go down. Louise will be home soon from Denise's house and Blue Peter must be coming on.'

Esther suddenly longed for Louise to be there. She wouldn't cry, she'd make light of it, not care, dash in and ask them all directly – *Dan's not going away, is he?*

Heart sinking, she knew he would, for she had heard the conviction in his voice. Dan, who never argued or got in a state about anything, Dan, who hadn't been the same since that dreadful night when Louise had come running into the living room, her eyes wide with horror. *There's been an awful accident. Caroline's just phoned – they're in a police station.*

It had made no sense then and made little more now. I wish we could go back, Esther thought, I wish we could undo that whole night.

It was one thing to tell his father; another to tell the rest. He was sorry Janet had heard the argument, sorry he had let it out to Gordon first.

Second. Caroline was first, of course she was.

She had not tried to stop him. The difficult thing was preventing her from throwing it all up and coming too. Saying to her 'I need a while on my own,' was reasonable, he knew it was. It was a reasonable thing to ask: to be alone, without his family, without his twin sister. Other people did it.

He had dreaded telling her.

'I know,' she said. 'I know you want to go. I've seen those books on your desk, the same books, open at the same pages. I know you're not working, I know you've given up in your head already.'

'I'm glad you see it. I don't think anyone else does. They think I'll be fine after New Year, back in uni, back working again. But I won't.'

She sighed. 'I'll come with you.'

'No!' He put a hand on her arm, conciliatory. 'Think about Janet and Harry. Granny. We can't both go at once.'

'Is it just a year out you want? It will be hard coming back, though.'

'No. Well, maybe. How can I tell? I just know I can't go back to pretending to be a doctor, after what happened.'

'It was – '

'Don't say it wasn't my fault, that's what they all say, and it isn't the point. Not at all.'

'I was going to say it was mine.'

'No.'

'I was in such a hurry and – '

'No. Don't. It's not your fault. It was my responsibility. All of it.'

The accident had been reported in the *Press & Journal* with a photograph of the car in the ditch since there was no photograph of the victim. If he was a victim. It seemed to Caroline that they were the victims. It was news in that quiet spell before Christmas when nothing much happens because people are preoccupied and busy.

They were sitting in a bar in Union Street, not Ma Cameron's or one of the other student bars, but a place much frequented by working men and the unemployed at lunchtimes and five o'clock. It was quiet on weekday evenings. There was a long mahogany bar behind which a poker-faced barman, who had seen everything there was to see as far as drinking men were concerned, and a plump barmaid spoke quietly to each other and polished glasses or did nothing at all. The smoke from the woman's cigarette curled upwards, its faint skein reflected in the mirror behind the optics.

Caroline and Daniel sat on hard chairs at one of the scarred wooden tables, turning beer mats for Mackeson Stout and Tennants Lager in their hands, making them spin. The place smelled of beer and cigarette smoke and furniture polish.

'Other people – ' Caroline began.

'Not to be relied on.'

'No.'

'Hell too.'

'What?'

'*Hell is other people.* Sartre. *Huis Clos.*'

'How do you know that?' She resented his knowing things she did not. Not about football or rugby, that sort of stuff, but about *books*, yes, she ought to know as much as he did.

'Gillian. Back in third year.'

'Oh yes, that girl doing the French degree.' She had been going out with another medic that year. She had not gone out with anyone doing a different degree since first year. That hardly counted.

'You're right,' she said suddenly. 'Our world is very narrow. If you don't go now, when can you? When can I?'

'You can go later.'

'You want to go on your own.' She could hardly be surprised, but something gave way inside her. If she had not been a medical student, she might have called it her heart.

'That's the point. But you'll have your turn to go off, do whatever you like. I promise.'

'What do you promise?'

'I'll make it all right with Janet and Harry if you drop out later, go abroad, stop being a doctor, marry a criminal mastermind or a Conservative politician.'

She laughed, despite herself. 'Oh Daniel, that's the first joke you've made since – ' She stopped.

'I don't call getting hitched to a Tory a joke, my dear.' He swallowed the last of his pint. 'Do you want another drink?'

'All right.' Before he could rise to go to the bar, she said, 'You want me to make it all right with them for you, persuade them they should respect your decision, let you drop out of medicine?'

'Yeah. That's it.'

'I'd rather come with you.'

This would not happen. He had made up his mind to go, and he had equally made up his mind she would not come with him. She thought of all the work she had done, of the fight it had been to get to the place she inhabited. *Doctor Livingstone, I presume.* . . .Their old joke to each other so that when other people made it, it was not too tiresome. No, if this was what she had to do to make it all right, she would carry on, she would not give up now. After all, it was getting off lightly.

'Where will you go?' she asked him when he sat down again with his pint and her shandy.

He shrugged. 'Don't know yet. Away.'

'You'll tell me though?'

'I'll send postcards.'

She shook her head, smiling at him. Not for one minute did she think this was all she would receive from him while he was away. He would phone, he would write, he would come back to see them, he would not be gone long.

When she spoke to Janet and Harry, when she talked to her father (not caring really what any of them thought), she made a good job of reassuring them, knowing she was the only one who could. She made them believe he just needed a break, that he would be back and would eventually finish his degree. She led them to believe Daniel had discussed this with the university, the faculty, his tutor. It was weeks before they found out otherwise and by then it was too late. When they rounded on her it meant nothing, because by then she had lost Daniel.

At first she thought it must be liberating, to go where no one knew you and you had no roots or base. She envied him with an ache so powerful her head hurt, thinking about it. Then she realised it was not like that at all.

He had found the little pebbles dropped long ago on the forest floor and followed them out to the wide world beyond. Not home though, he would not come home.

III

The Crack in the World
1967–1970

So Inge put on her best clothes, and . . . set out, stepping very carefully, that she might be clean and neat about the feet, and there was nothing wrong in doing so. But when she came to the place where the footpath led across the moor, she found small pools of water, and a great deal of mud, so she threw the loaf into the mud, and trod upon it, that she might pass without wetting her feet. But as she stood with one foot on the loaf and the other lifted up to step forward, the loaf began to sink under her, lower and lower, till she disappeared altogether, and only a few bubbles on the surface of the muddy pool remained to show where she had sunk.

The Girl Who Trod on the Loaf,
Hans Christian Andersen.

Hogmanay

1967

'Didn't your cousin kill somebody in an accident?' a red-haired student asked Esther at the Hogmanay party. 'He was a medic, wasn't he? My brother was in his year.'

He was drunk, she realised later, but at the time all she could think was *how dare you?* All she felt was fury. Three years on, she was still defensive and this was a stranger who had no right to an opinion.

'He didn't kill anybody,' she said. 'A man – *a drunk* – ran in front of the car. Dan wasn't even driving very fast. It was snowing. It wasn't his *fault*.' She glared at him.

'God, sorry,' said the student, shaking his head. 'Sorry – no – yeah. Sure – I didn't mean . . .'

Esther walked off, leaving him leaning on the wall at the bottom of the stairs, gesturing apologetically at her with a bottle of stout.

It was her first Hogmanay party – and my last, she was thinking bitterly, if this is anything to go by. She had been so keen, so insistent to her parents that she would be with friends, girls they had met. I'm sixteen, she kept saying to them. For goodness sake.

She had not told them she was going with Colin, who was in sixth year at the Grammar, and who had met her at the pillared corner on Union Street they called the Monkey House, where everyone met, to take the bus over to Devanha Gardens, where the party was being held. She didn't know this part of Aberdeen well and hoped some instinct would lead her home again if she had to walk on her own. She couldn't rely on Colin. He was already slumped hiccupping on the living room floor next to his best friend Bill, who was no better. She did recognise one or two other people, but not as many as she had led her mother to believe.

There seemed nowhere to go except the kitchen, where most of the party was taking place. On a small table opposite a sink full of dirty dishes and empty beer cans were plates of dried up chunks of French bread, a half melon spiked with cocktail sticks loaded with pickled onions and squares of pineapple and cheese, and bowls of crisps. That was the food. No wonder people were being sick she thought, recalling her one unpleasant visit to the bathroom upstairs. There was plenty of alcohol, but she knew better than to risk going home smelling of drink. Perhaps if she stayed out long enough they'd all have gone to bed and she could sneak upstairs. How much did you have to drink for other people to know about it? She had never had anything at home stronger than Babycham or Advocaat with lemonade; neither had had the least effect. She tilted her wrist to look at her watch. Five to twelve. In a few minutes it would be 1968 and in a few weeks she would be seventeen. That was almost grown up.

'Here,' said a boy in a long brown jersey, handing her a glass. 'You've got to have something to toast the New Year.' He was pouring everyone drinks from a bottle of golden liquid. *Grouse*, she read on the side. Whisky. 'No,' she began, 'I don't drink, actually.'

He laughed. 'You're kidding?' He put his arm round her, saying loudly to the assembled company, crammed into the narrow kitchen, 'Hey, it's Hogmanay and she says she doesn't drink!'

Someone cheered, someone else laughed. They were all drunk except her so with sudden resolution she took a gulp of the whisky. It burned in her throat, then apparently shot straight to her legs. 'Oh,' she said. 'It's strong.' The boy tightened his grip on her shoulder. 'I have to kiss you – we'll soon be a year older.'

She turned her face to him, indignant, but his mouth fastened on hers, warm and tasting of tobacco, his breath whisky-tainted, his floppy dark hair brushing her forehead. She gave in and let him kiss her, after a moment giddily kissing him back. Someone turned up the radio and there were bells ringing and people cheering and the boy put both his arms round her and held her tight, his mouth still on hers, his heart beating almost audibly so that hers seemed just an echo, as if they were fused, one person. His hands came up under her jumper hot on bare skin. She tried to pull back but he wouldn't let her. Then he took his mouth from hers and shouted 'Happy New Year!' and she laughed and didn't care any more. She drank another whisky and held out the glass for him to pour her a third. Her head reeling, she let him kiss her again and one of his hands crept up and onto her breast, squeezing, making her gasp. *Daniel, he is like Daniel,* she thought, pulling away and seeing his dark eyes on hers, heavy-lidded, as if he were drowsy. Then they were in a circle in the hall holding hands either side with other people and singing with them – *For Auld Lang Syne, my dear. . . .* The crowd thickened in the hall and she was swept into the living room.

Minutes later she had lost him.

As she stumbled back into the hall, the red-haired student said – 'Happy New Year!' and raised his bottle – not the same bottle, I bet, she thought as he staggered towards her as if to take her in his arms. She dodged him, running upstairs to find her coat. In the bedroom a girl with fair hair lay beneath a boy in a white tee shirt sweat-stained under the arms. He was panting and her skirt was up round her waist, his hand in her knickers. Esther felt her face on fire with embarrassment, but they did not even turn. 'I have to – ' she gasped, foraging for her coat. Finding it, she hauled it from under them, yanking it free, and fled.

There was no one in the hall now but the red-haired student who had collapsed on the floor, his bottle of stout fallen sideways in his loosened grip, spilling on the carpet. She caught the rank beery smell as she went past, kicking him on the shins as she stepped over him, not caring, half meaning to do it.

Outside, the cold air was a relief. She steadied herself on the gatepost, then buttoned her coat against the icy wind as it cut round the corner of the street. Which way? After a moment she felt less giddy so turned left, almost sure this was how they had approached the house.

There were small groups of people first-footing from one house to the next, all cheerfully wishing her 'Happy New Year' as she passed them, some waylaying her to offer a drink from a half bottle of whisky or a can of beer. She smiled and shook her head and went swiftly past, heart knocking, but nobody stopped her, nobody minded, they were still at the happy and loving everyone stage of being drunk. She began to worry about crossing the city centre on her own. It might be different there.

'Hey!'

The shout behind her spurred her on, whether or not she was the one he was hailing.

'Hey! Wait a minute.'

She half-turned her head to check who was behind her, all the while walking faster. Then hesitated, waited. It was the boy with the brown jumper. He had no coat but a long striped scarf was wound twice round his neck. The ends fell to his knees and swung wildly as he ran towards her.

'What a speed you walk at,' he complained, skidding to a halt. 'Where are you going?'

'Home.'

'No? Want to do a bit of first footing with me?' He took her hand. His was warm; she had not picked up her gloves or scarf from the occupied bed, she now realised, and hers were freezing.

'I should go home, it's late.'

'Come on – there's a really good party just round the corner from here.'

'I don't even know your name.'

'I don't know yours. Does it matter?'

He was not like Daniel at all – how could she have thought so? His hair was long and dark and he had brown eyes, but his features were much sharper, his nose aquiline.

'I'm Esther.'

'Say that again?'

She blushed, embarrassed as usual by her name, by having to repeat its sibilant sounds to a stranger. 'Esther Duthie.'

'Esther. I like it.' He squeezed her hand and began walking, very fast. She trotted to keep up with him, feeling like Alice seized by the Red Queen, having to run, not knowing why, or where she was going.

'You didn't tell me yours!' she gasped.

'Jack,' he said. 'I'm Jack Murray, I'm a student and I'm going to be a poet. I'm reading James Thurber right now. I was reading Hemingway but I think he's overrated. I like the Rolling Stones and Jimi Hendrix, but the best guitarist in the world will always be Eric Clapton.'

He did not seem to require an answer to this, so she did not attempt one. But the night had brightened, the cold wind no longer cutting her, the New Year promising more than it had only an hour or two earlier.

When Janet went upstairs to check on Margaret she found her still awake.

'Are you not sleeping?'

'I'm bored. Is it the New Year now – I heard you all downstairs.'

'Yes, it's 1968.' Janet straightened the covers and tucked Margaret in, firmly and neatly, making her at once more comfortable. 'Happy New Year, my dear.'

'Happy New Year.'

'Do you need anything? Will I get you some fresh water?'

'Yes please.'

She watched Janet go out of the dark bedroom into the warm orange light on the landing. With the door wide open like this she could just see the glitter of the fairy lights on the tree that stood in the hall, and would be there for another few days. She did not need the water, but it meant Janet would be here for a little longer. She was so kind when you were ill; she made everything seem all right.

'When will Esther be home?' Margaret asked as Janet set the glass of water down on the bedside cabinet beside Margaret's little pile of books: *Little Women, Treasure Island, Pride and Prejudice.* A funny mixture, Janet thought, but she had not had time to go to the library before it closed for Christmas and they'd had to make do with a selection from their own bookshelves.

'I've no idea. She said she wouldn't be too late, but she's got money for a taxi home. Louise is staying at the Frasers with Rhona.'

144

'I know.'

'I'm sorry you're here on your own.'

'It's all right. I don't want to do anything anyway.'

Janet thought she looked unhappy, all the same. 'Do you need to go to the bathroom?'

'Yes, I think so.'

Janet went with her. 'My legs are still shaky,' Margaret said.

'It's because you've been in bed so long.'

'I'm getting better though.'

'Yes, I think you are.'

While Margaret was in the bathroom, Janet remade the bed properly, pulling the undersheet taut, folding new hospital corners. Margaret slipped into the narrow space left for her, like someone being put into an envelope. She was so thin she did not make much of a bump in the bed.

'Don't go,' she said to Janet, reaching up a hand to catch her aunt's arm. 'Stay here.'

'Just for a minute, then.' Janet sat on the side of the bed and smoothed Margaret's hair off her forehead. Not so hot now, so perhaps she was getting better at last.

'Let's make our New Year resolutions,' Margaret said. It was a way of keeping Janet here longer.

Janet laughed. 'For a minute I thought you said *revolution*,' she said. 'With some people, I think that's what it would take to change anything.'

'What's yours?'

Janet thought for a moment. *Find Daniel.* The shadow crossed her mind and slipped away.

'I think it should be to redecorate this room. Don't you think it's time? Even if . . . I know you didn't want to when Daniel had just left, but now we could. Make it yours, properly.'

145

'It is anyway. I like it being the way Daniel had it,' Margaret said.

'Think about it – '

Margaret interrupted her, sounding sure and steady, for the first time since glandular fever had taken hold, weeks before. 'I think Daniel will come home this year. In 1968.'

For a moment, dismayed, Janet said nothing. Margaret had not mentioned Daniel once in the last year, she was sure of that. Esther and Louise referred to him; Margaret did not. Sometimes, she thought this was why she kept being ill, if that wasn't too far-fetched. But she had always been a child who got ill.

'He will,' Margaret repeated. She reached up and touched Janet's cheek with her hot hand. 'I'm sure.'

'My dear, it's been three years, and we've had no word for months.' She relented, seeing the little worried frown reappear on Margaret's forehead, shiny with sweat from her rising temperature. 'Still, who knows? I'm sure he will come back.'

She had been sure, for a long time, though so angry with him, as they all were, disappointed, frustrated. The postcards, addressed to the Harrowden Place house, but for Caroline, and so always forwarded to her, had been frequent at first. Paris, Vienna, Budapest, moving eastwards. Morocco. Then a long silence. Athens. Finally, through the year just gone, only one in March from Ankara, and nothing more. Despite her anxiety, she had been the one persuading Gordon and Harry to leave him be, not to try to find him. Caroline seemed so sure he would come back, and she was the one who would know.

She kissed Margaret before she went out of the bedroom, leaving the door ajar, as the child liked. She must be tired of being ill, Janet thought, what a year she's had.

Downstairs Harry and Gordon were talking about going to bed now that the New Year had arrived.

'I think the Stewarts might come in for a drink,' Janet said, thinking of their neighbours.

'We'll give them fifteen minutes or so.'

'How is she?' Gordon asked.

'Better. Cooler. But she's going to be weak for a while yet.'

'Do you want a drink?'

'No.' Janet sighed. 'If they're coming in, I wish they would. I just want to go to bed now.'

'Some Hogmanay,' Harry said with a smile. 'Is this middle age, do you think, being so tired when other people are up all night celebrating?'

All at once, Janet realised they were thinking about Daniel too, and that was what made them so dull, so unable to rouse themselves to think of the year to come.

'Margaret said – ' she began.

'What?'

She was on the sofa beside Harry and she put her hand on his thigh, for the reassurance of it, knowing he was here and solid and unchanged.

'She said Daniel would come home this year.'

For a moment, neither of the men spoke. Three years of absence and silence, like a reproach. But what had any of them done wrong, that he should do this to them? Gordon was still angry.

Harry put his arm round his wife. 'We'll see,' he said. 'Maybe he will.'

The doorbell rang long and shrill and they all jumped.

'Oh God,' Gordon said. 'Bloody Hogmanay.'

147

Daniel

1968

She snatched up the receiver and said 'hello' briskly. She was just about to leave for work and was running late. When she heard his voice there was a long moment when she could not breathe.

'Caroline?'

'Daniel?'

'Yes, it's me.'

'It is you – it is *you?*' Even her legs were shaking. 'Where *are* you?'

'Glasgow.'

'*Glasgow?* But . . . how did you know where to find me?'

'You're in the phone book.'

'Oh. Yes.' She took a deep breath. 'But how did you even know I'm in Edinburgh?'

'Directory enquiries. I tried other cities too. I've looked in a lot of phone books. But I thought Edinburgh was most likely.'

'You've been looking for me.'

'Yes.'

Caroline could hear a commotion in the background. 'It's very noisy, where you are.'

'I'm in a busy street and the phone box has a lot of panes

148

missing. If you listen you'll hear me crunching broken glass under my feet.'

'Oh God.'

'I'm ok. I've got somewhere to stay – flat-share with a couple of students.'

She said nothing, the words choked in her throat.

'I've got a job. It's all right, Caro, *I'm* all right.'

'A job – what job? Where have you *been?*'

'Here and there.' A pause. 'We could meet.'

She tried to conjure his face, but could picture only a vandalised phone box in a Glasgow street full of noisy traffic and probably thugs and drunks. It was Friday night.

'I'm working till Thursday but I'll see if I can change my shift. I'll come and see you, or can you come here? I've got a nice wee flat, you'd like it, you could come and stay here.' She was gabbling, unable to think.

'I've got a job in Glasgow.'

'How *long* have you been here – you're *working*? You could get a job *here.*'

Silence. No, she thought, no, I mustn't lose him again.

'I'll come and see you. Dan?'

'Yes.'

There was a change in his voice and it frightened her. Before she could speak again he said,

'I'm working till Thursday too. Don't worry. I'll see you then.'

'That's ages. After *three and a half years.*'

'I know, Caro. But it's all right.'

'Is it? Where do you want to meet?'

'I'll come to Queen Street station,' he said. 'I'll meet your train.'

'I'll have to get a timetable – '

'Just come on one that gets here about lunchtime – any time between twelve and two – and I'll wait for you. Can you do that?'

'Yes, yes, I can do that. Thursday. You'll look for me when the Edinburgh trains come in?'

'I won't miss you. Promise.'

She was comforted: he had promised, so it would be all right. For a moment, jealous, she wondered if he had called anyone else – Granny or their father. More likely Janet, he would call Janet, wouldn't he? Yet she knew he had not.

'I have to go,' Daniel said. 'There's someone waiting for the phone box. See you on Thursday.'

'Don't go yet – '

There was a click on the line, then silence. 'Daniel?' She put down the receiver, feeling sick.

It was a long time till Thursday. Should she tell someone? Who? She wanted to tell someone, but an instinct she could not make rational told her not to, to say nothing at least until she had seen him. What about Margaret? No, it would be unfair to tell her yet. She sat down, still shaking, unable to move, knowing she was going to be late.

He was back, he was here, he had got in touch. She had dreamed this, imagined it, over and over after he left. Then, the postcards getting fewer, passed on by Janet after she moved to Edinburgh, she began to see that whatever she did, she would have to do it on her own. That still meant being a good doctor. She had promised him; she would not break that promise. It would not be true to say she had given up hope of being with him again. Nothing but death could make her do that and she believed – was *certain* – he was somewhere in the world.

Outside, traffic went by and someone called out. A hiss escaped from a lorry as it braked. Inside, silence became oppressive, like a blanket, a shroud. Still she could not move.

Daniel, where have you been without me?

Something cracked and seemed to break in pieces around her. She put her face in her hands and cried.

The next morning Caroline's shift did not start until two, but she was up early because she had been awake for hours. She felt light-headed. There was a little Italian café on the corner of her street. She put her shoes on and went out. After Easter, pretending it was Italy and not Edinburgh, they put a few rickety chairs and tables outside. They didn't seem to mind how long you sat there with one drink. She went in and asked for coffee.

'I'll sit outside,' she said. The waiter was Gianni. She knew his name now; the boss, who was surly and never looked at her, called him that.

Gianni grinned. 'For you, I bring outside. You have smoke, and wait.'

'You know fine I don't smoke – and neither should you!'

If the café was quiet, Gianni sometimes came outside and stood near her with his cigarette.

'You medical people – full of good advice, eh?'

She shook her head at him and went to sit on one of the uncomfortable metal chairs. It was not really warm enough to be out of doors. She fastened her jacket and tucked her hands between her knees, warming them. A gleam of sunshine moved between buildings and cast its pale warmth across the table. She shivered, grateful for it.

When Gianni set down the cup and saucer with a flourish, her bill tucked beneath it, she said,

'My brother has come back. I'm going to see him on Thursday.'

'He has been far away?'

'Out of touch. It's been a long time.'

'You're pleased to hear from him, heh?'

'Yes. Yes, I am.'

He looked at her for a moment, assessing. 'I think you could use a cigarette this morning. Or a glass of Chianti?'

She smiled. 'A bit early in the day perhaps. For the wine. But yes, it's a special day.'

Later, getting ready for work, she thought, you can tell strangers anything. Truth, lies, secrets – anything you like. All you have to do is make sure they remain strangers.

In the hospital, time flew past, unmarked. Often she did not even stop to eat. She was constantly on her feet, walking between wards, up and down wards, along corridors, standing by beds, trying to find time just to sit and think but not ever having a minute. Your head was full of the patients, but more than that, of the rapid decisions you had to make, scarcely one of them without a nag of anxiety – am I right, is this really the thing I should do, say?

She did not finish until late on Wednesday night and when she got back to the flat was too tired to eat. She had hot milk and a biscuit, and went to bed.

She woke with the drugged feeling you have coming up from deep sleep, the kind of sleep where you wake in the same position in the bed as you were when the last conscious thought left. For a few seconds she had no idea what day it was, whether she was working or not. Then she remembered: it was Thursday and she was going to see Daniel. She had bought thick lined curtains for her bedroom, since she often came home at dawn and had to try to sleep then. Despite the traffic the summer mornings did not wake her as they had at Braeside.

She checked her alarm clock: after nine already. She lay back, still coming to the surface, for another ten minutes. Then she got up and went to have her shower.

All the way over to Glasgow on the train she worried that Daniel would not be there. It was as if she had imagined the telephone call, so much had she longed for it, willing it to happen. He might simply disappear again. No, he said he had somewhere to stay and a job. He meant to be in Glasgow for a while. He had called her; she had not found him. It would be all right.

At Queen Street the station was busy. She walked down the platform head high, looking for him, feeling sick, her stomach churning. *Be there, be there.*

Then she saw him. He was scanning the arrivals board. He turned and began walking towards her, seeing her almost immediately. She broke into a run, desperate to reach him, terrified he might vanish, as he had in all her dreams the last three and a half years.

'Hello,' he said and put his arms round her.

She held him tight. 'You're here, you're here.' Eventually she drew back and looked at him. He was the same and not the same. Thinner perhaps, with an inch of beard and his hair longer, but she could see past that, she *could*, he was still in essence her mirror image, he had not changed so much.

They walked arm in arm out of the station into George Square. A thin rain had begun to fall.

'Where do you want to go, what will we do?' he asked.

'I don't know – somewhere out of the rain, I suppose. We need to eat, don't we? Have you had any lunch?'

'No. '

'I'm so hungry – I haven't had much to eat the last couple of days.'

153

'Let's get some food. Maybe we could go to Kelvingrove or something? It's quiet there, we could just walk round, look at paintings? I do that quite a lot.'

This took a moment to register.

'How long have you been here?'

He looked uncomfortable. 'About a month.'

'Why on *earth* didn't you – ?'

'I had to get settled a bit first. Had to be sure I was going to stay for a while.'

'I could have helped.'

'No.' He smiled, softening this. 'Come on, there's a wee place round here we can get something to eat, then we could head up to Kelvingrove.'

She looked at him, uncertain and frightened. It was too like a dream: he might vanish if she turned her back. He seemed less familiar than he had even a few moments ago; the beard made him look older. She let him lead the way to a small steamy café tucked into a side street about ten minutes' walk from the station. They had bacon and eggs. The bacon was crisp and salty, the eggs with soft fresh yolks they mopped up with floury rolls. They sat on with mugs of tea in peaceful silence.

'That was just what I needed, after the last few days I've had.'

'Good.' He smiled, wiping a smear of egg from the corner of her mouth. Then his knuckle touched her cheek, just under the eye socket. 'You're tired. Dark shadows.'

'Of course I'm tired,' she said, dismissing this. 'I'm tired all the time – it's just what it's like.'

'So you stuck with it.'

'I said I would.'

'Unlike me.'

'Unlike you.'

'Sorry.'

'I said I would, that was the bargain. But I didn't think you would do *this* to us, stay away so long. Why did you?'

He did not answer. 'Tell me,' he said, 'tell me about it. Tell me you're not sorry you're a doctor.' He seemed to be pleading. Giving way, she said,

'Well, sometimes it's utterly grim. I'm not even going to pretend I've liked it all. But something makes you keep going. I don't know – a sense of doing what you're meant to do.' Their eyes met again across the table. 'I never thought I'd feel like this.'

'You've changed then.'

'Yes.' The words *so have you* hovered unspoken. Before she could ask him about himself, however tentatively, he got up.

'I'll pay for our food and we can walk up to the gallery.'

'I've got money – '

He was already at the till, getting a crumpled note and some coins out of his jacket pocket. It was an old tweed jacket with leather elbow patches, frayed at the cuffs and with a piece of the lining hanging loose, the hem unpicked. He looks poor, she thought with a flush of shame and pity. He was clean, his hair soft, his fingernails short and scrubbed looking, but his skin was sallow and he was, she saw, bone-thin. The jacket hung loose and the belt of his jeans was drawn so tight he had punched another rough-edged hole in the leather to make it fit.

Outside the fine misty rain had thickened: *real rain now,* Daniel said.

'We'll get soaked walking all the way to Kelvingrove.'

'We could go somewhere else.'

'Let's just get a taxi.'

'Well – '

155

'Come on, you paid for the food so I'll get the taxi – they're not that expensive.'

'I suppose you're a high-earning doctor now?'

'Hardly. Not yet anyway. But I can afford a taxi.'

In a few minutes they caught one and got into it, grateful the driver wasn't the talking kind, as he so easily might have been. They sat in silence as the rainy streets went by and they drove toward the West End.

In the cool quiet spaces of Kelvingrove Gallery, they stood uncertain for a few minutes on the black and white flagstoned floor.

'Have you seen the Dali *Christ*?' Daniel asked.

'No, I don't think so. Or not for years.'

'Come on then.'

They reached *Christ of Saint John of the Cross* quickly, since Daniel knew exactly how to find it, and stood for a long moment gazing.

'He's a very modern-looking Christ,' was all Caroline could think of saying. She was uneasy at how absorbed Daniel was in this vision. 'Shall we go and look at the Colourists now?'

He seemed reluctant to move, to take his eyes from the Christ figure suspended above a dreamlike landscape.

'Daniel?' She touched his sleeve.

'Sorry, yes, let's go.'

In the room with the Peploes, Cadells and Fergusons, there was a bench, and when they had gone round the walls they sat down in front of Cadell's *Orange Blind* as if by silent mutual agreement.

'I like this elegant lady,' Caroline said. 'I imagine her waiting to have tea with her lover in a grand hotel.' Daniel nodded, *Mm*. 'Are you ok? We don't have to stay – what would you like to do?'

'It's fine. I'd rather be here.'

After a moment, he said, 'Don't you think it seems a kind of suicide, the crucifixion?'

'*Suicide?*'

'He decides for himself. He doesn't have to die.'

'But it's about God, isn't it? He's doing his Father's will, dying to save us.' She was tempted to add, *except it didn't work – we're not saved.* 'We never believed in all that, though, did we? Despite Granny taking us to Sunday School.'

Every Sunday morning of early childhood they had been dressed in their best, kept clean and tidy and not allowed out in the yard or near the steading. They had walked to church in fine weather, and she could remember the sound of the church bells as they approached Drumoak and joined other people in their Sunday best. This was a vital social event in their grandmother's week, especially the half hour or so after the service when they had shaken hands with the minister, and stood talking to neighbours while the children ran out of the church hall to join them for the walk home. Caroline struggled to remember much about Sunday School except the hard benches they sat on and the books given out as prizes in June before the summer holidays, each with a coloured plate inside, inscribed with your name. She had learned the Lord's Prayer and heard the same Bible stories over and over, so that in the years since they had stayed folded in her mind like memories. Going home from church, they were not watched so closely and were inclined to dawdle, to dive into ditches after a rabbit or scuff their shiny shoes in the dust, racing each other up the road.

None of it had seemed much to do with God, or having faith, which she did not.

'I probably think much more about God now than I did then,'

Daniel said. 'Although, whether or not He exists, He's pretty capricious. He favours some of us, but not others.'

Caroline did not know whether he meant something personal, or if it was a general remark about – say – famine in Africa. She wanted to steer him away from this, feeling they were on dangerous ground, without understanding why that might be.

'What are you doing?' she asked. 'You said you had a job, but you're not working today?'

'Not till six. I work in a restaurant.'

'Cooking?'

He laughed and his face brightened for the first time, so that she caught a glimpse of him as he used to be and her heart leapt. 'Definitely not! I'm a kitchen porter.'

'Oh.'

'I quite like it. No responsibility.'

'Not like medicine then,' she said before she could help it, and keep the caustic note from her voice.

'I think I've had enough of pretty women in hats,' Daniel said, getting up with a nod to the *Orange Blind*.

'Better than men dying on crosses,' Caroline retorted. She followed him out of the room. He did not linger or look at paintings as they went past them. 'Wait!' He stopped. 'What about a cup of tea – there's a café here isn't there? Then we don't have to look at paintings or anything but we can sit and talk.'

Daniel said nothing for a moment but gazed at her, as if working out what should come next. His dark eyes told her nothing, nothing but that he was profoundly sad. Her eyes filled with tears and she reached her hands out to him. He took them in both of his and they stood for all the world like lovers who cannot bear to look away from each other.

'I'm sorry,' he said. 'I think this is as much as I can cope with today.'

'What do you mean?'

'I should go. You should go back to Edinburgh.'

'But we've only just – '

'I'm sorry.'

'I can't bear it if you disappear again – I just can't bear it. You've no idea what it's been like – for all of us. But worst for me, did you think of that, did you think about how *I* might feel?'

'Yes. I did. That's why I kept sending postcards, so you would know I was all right.'

'That wasn't reassuring, actually. Getting an occasional postcard sent on by Janet. They were all so angry with you when you didn't keep in touch properly – I couldn't argue them out of that. Granny didn't seem to understand you weren't even in this country, and Janet was cross because she was upset. Harry never said much, but Dad's just gone on being angry. I think it's partly guilt, but you can't speak to him about it. They were *all* so worried.'

'I did sometimes start writing a letter but it never got finished somehow, and I didn't want to get any back. I had nothing more to say, just, here I am and I'm ok.'

'Were you ill?' she asked. Something more than distance had separated them. Professionally, she knew this and both hated knowing it and was relieved. An explanation.

'I don't know. Maybe.'

'Are you ill now?'

'I don't think so.' He squeezed her hands. 'There's nothing *wrong* with me. Nothing physical.' He sighed. 'Look, let's have the cup of tea, and you tell me about your job, what you've been doing. I'd like that. Then maybe – '

159

'We will keep meeting, though.'

'Yes. I promise.'

Reassured, she slipped her hands from his and they went downstairs to the café.

Once she had begun, it was easy to talk to him about work. He understood, for all he had abandoned medicine more than three years ago.

'I haven't finally decided what to do next,' she told him, letting her tea grow cold, not wanting it. 'But I'm considering neurology. I did think of psychiatry, but then I realised I want some answers. I want to understand the relationship between the brain and the central nervous system, I want to know how it all works, what that means for human beings. Psychiatry has no answers it seems to me; one explanation for human behaviour is as good as another.'

'You're really interested in it. You must be a good doctor, Caro.'

'Oh no, I don't think so. I'm still terrified of making a mistake. They leave you in charge when you're barely competent, a whole ward full of sick people relying on you. And some of the nurses can be so snooty, waiting for you to make a hash of it, knowing better.'

He smiled. 'Yeah, I remember that.'

'Would you think of coming back, picking it up again?'

He looked down at the cup held between his long hands, the nails short and scrupulously clean, and she saw his shirt cuffs were frayed. He did not answer.

'That means no, does it? No for now, or no for ever?'

'No for ever, I think. But we'll see. It's done me good to be with you. I feel better.'

'Oh, I'm so glad.'

She was able to accept it now when he said he must go. The

rain had stopped and they came out to the freshness of wet grass and a watery sun making its way through thinning cloud.

''I'll get the bus from here.'

'How will I reach you? Do you have a phone number?'

'I'll phone you next week.'

'No – no, that's no good, I'll worry too much if I don't hear and I can't bear not to know how I can find you.'

'I'll write down my address. Will that do? There's no phone but you can leave a message for me at the restaurant if you call in the morning after eleven. Don't ring them at lunchtime or in the evening. They're too busy then and they won't bother to tell me.'

She found a small notebook in her bag and gave it to him with a pen, so that he could write his address and the restaurant phone number. He handed it back to her with a bow.

'Here you are, ma'am. But I will call you.'

'If I'm working – '

'I'll just call another time, till I reach you.'

She took a deep breath, accepting this. 'All right.'

'Come with me to the bus stop.'

'Can't I get the same bus?'

'I want to sit on the top deck and look down and see you wave me off.'

She laughed. 'Why?'

'I just do.'

'All right. I might walk back to the station now that it's fine.'

They had stood at the stop for only a moment when a bus came along and Daniel said he would take it. He put his arms round her and they hugged. She felt the warm boniness of him through jacket and shirt, almost felt his ribcage, the core of him, and breathed in his clean dusty scent, familiar all over again,

Daniel her brother, her twin, her self. *How can I let him go?* But she must.

From a seat at the front of the top deck he waved and she waved back, waving and waving until the bus was out of sight. Then, hardly able to see the pavement for tears, she began to walk towards the city centre.

Going back to Edinburgh on the train, Caroline was tormented by questions she had not been able to ask. It was not only Daniel's strangeness, his reserve that had stopped her but her own wish to be with him quietly, as they used to be. Wherever he had been, whatever he had been doing while he was away, she would know in time. It scarcely mattered, as long as she could be with him now, and be sure he would not disappear again.

She was not sure. She took out the little notebook and read over and over the address he had put there: *Flat 1/3, 102 Cessnock Crescent*. He had written the capital 'Cs' like crescents themselves, large and curving around the rest of the words they headed. She was comforted by that, wanting to recognise as much as she could of the Daniel he had been, though he was changed. They both wrote capital letters larger than they needed to be; their handwriting was very alike.

Her heart seemed to be beating louder and faster than usual, as it does with fear. She *was* afraid. Before they met she had decided to wait before telling anyone else, but had imagined herself calling them: Margaret, then Granny and Janet, telling them she had found him, he was back, he was all right. She had rehearsed the words she would use, the calm and almost casual way she would break the news.

Now she did not think she would tell anyone else – yet. All her attention must be on him, on convincing herself he was real

162

and she was with him. She wanted only to keep him by her, not to take a single risk with his attention, his presence, his affection. She had been sure of *that* at least. Whatever else, he had not changed towards her. There was a barrier she did not understand, but she didn't believe it was a barrier he had put there. It was as if he was powerless to reach her. She had waited and he had tried, but he could not do it. All she could do was go on waiting, but at least she would be with him while she did.

She was sure Daniel did not want anyone else to know. If she told them, he might disappear again and she would never take that risk.

They met again just over a week later, this time in Edinburgh. Caroline had been on nights and those nights usually stretched far into the morning. There were times when she was light-headed with being on her feet so long, giddy with a sensation of being dissociated from the rest of her life, from the world itself. The hospital engulfed her; it was the world.

Work kept her from the madness of worrying that she would never hear from Daniel again. When she eventually had the chance to sleep, the terror of that reared up. She saw herself going to the flat in Glasgow and some stranger opening the door to her knock. *No, nobody called Daniel here, never has been,* he would say and look at her with pity, thinking her a duped girlfriend.

He did call her. She was just through the door of her flat, kicking off her shoes, desperate to sleep but so far beyond herself she did not think she could. Her head was full of the night gone past. When the phone started ringing she stared at it, dazed. Then with a jolt she dived across the room, snatching up the receiver.

'It's me,' he said as those we love and live with do say, knowing they will be recognised from two syllables.

163

'Hello. *Hello.* Are you all right?'

'Yes. Are you?'

'I'm just off nights. I'm a bit – never mind – I'm glad you called me.'

Her legs were aching, burning, so she caught a stool with her foot and dragged it close to the phone so that she could sit down.

'Do you need to get to bed? I can call later.'

'Yes, but it's all right. Will we – when will we meet?'

'I'll come to Edinburgh if you like,' he offered. 'When will you have had enough sleep?'

'Never, at this rate. But it's fine – I just won't be fit to speak until really late tonight.'

'Tomorrow then,' he said. 'I have two days off, so – '

'Oh that's good, so have I, come tomorrow, come to Edinburgh. I'd like that.'

He sounded different, better, this time. Perhaps, after all, everything would get back to normal. A different normal, but she accepted that, and was hopeful as she lay in her darkened bedroom, listening to the traffic in the street taking other people to their ordinary lives, and drifted at last into sleep.

The exigencies of their jobs, utterly different and yet with similarly antisocial hours, meant they could not establish any kind of routine. They did however meet as often as possible. The train journey between Glasgow and Edinburgh became familiar, though she often dozed for part of it, never quite catching up on sleep.

He took her to his flat and she met the two students he shared with. Daniel's room, and the part of the kitchen where he kept his things, were sparely furnished and immaculate. The rest of the flat was chaos, but Caroline found it endearingly comfortable. There was no threat to Daniel or her from these thin boys in jeans and tee shirts, eating bad food and leaving piles of dirty clothes and empty mugs and plates everywhere. Joe was an art student whose main study was photography. 'Good,' he said when he was introduced to Caroline, 'brilliant, can I get you both together, right? Twins, yeah? *Magnifique.*' Kenny, who was often irritated by Joe being arty, raised his eyes heavenwards. 'He's a maniac with that camera,' he said. 'Nobody's safe. He keeps taking shots of the fucking door. Sorry, Daniel's Sister. *Boring* door.' He grinned.

'It's a *supercalifragilistic* door, you moron,' Joe said. 'Go on, can I?'

He made them stand outside the main door of the flats, a door with peeling paint and one of its numbers askew – the 2 of 102 leaning sideways, a nail missing. He photographed Daniel first, then pushed the door half open. 'Now stand behind him, right, yeah, that's it.' Behind her, Kenny said something and laughed, and she half turned, missed the first one, was too far back or something. They did it again, but they were all laughing, and Joe gave up. 'Hopeless,' he said. 'I want moody and mysterious. Not hysterical.'

A few days later, he was attaching his bicycle to the railing with its chain lock when they came out, Daniel first, Caroline a few seconds after. Joe dragged his camera out of his bag with rough haste, calling 'Wait!' and caught them, unwary and unready, Caroline still in the shadow of the doorway.

'They make me laugh,' she said to Daniel afterwards.

'Me too,' he said, and smiled.

In Edinburgh, her own flat seemed still and empty in contrast, her life quiet. Daniel said he liked her place, but she could not persuade him to look for a job in Edinburgh. He was more cheerful, but she felt she had to treat him like an invalid who must be allowed to have his way, at least for a while. She had raised the matter of telling the rest of the family. They were having coffee inside the Italian café because it was a chilly June day with an Edinburgh East wind.

'I haven't told anyone yet, but I can't keep on not telling them.'

'Right.'

'Will I call Janet or Granny?'

Daniel stirred brown sugar into his coffee, watching the crystals dissolve in the foam. 'It's up to you.'

'You don't want me to?'

'I should call them myself. I will.'

'Right. So when – '

'Soon.'

'Do you promise?'

'Promise.'

After a moment he said, 'I won't disappear again, I won't do that.'

Relief flooded through her, but all she said was, 'Good.' Then, remembering, making light of it, she said, 'At least they noticed you'd gone. You know that time when you all left the theatre without me? I still can't believe we were right and it was only Esther tried to tell them.'

Daniel smiled. 'Yeah, the disappearing twins. Best we don't do it together.'

She wondered why not; the idea, all at once, appealed. 'It's awful being the one left behind.'

'I know.'

'*I* came back next day!'

'Did you ever tell them where you were?'

'Told them the truth – I stayed with a friend.'

166

It had not been the plan. They had withdrawn themselves quietly from the crowd to stand talking in the foyer.

'He wouldn't notice we'd gone, I bet, for days,' Caroline had said. 'The only person he pays attention to is her.'

This wasn't new, and it was just as true for Margaret, Daniel pointed out.

'One of us,' Caroline said, 'could just disappear – tonight – and I bet you a tenner they wouldn't notice at least until tomorrow.'

'I won't bet,' Daniel said, 'because I suspect you're right.'

It had to be her; he was the only boy, and more noticeable, after all.

'Where will you go?'

She had wondered if she might just walk out of the theatre, down Union Terrace, and head for the country bus. She would go to Braeside. Stay there till her grandparents came home next day.

'Eddie's there, though, isn't he?'

'As if Eddie would bother. He only thinks about the beasts. He'll be in bed, up early for milking.'

She had simply disappeared into the Ladies as the rest of the family put on their coats, ready to go home. They would look for her here, if anyone asked where she was, or counted them all back into the cars.

No one did.

She waited half an hour, to be sure, with increasing indignation at being proved right.

On Union Terrace, the idea of going all the way to Braeside lost its appeal. She thought she might just go back to Harry and Janet's after all, getting a taxi after the last bus had gone, to give them a fright at least. She did not believe they *would* all go to bed

167

without realising she was not there. But Daniel had promised to say nothing, to wait and see.

At the next bus stop was a student she knew, not a medic, someone she had come across at parties, with other people. She knew he liked her.

'Come to the folk club?' he asked. So she went. The session was all but over by the time they got there; she ended up sleeping on the sofa in his student flat.

'It was very strange, being in hiding. It felt like that,' she told Daniel now.

'I took the easy way out,' he said. 'Went overseas.'

'Tell me about it,' she said. Hesitant, he began, but for all he told her, she knew there was more. How much time, she wondered, did they have? She was uneasy about keeping so much from their family and beginning to feel like a liar.

Janet wrote to her every week, Granny once a month, both of them letters with news that often made her miserable with longing for home when she was alone and struggling with work. Now she felt her replies – always brief – had become deceptive. Not knowing her hours of work, they did not telephone; Granny distrusted the instrument and had never acquired the facility to talk on it for more than a moment. It was easy to deceive them.

When she told Daniel about the letters, he wanted to read them.

'I've got every single one,' Caroline said. 'You can read them all.'

He looked in astonishment at the shoebox she handed him. 'There are hundreds!'

'Almost two years of letters, coming weekly. I've been home

of course, Christmas and some holiday, but still, there are a lot. If a postcard had come from you, she put that in with them. I could tell by the stiffness of the envelope, if there had been one that week.' She paused, remembering the lurch of disappointment when she knew there was nothing enclosed. Janet had not commented, had written only, 'I'm enclosing Daniel's pc, or something like 'We can't make out the postmark, but it's the Acropolis so he must be in Athens.'

In the pause, Daniel said, 'Sorry,' and their eyes met.

Caroline put her hand on the box. 'There's nothing exciting in the letters, I hope you don't expect literature – it's just the day to day stuff. Granny tells me if the hens aren't laying, and what the weather's like and quite a lot about people's illnesses and operations. All her friends are old now, like her.'

'Is she all right? She must miss Grandpa.'

'Of course she does. And – ' She had been about to say *and you* but stopped, biting her lip.

'Let me read the letters, then – '

'Then what? You'll get in touch, let them know you're all right? That's what they want, that's all that matters.'

Gianni's little café was an easy place for them to sit and talk, part way between Caroline's flat and Waverley Station. They liked it and Gianni saw them as old friends, persuading them to have minestrone at lunchtime, adding extra garlic bread without putting it on the bill. Before Daniel went for his train, Caroline taped up the shoebox and they stopped at the café for their last coffee together for nearly two weeks. Their hours did not match and Caroline anyway had an exam coming up. She could manage the weeks without seeing him, now she had stopped being afraid he would vanish.

'You've been so good to me, Caro,' he said. 'I wouldn't blame you if you went ahead and called Janet. But they won't be like you – they'll want all the details, a real explanation. Where I've been, what I've been doing, why I didn't get in touch.'

'I want to know all that too.'

'Yes, but – well, I guess you've changed too. You'd have nagged me to death a few years ago.'

'Maybe. A few years ago you wouldn't have gone off on your own, given up medicine, your career, your *vocation*. Your whole life.'

A flash of pain sharpened his face and his cup went down with a clatter. 'I know.'

'Well – '

'Look – ' He turned to her at last. 'I will tell you, I'll tell you all about it. Next time we meet. I need to read these letters first, I need to think myself back to the guy I was then, the *boy*. That life. Being us, at Braeside.' He paused. 'What about Dad?'

'He's always known it's me you were most likely to contact. He's still in London, but he's talking about moving back to Scotland. I think he's had an offer from an oil company now that there's so much going on with North Sea oil in Aberdeen.'

'So I should contact him.' Caroline did not answer. 'Right,' he said, 'I will.'

They sat in silence for a moment. Then Caroline said, 'Did you use much of your money? Travelling around.'

'What do you mean? I stayed in hostels and stuff, slept on people's floors. Did temporary jobs in hotels, on farms, in a vineyard once. I didn't spend all that much.'

'So you've still got some left – of our mother's money.'

'Oh – *that* money.' He seemed suddenly to realise what she meant. 'Never touched it. Not a penny after – afterwards. If you subtract the cost of the car and what we spent on the flat, the rest is still there in my savings account, and whatever that investment was Harry sorted for us.'

'So you could buy a flat or something. That's where mine has gone. Harry thought it was the best thing to do. He says property always rises in value.'

Daniel smiled. 'Harry would. No, I don't want to use the money for that.'

'What then?'

'I don't know that I feel entitled to it.' At Caroline's flush of resentment, he added hastily, 'I think *you* did the right thing – you need a place of your own, working the way you do. It's me – I don't think I can . . . what's the expression? I don't feel I can lay claim to that money. Not for myself, not yet.'

Caroline sighed. 'Oh, Daniel.' She glanced at her watch. 'We'd better go if you're planning to get the four-thirty.'

He put a hand on her arm, keeping her in her seat.

'After the accident – how could I be a doctor? Doctors are supposed to have integrity. They preserve life, they take responsibility. I didn't do that, I was careless.'

'But so was I. Still, it *was* an accident. I don't feel guilty about *that* any more. It wasn't our fault.' She knew she sounded as if she were pleading and that he still did not believe it.

'I decided to put myself out of the picture, as far as anything medical was concerned,' Daniel went on. 'I know we don't believe in God, any of that, but when something you do leads to a terrible thing happening to someone else, you have to make up for it in some way.'

'Atonement,' she said, thinking of herself.

'Well, yes. When I thought about it, the money seemed to be part of the guilt I felt. I used that money to buy the car.'

'So my atonement is to be a doctor, and yours is to work as a kitchen porter?'

'That's just to keep body and soul more or less together. Though there were times I thought they might be better apart.'

'No!'

'Don't worry. I haven't the right to take another life, even my own.'

'It's crazy. You should be using the brains you've got, making the most of your life.'

'Like you.'

'You know it wasn't my choice. I wanted to come with you.'

'But it has worked out all right?' Now *he* was pleading.

She was silent for a moment. 'I had to let you go away. I owed you that much.'

He sighed. 'You made it possible. And though – though it might not look like it right now – that was the right thing for me. I'm grateful to you. I just want to know that – in the long run – it was the right thing for you.'

She shrugged, not answering that. 'We're quits, then?'

'Oh yes, we're quits.' He put his hand on her arm. 'You've worked bloody hard, I can see that.'

Caroline put her hand over his and they sat in silence for a moment till she glanced at her watch, knowing he did not wear one, neither Gordon's nor any other. Fleetingly, she thought of her ring, left at Braeside nearly three years ago. 'We have to go.'

'There's something I should tell you, before we do.'

Panic swept her off kilter – *what?*

'I can get the five-fifteen, that will do.'

'What is it? You're not going away again – please say you're not doing that.'

172

He squeezed her hands between his. 'No, of course not, no. Don't cry.'

'I'm not.' She fumbled for a tissue and blew her nose. Then, tucking it away, she put her hands in his again, wanting the reassurance of touch, of knowing he really was still here. 'What is it, then?'

'It's about Margaret,' he said.

'She's all right. She was ill a lot – the way she was as a little girl, with mysterious fevers – but – ' She stopped. He wanted to tell her something about Margaret, not to ask. What could he know, that she did not?

'It was Janet. Before I went, long before. Just after Diana died she asked me about blood groups.'

'Janet asked you about *blood groups*. Why?'

'Parents and children. She asked about blood groups of parents and children.'

'Oh God.'

'I guessed it was to do with Diana.'

Fleetingly, they tried to conjure Diana, but all that seemed so long ago, and she had become unreal to them.

'Diana? Had Dad said something to Janet? Or was it Diana herself?'

'I don't know. Janet didn't say, but she'd just come back from seeing Diana in London, before she died.'

'You never told me *any* of this!'

'Hush.' He glanced round, since she had raised her voice, but nobody was paying any attention. 'It wasn't my secret to tell.'

'You kept this *secret* from *me*.'

'I'm sorry, I don't even know if there was a secret. I didn't think anything about it at the time, really. It was only later, when I was going away and I was thinking about Margaret, leaving her behind.'

173

'You were leaving *me* behind without a backward glance!'

'Hardly!'

'Well?'

Something changed in the air around them, a mist lifted, and Caroline saw him as if for the first time since he had gone. Here he was, Daniel, straight, without the layers of mystery he had seemed to accumulate in his absence.

He smiled, putting his hand over hers, twisting with fury in her lap. 'Sorry,' he said. 'Don't be cross with me. I relied on you to be ok, but I felt guilty about Margaret. Then I thought it doesn't make any difference, what Diana might have said when she was dying. If that was it. Margaret's still Tilly, still our sister, isn't she?'

Caroline, not answering this, thought, maybe not. With a sigh, she opened her hands and held his, warm between them. 'I'm not cross,' she said. 'At least, no more than usual.' She smiled back at him.

'I'm telling you now,' he said, 'because . . . well, because I'm back.'

Within the space of this strange conversation, Caroline realised she had stopped feeling afraid. I've been rigid with fear since he came back, she thought. And now I'm not.

They sat gazing at each other in silence.

'There's nothing to be done,' Daniel said. 'We just carry on as if nothing's changed. Maybe it hasn't.'

'What about Dad?'

Daniel shrugged. 'We don't even know if he knows'

'So, Diana, on her deathbed, says to Mum – ' She could not imagine it.

'It's all speculation. You can always stack up what you think is evidence, but it's not, not really. The thing is – we mustn't say anything to Margaret. She needs to be protected. She always will, probably.'

'All right,' she said, not agreeing, but for the moment not much caring. After a moment, she took her hands away and looked at her watch. 'You'll miss the five-fifteen if we don't go now.'

They got up and paid for the coffee. Outside, the sky had darkened and the day was cold as November. Caroline tucked her arm in his. In his other hand he gripped the string she had tied round the shoebox of letters.

'Don't you dare lose that,' she said. 'My precious letters. I love to get them, you know.'

'I'll look after them.'

At Waverley, as they waited to see which platform his train was to leave from, he said, 'You remember George's cottage – that place near Ullapool?'

'Of course I do!'

'Is it still there – I mean, does George still have it?'

Caroline bit her lip. 'George died,' she said. 'About two years ago. He had a heart attack while he was climbing and he was dead before the Mountain Rescue people could get to him.' She put her hand on Daniel's arm, afraid of his reaction. 'I don't know who owns the cottage now.'

'Ah. Oh well, things don't stand still just because I've gone off travelling,' he said lightly.

'What made you ask?'

'I thought – I thought we might go there, that's all.'

'We can find another cottage. I'll look, we can organise that.'

'You can,' he said with a smile.

'OK, I'll do it.'

'But we have to tell them – don't we?'

'Yes.'

'All right,' he said. 'I will do that. I promise.'

When she left him at Waverley she was weak with relief. She took the bus back to her flat instead of walking.

He would read the letters, then he would get in touch with their family so that she need not lie to them any longer. After that, they would find a cottage and have a holiday together. It would not be the same – they were older and too much had happened. But it would be fine, it would be wonderful. As for Margaret – by now, only an hour later, she had convinced herself it wasn't true anyway, and if it were – what difference was it going to make? Still, you could not forget that, not altogether.

She had an hour in the flat before she had to go to work, and was tidying the living room when she realised she had not looked at her post, that Daniel had laid on the table for her. Tucked under the electricity bill, unnoticed by either of them, was a letter from Janet.

Dear Caroline

I never know when to telephone because you are working such odd hours, so I thought I would just write an extra letter.

I've decided to come down to Edinburgh at the end of the month to see Sunset Song *while it's on in the theatre. Uncle Harry and I will be away on holiday when it comes to His Majesty's. I just can't let this go by, though it seems extravagant. I've always loved the book so much. I'm taking Esther with me because she's reading it. It's one of her course books. We can stay with Doreen at Linlithgow if you're working. I know how busy you are.'*

Caroline was cold with apprehension. She turned over the sheet of blue Basildon Bond and read on the back,

I've booked for the Saturday night, so we'll travel down during the day and go home on the Sunday or Monday depending on the hours you're working, if that suits you all right.

Two weeks away.

Janet missed nothing. The slightest shift in a tone of voice, the merest hesitation told her more than you wanted to reveal. How could Caroline lie to her when she was here? It was not possible.

Daniel would still be on the train and she had to leave for the hospital in a few minutes. She must find a time next morning to call the restaurant and leave him a message. Perhaps it would be quicker to write. Anxious and flustered, she left for work. In a fortnight she would have to meet Janet and Esther, would indeed have to offer them a bed for the nights they were going to be in Edinburgh.

Janet had read and re-read *Sunset Song*, had tried to interest Caroline and Margaret and her own girls in the novel, but it appealed less to them. It was certainly not of interest to Harry. And yet, Caroline had never known Janet do such a thing on her own – travel to another city just to see a play. Perhaps it was to help Esther. What she was afraid of was that Janet had guessed something had happened. She had an instinct sometimes that was uncanny.

I bet she knows there's *something* going on, Caroline thought. You could never keep secrets from Janet. That was one reason Dan left, why I had to go too.

She raced for the bus, breathless with anxiety. There was no longer any question of giving Daniel all the time he wanted. Their family had to be told.

Caroline and Daniel had been writing to each other, usually a few words on a postcard, if they weren't likely to meet for a couple of weeks. Daniel's were more frequent. She kept all his notes in her bedside cabinet, along with the postcards he had sent during his long absence. Her shifts made it more difficult for her to write and send notes, except on her days off, but she felt she couldn't wait to let him know about Janet. In the first break she managed to take that night, she went along to the day clinic and found some stationery in a drawer behind the reception counter. The envelopes were brown hospital ones, used for sending out appointments. She scribbled a note and sealed it up. The hospital mail was franked, but she had a stamp left in her purse and she could post her letter in the patients' mailbox at the hospital entrance. Once there, she hesitated – *no, I have to tell him* – then dropped it in and strode to the revolving door. She stood outside for a moment, breathing cold air. The sky was clear and there was a faint light low on the horizon, as if somewhere dawn was lurking. With a sigh, she turned and went back to work.

Four shifts passed, but she did not hear from Daniel. He must have got her note by now. He might have phoned the flat but she had hardly been there. Two more shifts and she would have a day off; she could call the restaurant then and try to reach him.

When the policewoman had gone, Kenny and Joe went back into Daniel's bare room and stood looking at each other in disbelief.

'You think we should try and get hold of his sister?' Kenny asked.

'They're going to do it, she said. That's why they wanted her address – why she took away all that stuff.'

'It wasn't much, just that notebook he wrote in and his driving licence and passport. He didn't have any ID on him she said, only that letter from his sister that came in the post the other day. I remember Dan saying, that's her using the hospital envelopes again, joking. He put it in his jacket pocket when he was going out.'

'Oh, right.' Joe thought about this and about what the police-woman had said. 'The envelope had our address on it, then.'

'What's *that*?'

'What?'

'Under the bed.' Kenny pulled out a shoebox. 'God, I knew he was a poof – he keeps his shoes in *boxes*.'

'No he isn't,' Joe said, knowing this because he was queer himself, but hadn't told Kenny, who was not. '*Wasn't*. Jesus.' He looked at the shoebox more closely. 'It's tied up with string – even poofs don't tie their shoes boxes up with fucking string. And it's for high heels, you moron, girls' shoes – look at the picture.'

'Should we have given this to the bobby as well?'

'What's in it?'

'Is it ok to look, do you think?' Kenny asked.

They were silent, realising there was no one to mind, whatever they did in Daniel's room.

'We should give it to Caroline,' Kenny decided. 'I guess she'll come over and collect his stuff.'

Joe sat on the bed. 'I feel like I need a drink.'

Kenny dropped to the floor and sat with his back to the wall opposite the bed. 'Me too. Poor guy.'

'They're twins – she's going to be *shattered*.'

Each of them was wondering how they could manage not to be here when Caroline came for Daniel's things, as she must.

'We should both see her,' Kenny said at last, before Joe could find some reason to be absent. 'Right?'

'Right. Yeah, ok.'

After a moment, Kenny said, 'I never knew anybody who died before. Well, my grandparents, but I was three when my gran died and ten when my grandpa had a heart attack. They were *old*, though.'

'I knew somebody who died of cancer,' Joe offered. 'Well, my mum knew her.'

It was not the same. Daniel was only a few years older than they were. They knew of course that people their age died in war, in accidents, in all sorts of ways. They knew it happened, but it still did not seem possible that Daniel, who had made them spaghetti Bolognese, who liked Pink Floyd and who had anyway walked out of the house that very morning, was no longer living and breathing.

'In front of a van,' Joe said, thinking about it. 'She said it was a van. You'd think you'd see a van coming, wouldn't you?'

'Some of these drivers in Glasgow – they're lunatics.'

'Yeah. I suppose.'

They went on sitting in Daniel's quiet tidy room for what seemed a long time, feeling frightened and shocked, and unable to get up and do anything at all.

Caroline was in the ward with an elderly patient when Dr Grainger and Staff Nurse MacLeod came to find her.

'I was just going to – ' Caroline began, but Dr Grainger said,

'Staff Nurse will deal with it. Will you come with me, Caroline?'

She wondered at the use of her first name in front of the patients. There was something odd about the way Dr Grainger, usually so aloof, spoke to her. Suddenly afraid, she wondered if she had made some terrible mistake – given the wrong dosage of a drug, missed something vital in a diagnosis. She was frightened, when she followed the consultant down the ward, but it was the wrong thing she feared.

Caroline

1968

Frost lies on the fields along the top of the ruts the plough has made, a faint whitening. Shreds of mist cling to the edge of the woods, a wispy scarf for the trees near the edge, wrapping their throats from the icy air.

Caroline has risen early and dressed in the dark, her clothes carefully laid out the night before. After the brightness of the bathroom, the shadowy bedroom soothes. She puts her mother's pearl earrings in, finding the tiny holes for the spikes with the swiftness of practice. Daniel's chain is already round her neck, as it always is. She can brush her hair in the dark, easy when it's straight and falls in wings on either side of your face, the central parting made with a fingernail.

For a little while longer, she will have the silence of the house, its large cold spaces, instead of the stuffy heat and smells of the hospital. The kitchen will be warm and she can make herself tea before she goes out. These days, Granny does not get up as early as she used to, so it is as if she has the whole place to herself.

There's daylight when she goes outside and stands looking over the fields, that pure early morning light that comes in early November in the North of Scotland, the faint flush of the sun coming up on the horizon, the pearly blue of the night sky making its slow farewell, the stars gone, the moon a high transparent disc.

Across the yard she opens the garden gate and begins to cross the lawn. The frost is softening already and her city boots are quickly soaked. She should have remembered not to wear them, but they matched the other things she has chosen this morning, and they stand for something she hasn't quite named yet. She could go back for wellingtons, but the forgotten sensation of icy feet and hands (she has not thought of wearing gloves) is still more pleasure than pain. She breathes in clean air like a drink of cold water, and pauses at the far side of the lawn at the next gate, the one that leads to her grandmother's vegetable plot. Beneath the hedge there are tiny rustlings made by birds or perhaps mice, but nothing seems to move among the fallen leaves.

Today she will decide what to do. Since she realised that she is able to do this alone, that she holds her future in her mind, can direct it by her own actions and is answerable – now – to no one else, she has felt peaceful. The frantic dashing between one bed and another in hospital; the dread that haunted her for hours after she came off shift, worrying about mistakes she might have made; the aimless toing and froing of the rest of her life and then the breaking down, the helpless giving way that finally brought her home to Braeside – all that has stopped. It is as if she has moved into an empty space she did not realise was there. Despair has made its own place; she has found a way to live inside it.

Wherever Daniel is, he cannot help her. He is no longer her advisor and friend, her other self. There is no other self, she knows that now.

Everyone told her she was going back to work too soon, but what else was she to do? There was nothing that would fill up her mind as work does and make her so tired she could not think.

She had no memory of the funeral, or the days leading up to it, and now she could not remember those frantic weeks back at work, brushing off sympathy, getting on with it, being absolutely focused on each and every patient, each and every task.

They had been right, she supposed. She was not sure how it had crashed, only that it had. Janet's regular phone call and one day being unable to speak to her, that silence. Then there was a whispering at the other end of the line as she waited, her feet cold because she had taken off her shoes and was standing in her little kitchen on vinyl tiles. She remembered her cold feet, and Harry speaking to her instead of Janet, saying they were coming for her, just to wait, they were on their way.

For weeks now she had been at Braeside. She knew all about that, there was no fog around her any more. It was like being a child again, with Granny's broth on the stove and her oatcakes on the griddle, her scones coming out of the oven, the comfort of someone else doing everything. When she got up at last she was sent to bring in the eggs or told to sweep the kitchen floor, given the kind of jobs a child might get, that Esther had loved when she was little, but Caroline never had, resenting it all. She did not resent it now. Whatever she thought, Granny said nothing about Daniel, nothing about getting better, or going back to work, any of that. You could see Janet wanted to when she and Harry came out, but Harry wouldn't let her; they too kept their silence and left her alone.

She slept not in the attic but in the big back bedroom across the landing from Granny's. One day not long after she had got out of bed for the first time, she went upstairs to the attic rooms while Granny was outside talking to the egg man, who had come to collect her week's trays. On the top floor the house was still warm from risen heat. This was an afternoon full of sunshine, and she was dazzled when she opened the door of her old room and moved from the shady staircase to bright south-facing space. The room had been emptied out, nothing of her left but the familiar furniture, the bed stripped, its knitted patchwork cover folded neatly at the foot.

She opened the wardrobe door and found some of her school uniform, forgotten. On the chest of drawers was the little wooden box she had left here because she'd been given a larger, more elaborate one by her father which was – she supposed – still at Harrowden Place. It held the rest of her mother's jewellery; all she ever wore were the tiny pearl studs in her ears.

This box must be empty. She lifted the lid.

How small her ring looked, how little it mattered now. She picked it up and slipped it on the third finger of her right hand. It was loose. She had lost too much weight. Perhaps she would wear it now, but not on her finger. She pulled Daniel's chain free of the neck of her jumper and unclasped it. The ring slid along the chain, as it had before, when she had been too angry with Gordon to wear it, but not able to abandon it altogether. It was a pretty ring, unusual. She fastened the chain again and tucked it into her jumper.

There was something else in the box – a piece of paper, folded small. Oh – her will! As children, she and Daniel had each made a will, and this was hers. What had happened to his, she had no idea. Thrown out, years ago, in one of Granny's spring cleans, she supposed.

She folded the piece of paper again, crushing it tight in her hand, not wanting to look at Daniel's name. She would have to write another one now.

She had a bad night after that, almost as bad as those she'd lived through after the funeral. She must keep it from Granny, not worry her. At some point during the long wakeful hours she crept upstairs again with another piece of paper, an angry scribble of words, some scrawled out. She meant later to destroy that. It was childish. She put something else in too, because Daniel had not worn it or wanted it, and she was glad to hide it away.

The next day passed, and the next, another week, and another. It was the middle of October, and as the weather cooled and darkened, she felt lighter. She slept for hours, and walked, and did whatever jobs Granny asked of her, and read her way through Grandpa's collection of Reader's Digest Condensed Books that she and Daniel had mocked when they were students but were now the perfect way to read anything. The tight, hard pain in her chest seemed to move off a little, as if it was standing in the corner, not gone, but no longer inhabiting her so fiercely.

The first frosts came, and the vast autumn skies were clear as water.

Before her lies the familiar garden. The pea shaws that are left are brownish yellow and shrinking, but the kale is bushy and upright, and will go on far into the winter. The fruit bushes have long been stripped of blackcurrant, redcurrant and gooseberry, and only the apple trees have some fallen fruit still left on the grass for the birds. It is all familiar as her own skin, but she seems to see it as if for the first time. Beyond the wall is the South field with cattle still out of doors because the autumn has been mild. They are up early too and grazing, heads down, still as a painting in the first sunlight.

Although she knows she must – and will – make her decision alone, Caroline is waiting for a sign. She does not know where it will come from or how it will manifest itself but it is more likely to appear here, in what is still her home, than in the city.

She rests her cold hand on the wall and the moss seems a little less icy than her skin. She rubs it beneath her fingers; it's like some strange fabric, velvety but rough. For a few minutes she hears and sees nothing; she is lost. Then a sound calls her back. The cattle have noticed her. Hopeful and curious, they have moved across the field. They are in a row by the fence behind the wall, right in front of her, jostling each other as if to get the best view. She might be a film star on a red carpet and they the eager fans, so wholly do they concentrate their attention on her. She can smell the grass on their breath and the warm aroma they carry of milk and dung.

Caroline returns their gaze and for a moment they are all held in the suspended unreality of a communication neither could explain. Suddenly, she raises her hands and spreads them wide as if in greeting. The cows begin to back off, stumbling into each other so that she cannot help but laugh, they are so comical. It's too much: one panicky beast starts to lumber away, breaking into a run, the others following so that now they are all running, hooves thumping on the turf.

The spell is broken, but she has had her sign.

It's too cold to stay out here. She has to go indoors and change her shoes and tell them what she has decided to do.

IV

Good Wives
1971–1991

There was no bridal procession, but a sudden silence fell upon the room as Mr March and the young pair took their places under the green arch. Mother and sisters gathered close, as if loath to give Meg up; the fatherly voice broke more than once, which only seemed to make the service more beautiful and solemn; the bridegroom's hand trembled visibly, and no one heard his replies; but Meg looked straight up in her husband's eyes, and said, " I will!" with such tender trust in her own face and voice that her mother's heart rejoiced.

Good Wives, Louise May Alcott

Weddings

1971–73

i

The photograph of Louise's first wedding sat next to Esther's on the sideboard in Harrowden Place.

It was because of this poor show, as her mother called it, that Esther had the dress, the flowers, three bridesmaids, a four course meal, 150 guests and 50 additional cake boxes sent out afterwards with a few crumbs of cake and a dry corner of icing. Esther had what Janet called 'The Works': a proper wedding to make up for Louise's duplicity, not a Big Day in *her* case but a missed one, never to be recovered. However much Louise wanted to splash out on her second wedding, it seemed that was no substitute. A second marriage was not the same at all.

At her own wedding Janet had worn a grey costume with a rakishly tilted hat decorated by two sharp feathers, her only flowers a large corsage on her lapel. No bridesmaids, no big reception. Wartime, she said. War made things different.

There was just one photograph of Louise's secret wedding. She looked uncharacteristically demure but smiling and pretty, her thin legs half hidden in knee-high silver boots, the flowers in her hair trailing carelessly over her shoulder and the ragged bunch clasped in her hands reaching further than the hem of her mini dress. Next to her Peter was eclipsed by his shaggy hair and beard, his awful flared trousers and patterned shirt. Peter who was completely eclipsed now, no longer part of their family, if he ever really had been.

Next to this photograph on the sideboard in the dining room in Harrowden Place was the representation of the much grander wedding that had Esther and Jack shyly at its centre, dressed up and self-conscious, framed in silver.

Louise had gone to London to get married.

'I've got a summer job,' she announced in May. She was in the middle of first year exams and had picked her moment carefully. They were having breakfast and everyone was in a hurry.

'Have you?' Esther was startled. 'I've not even thought about that yet.'

'It's in London.'

'London? ' her mother exclaimed. 'How on earth will you manage there on your own? What sort of job is it?'

'I won't be on my own – three of us have found jobs in the same hotel. Live in, so we've got our accommodation sorted out.'

'I think we'll need to know a bit more about it than this,' Janet said, 'before we let you go trailing off to London with your friends. Who else is going?'

'Lesley and Peter. You don't know them.'

'You should have told us this last night, while your father was here. He'll not be back now till Thursday. I don't know what he'll say.'

'I'm *going*,' Louise said. 'You can't stop me anyhow.'

'Just a minute – '

Louise pushed her chair away from the table.

'I've got an *exam*,' she cried. 'You always do this – upset me when I need to stay calm.'

Mindful of the exam, and the apparently scant work Louise had done for it, Janet sighed and gave in.

'We'll talk about it when Dad's home. You need to get ready now.'

'That's what I'm saying. Honestly, I don't know why I couldn't go away to university like other people. How on earth am I supposed to broaden my horizons, the way you're meant to when you're a student? Especially if you won't even let me go to *London.*'

On this exit line she went out, banging the kitchen door behind her. Janet sat down.

'What do you think – do you know these friends of hers?'

Esther had been trying to keep out of it. 'Not really. She goes about with quite a big crowd.'

'Lesley I think I've heard of. But Peter – Peter who?'

'Munro. He's doing sociology.'

Janet raised her eyes. 'For goodness sake.'

It was bad enough that Louise had chosen Psychology instead of a real subject like French or History, or a career like teaching.

'So he's her boyfriend?'

'Yes.' Esther hesitated, torn between loyalty to Louise and duty to her mother. 'I think they've been going out for about six weeks.'

'Well,' Janet said, rising from the table and gathering plates together, 'it's news to me.'

It would be, thought Esther with a flash of irritation. There were things you did not confide in your mother. No one did. She went hot, thinking of Jack and his room in Halls.

As she went out, her mother said, 'What do you think about this holiday job, Esther?'

193

Esther had no wish to go to London herself, but for a moment was jealous of Louise's adventure there, for she was sure it would be an adventure. 'Well, she's managed to sort out a job on her own – and if they're living in, you won't have to worry about where she's going to stay. It might . . . oh, I don't know, it might have been better if we'd both gone somewhere else to get degrees.'

'What on earth for? Aberdeen's a perfectly good University – and on your doorstep. No need to pay for expensive halls of residence or flats.'

'I was thinking of looking for a holiday job somewhere else too.'

'Were you?' Janet looked startled, but at once turned away to conceal her surprise. 'With Jack?'

'Yes.'

Janet began washing up the breakfast dishes, and as she did not immediately protest, or indeed say anything else, Esther left her and went upstairs to collect her essay for the seminar at ten o'clock.

In the kitchen, Janet was weighing up greater and lesser evils, and reasons to be anxious or not. They're grown up, Harry told her when she worried about them. You need to let them make their own mistakes. But Janet went on worrying about these very mistakes. It did not occur to her that marriage might be among them – at any rate, not yet. Inevitably, she started to think about Daniel again, and Caroline so estranged from them since his death. They had to keep their girls close, after all that, she thought, had said so often to Harry. It was easier said than done, with Louise. Nothing, Janet found, had prepared her for the row which erupted over Louise's wedding.

*

'You've *what?*'

Louise, waving her hand with its shiny gold ring, so broad it seemed to take up half her finger, still had a dazzling smile on her face. She just doesn't see what she's done. Esther thought.

'I got married. Pete and me – in London in Marylebone Register Office. Loads of famous people get married there. We were lucky the hotel was near so we were in the district. You have to live in the district for – '

'You got married.'

Louise stopped waving her hand. 'Yes.' She shrugged her shoulders. 'You don't mind, do you? We can have a party if you want a proper wedding do for me, I wouldn't mind that. It was just, we didn't want the fuss about a dress and bridesmaids and things. We thought,' she added with an air of conscious virtue, 'that it would save you loads of money and we just wanted to be together.'

'You just – '

Esther had not often seen her mother speechless. Harry, who until now had not moved from his arm chair, got up. His height, his frown over the top of his glasses, caused Louise to step back, suddenly tremulous.

'Louise,' he said, 'are you seriously telling your mother and me that you got married in London to this lad – Pete? – a boy we met once at the station before you headed off to your hotel job?'

'Yes.' She would brazen it out. 'We're both over eighteen, so we didn't need anybody's permission and we got copies of our birth certificates from that place where they keep them – Somerset House or something. It was easy.'

'*Easy?*' Janet burst out. '*Easy* doesn't make it *right!*'

'And Pete – has he told his parents?'

'Not yet.'

195

Louise looked sullen now. It was as if she was trying out suitable expressions to withstand the onslaught that Esther was afraid had only just begun.

'Lou,' she said, 'why didn't you tell us?'

'Och, it was just the way we wanted to do it. Make it special. But I keep saying, we can still have a wedding party.'

Harry removed his glasses and looked at her without a smile or change of expression. 'If that's what you want, you go right ahead. I just hope you can pay for it.'

Louise went scarlet. 'I thought *you* wanted it.'

'We,' Harry said, 'have not been consulted, so I don't see what it's got to do with us.'

'I don't know *why* you're being so horrible,' Louise yelled, red and furious. 'Honestly, most people are really pleased when their daughters get married.'

'I dare say,' Harry said dryly, 'if we'd had a bit of notice we'd have been over the moon.'

Janet had rallied by this time. 'You've been very silly indeed. But if you're married, it's done, and can't be undone. You'd better bring Peter, or whatever his name is, over to meet us properly.'

Louise, crying now, started searching in her bag for a hand-kerchief, gave up and rubbed her face on her sleeve. 'I'm leaving,' she said. 'I'm going to Pete's, I only came back to tell you and collect my stuff.'

She waited for a few seconds, poised, but nobody stopped her, nobody said a word. She flung herself out of the room, slamming the door. They heard her thudding upstairs.

'Well,' Janet said, rounding on Esther, 'you needn't think you and Jack are going to go off and have a hole in the corner wedding like that.'

'Mum!' Esther cried. 'That's really unfair – I didn't know anything about this.'

'No?'

'*No!*'

Harry put a hand on Janet's arm. 'Maybe you should speak to Louise,' he said to Esther. 'You'll be able to get her to calm down. As your mother says – it's done now.'

Janet sighed. 'Och, I'm sorry, Esther. I'm upset.' She sat down on the nearest chair, looking all at once smaller and older. 'This boy – Pete – did you say you know him?'

'Not really.'

'Is he – ?'

What was the question she wanted to ask? Was he respectable, sensible, clever, did he have a future, what were his parents like, what kind of background did he have – all those things. Too late, though, whatever the answers were.

Esther looked at her father, who nodded.

'Off you go,' he said.

As she went upstairs, Esther could hear drawers being banged shut and Louise cursing as she dragged her suitcase across the room. She was still hurt by her mother's outburst. *I want a proper wedding,* she thought. But that's it now – we'll not be able to do it until we graduate. I wouldn't dare ask.

She and Jack knew it was something they would do one day. An assumption had been made, a potential future appearing in both their minds, that they did not talk about, as if talking would make one or other of them shy away and deny it was going to happen. Her main feeling right now was that Louise had somehow spoiled all this, the lovely future they were both going to have one day, white weddings and being each other's bridesmaid. She felt betrayed.

Pushing open Louise's bedroom door, she had again that sensation of being temporarily in a different world. When Caroline disappeared, when the accident happened, when Daniel left and did not tell them where he was and then, worst of all, when he was killed: she had had this feeling then, of being disconnected from her own life. Where had it gone? She wanted it back, wanted back the life she had often thought boring and pedestrian. Now, as at those times, it had all the poignant desirability of something beloved that has been lost.

The front door opened. Margaret called 'Hello, I'm home,' and her school bag landed with a thud beside the hallstand. She must have seen Louise's presents from London, the bags printed with 'Biba' and 'Habitat' – those magical names – abandoned in the hall, and as her mother came out to meet her, she said, pleased and expectant – 'Is Louise home?'

ii

By the time Esther married Jack in 1973, Pete was back in Dundee and Louise, while still legally his wife, had begun to behave like a single girl again. When her mother referred to her as Esther's 'Matron of Honour' she exploded with laughter.

'You're joking! I'm not a *matron.*'

'You're married,' Janet said, offended. 'That's what it's called, when a bridesmaid is married.'

Louise stopped laughing and bit her lip. 'Oh,' she said. 'I see what you mean.'

They did not talk about Louise's marriage. Since it could not simply be wished away, Janet was torn between wanting her to be divorced, so that she could at least look forward to a more sensible match, and anger that she was not trying harder to revive and mend her existing one. 'No one in my family,' she said to Harry when they were on their own, 'has ever been divorced.'

'Except Diana. Do your mother and father – did Gordon ever tell them she'd been married before?'

'They've never mentioned it.'

'Ah.'

'Anyway, she was Gordon's wife, not my family. And it wasn't Gordon she divorced, it was her first husband.'

'Am I not your family?' he asked, teasing.

'I'm sure there are no divorces in your family either!' she snapped.

To this, there was no answer, since it was true, so he did not attempt one. He knew her opinion of Diana. All things considered, he did not think it was a good idea to rake that up.

The invitations were out and the cake had been made by Janet (one tier at a time, over several weeks) and taken to the baker for icing. The bride and bridesmaids all had dresses hanging in what had once been Caroline's bedroom. It was a spare room now, redecorated and with a new plain carpet, startlingly different from the carpet with green swirls and the pink rose-patterned wallpaper it had had all the time she lived with them.

'It doesn't look like Caroline's room any more,' Margaret said, as she took out her blue lace-trimmed dress yet again, just to gaze at it.

'That's what I was thinking. Ironic, really,' Esther said. 'She'd like this much better.'

'How do you get divorced?' Louise asked, sitting on the bed with a thump.

'What?'

'I said – '

'Yes, I know.' Esther hesitated. 'Are you and Pete – ?'

'Don't go on about it. Mum's bad enough.'

'He has to be unfaithful,' Margaret said. 'Or you have to.' She blushed as the other two turned to stare at her. 'Or it could be desertion,' she ploughed on. 'Or one of you has to be incredibly cruel. It's usually the man.'

'I thought you were planning to be a primary teacher, not a matrimonial lawyer?' Louise said.

'There's no need to make fun of me.'

'Look, the point is – " Esther began, but Louise spoke across her, impatient.

'The point is I want to get divorced. I can't keep on like this, it's stupid. My life's completely stuck.'

Even here, the air seemed thick with the unspoken words 'I told you so', or worse, 'You've made your bed . . .' It was impossible to be in the same room as their mother for more than five minutes without being aware of these rebukes. Janet did not need to utter them for Louise to know exactly what she was thinking. What they were all thinking.

She left Esther and Margaret to yet another discussion about how well the shoes matched and what their bouquets were going to look like. In her own room, she went back to the story she was writing about a marriage that had gone wrong. By now it bored her, so she had allowed it to veer from kitchen sink drama to romance, with the heroine confiding in a sympathetic but mysterious older man who also happened to be extremely good-looking.

For a while, the story comforted her, the other world taking over. It was no use though. She must somehow get unmarried. To do that, she had to speak to Pete.

She was still thinking about this when they were having dinner and was so far from the table in her thoughts that it was only when Harry spoke to her directly, she realised what they were talking about.

'I said,' her father repeated, 'have you had any contact with Caroline?'

'What? No, of course not. I'd have told you.'

'She hasn't replied to the wedding invitation and Esther's wondering if we should try to find a phone number for her, or write again.'

Louise thought about this. 'We could just go and see her. Any reason why not?'

'She's in London!' Janet said.

'We could go there – why not?'

'I bet you'd find a wedding outfit there,' Esther said to her mother.

'You want me to come too?'

Louise did not, but waited to see what Janet would say.

'I'd have to think about it.'

Later, when they were on their own, Louise said with a sly grin, 'Mum only wants to come in case I find another unsuitable man in London,'

'I can't see the point really. It would make more sense to telephone.'

'Ring up Directory Enquiries,' Louise said. 'We've got her address, haven't we?'

Janet had gone to Braeside after lunch to see their grandmother; Harry was at work. In the house on their own, before Margaret came home from school, Esther and Louise got out their mother's address book and looked up Caroline's addresses, each one eventually crossed out and replaced by another. Edinburgh, Glasgow, Edinburgh again, and now London. There was no telephone number but Janet had added *St Bartholomew's Hospital, Neurology Dept.*

A call to Directory Enquiries established that the telephone number for Caroline's home address was ex -directory.

'That's that,' Esther said.

'Let's try the hospital.'

'What, ring it now?'

'Yes.'

'Go on then.'

Having called Directory Enquiries, Esther considered she had done her bit, but she also felt nervous of doing more. Caroline had made it clear she did not welcome anything other than the most perfunctory contact. She hadn't even been sure the wedding invitation would elicit a response, though she had gone on hoping for one.

Louise secured the main number of the hospital and dialled it. 'I'll just ask for Dr Caroline Livingstone, right?'

'Yes, unless she's got married.'

Louise put the receiver down with a clang. 'Really? Do you think so, without telling us?'

'Well, you did that, and you were still in touch with us.'

'That was different. I was young.'

'You were an idiot.'

'Yeah, well, I think we all know that.' Louise sighed. 'These violent delights have violent ends, as they say.'

Esther laughed. 'I can't say I saw you and Pete Munro as Romeo and Juliet!'

'I think she would keep her maiden name. Doctors often do. But I bet you anything she's not married.'

Esther did not see why not. She glanced across the den to the bookcase where there were framed photographs of them all as children, crowding in front of the faded one of Gordon and Bess. In one of them Daniel and Caroline, aged about sixteen, were in the garden at Braeside. Even then, she had been striking. After Daniel's death, as if shock and grief had drained her of imperfection, she had seemed to Esther quite lovely. Daniel's grave ascetic beauty was there, at last, in Caroline's own face.

Louise was speaking to someone in London. There was a pause. 'Louise Duthie,' she said in answer to a question. She covered the receiver. 'They're looking up her number in the department I think. Anyway, they didn't say 'who?' I think she is there.'

Someone spoke to her, and Esther waited, a knot of anxiety in her stomach. She must come, she must speak to them.

'Yes, thank you. When will she be back? Oh. No, it's ok. I'll try again.'

'What?'

'That was her secretary. She must be quite important, do you think, having her own secretary?'

'But she's not there?'

'On leave. Back in a week.'

Just as well, Esther thought, they hadn't gone rushing off to London.

When they told their mother, Janet looked relieved. 'Oh, that's why she hasn't replied. She's on holiday. We'll just wait.'

'How was Granny?'

'Och, she's fine. It's fortunate Eddie and May can pop in most days. Though they're getting on too.' Janet was coating fillets of haddock with breadcrumbs so she did not look up as she added, 'She's looking forward to the wedding.'

'Maybe everybody will be there after all.'

Janet paused, a shadow crossing her face, vanishing. 'Oh aye, if Caroline comes.'

'And we'll meet Uncle Gordon's lady friend from Richmond.'

'She's very nice,' Janet said. Something in her tone suggested there were other things she might say, but would not. She and Harry had visited Gordon in his house in Richmond the previous year; he had not yet brought the woman Janet still thought of as Mrs Ashton to Aberdeen.

'Do you think they'll get married?'

'Oh, I think they're fine as they are,' Janet said, surprising Esther. 'He's been married twice already, after all.'

Perhaps the implication was that it was somehow immoral to keep getting married, or that Gordon himself wasn't successful in his choices. Esther was much more concerned that Caroline should get in touch. She counted the days till she was supposed to be back in London, and they could try again.

Esther and Louise had been teenagers who were out a lot: with friends or boyfriends, at other people's houses, in cafés or folk clubs. In summer they had been down at the beach or at the other end of the city gathering in Hazlehead Park. Margaret was a teenager who stayed in her room a lot, playing music and reading, or in Janet and Harry's bedroom, on the newly installed telephone extension, having long conversations with a best friend, or occasionally, a short-lived boyfriend. Now she was going steady with someone called Alan. Janet worried less about Margaret than the other two, partly because Margaret was the third, and she had less energy and fewer doubts these days. It was also because Margaret, apart from being timid and quiet, and ill a good deal as a child, had not given her a sleepless night or anxious day.

Margaret was out with Alan now, and would not be home until later in the evening. He would walk her home, despite living himself on the other side of the city, but so far she had not brought him in to meet her aunt and uncle.

'Don't you think that's strange?' Louise said. She had unworthy hopes of finding Margaret out at last in some terrible indiscretion. For once, not me being the bad girl, she imagined.

'Oh, I'm sure she'll bring him in to meet us soon,' was all Janet said. Louise and Esther made faces at each other behind their mother's back, but Esther, in the bliss of being about to be married, gave other people's love affairs very little thought.

Esther and Jack were in the den; Louise was upstairs getting ready to go to a party. Harry and Janet were watching television in the sitting room. No wonder, Harry said, the central heating bills were so high: they were heating too many rooms. Once all these girls have left home, he told Janet, we'll be able to turn off about half a dozen radiators.

Because Esther had firmly closed the door of the den, and they were anyway listening to Simon and Garfunkel, they might not have heard the front door opening and Margaret coming in. But the LP had come to an end, and Esther had just got up to go and make them coffee. As she went to the door she heard Margaret calling 'I'm home – Mum – Dad – it's me – where are you? You'll never guess – '

She did not even sound like Margaret, usually so calm and soft-voiced. The television was on and Janet and Harry, also behind a closed door, had not yet heard. It was Esther on her way to the kitchen and Louise at the top of the stairs, who saw her first.

Margaret was there in her coloured maxi skirt and army surplus jacket, face flushed with excitement – or shock. Later, Esther thought it was just shock.

Behind her, framed in the doorway, with her loose coat open and a leather bag over her shoulder, another larger one at her feet, was Caroline.

Dividing the Spoils

1973

Caroline had taken possession of her old room. Some of her clothes were hanging in the wardrobe and on the dressing-table sat jars of Clinique cream and her silver-backed hairbrush, a long ago present from Gordon and Diana. The air was fragrant with *L'Air du Temps* and a silky white kimono patterned with blue and green lilies sprawled across the bed. Esther, who had been in love with her trousseau, saw that nothing she had bought so far was anywhere near the elegance of any single thing Caroline owned.

She stayed a week.

'When I got the invitation,' she told Janet, 'I thought I should come and see you all. Esther getting married – I could hardly believe it.'

'I can hardly believe it myself, sometimes,' Janet said but she did not smile in answer. 'At least we're prepared – this time.'

Behind her back, Louise made a face and amusement crooked the corner of Caroline's mouth. With Harry and Janet, she was all courtesy and complaisance – or so it seemed to Esther, watching them, hearing the talk in the sitting room when she found them there. What her mother thought she could only guess, and wondered if she would dare ask, when Caroline had gone.

Louise, aloof at first, came round in a day or so, as fascinated as the others by this changed, almost glamorous Caroline. Or not changed, Esther thought, remembering the seventeen-year-old reading *Alice* to them in the garden at Braeside, doing the different voices with such skill. Perhaps that was what gave her the ability to enter into her patients' lives and sickness. Esther wanted to ask her, but there had been no opportunity.

'I spoke to your secretary,' Louise said. 'Did she give you the message?'

Caroline laughed. 'God, I don't have a *secretary!* There's a department one – that must have been who you spoke to. Marion. I'm not grand enough to have my own. Not yet.'

'You will be,' Margaret said. Caroline smiled and tucked a stray curl behind Margaret's ear for her, lightly, lightly, a gesture which might have been loving or mean nothing at all.

Margaret had succumbed. She was wholly in love with Caroline as she had never been before. There was no Daniel now, no brother to idolise. They did not speak about him.

'I like this,' Caroline said, admiring her former bedroom. 'Much nicer.'

'I knew you would.' Esther sat in the basket chair with its new tapestry cushion, stitched by Janet on winter evenings. Caroline swung her legs up on the bed and piled the pillows behind her head.

'Where's my wooden box?' she asked. Margaret, examining the jars on the dressing table, knew at once what she meant.

'The box with your jewellery? Is it still here?'

'Yes, I didn't take a thing away with me, apart from clothes and books.'

'Mum put it in her wardrobe.'

Margaret looked at Esther, surprised. 'Did she?'

'For safekeeping. This room is supposed to be the spare now, not that many other people have stayed.'

'I'll go and ask her,' Margaret said.

'No hurry.' But Margaret had already gone, running downstairs.

'I thought I'd go out to Braeside tomorrow,' Caroline said.

'Granny's pleased you're coming to the wedding.'

'Oh. Yes, yes, I suppose I will.'

Esther's stomach gave way: *might she not come, after all?* She did not dare ask. Just assume, she thought, just go on assuming she will, so she can't get out of it. She did not at that moment question why Caroline would want to.

Margaret had fetched the box from Janet's wardrobe. 'Here,' she said, breathless, putting it on the bed.

'Thanks,' Caroline said, but she did not open it. In a few moments they all went downstairs and the box was left in the middle of the bed, as if after all, she had lost interest in it.

Caroline spent the next day at Braeside. She had never learned to drive, so Janet took her. Esther and Louise had other things to do, but anyway were not asked to go with them. Margaret was still at school until the following week.

'I wonder what Mum and Caroline will talk about, all the way out to Braeside on their own,' Esther said, thinking of what they would *not* be discussing: Daniel, Caroline's cold withdrawal from the family; Gordon and Mrs Ashton. Though perhaps they would speak about *that*.

'I bet it's all about Granny and how she's going to manage if she gets ill or loses her marbles,' Louise said.

Their bus for the town centre arrived. In the business of paying for tickets, Esther's mind turned to the afternoon's shopping, but when they were settled in their seats, Louise said,

'I asked Mum about Granny's house.'

'What?'

'Braeside. When Granny dies, it will belong to Gordon and Mum. Well, Gordon and Mum and Dad. I said, would they sell it, or what?'

'Sell it!' Esther stared at Louise, her hand to her mouth. 'It *belongs* to us – *sell it?*'

'Mum doesn't want it. That big draughty place, she called it. She said it would take thousands to bring it up to date and she and Dad had spent enough on our own house. Braeside doesn't even have central heating and apparently some of the window sills are rotten. And no fitted carpets . . . that sort of stuff. Not that I've noticed, it seems fine to me.'

'It's lovely,' Esther said. 'It's a wonderful house.' After a moment she asked, 'What about Uncle Gordon?'

Louise grinned, imitating her mother. 'She said *he* wouldn't be interested, not now he's *in tow with that Mrs Ashton.*'

They both laughed. 'Don't think Mum liked her much that one time they met,' Esther said. 'But I wonder what Granny would want.'

'She won't care, will she? She'll be dead by then.'

'Louise!'

'Well, she will.'

'What about – ' Esther felt sure her grandmother *would* know what they had done to her house. They never talked about it, but it seemed Louise no longer believed in God. I do, though, she kept reassuring some other voice in her head, it's not just because Mum and Dad brought us up like that.

In a month she would be taking vows in King's College Chapel, in a month she would be marrying Jack in front of God. A God Jack also didn't seem to have any interest or belief in, but that didn't matter. In time, the minister had said, he may come to God, if you continue to be strong in your faith.

She blushed at the memory of this conversation which had taken place in the stuffy little vestry one Thursday evening, after the Women's Guild had finished and the Minister saw individually young people who were preparing for membership of the Church. Though she liked their minister, having known him all the way through Sunday School and teenage years, Esther had had no more intimate conversation with him than the pleasantries of chat after church or – long ago – the Brownies annual fair. To speak to him about Jack and marriage and the duties that apparently awaited her, had been excruciating. And yet, it had also been a conversation charged, for her, with emotion. Afterwards, walking home, clutching the booklet the Reverend John Simpson had given her *(Preparing for Christian Marriage)*, she had been brimming with tears.

She could not say any of this to Louise, bright and careless beside her. Perhaps to Margaret. Margaret still went to church with Harry and Janet, and Esther suspected her of a more devout faith than even she could manage.

Religion, Jack declared, is something you grow out of, if you've grown up with it. And something you can get fanatical about if you don't. He said that sort of thing a lot, which had at first surprised Esther, since his father was a minister. Harry had said that was probably why. 'Too much too young,' her father had said, and laughed, as if it didn't matter. Though still hanging on Jack's every word, Esther could not quite agree with him about God – or his absence.

Lightly, she said to Louise, 'I wonder what Grandpa thinks of it, looking down on us all – bet he would have something to say if Braeside was being sold.'

To this absurdity, Louise made no reply except to say, 'Are we getting off at Union Terrace, or what?'

On the evening before she went back to London, Caroline and Esther were alone for a moment in the kitchen.

'Would you come upstairs with me?' Caroline said. 'I've got something for you.'

Now that she was about to leave, it was impossible to ask any of the things that had been burning in Esther's mind all week. She was curious, as she followed Caroline to her room. It must be a wedding present, but not, she was sure, a toaster or bed linen or any of the things people seemed to think were suitable. Most of it was boringly utilitarian (iron, chopping board, toaster, sheets and pillow cases) or hideous – how could you be grateful for such things, let alone love them? The tea set from Harry's aunt Ethel had already arrived and was waiting for her in the dining room. Ethel had – unexpectedly, given her age – decided she would travel from Perth for the wedding, but had had the richly red and green rose-patterned tea set with fluted cups sent ahead directly from the china shop. Esther wondered if she could just quietly leave it here. Surely there would not be room for it in their tiny flat? All they needed – wanted – were coffee mugs and a few plates. Janet had laughed when she said so. 'You should be grateful for her generosity – she's an old lady so her taste is a bit old-fashioned.' ('A bit!' Esther had exclaimed, not grateful at all.)

Caroline had not bought them another tea set.

They sat on the bed with its faded pink quilt and Caroline opened her wooden casket. 'Here,' she said. 'I know you have your pretty engagement ring and you'll have a wedding ring, but I thought you might like this too.'

211

It was the emerald and diamond ring which had been given to Bess many years ago, when she agreed to marry Gordon.

'You can wear it on your right hand – I would. It's big enough to be a dress ring,' Caroline said.

No need to pretend to be grateful now.

'It's beautiful – I'd love to have it – but – don't you want – ?'

'I want you to have it.'

There had been the little piece of paper in the box at Braeside – *my ring to Esther.* Was this, after all, the ring she had meant? Glancing down, Esther saw no sign in the box of the gold ring Caroline had worn, and lost, and that had been found again. Caroline was not wearing it or any jewellery except Bess's pearl studs in her ears, and Daniel's thin gold chain round her neck, glimpsed, but tucked inside her blouse.

'Thank you. This is the nicest wedding present I've had. Will have.'

'Ah, it's not a wedding present. It's just for you. I'll give you a cheque later. You'll want to choose your own things for your house.'

Flushed with gratitude, Esther longed to do or say something in return that would be right and perceptive and bind her for ever to this familiar and strangely unknowable cousin.

'You understand much better than anyone else. I'm so sorry – '

'It's all right. Come here.'

For a brief moment Caroline embraced her and she was caressed by the sweetness of her scent and the cool silk of her hair brushing her own hot face.

'You will come to the wedding, won't you?'

'I'll see. I'll try. Promise.'

When Daniel said *promise* it meant yes. Or it had, for as long as he was able to keep his promises. Caroline knew that better than Esther, knew what weight the word had.

What Esther wanted to ask now was whether Caroline intended to give Louise and Margaret some precious thing too. Was the ring because of her marriage, though not a wedding present, or for some other reason? What about Louise's wedding? 'The sooner she's divorced the better,' Janet had said to Harry in Esther's hearing, 'and that's not a thing I ever thought I'd say about a daughter of mine'. If Caroline thought the same, was there any point in marking it now with a gift or gesture? Esther wanted to ask, but could not, even to square things with Louise, as she was obviously going to have to do, when she showed her the ring. She would keep it to herself till after Caroline had gone; she had to pick the right moment.

When Caroline left, some brightness went with her. For a while, even the wedding seemed less exciting than it had before.

'I'm glad she came,' Esther said to her mother. 'Are you?'

Janet, clearing space in the dining room to store the new presents which had arrived in the last week, paused and straightened, a hand in the small of her back, where there was a new ache.

'Yes,' she said. 'Your Granny was very pleased to see her.'

'Mum – she gave me something.'

'Oh?'

'I'll show you. Just a minute.'

She brought the ring in its leather box. The corners were rubbed and it had faded, but the ring itself gleamed on dusty black velvet, as good as when it was first given to Bess.

'It's her mother's engagement ring – it belonged to Aunt Bess,' she said.'

Janet took the ring from the box and held it up. 'Yes,' she said, 'I remember this ring, how unusual it was. I didn't know anyone else who had an emerald.' She tucked the ring into the box and handed it back. 'That was very generous,' she said.

'I'd have thought she'd want to keep it,' Esther said. 'I felt quite bad, taking it. But she was so definite.'

'You could get it cleaned,' Janet said. 'The jeweller will do that for you – it doesn't cost much. It looks fine, but you'll see a difference if you do.'

'Mum – '

'Oh, don't ask me about Caroline,' Janet said. 'I can't tell you anything. She's a mystery to herself, I sometimes think, never mind the rest of us.' Janet turned back to the boxes on the floor. 'Now, where's the card for this one? I think this is Mrs Graham's – she said it was a kettle.'

'I have to tell Louise and Margaret about the ring – I haven't said anything to them yet.'

Her mother knew, she always knew, you did not have to explain.

'You're the one getting married, and you're the eldest. Their turn will come.'

Neither of them mentioned Louise's wedding. It doesn't count, Esther thought. Maybe you had to have this ritual for everyone to recognise the reality of your marriage. And you have to stay married, you have to mean it. She and Jack did mean it. They were going to be married for the rest of their lives.

Sometimes this idea was a great comfort to her; sometimes she feared it. Trying the ring on again, she looked from it to the little garnet and opal ring on her left hand that Jack had bought second-hand from an antique shop. One day perhaps they would be rich enough for Jack to afford emeralds and diamonds but that future was too far away even to be interesting.

'You're her favourite,' Louise said, when Esther showed Margaret and her the emerald ring. 'That's why she gave you her mother's ring.'

Margaret said, 'There are other things. Maybe it wasn't a will after all.'

'What wasn't?'

'The list of jewellery in the other box.'

Had they ever told Louise? Esther was sure they had. 'You remember – Caroline was going to leave her jewellery to us, and everything else to Daniel. I could hardly remind her of it, could I?'

'Oh yeah, I think I remember something about that. Do Margaret and I have to wait till she's dead then, to get our rings or whatever?'

'Maybe she's changed her mind,' Margaret said. 'So she's going to give us stuff when we get married.'

'Or in my case, maybe,' Louise said, going red, 'get *unmarried.*'

'I feel awful about it,' Esther said, 'but I could hardly say – what about Louise, aren't you giving her anything? Or Margaret?'

'It's because you're getting married,' Margaret said. 'I mean, nobody was invited to your wedding, Louise. It was different, you said you *wanted* it to be different. If Caroline was just *giving away* her jewellery, or her mother's jewellery, she'd give all of us something.'

When they were on their own, Louise said, 'Ok, I admit I'm a bit put out, but it's my own fault. It's worse for Margaret – a bit of a snub for her.'

'Why?'

'She's Caroline's sister, isn't she, and we're not?'

'I keep forgetting,' Esther said.

'*Once upon a time there were three little sisters,*' Louise quoted.

Esther felt in the wrong – she had not thought about Margaret's feelings. She had been insensitive, which was not how she saw herself. There was a hard knot in her chest. The day was spoiled, the gift tainted.

Louise was offended, but would get over it by teatime. Margaret was hurt, and would not.

'Oh, I wish she'd never given me the ring!'

'No you don't. It's beautiful, and it was Bess's ring, so it was hers to give away to whoever she liked.'

'Margaret will get Diana's stuff, won't she?' Esther said, comforting herself.

'If Uncle Gordon doesn't give it to Mrs Ashton instead.'

'No!'

'I'm kidding. Forget it.'

Esther could not. She went on feeling uncomfortable and guilty for days. In the end, she spoke to her mother when they were quietly on their own, going through the replies to the wedding invitations, ticking them off on the list written out in Janet's neat rounded hand.

It was a cool July day of repeated showers, the sun gleaming falsely now and then, but never breaking the cloud. Rain sprayed the window of the den but at the back of the house they heard nothing apart from this fitful spattering. The cups of tea they had made for themselves after lunch cooled on the low table in front of the empty grate as they talked.

'So there's still the Mackies' reply to come, but Sheila's always at the last minute. And Jack's uncle and aunt from Devon,' Janet said. 'Did you ask Jack about them?'

'I forgot. I'll ask him tonight when he comes round.' As her mother gathered up the envelopes and put them away in the bureau drawer with her list, Esther said, 'I want to ask you something. I don't know what to do.'

'Oh?'

She had her mother's full attention these days; Esther was a grown-up now too. She was someone to be listened to and

216

consulted. Janet was still in charge, but Esther was catching up. Beyond the wedding was the world of being married. She could not imagine it, could not think how it would feel, to have crossed that divide between the unmarried and the married. Something would be revealed to her, a mystery she knew her mother could not explain and that anyway, she did not want explained. It was something you had to find out for yourself.

They talked about the wedding all the time. They did not talk about the marriage coming after it except in the most practical terms – money, the flat, furnishings, how to cook nourishing meals.

'You know the ring Caroline gave me?'

'It's come up beautifully,' Janet said. 'Sparkling.'

It had come back from the jeweller with the stones dazzling, the gold shining like new. This made it even worse, the guilty uncomfortable feeling.

'I wish in a way she'd never given it to me.'

Janet sat down again and waited. Esther, stumbling through her explanation, gave up and stopped.

'Do you see what I mean?'

'Louise will be all right – I wouldn't give that another thought.'

'Louise is all right about it actually.'

'Is Margaret upset?'

Margaret had said nothing more, so Esther could not answer this. 'Louise said she would get Diana's engagement ring and things – she will, won't she?' Esther tried to picture the long ago Diana, her pretty clothes, the glitter of her earrings and necklaces as she turned her blonde head.

'Will I have a word with her?' Janet said, not answering the question.

'If you think – what will you say?'

217

'Not a word about Caroline, you can be sure of that.'

'I wish – '

'It's not your fault. You couldn't say no.' She sighed. 'But oh, how like Caroline to cause trouble amongst other people.'

The guilt weighed less heavily now. Her mother would take care of it, and her mother had absolved her. It would be all right.

A week before the wedding, a call came from Caroline while Esther was out. She spoke to Janet who was the only one at home. A colleague was very ill, so they were short staffed. Caroline was unable to take leave and would not be at the wedding after all. A cheque for Esther was in the post, and she would send a telegram on the day.

'I knew it,' Esther said when she heard. 'I knew she wouldn't come.'

'And she promised too,' Margaret said, dismayed.

'No, she only promised to try, she didn't promise to come. That's how I knew.'

On the eve of her wedding, Esther lay in bed in the pale summer dusk, gazing at her white dress suspended on its hanger from the wardrobe door, the veil spread across a chair, the white shoes neatly side by side on the floor. On her bedside cabinet were two little boxes, one with her engagement ring, the other with Bess's emerald.

She could not sleep. Jack had phoned at seven but the conversation had been short and unreal. *See you tomorrow then. See you. Are you all right? I'm all right, are you? I think so. It will be fine, he said, it will be all right. Soon it'll just be me and you anyway, the whole thing will be over.*

That was what she feared and wanted in equal measure.

She sat up and looked in the little boxes again. Her ring, Bess's

218

ring. She would not wear Bess's ring yet, not for a while, since someone had told her green was unlucky at a wedding. Poor Bess, unlucky for her.

Perhaps she could read, since she would not sleep yet, maybe not at all. Then she would look terrible tomorrow. She propped the pillow up and got her book out, but the words danced and would not resolve themselves into sense. She was wearing an old pair of summer pyjamas with a broderie anglaise trim that was coming off at the neck and sleeves, the stitching worn. *I will never wear these again.*

She had begun to climb out of the old life; she was standing on the cusp of – what? Being an adult, a woman, a wife – somebody else. She lay back on the slouching pillow, running her hands over the thin cotton sheet, fraying at the hem, and down over the cool blue satin of the quilt. Then she crossed her arms, feeling the soft cotton of the pyjamas that she'd worn every summer for years, and they were faded like the wallpaper with its forget-me-nots and daisies and the blue curtains whitened at the edges by the morning sun. Everything here was old and fading, not worth replacing when she was so soon to be gone, and as if it was all slipping into memory already.

She spread her hands out and looked at them, the nails carefully tended for weeks and filed smooth so that the new wedding ring would be suitably housed. If she were like her mother and never took that ring off, her hands would not be naked again like this. Abruptly, she pushed the covers off and got up, crossing to the window in bare feet, on carpet and then lino at the edge of the room, cold beneath her soles. She pulled back the curtain a little and looked down into the street.

When they were little she had stood by this window on summer nights and told Louise and Margaret what was happening below:

a black cat stalking a bird, a man going home swinging his brief-case, a woman with a walking stick, moving slowly, a black car gliding by and disappearing round the corner at the end of the street. She had described it all, and Louise had made up stories about them, until their mother came upstairs and took a drowsy Margaret off to bed and they had to get into bed too.

They had vanished, all these ghosts. The street was empty and silent.

Somebody or something must come, Esther thought, to give me a sign. What the sign was to portend, she did not know, or what shape it should take.

Nothing happened.

Then, like a shadow, a grey cat leapt onto the wall of the Donaldsons' house opposite and halted, poised, before slipping down and running along the pavement. At some unheard signal, it paused again, then turned its head in Esther's direction, looking up. Its eyes gleamed in the street light's beam. A few seconds later it was gone, darting between gateposts, out of sight.

It was too ambiguous a sign to be satisfactory, but it would have to do. Esther let the curtain fall and went back to bed.

By tomorrow night she would be clear at last of the treacle well. When you are in it, there seems no way out, no imaginable time when you will be free to make your own decisions and know what is coming next. When you are out of it, it becomes a dream, short and transitory.

This time, when Esther lay down, she was able to close her eyes, growing drowsy at last. However long it seemed, it was only one night and it would soon be over.

In the Snow

1978

In one kind of extreme weather it is difficult to imagine its opposite. In the heat of Tunisia, recollecting her grandmother's funeral only a few months ago, trying to describe it to Eric who was with her – despite the dangers this posed to both of them – Louise struggled to find words for the landscape of that January day.

The reason she wanted to speak about it at all was nothing to do with Eric or indeed her grandmother. It was because while they were at Gatwick airport, skulking in case anyone they knew saw them together, she had seen Caroline.

Celia died of a second stroke a few days after the minor one which had put her in hospital soon after New Year. After a mild Christmas, it was piercingly cold. On the day she died the air seemed to soften, but that was an illusion: in the afternoon snow began to fall. Janet was on her way to the hospital with a clean nightdress and a bottle of orange squash, hoping to see her mother a little better, more wakeful than the day before. They all thought she was improving and might even be able to come home soon, not to Braeside but to Janet and Harry, to convalesce.

Because she was in the bus on her way to the hospital, not

risking the car in heavy snow, Janet was not at home for the telephone call from the Ward Sister suggesting she get to the hospital as soon as possible. She was too late anyway. They met her at the entrance to the ward, their concerned faces giving them away. How to break bad news to relatives, she thought afterwards – just look like that. It was not an expression that could be misinterpreted.

Celia was in a small side ward with a single bed. Janet sat with her mother, holding her hand that was still warm, the thin hand with its loose wedding ring, and looked at the face that had fallen away from life, or life had fallen from it, leaving it ashen and empty. She thought she would cry, but did not. She sat dry-eyed, gazing at her mother, unable to believe yet that she would not reply with so much as a blink or movement of her head if Janet said to her, 'I'm here, Mum, it's me'.

A little staff nurse with curly hair brought her a cup of tea, milky with two lumps of sugar dissolving brown in a pool of tea in the saucer, spilled over when the nurse set it down on the swivel tray by the bed. On a separate plate were two Rich Tea biscuits. The nurse put her arm round Janet's shoulder and squeezed. 'I'll leave you for a wee while. Just tell me if you need anything – we're at the nurses' station.'

Janet, resenting the familiarity of the hug, nodded, not trusting herself to speak, not wanting to speak. What she wanted was the silence in the room, the silence between her and her mother.

In the ward beyond there was plenty of noise: nurses talking, a trolley rattling along a corridor, a shout, a bell ringing, but it all sounded far away and unreal.

After a few moments, Janet got up and went to the window. Eventually she managed to move the catch and open it a little. Icy air crept in over her hands and touched her face. When she turned back to the bed, some last shred of consciousness had gone from it, and her mother, she now knew, was dead.

She called Harry from a public telephone in the hospital.

'I'll come right away.'

'It's all right,' she said, 'you don't have to. There's no point really and I can get the bus home. It's still snowing, isn't it?'

All she wanted was to leave the hospital as soon as she decently could. She saw the Sister in charge, collected her mother's things and arranged that Harry would pick up the death certificate the following day.

Then she set off for the bus stop and home, where she would try to reach Gordon, who was in Texas, and begin the other telephone calls she had to make. The bus crept down the hill in a blizzard but by the time she got off to walk the rest of the way home, rather than change buses nearer town, there were only a few stray flakes still floating in the air.

Just me, she kept thinking, just me now, and Gordon. We have no parents, Harry has no parents, there is no one behind us. With a dusting of snow, a new mantle seemed to have landed lightly on her shoulders.

The funeral took place a week later, giving everyone time to get back to Aberdeen: Esther and Jack from Glasgow, Louise from Newcastle, and at the last moment, Caroline from London. Margaret and Mike were only on the outskirts of the city in their newbuilt house at Westhill.

Caroline had not come for Margaret's wedding a few months ago. She was a registrar now, still working long hours. They did not often hear from her so Janet, managing to reach her by telephone to tell her about her grandmother, was half surprised by the swift response.

'When is the funeral? Tell me as soon as you know – I'll make sure I can take a few days off.'

Weather intervened. Snow went on falling all week across the whole country. Planes were delayed or could not land; trains were late or cancelled; nobody drove further than they had to. Louise came by car but no one knew that she had been driven from Newcastle to Aberdeen in Eric's Volvo that he said was built like a tank, and drove like one too, slowly but safely, and with a wonderful heater which made the winter landscape seem like a film going steadily past them all the way north. To the indolent soundtrack of Miles Davis in the cassette player, she began to imagine a story based around a dramatic mountain rescue. When they reached Aberdeen, she took a taxi to Harrowden Place, where she pretended she had come from the station. Harry drove out to Braeside with Jack next to him and Louise crammed between her mother and Esther in the back. Eric, still foolish with love, began driving back to Newcastle but was stuck for three hours near Perth because a lorry had skidded and jack-knifed across the road. He had plenty of time in which to work out which explanation to give his wife.

Esther and Jack came by train, where the heating broke down in a full carriage crowded with families going home after New Year. They all seemed to have loud undisciplined children and Esther, wrapped up in as many jumpers as she could drag out of her suitcase, but still shivering, went off the whole idea of having a family. The decision had been postponed anyway until they could afford a better house and, though Jack wasn't fully aware of this, move back north. Esther was miserable in Glasgow though she had wanted so much to leave Aberdeen. Jack came home exhausted and angry from a school apparently peopled by the offspring of Glasgow gangs. Esther, thankful she had resisted teaching for herself, despite Janet's urging, worked in the University library and was bored. She was learning how slowly afternoons can pass. They had been in Aberdeen for a long break over Christmas and would not be able to stay on after the funeral. Term started the following Monday.

Mike and Margaret drove, since they lived so near, but because of the snow it took them longer than Mike had anticipated and they arrived at Braeside not speaking to each other. Janet and Gordon agreed it would have been easier if the funeral had taken place in Aberdeen, but Celia was to be buried in the Drumoak churchyard with her husband, so there was no question of starting from anywhere but her home.

Since he had begun working in the Aberdeen office of an oil company Gordon had been living at Braeside, letting out his Richmond house. He had been called to its head office just before his mother's first stroke. Coming back, he realised he would always in future return to an empty house.

'What are you going to do with this place now?' Harry asked him as they stood about waiting for the hearse to arrive and the cars to take them to the church.

'Do?' Gordon had not thought of doing anything. He seemed to have run out of the ability to see ahead. 'Ach, no idea. Carry on, I suppose.' He tilted his wrist to look at his watch. 'Caroline's cutting it fine.'

'She is coming?'

'Said so. She called me last night. A surprise, can't remember the last time. Oh well.'

'Is that a car?' Janet asked.

Esther was nearest the window. 'I think it must be the under-taker – it's black. No – it's a taxi.'

225

For the last hour, it had not been snowing. The sky was a brilliant deceptive blue, as if innocently promising the rest of the day would be fine. Caroline got out of the taxi and paid the driver. She was in black, a long coat and boots, and carried a dark grey suitcase.

'It's Caroline,' Louise said, at the window with Esther. They turned to look at Margaret, perched on a sofa arm on the other side of the room from Mike.

The funeral service was short but the minister kind and sorrowful; he had known Celia for many years, and Andrew too. He was newly retired himself and had moved from the draughty manse to a cosy bungalow in Peterculter, but wanted to take this funeral himself. He shook hands warmly with the family and came back to Braeside afterwards, where Janet and Margaret heated the soup they had brought and Esther and Louise cut sandwiches and slices of fruit cake, and made pots of tea.

It was just as well, Janet thought, that there was so much crockery in the china cabinet, unused for years. The house was full and for once, very warm. They had lit fires to make the big rooms welcoming but the central heating Gordon had installed, despite his mother's horror at the cost, was also on, turned high.

'Did you know there would be such a crowd?' Esther asked her mother as they piled sandwiches on plates and gathered cutlery.

'I wasn't sure. The house was full like this for your Grandpa's funeral, but some of the folk who came then are . . . well, they're dead too. It's a smaller group now, the old friends.'

'Have you spoken to Caroline?' Esther asked, pausing in the kitchen doorway with her tray.

'Not really. It's been all go since we got here.' Janet looked up from the cake she was cutting. 'Have you?'

'I thought I'd look for her now – see how long she's staying.'

226

'Staying?' Janet had not thought of that. 'I don't know – ask her, Esther. Gordon won't have thought about making up a bed.'

Esther went round with sandwiches. 'Have you seen Caroline?' she asked Louise.

'No – not for a wee while. I was just going out for a fag.'

'Mum wants to know about making up beds, I think.'

When Louise went outside it was getting dark already at half past three, clouds like a pewter blanket closing down the light, full of snow. On the far side of the yard, someone else was already there, a tall thin figure in a long coat: Caroline, pacing up and down against the cold.

'Hi,' she said as Louise joined her and flicked her lighter twice, three times, without success.

'Bloody thing, never works outside.'

It flared at last and the cigarette caught in her cupped hands. They walked up and down the yard for a moment in silence, their boots making neat footprints in the snow, side by side.

'Time I stopped really,' Louise said after a moment, indicating the cigarette.

'Out of doors,' Caroline said, 'I occasionally fancy it myself.' She smiled.

'And you a doctor!'

'Well, at funerals only, perhaps.'

'Ah,' said Louise. 'I suppose they are stressful, eh? I'm supposed to ask you – are you staying here or Harrowden Place? Mum's wondering – she has a pretty full house with all of us but there's space if you want it.'

'I'm staying here with Dad,' Caroline said. 'I thought I might get a flight back tonight, but it wasn't possible. I'll get a taxi straight to Dyce in the morning.'

'Ok.'

More silence, more walking. After a moment, Louise put out her cigarette on the snow then picked up the stub to put in the kitchen bin later. How well brought up I was, she thought with a spurt of amusement, and still stick to it. Mum would be proud.

'Better go in,' she said. 'Collect empty plates or something – earn my keep.'

'How do you?'

'What?'

'Earn your keep. What are you doing now?'

Louise stared. 'Don't you know?'

Caroline shrugged. 'I must have, once. Tell me again. I'll listen this time.'

Louise laughed. 'Oh don't worry, I'm not offended. Why should you remember? I'm a psychologist. I work with adolescents, mainly in youth custody, children's homes . . . that sort of stuff.'

'Oh.' Caroline stopped walking. 'God, sorry I didn't know.'

'What about you?'

Caroline reached out and put a hand on Louise's arm, gripping it. 'Don't. Don't ask me questions. I'm fine, I'm all right, work is all right, I'm lucky to have such a good job. That's all there is to know.'

'I see,' said Louise, who did not. At least Caroline was talking to her, at least she had stopped mouthing platitudes, which were all she seemed able to offer her family these days. The light was almost gone and their faces were in shadow. Louise took courage from this anonymity.

She would say what she knew her mother would want her to say. And perhaps Gordon as well, who knew? After all, Louise decided, as they turned by tacit agreement towards the door of the farmhouse, what have I got to lose? She's not close to any of us now.

'Pity you couldn't come to Margaret's wedding.'

They were at the back door and could hear the rise and fall of voices inside, the sound of the first farewells. In a moment, the door would open and someone would come out to be seen off into their car parked in the lane, urged to get safely home before the snow began again.

'Work,' Caroline said.

'Oh sure – but you could have booked leave, couldn't you? She was upset.'

Caroline bit her lip. 'Was she? I sent a present.'

'That's hardly – '

'No, you're right. I should have come. I'm not keen on weddings.' She managed a grim smile. 'I seem to cope better with funerals. You're right, of course, I should have come – whatever the circumstances. Not Margaret's fault, what happened.'

Louise, astonished, saw that for all the indifference of Caroline's tone, there were tears glittering on her lower lids. In the dusk, she felt as much as saw a sudden distress.

'Oh *there* you are,' Harry said, opening the door to usher the minister and his wife out. 'Are you not frozen stiff out here?'

They were, and went indoors grateful for the rush of heat that greeted them in the kitchen, the fresh pot of tea Janet had just brewed for the remaining guests.

Louise, coming into the sitting room with her cup, raised her eyebrows at Esther – *tell you later* – and Esther frowned slightly – *what?*

In an hour they had all gone but the family. They sat around in the sitting room with its extra chairs – brought in from bedrooms and elsewhere – empty now, so that the room looked both crowded and vacant, a room where something has happened, but it is impossible to say *what* from the furniture or the expressions of the remaining inhabitants, all too tired to get up and put another shovelful of coal on the dying fire. Eventually Janet said, 'That fire's going out' and Gordon rose with a grunt and went to fill the coal scuttle.

'This is the warmest the house has ever been,' Margaret said. 'Thank goodness.'

'Oh, you'd like to live in an oven,' Mike teased, but she would not look at him. Esther realised there had been something wrong with Margaret all day. They had exchanged only a few words, the day being too full of other people for anything else. Soon they would leave Braeside all except Caroline and Gordon, but only Louise and Esther would be staying at Harrowden Place. They could not conduct their three-way sisters' analysis of the day, as they'd done all through childhood and adolescence. If she was to find out what was wrong, she would have to speak to Margaret before they left.

'Does anybody want anything to eat?' Janet asked as Gordon reappeared with coal.

'I'm stuffed with sandwiches,' Esther said.

'What about a curry?' Jack asked. 'We could get a curry in Aberdeen, save cooking.'

'Curry!' Janet looked disbelieving.

Mike thought that was a good idea. 'Will we just take it back to your house?' he asked Janet. 'Eat together?'

'Well, if that's what you want to do – '

Janet liked her sons-in-law, more than Harry did, though he had wanted a son. She supposed daughters' husbands are not always so welcome to men. They were nice boys, *mannerly,* as her mother would have said. She sighed, seeing for a disorientating moment, her mother's dead face, her mother no longer herself. A sob rose in her throat but she quelled it, rising briskly. 'Now then, curry or not, we'd better get going. That road will be terrible if we wait till the snow starts again.'

It had already. Louise went to the door to check and came back saying, 'Do you really think we should set out in this?'

They went to the windows or stood in the doorway, unable to see the other side of the yard or beyond the hedge that bordered the lane. Snow obliterated, whirling past, blown by a northerly wind driving Louise indoors, shivering. 'Shut the door somebody – it's perishing.'

'What do you think?' Janet asked Harry.

'We'll wait for a bit,' he said. 'It might clear.'

'It's only going to get worse,' Gordon said. 'They won't send a snow plough out till tomorrow morning at the soonest.'

It was already deep on the wall, on the roof of the steading, weighing down the branches of the rowan near the back door. In the near dark, the snow glimmered, lit by the light from the house, the open doorway, the uncurtained windows. Harry shut the back door and they all returned to the sitting room. Gordon got out a bottle of whisky and offered it round. Harry, catching Janet's eye, began to say no, then changed his mind.

'We could all stay, I suppose,' Janet said. 'That might be best. Though goodness knows where everyone will sleep.'

'Don't fuss, woman.' Gordon poured generous tumblers, while Harry went to get a jug of water. 'If there's one thing we're not short of here, it's space.'

'What about the rest of us?' Esther said. 'I don't like whisky.'

'There might be some sherry – even a couple of bottles of stout – in the sideboard. Help yourselves.'

'Advocaat!' Esther peered further into the cupboard. 'How long has *that* been here?'

'Guess we're not going to have a curry,' Jack sighed as he and Mike gulped whisky, not their usual drink, and going far too quickly to their heads.

'There are eggs,' Gordon said, cheerful now that he was going to have a full house for at least tonight. 'Plenty of eggs.'

'You're glad we're staying,' Janet smiled as she sat down next to him on the sofa.

'Ah well.'

'Eggs – ' Esther turned to her mother. 'What about the hens? Who's going to look after them now?'

Gordon laughed, not caring after his large whisky, and poured another.

'Mum's hens. She would insist on keeping them,' Janet said. 'I'm sure May will go on doing it for a bit longer till we sort it out. We might just take them up to Easter Logie. I should have asked Kathleen today.' She closed her eyes, leaning back in her chair, wearied by the long difficult day.

Upstairs, making up beds, Esther and Margaret talked about the funeral.

'It seems strange, everybody laughing and being quite jolly,' Margaret said. 'And Granny – '

'I know. I think it often happens – it did at Grandpa's too, but not so . . . more subdued, I think. Because of Granny.'

'Give me that pillow case. Thanks.'

'Are you ok?'

'What?' Margaret did not look up from the pillow she was stuffing into a pillow case so long unused the creases were sharp. It smelled of lavender from the linen cupboard on the landing, a scent overlaid with something musty, old.

'You're very quiet.'

'It's a funeral!'

'Yes, but – '

Margaret paused, the pillow in her arms, hugging it. She looked up. 'Och, I'm just annoyed with Caroline. Turning up like that, last minute as usual, but she didn't manage to come to our weddings, did she?'

Louise, appearing in the doorway, heard this.

'I came to help. Told Mum to leave it to us. She looks done in, I think she's had enough. Pity we can't go home.'

'I hate the idea of getting up in the morning and putting on all the same clothes,' Esther said.

'Knickers, you mean.' Louise grinned at Margaret.

'Well – ' Esther, defensive, dissolved, laughed too. 'Ok, I especially must have clean knickers to put on.'

'I'm sure there's some of Granny's you could have.'

'Lou!' Margaret was shocked.

'Nighties though,' Esther suggested. 'There's a thought – if Mum doesn't mind.'

'I'll need a winceyette nightie,' Louise said. 'It's all right for you two with your nice warm husbands.'

Esther laughed. 'You should hang onto yours a bit longer then.'

'Touché.' Louise shuddered. 'But not Mark. My worst enemy wouldn't want me to hang onto him.'

Esther sat on the newly made bed with a bump. 'What?'

Margaret put down the pillow gently, like a baby being laid in bed, smoothing it. 'You seemed very happy on your wedding day. We all thought he was nice.'

Louise let out a puff of air between her lips. 'Puh!'

'Well then,' Esther said, 'you'd better tell us.'

They were all sitting on the bed now, Margaret hugging the pillow again, Louise curled up, arms round her knees, Esther primly at the end, waiting.

'He hit me,' Louise said. 'So I left.'

'Oh no!'

'Why, what had you done?' Both of them rounded on Margaret who went scarlet. 'You know what I mean – why did he?'

Louise had once spoken to the girl Mark had left for her, had actually abandoned at the party where they'd met, taking advantage of the girl being drunk and escorting Louise home instead. It was a month before a mutual friend told her about the other girl and by then she was in love with Mark, or thought she was. The girl was not friendly when they finally met, but she did say Louise was welcome to him.

Recounting this now, rueful, she told Esther and Margaret, 'I think he must have hit her too.'

'What happened?'

'We weren't long back from our honeymoon. I wasn't going to put up with it, though. I packed up my stuff and thank God I still had my flat, hadn't managed to let it yet, so I just went home. Locked the door. But he wasn't the mad pursuer type. Just lazy and arrogant. You can keep your good-looking men from now on. Your chiselled features and crooked smile, your rippling muscles and permanent sun tan.'

'You make him sound like somebody in a Mills and Boon romance,' Margaret said. She sighed. 'He did look like that. How awful. Weren't you frightened?'

'You did the right thing,' Esther said. 'I think it was brave, to leave right away.'

'Brave – I don't know. It was bloody humiliating, lying on the floor, my lip bleeding. I didn't really know what had happened. We were both a bit drunk. I was screaming at him – then somehow we ended up in bed. It was always like that with him. Next morning he was really apologetic, said it was an accident. I said fine, ok, couldn't altogether remember how it had come about, I'd had a fair bit to drink as well. But somehow, after that, he didn't look the way he used to.'

He had become a paper man, she thought, but did not say. He was like a cartoon character, just muscle drawn on the page like those guys in Jackie magazine, with a star shaped speech balloon beside them – a girl saying *What a hunk!*

'You were drunk,' Margaret said. She sounded thoughtful.

'That's no excuse!' Esther said, but wondering. *It was always like that with him.* And yet Louise had said – he hit me, so I left. It didn't altogether add up. There were gaps. Still – 'You did the right thing,' she repeated.

So immersed in Louise's story were they, they heard nothing else, not a door opening or a footstep on the stairs.

'Well, here you are!' Caroline leaned on the door jamb, smiling at them. 'Once upon a time there were three little girls and their names were – '

'It's an Elties meeting,' Louise confirmed. 'But you can be an honorary member.' She patted the bed. 'Come in and be the Dormouse.'

'The men all seem to be hungry,' Caroline said. 'So I was sent to ask you what you'd like to eat.'

'We're really snowed in then?' Margaret asked.

'Looks like it.'

Caroline sat on the edge of the bed. Close up, she looked tired. 'It's been a long day,' she said.

'For all of us,' Louise agreed.

'You had a point, you know,' Caroline said to Esther. 'The hens. My father can't look after them. He's at work, he goes away regularly . . . He won't cook for himself either. There are things in the freezer – Granny had really got the hang of that. Janet is searching there now for stuff we can heat up in the oven. But when that's all gone – don't know what he'll do.'

'He must be able to cook. He's lived on his own for so long.'

'No, Margaret, he can't. He'd rather spend money in a restaurant than cook a meal.'

Margaret frowned, then flushed and looked away. Esther thought she must still be annoyed with Caroline. She wanted to put things right, without knowing how, and feeling guilty all over again about the ring Caroline had given her.

'Anyway,' Caroline said, looking from one to the other, 'what were you talking about so seriously when I came in?'

'Marriage,' Esther told her.

'Well, my lack of success at it,' Louise said.

'Best avoided altogether in my view.' Caroline smiled and tilted her head at Esther and Margaret. 'Saving your graces.'

'Oh they're both better at picking than me.' Louise got up, tired of the attention on her past, her failure, her half-true confession. Even to find out about Caroline, she would not stay. Let the others, if they wanted to.

'I'll just have scrambled eggs,' Margaret said, 'if you're going down to see Mum about food.'

'Me too.'

'Ok – I'll say. Caroline?'

'I don't mind. Soup, if there's any left.'

Perhaps she knew there was danger in being alone with Esther and Margaret, whose weddings she had failed to attend. Caroline slid off the bed and followed Louise to the door.

'I'd better unpack,' she said. 'I'm going to sleep in my old room up in the attic.'

'It will be freezing – the heating doesn't go so far.'

For a moment, she was crestfallen. 'You're right – I'd forgotten. But there's a wee electric heater up there, if it still works. I'll be fine.'

Left on their own, Esther and Margaret looked at each other. 'Well.'

'I know,' Esther said. 'But she came in, she sat on the bed with us, she was quite – friendly.'

Margaret bit her lip. 'Sometimes Essie, honestly – '

'What?'

'Nothing. "*My* father . . . " '

'Tilly?'

Margaret had gone out. In a moment Esther heard her bang the linen cupboard door and go off to the room she was to have with Mike, to make up the bed there.

Upstairs on the top floor, Caroline dragged an electric heater into her room and switched it on. Some heat had risen from the floors below, but it was still cold here. She felt herself cooling and her hands that were always cold, felt stiff as she opened her suitcase. As she put her hairbrush and sponge bag on the chest of drawers, she saw the little box where she had put Daniel's watch, with its bit of paper, written in madness, a scrawl. She thought of what she had written. She had not forgotten, but had no wish to look at any of it again. I'll hide the box, she thought, not sure why that mattered. Perhaps she did not want to look at Daniel's watch.

No, it was not that.

She took out the watch and put it on her own wrist, too loose even on the last fastening. Then she slipped it off and put it back, leaving the piece of paper untouched. Where should she put the box? The chest of drawers, in this full house, seemed too exposed.

Despite the comfort of Jack's warm length entwined with hers, Esther lay awake, trying to remember the last time she had slept at Braeside, the last time the family had been together. Not their weddings, unless you didn't count Caroline and you could not do that. She was their cousin, Margaret's sister, and there was Daniel. Somehow you had to be more her cousin, more her sister because of that loss. Only Caroline wouldn't let you, wouldn't let anyone get near. Was it so bad for her? Yes, you idiot, Esther told her drowsy self, yes it was that bad. She thought of how it would be for her to lose Louise or Margaret, and then suddenly, of how it would be if Jack were killed, run over in a busy street by a van hurtling round a corner unheeding. Now I understand, she thought, and the image came at her again in her half dream, the van looming out of nowhere and Daniel strolling across the street, perhaps absorbed in thought, not seeing, Daniel flung up in the air like a dummy, a toy, a piece of rubbish caught by the wind. Then crashing to the road, hitting it with a smack – only in her dream it was noiseless, a silent film, the music reel broken, nothing but the indrawn breath of the cinema audience as he lay still at last.

In her dear familiar room, next to Daniel's, Caroline lay awake too, but she had long trained herself to think of work or of nothing at all in these empty moments. This time, though, she thought of her grandmother, heard her quick step on the stair or the clucking sound she made, calling the hens, saw her stooped in the garden in her flowered pinny, wrapped tight round her spare frame, pulling carrots for their dinner, or strawberries, fat and red, in summer. Think of these things, she told herself, think of Granny and being a child, when it was safe and everyone was all right.

'She just went off,' Louise said to Eric as they sat outside the café they had decided to adopt as their favourite during the holiday. The chairs were metal and those in full sun burning by ten o'clock, but they had a table in the shade. Eric did not take to the sun; he was fair and freckled. At night they compared Louise's developing tan with his pink skin and he admired her beauty all over again while she rubbed after-sun cream on his neck and shoulders as a brief but satisfactory prelude to love-making.

Eric was having a beer, Louise citron pressé with ice. She stirred it with her straw, watching the ice cubes dissolve fast in the heat.

'Next day, when we were still wittering on about whether the snowplough would make it, she telephoned for a taxi and believe it or not, got one. Came out from Culter – guess he wasn't getting many fares that day – took her to Dyce and she caught her plane.'

'Well, well,' Eric said, not altogether following, but willing to take Louise's word for it that her cousin was odd.

'So *probably* – and here's the daft thing – she's the one person I could have spoken to at Gatwick who wouldn't care who I was with.'

'Do you think she would have recognised me?' Eric asked.

'Don't look so wistful!' Louise laughed. 'I don't think she's a literary type. That's not the point. She wouldn't care if she saw us and she definitely wouldn't mention it to my mother. Or anyone else.'

'Ah.' Eric waited a reasonable moment or two, then he said, 'Do you want another drink or shall we just go back to the hotel for more sex?'

239

Louise lifted his large freckled hand and kissed the back of it. 'Sometimes I almost wish you *weren't* someone else's husband.'

'I'm not such a catch,' he said, 'for a beautiful young woman like you.' He looked pleased though, and she laughed at him again as she pulled him to his feet. He paid the bill, she tucked her hand into the crook of his arm and they walked up the street, baking in the morning sun, bathing them in heat.

Louise forgot about the funeral, the snow, Caroline leaving. Later, lying in Eric's arms as he snored gently, creating a tiny draught through her hair, she thought of Caroline at the airport, not seeing them, intent on the arrivals board. *Arrivals.*

Caroline wasn't going anywhere, she was waiting for someone. Perhaps a lover after all, though she was so scathing about marriage. How little they knew. For a while, until she too fell asleep, Louise speculated, planning to call Esther as soon as she got home.

She might even tell her about Eric.

All Good Things Come to an End

1979

'I told you Jack stood for the Council this time, didn't I?' Esther said. 'Much good that was. I was quite glad he lost. Honourably – I mean it wasn't his fault. The wrong election to try, as it turned out.'

She was sitting at the bottom of the stairs in their tiny house in Linlithgow, where Jack was now teaching, winding the spiral of the telephone cord round her fingers. Louise had called to say she'd got the job in London she was hoping for, but mostly they talked about the election.

'I thought it was devolution he was campaigning for?'

'Oh, don't. That too. He got very tetchy with some of the people we met out canvassing. A lot of them were quite stupid. So maybe it's just as well it's all come to nothing.'

'Devolution?'

'No, being a Councillor. He feels sold out about devolution. It was such a stitch up. Most people *wanted* it.'

'You agreed with Jack then?' Esther always did, when it came to politics. 'You voted for it?'

'Oh yes. And not just because *he* did – I know what you're thinking.'

'Oh well, chance missed then.'

'Not for ever,' Esther said. 'Jack says it has to be raised again.'

'Mum said, wasn't I pleased we were going to have a woman prime minister at last? She thinks that's what feminism means.'

'It does, in a way.'

Louise thought that if Margaret Thatcher was a failure, everyone would say it was because women couldn't lead countries, and if she was a success, people would say she was unique, or it showed how like a man she was. And a Tory too. She missed Eric, the long talks about politics she had had with him, his Socialist ideas she could mock and next minute be convinced by. She just missed Eric, that was the trouble. She had not thought much about devolution at all. She did not tell Esther this.

'Before I start the new job,' she said, 'I've got some leave to take. 'Could you take some too – maybe come to London and help me look for a flat?'

'When?'

'First week in June?'

'Will I ask Margaret too?'

'Why not? All for one and one for all.'

'Oh no, it's term time, what am I thinking about? She won't be able to.'

'Does she still like it?'

'Oh yes, she loves her little Primary Twos.'

'You come then. And I was thinking – I'll see if Caroline will put us up.'

Taken aback, Esther said, 'Are you in touch?'

'No. So what? Time I was. Time she was. Let's not wait till the next funeral.'

It would save money if they could stay with Caroline. Esther wondered whether she could afford a week in London. She did not have a new job yet and it was tight on one salary with their mortgage. She had resigned her hated library job on the excuse that she was moving out of Glasgow, but she could have travelled there by train. Jack, full of confidence about his promoted post, agreed she should give it up. Now she cleaned and cooked with vigour, feeling guilty she was no longer earning. Some feminist you are, she scolded herself.

Still, there was her birthday cash and she could dip into the money they had each been given when their grandmother died.

'All right,' she said. 'If the flights or trains – whatever's best – aren't too expensive.'

'Let me know. I'm in funds – I can help out.'

Esther would not let her do that, but she was grateful. Even before she had broached it with Jack, she began to look forward to seeing Louise. Perhaps Caroline too.

London made you breathless. Everyone was in a rush but knew exactly where they were rushing to; she felt alternately swept along and swallowed up. Louise seemed familiar with the Underground already, while Esther hopped behind her, worried they might be setting off in the wrong direction. She had a dread of the train stopping in a tunnel. What if it never started again? Would they suffocate before help came? She refused to get on the next train at all when she saw the surge of bodies cramming themselves in. She made Louise go all the way back up several escalators until they reached London's approximation of fresh air. It was very warm and Esther had come in the kind of clothes you need in Scotland in spring.

'Where *is* Caroline's flat?' she gasped, sweating with the effort of dragging her suitcase in the heat.

'We'd be there by now if you'd let us get the tube instead of waiting for a bus,' Louise said. 'I'm not even sure this *is* the right bus. Let's get on anyway – here's hoping.'

Caroline's flat was in Palmer's Green, unfashionable but somewhere she had been able to afford, with generous rooms and a view of a dusty park with an avenue of plane trees, where dogs were walked and prams were pushed, sometimes by nannies who may have strayed from more prosperous parts. Louise had arrived the previous day and been given a spare key. They climbed the stairs to the first floor, Louise finally taking pity on her sister and carrying the suitcase. The staircase and landing were scuffed and worn, but Caroline's front door was red with a shiny black knocker and letter box. Esther cheered up when she saw its bright paint and followed Louise gratefully into the narrow hallway.

'This is where we're sleeping,' Louise said, opening a door on the left. Here too the paintwork was fresh. The carpet smelled new and the bed linen was crisp blue and white. It was an immaculate room made untidy by Louise's clothes scattered on bed and chair.

'Her stuff is from Habitat or somewhere like that – really nice. She's been decorating all the way through.'

'I can see that. What about the rest?'

'Kitchen next,' Louise said. 'I'll put the kettle on. Caroline won't be back till late, she said, so we're to help ourselves.'

As they came out of the bedroom a key turned in the lock of the front door and they stopped in surprise. Caroline, they thought, some mistake about the time.

A man came in. Seeing them he checked, stepped back, stared.

'Who are you?' Louise said.

'I might ask you the same thing.' He did not sound pleased to see them.

'We're Caroline's cousins. We're staying here.'

'Ah.' He gave a little bow, inclining his head towards them. 'My apologies. I had no idea.' He backed off, seeming to change his mind about coming in.

244

'You've got a key,' Esther said.

'Yes.'

They waited while he hesitated. Just as the silence was becoming too long for comfort, he said, 'I stay here sometimes'.

'Would you like a cup of tea?' Esther asked, having for once greater presence of mind than Louise, who was just staring at him. 'We were going to put the kettle on.'

He was a tall fair man, at least ten years older than they were – perhaps even older than Caroline herself. So they judged, not having an idea really, just that he was older, another generation. It was only when he had gone, courteously turning down their offer of tea, retreating still puzzled, they felt, that Louise said,

'He's her lover.'

'No!'

'Well, what else? He had a key, so I don't suppose he was a burglar.'

'Oh help! Maybe he was and we let him go.'

'What else were we going to do? Pin him to the ground? If he is a burglar he's not the kind you see in the *Beano*, anyway. Bag marked *Swag* over his shoulder and a striped jersey.'

Esther began to laugh. 'A gentleman burglar?'

'Was he a gentleman then?'

'Oh yes.' Esther was sure of that, at least.

'God.' Louise was laughing too. 'You're as bad as Mum. An instinct for class distinctions.'

In the neat kitchen with its tub of parsley on the window sill and pottery jars for coffee and tea, Louise filled the kettle. 'I guess that's where I went wrong,' she said. 'Marrying out of my class.'

'For goodness sake, all that stuff went out years ago. Not that we're exactly upper class, eh?'

'It's not about that. It's about . . . You think it all disappeared in the sixties?'

'It seemed to.'

'Don't kid yourself. And wait and see what our new PM does. When she gets going.' Louise dropped tea bags into mugs. 'Even if she is a grocer's daughter.'

Esther thought Louise was the snob, not her, but she didn't pursue it. There was too much to look at in Caroline's flat, so much that might reveal her to them. Or not.

In the living room they sat on beige sofas hoping they wouldn't spill a drop or a crumb to mark them, and ate chocolate biscuits. It was a relief to find that Caroline had such ordinary things as tea bags and Penguin biscuits in this carefully chosen and anonymous place. It's a different world from the one where she was brought up, Esther thought, her mind going to her mother, and then to Braeside.

Louise had made up her mind about the man.

'No, I'm right. A lover. Though clearly he doesn't live here, or she could hardly have avoided telling us about him.'

'Or him about us.'

'So do we say, casually, this chap dropped in – '

'Something like that.'

'Ok. What do you want to do now – I have to ring up about some flats to view.'

'Go ahead. I'll have a wash and unpack.'

When Louise had made her appointments for the next day they went out to walk in the little park and explore the near neighbourhood. They began to feel reckless; there was something exotic about London. Instead of cooking, they ate out in an Italian restaurant not far from the flat, in a row of shops with a hairdresser and laundrette, like a village street tucked away in the city. When they came back late, full of food and a little hazy with the carafe of wine they had shared, Caroline was home.

She was heating a tin of soup. There was a glass of white wine in a tall stemmed glass beside her. Esther was entranced – having had more than usual herself – by the extravagance of opening a whole bottle of wine on a week night, to drink some on your own. Even stranger, just to have it with soup from a tin and bread and cheese, which was all Caroline ate. Later, dropping something in the kitchen bin, Esther saw the tin and read on an unfamiliar label the words 'Lobster Bisque'.

Caroline put out two more glasses and offered the wine. Esther, sobering up, refused, explaining, 'We had quite a lot in the restaurant, so – '

'Not that much,' Louise interrupted. 'I'd love some.'

'What are your plans for tomorrow?' Caroline asked.

'Flat hunting. We're going to see four.'

'Where are they?'

Louise got out the agent's details and Caroline looked through them. 'This one,' she said.

'Oh do you think so? It's not as big as the – '

'Not such a good area.'

'Oh. Right.'

'You'll see when you go.'

Esther, curled up in the corner of a sofa, listening sleepily, thought that in the shadowy dusk, with one lamp lit, Caroline looked no older than they were. The years mattered less when you were all grown up. If we are, Esther thought, not feeling it. She was missing Jack, yet found herself wondering about being a single woman in London, as Louise planned, as Caroline was.

'There was a man,' she exclaimed, waking up, remembering him. 'We forgot to say.'

'Sorry?'

'He came in when we'd only just got here. He said he stayed sometimes. But he – '

'Well, he didn't stay,' Louise giggled. She really had had too much wine now.

Esther broke in. 'I think he had a bit of a shock, seeing us. Anyway, we did invite him in, but – '

Caroline looked down at her glass. Her colour did not change, or her voice. 'I didn't think he was back yet, or I'd have said.'

'Is he – ?'

Even Louise did not have courage to continue. There was a pause, lengthening in the dusk; outside a car went by. For London, this was a quiet street but if you listened, you heard the hum of traffic, a shout far off, then shrilly a police siren wailing into the distance.

'His name is Martin,' Caroline said. She looked directly at Esther. 'How's Jack?'

Later, as they talked quietly in bed, Esther and Louise agreed that having had a bit to drink themselves made everything easier. 'You don't think she's an alcoholic, do you?' Esther wondered, 'drinking on her own?'

'She did offer us some.'

'She had to, really.'

Louise laughed softly. Esther was very unworldly, but it was no use telling her so, she would be hurt.

Esther had been thinking about having a baby. She had tried to talk to Jack about it, but his mind was on his new job. 'Whenever you want to,' he said. 'It's up to you.'

'I don't want to have a baby just because I can't think what , else to do.'

248

In London, she had begun to be aware of other possibilities, things she might have done had she not married Jack. Linlithgow was not London, and however near Edinburgh and Glasgow were, she no longer lived in a city and was not part of one as Caroline was, as Louise soon would be. She was jealous when she thought Louise and Caroline might meet and be friends, as you could be, she saw now, the eleven years between the two of them vanishing. For the first time since her wedding, she wondered if she had done the right thing, if she had not missed something important.

Louise found a flat to share with another woman, a staff nurse at University College Hospital near the clinic where she was going to be based. In time, she planned to buy her own place, but for now she was too poor, she concluded, too junior.

Full of excitement and courage, she had rushed headlong at London and was – at times – rebuffed, thrown back on her old provincial self, the person she was rather than the person she spent most of her time imagining she was. The imagining began, in the long evenings when the nurse was on shift and she was alone, to turn into stories, scribbled in blue notebooks bought from the corner shop. The shop was run by Mr Patel, who was avuncular and helpful and the person she was probably most comfortable with in the whole city.

She would not go to Caroline for friendship or support. She would make it on her own.

She was missing Eric.

'All good things must come to an end,' he said when they parted for the last time. Then, because language was what he worked with, he added, 'all things, if you think about it, good and bad. Us too.'

'Don't,' Louise said, closer to despair than she had been at the end of either of her marriages. 'That's not a comfort.'

'Nor for me,' he agreed. 'I'm sorry.'

He folded her in his large familiar embrace, and she inhaled again his dear smell of tobacco and tweed, his dusty, academic, unfashionable smell, and she cried, ashamed and sorry and angry with herself and him. How had they let it get so out of hand, their little affair, what he called their *tendresse,* that was not meant to last or matter?

'I can't leave her,' he said again. 'Them. I can't leave them. I'm a weak man, not good enough for you.'

'Stop saying that!' She was furious with him. 'It's a poor excuse.'

'I'm sorry – "

'We must also stop saying we're sorry. It's pathetic.' Louise had braced up. She was stronger than he was and she was younger. She had the better chance of being happy again. So she told herself, even if on nights alone in London, it was not how she felt.

The months passed. Caroline stayed in touch more often, but no more satisfactorily. She met Louise for coffee now and then; she recommended restaurants and the best places to buy clothes or food. She said she must invite Louise for dinner sometime, but it did not happen. Louise, not languishing long in self-pity, met new people and began going to parties and the theatre.

Esther took a job in her local branch library, which she intended to be temporary, but it was not like the University, where she had felt inexperienced and inadequate. Here, the staff were gossipy and kindly, their idea of a good book Catherine Cookson or Georgette Heyer. They were delighted to have Esther there to keep them right about anything more academic. They thought she was young and trendy and clever, and spoiled her, believing she needed mothering. They gave her recipes for casseroles and puddings and a day to day life that was undemanding but never dull.

Jack, growing more ambitious, began applying for promoted posts. In February of 1980, he was appointed to an Assistant Head's job in Aberdeen.

By April, Esther knew she was pregnant.

Grown Up

1985

'Do you remember the time Caroline vanished – she didn't come home all night?'

'That was the night we went to the theatre – the whole family together,' Esther replied.

'I don't remember,' Margaret said.

'We got to meet the actors. Oh, and there was champagne after the play. I was so impressed,' Louise said. 'I'd never so much as seen it before and everyone had these little thin glasses. They gave us some too.'

'No they didn't,' Esther protested. 'They never gave children alcohol in those days.'

'I don't *now*,' said Margaret.

'Poor Anna – you're not preparing her properly for adult life.' Louise watched her niece jumping off the low part of the wall into the paddling pool. There was not much water left in it because the children had been taking turns to do this all afternoon. You're wrong, she thought, there was definitely champagne and we definitely got some. 'If you think about it,' she said, 'Daniel and Caroline must have had a good bit – they were very lavish I remember, the people taking it round.'

'I remember Mum said to Dad, better not have any more if you're driving us all home.' Esther was surprised by this sudden recollection. 'You know, I think you're right, I remember those little glasses. But I thought they just gave us lemonade.'

'I'm sure that's what gave me a taste for champagne,' Louise said with a grin.

'I can't believe you remember all that – I don't.'

'You were tiny,' Esther said. 'No wonder.'

'I have a good memory.' Louise looked smug. 'Writers need it.'

'What for?' Margaret asked. 'Your stories are all fantasy, aren't they? Rugged handsome men and flame-haired beauties riding off into the sunset on a black charger.'

'Exactly,' Louise said, laughing, 'just like our own youth!'

Margaret, feeling annoyed without knowing why, thought Louise had had more romance than she or Esther had managed. Two marriages already, and goodness knows how many boyfriends. She got up and went to tell the children to do something else. They were going to wreck that paddling pool, and it was quite new.

They were at Braeside. None of them had a house big enough to accommodate all of them and Louise came up from London only two or three times a year. This was the best way to get together. It meant Esther and Margaret had to come out a day early to clean and make up beds, but Gordon was content to let them have the run of the place. He had retired last year, and sat in the sun wearing the white trousers he had had in Egypt years ago and a battered straw hat to provide enough shade for him to read. He read the sort of books nobody else was interested in: colonial and wartime memoirs; histories of both world wars; biographies of generals and dead politicians. Even he seemed to be bored by them this hot afternoon, for he'd fallen asleep under the apple tree and the book had slipped from his lap to the grass and lay open, the pages turning in a tiny breeze.

'I don't know how you can sleep,' Esther said to him when she picked up the book. He opened his eyes with a grunt.

'What? What time is it?'

'Half past three. The children have been making such a racket.'

'Have they?'

He was getting deaf. Sometimes it was necessary to say things again, enunciating more clearly. Not that she would have commented on it; in every other way he was as fit as he had ever been. He still tramped the paths and hills of Scotland, alone or with his old friend, Bob Douglas.

'Cup of tea?' he asked.

'Sure. I'll see if Tilly and Lou want one.'

Half past three, Esther thought, going up the garden to the house to put the kettle on, that dead part of the afternoon, too long after lunch to go out, too soon before dinner to start going indoors and getting ready for that. It was the children who would give half past three some meaning, when Andrew went to school in August, for that was when she would be at the school gates to meet him. She had a flicker of pleasure and excitement at the thought of it. Ross and Anna were toddlers, barely fledged, but Andrew gave her hope that their children would one day be grown up and independent.

Gordon had followed her into the house. He had begun to modernise the kitchen when he first moved in, to make it easier for his mother to use, but since her death he had done nothing further. In this process, the place had somehow lost the warmth and familiarity Esther associated with it when she was a child, but it was still not convenient and no longer even comfortable.

'Too hot to sit outside.'

254

'You should be used to it!' The water drummed into the kettle and she raised her voice above it.

'Ach, it's years since I worked overseas. It's not the same here anyway – a different heat. Nobody sits out in it in hot countries. More sense.'

'We're very glad of it – keeps the children amused for one thing, being outside all the time.'

She began to get out some of the old cups; Gordon's improvements had not extended to buying crockery. Esther liked to use the familiar cups and plates with the green and gold rim.

'If Granny was here she'd be making pancakes,' she said.

'There's some shortbread in that tin,' Gordon offered. 'But mind, it's been there a while and it's only bought stuff.'

'It's all right – I brought fairy cakes and Margaret made a fruit loaf.'

'So you still bake, do you, you young women?'

'Scotswomen all bake, Uncle Gordon, you should know that!'

He had married two Englishwomen, so maybe he didn't know, though Janet had always baked, just as much and as well as Granny. When she stood with the baking bowl in front of her, sifting flour or beating butter and sugar together, Esther felt she was doing something traditional, taught to her at home, a skill she might one day pass on to her own children. The boys too, of course, but the thought was in her mind now that this third child, when she came along, might be a girl. She was at that early stage of not being quite sure, so only Jack knew. Should she say anything to Louise and Margaret? Not yet. She hugged it to herself, liking for once to have a secret.

Her own children had also followed her into the kitchen to complain about the loss of the paddling pool, but seeing her with a Tupperware box full of cakes, Andrew changed tack.

255

'We're hungry.'

Ross came round to where she stood at the table, putting slices of fruit loaf onto her grandmother's cake stand, and clung to her legs, wiping his nose on her skirt.

'Cake,' he said, hopefully.

In the garden, Anna lay on Margaret's lap where she and Louise sat on the old travelling rug, making daisy chains. Anna had shown interest at first, but now she was falling asleep, her head a hot weight on Margaret's thighs through her thin cotton trousers.

'She's very blonde, isn't she?' Louise said, stroking Anna's hair with light fingers. 'You were fair like that when you were wee.'

'You used to say,' Margaret remembered, 'that I was your 'almost sister' but, you know, I don't look like either of you.'

'Elsie, Lacie and Tilly.'

'Oh. I'm so dim – I've just realised.'

'What?'

'Your name, when you write those romances – I never even thought. That's why.'

'Lou Lacey.' Louise grinned. 'I can't believe you didn't get that! Yes, a lot better than Louise Duthie. Or either of my married names.'

'Either!'

'People do marry more than once,' Louise said, still lightly, but with an edge of irritation. She was never allowed to forget she was the only person in their family who had been divorced.

'You were really young when you and Pete – '

'Yes, I was. Nineteen. Nobody gets married at nineteen and expects it to last, surely.'

'Didn't *you* – when you ran off like that?'

'Oh come on, we didn't exactly elope. We just had this idea, the summer we were working in London. *Why not do it now?* It was a laugh. And it was doing something without asking permission. We were there just long enough to establish residency – but we got a special licence. For once I was beyond parental control. And so was he.'

'We never met any of his family, did we?'

'Well, they lived in Dundee and it wasn't somewhere they seemed keen on leaving – God knows why. They were even less pleased than Mum and Dad. He didn't have any sisters and his mother was hoping for a big white wedding – like Esther's.'

'So what happened?'

Louise shrugged. 'We lived in a tiny flat with two other students, till Mum and Dad got over it and helped us out so we could rent our own place.'

'I remember that. I meant, what happened that you didn't stay together?'

Louise looked down at Anna, flushed with heat and sleep, her thistledown hair, smooth unmarked skin and pale pink finger- and toenails, the soft perfection of having had only two years of life.

'When we actually knew each other better, we just got on each other's nerves. It turned out we didn't want the same things. The same sort of life.'

Abruptly, she got up. Daisies scattered, the half-finished chain drifting down to land on Anna's hair like a crown.

'I'm going to see if Esther wants a hand,' she said.

Margaret sat on quietly with Anna. Her legs were aching, but if she moved, Anna would wake. Where was Pete now? Had he married again, had a family? Louise probably didn't know. Then there was that second husband, the time she'd had what Margaret thought of as the proper wedding. That hadn't lasted either. He hadn't looked like a wife beater but it turned out this was something that happened to all sorts of women. Still, you couldn't overlook the fact that Louise had had two very short failed marriages. She thought of her own wedding, how kind Janet had been, how pretty she had felt, all day. She looked down at Anna. It was worth it.

She arranged the daisy crown more carefully on Anna's hair. *My love,* she thought, *my dear, dearest little love.*

Louise had brought some work with her, so she went upstairs after tea to spend an hour on her own with the romance she was writing. Her heroine was a primary school teacher, which meant she had been able to get some useful background material from Margaret. She thought of it as *colouring in*, this inclusion of realistic detail, intended to give her readers the illusion their dull primary school or shop assistant lives could be miraculously enhanced – or more often, transformed – by the kind of unlikely adventure her heroine was thrown into.

Writing romances had started almost as a joke, a way of proving she could do something unexpected. Eric's idea. When she flung another rejection note in the waste paper basket after yet another angst ridden novel had been turned down, he said, 'Try something different'.

'What sort of different? Are you just telling me I can't write?'

'You can write,' he said, for once with no hint of humour in look or voice. 'Just not the literary stuff, I suspect.'

'What then?'

'Romance, crime, I don't know. Humour is difficult, but – '

'Give me a start,' she said, liking the challenge, if only to prove him wrong. 'Give me – I don't know – an outline or something.'

Instead, he told her which publishers to approach, and from the first, and least likely, she received a template, and instructions. This was what they wanted; these were the rules. Rules! She hated rules and regulations.

'I knew you'd give up at the first hurdle,' Eric mocked. 'Go back to your tales of misunderstood women.'

'All right, you win,' she said. 'I'll give it a go.'

The affair with Eric had been full of that kind of thing. Nonsense, she called it, never taking anything seriously, a *truth or dare* kind of relationship. Appropriate, perhaps, for someone recovering from the end of a marriage that had been her major attempt to be serious and grown-up.

Well, she thought, feeding a new sheet of paper into the Olivetti, that didn't work. She wasn't meant to be grown-up. Look at Esther and Margaret with their husbands and toddlers and the cakes they baked and the nice houses they had: they had grown up.

Two failed marriages, Janet had said, when she told her about leaving Mark. It had taken courage to tell her mother. She was still in awe of her, still wanted Janet to admire and believe in her as she apparently believed in Esther and Margaret. But she could not reach her. Different generation, different education, outlook, personality, *everything*.

'We weren't happy,' she said, knowing this was feeble and would sound like an excuse to Janet.

'Happy! You have to work at marriage, Louise, it isn't all hearts and flowers.'

Was it pride or shame made her unable to tell her mother about Mark? Already it was too late to confide and it had taken years for her to tell even Esther and Margaret. She felt stupid, that was it. How to admit to your mother you're stupid, when her opinion is already low? She had a sneaking fear Janet would not even believe her, or if she did, say it was her own fault. Better not to talk about it at all.

Her books supplied all the hearts and flowers she needed. She could be cynical talking about them, but write with happy commitment to the ideals of romantic love. All her heroines obeyed the rules set by the publisher: they married their one true love after setbacks and confusion. Sometimes the confusion was occasioned by not realising who the one true love was, but it always worked out fine in the end.

As for marrying again herself – that would never happen. She was only thirty-two, but she had rushed through too much too quickly. That was that, then. Love.

She was between lovers, she told herself, now that Eric had taken a new job at the University in Bristol and was going there with the wife who – he claimed – bored him, and the teenage children who merely bewildered. The wife who had known about Louise all along. A martyr, was how Louise had thought of her, a fool. But perhaps not – she was the one with Eric, after all.

Louise stared at the last page she had written, trying to think her way back into the scene. *Concentrate,* she scolded herself. The window was open and she could hear faintly the voices of Esther and Margaret as they sat talking on the wooden bench at the back door, without being able to make out the words. Then she heard a car in the lane: Jack and Mike were back from golf. She got up and shut the window.

She only needed one line, then she'd be off again.

Harriet unlatched the wooden gate in the wall. It was stiff and creaky. Suddenly it opened wide and she was gazing for the first time on the gardens of the house that she had been dreaming about for so long.

'Louise?' Gordon had tapped at the door without a response, but hearing the typewriter, he came in and stood on the threshold.

Louise pulled herself out of the other world. 'Oh – hello. Sorry, deep in my new masterpiece.'

'Sorry to interrupt – do you have any indigestion stuff? Milk of Magnesia?'

'Me? No. Is there nothing in the bathroom cabinet?'

'Esther and Margaret cleared it out yesterday. They said everything was too old to be safe.' He smiled. 'I doubt that. But your grandmother did hang on to medicines for years.'

'I bet Margaret has something – did you ask her?'

Gordon shook his head. 'No, no, I've been having a lie down.'

Louise got up. 'Are you all right? D'you feel ill?'

'Not at all. Just tummy trouble.'

'Ok. I'll go and ask Margaret.'

'You get on with your story – I'll ask her myself.'

'Are you sure?'

His colour was high, but he had always had a ruddy skin, weathered by years of sun. Louise sat down, but it was a few minutes before she could begin writing again.

When Gordon had come to live at Braeside he spent money on what he saw as essential maintenance and repair. Thinking as an engineer, he took care of the fabric of the house: roof, windows, heating, believing they were what mattered. Since he had been on his own, the house had gradually and subtly altered in less visible ways. Her grandmother's absence was powerful as her presence had been. Eileen had died last year, but had anyway been too stout and arthritic to help for some time. A girl from Echt with children at the primary school had come in to clean for a while but she had had another baby and now nobody did it. When they visited, Esther and Margaret took turns to go through the house, doing what they could. Still, the neglect was visible in a house no longer cared for, in the corners and the cupboards, the grimy kitchen floor, the smeared cooker, the mould at the back of the fridge, the green rusty stain along the bottom of the bath beneath a dripping tap. The bloom of the house had rubbed off. It no longer felt lived in, as if Gordon only half inhabited it. Until January he had continued to work away from home on contracts on a consulting basis, so the house had often been empty.

Tomorrow, Esther said they should tackle some weeding and tidy the garden. This was not Louise's idea of a holiday, but it would be good exercise and as Margaret said, they could make a difference in a morning if they all worked at it. Gordon was not a gardener.

Watching her uncle walk slowly along the landing and downstairs, a hand on the banister rail as if to steady himself, Louise was overcome by a sensation that was close to fear. What would happen to Braeside if Gordon was no longer here? Don't be squeamish, she told herself. When he dies.

She had not realised she loved the house. Not like Esther, not in that way, Esther who had spent so much time here with their grandmother. But it belonged to their family and the idea that it could belong to anyone who was not one of them was appalling.

Louise sat down at the typewriter again, but had lost all interest in Harriet and the handsome gardener she was about to encounter in the orangery. What was an orangery, anyway? She must look it up.

A few moments later she heard Margaret running lightly upstairs and along the landing.

'Lou – are you there?'

'Yes, what?'

'You don't have any Rennies or anything? Dad has indigestion.'

Louise got up and went to the door. 'No. He asked me, and I said to try you.'

'The shops will all be shut now. I'll get him something tomorrow.'

'You shouldn't have emptied the bathroom cabinet – I bet there was stuff in that.'

'Oh yes, with its own penicillin growing on it probably.'

'Is it just indigestion?'

'What?' Margaret looked surprised. 'Sure. Of course.' A pause. 'What else could it be?'

'Where's our cousin Caroline when we need her?'

Margaret hurried past that thought. 'Oh, he's not *ill*. He says he often gets it.'

Louise went back into her room. Third time lucky, she thought. This time, staring at the next empty page, she started to think not about her grandmother or the house, but about Caroline.

Useless, this, of course – another train of thought that would never lead her towards romantic fiction.

It was definitely not Esther's turn to tell the bedtime stories. Though she was not the author in the family, it seemed she was best at it, so here she was anyway, with all three children.

'Tell about the Elties,' Andrew said.

The children were in a row in the same bed, crammed together. Eventually, Anna would have to move across to Mike and Margaret's room and the travel cot. Meantime, for the stories, she was an honorary Murray and sat up between Andrew and Ross, clutching a wilting teddy and sucking his ear.

'Once upon a time,' Esther began, 'there were three little girls and their names were Elsie, Lacey and Tilly.'

The stories were based on childhood memories, embellished to make that distant time more exciting than it was. Margaret, leaning on the door frame listening, was amused.

'I don't know where you get it all from,' she said as Esther came to an end and Anna was lifted from the bed, protesting. 'You and Louise, with your stories. I couldn't be bothered. I just read Anna the same books over and over. That's what she wants. I could scream sometimes, I didn't know it was possible to dislike a fictional character as much as I hate the Hungry Caterpillar.'

'And I don't know how you came to be a primary teacher,' Esther retorted. 'Aren't you supposed to like reading stories?'

To this ignorance, Margaret made no reply. She had, in any case, left being a primary teacher behind, and had no intention of returning. Perhaps one day, she said to Mike, when Anna is at school. That seemed a long way off.

She carried Anna through to the cot in the room across the landing, murmuring to her, settling her for sleep. Esther's boys, tucked up with a tractor and a cloth rabbit, were still wide awake, but she left them with a kiss, hoping they might sleep soon.

In the living room, Jack and Mike had opened two bottles of wine, and Louise had joined them, having given up on her romance for the night. Gordon nursed a whisky, his glass perched on the swell of his uncomfortable stomach, and read his book beneath the light of the standard lamp.

'All well?' he asked, looking up over his glasses.

'All well.'

'Peace reigns at last,' Mike said, getting out glasses for Esther and Margaret.

'Can I have white, please.' Esther sank onto the sofa next to her husband.

Jack put his arm round her. 'Are they sleeping?'

'Not yet, but fingers crossed. Andrew insisted on the tractor, so I just left it in the bed.'

On the other sofa, Mike and Margaret sat a little way apart. Margaret looked broody, Esther thought.

'I don't think you like me making up stories about us, about our childhood,' she said. 'They're not about us really. Mostly I'm inventing adventures for the Elties.'

'The *what*?'

Esther looked from Mike to Margaret. 'Hasn't she told you about the Elties? That's what we called ourselves, the three of us.'

Mike shrugged. 'She doesn't talk about that stuff, do you, Maggie?'

'Don't call me that,' Margaret said, but as if she had said it too often before and hardly paid attention herself. 'I can't see the point. It wasn't as marvellous as you make out, Esther.'

'Oh, I make it more exciting than it was.'

Margaret shrugged but did not answer. Perhaps she was thinking about Diana. Esther realised she did not know, never knew what Margaret thought about her own mother. She had always been more sister than cousin, so she had had just as much love and security, surely?

Jack looked from Esther to Margaret.

'Right,' he said, heaving himself out of the sofa. 'I'm going to get that box of chocolates Esther hid from the kids. Where did you put it?'

Gordon went to bed at nine. The rest sat up late, hoping none of the children would wake.

Esther took half a glass of wine but did not even finish that. As the evening went on she was aware the others were jollier

265

than usual, even Margaret, but did not mind feeling a little apart from them. She curled up against Jack on the old hide sofa and let them all talk over her. Jack put his hand on her thigh and squeezed it now and then, smiling at her. I'm happy, she thought, dangerously.

About eleven, too tired to stay awake, she decided to go to bed.

'I won't be long,' Jack said.

'I'd better go up too,' Margaret sighed. 'Anna still wakes sometimes in the night.'

On the landing, Esther said, 'What about checking Uncle Gordon's all right?'

Margaret frowned. 'Why? Are you worried?'

'No. Just, he didn't seem quite himself and he went to bed early.'

They stood in silence, listening. Faintly, from Gordon's room, once their grandparents', came an unsteady intake of breath followed by the wheezing growl of a snorer asleep. They looked at each other.

'Sounds ok,' Esther admitted.

Margaret laughed softly, as if louder noise would wake him. 'I think he's out for the count – I'm sure he's fine.'

'Goodnight.'

'Esther – '

'Yes?'

'Is Louise – is she *happy?*'

'Oh, you know Louise. She just moves on to the next thing without much thought.'

'Next man.'

'Well.'

'Essie – ' Margaret lowered her voice still further. She was gripping the banister, Esther realised. 'Does Caroline write to Janet? Or phone sometimes?'

'You don't hear from her?'

'Nothing. Well, if you call a scrawl on a card at Christmas hearing . . .'

'No, nor do I. You know I'd tell you if I did. Mum's the same – we'd always tell you. I think Lou sees her now and again.'

Margaret gave herself a little shake. 'Ah well.'

'She has her career,' Esther said doubtfully. 'She has such a responsible job now she's a consultant, Mum says. And the hospital is a big one, a teaching hospital.'

On an impulse, Margaret, least demonstrative of the three of them, put a hand on Esther's arm. 'You two are much more my sisters than she's *ever* been.'

'Oh, Tilly.' Esther put her arms round Margaret. It wasn't easy to hug her – she went stiff and didn't respond. Esther was on the verge of tears. *Yes,* she was thinking now, I definitely am. Or why am I so soppy?

'I'm fine,' Margaret said, disengaging herself. 'Sorry. Don't know what came over me.'

'Bordeaux?'

Margaret laughed. 'Yes, probably. Goodnight.'

'You don't still think about it, do you?'

'What?'

'You know, that she didn't come to your wedding? She didn't come to any of them. A big cheque and that was it.'

'I suppose the strange thing was the way she turned up just before you and Jack got married.'

'Strange?'

'It wasn't the start of Caroline being part of the family again, whatever it meant.'

'She came to Granny's funeral.'

They fell silent. Then Margaret, rousing herself, said, 'I'm going to bed. Goodnight.'

When she went into the bathroom, Esther was distracted by the green stain along the bottom of the bath which had bothered her when the children had been bathed earlier in the evening. Wide awake now, she shook some Vim onto the stain and scrubbed at it vigorously with the dried up cloth found hanging over the end. She ran water in, sluiced it away and surveyed the results. A bit better, surely?

After that, looking for something new to read, she went up to the top floor in nightdress and slippers, to Caroline's old room. She recalled a small bookcase by the bed, though they rarely used the top of the house and she had not been up there for years. When the children are older, she thought, they will love sleeping in the attic rooms. She was visualising years and years ahead when they would continue to congregate at Braeside and her children would have holidays here as she had. In their turn, they would wander through the wood with the dogs' graves or run down to paddle in the burn and follow it all the way to the wall where it dipped underground and reappeared on the other side of the road.

The remaining evening light seemed brighter in this room than on the first floor, perhaps because for some reason there were no longer any curtains in the window. In the shadowy dusk she looked round, remembering how Caroline had read to them at Braeside when they were little, a golden older sister, beautiful and accomplished.

Another memory – of being here with Margaret long ago – jolted her back to being thirteen and she saw again the wooden casket with the inlaid pattern, Caroline's scribbled list of bequests, and the gold ring. When her gaze rested on the chest of drawers, all that sat on it now was a dusty mirror. The box had gone. When had it disappeared – and who had it?

Esther had forgotten about being tired. She looked in the drawers and opened the wardrobe. They were all empty. Next to this was Daniel's room, but they did not go in there. Now she did, quietly opening the door and looking at it for the first time for so long she did not even try to remember when that might have been. This room was smaller, truly an attic, Spartan with its single bed stripped to the mattress on an iron frame. A chest of drawers, a small mirror attached to the wall above, a single wardrobe. Nothing of Daniel was here now.

And yet, standing there, Esther had powerfully a sense of who Daniel had been: years after his death, he still had presence – or at least it seemed as if he did, in this little room.

Taking a deep breath, Esther turned the key in the wardrobe. The door creaked and her heart began to thump. *This isn't good for me. I need to stay calm.* She was excited, she was not afraid.

It was empty. Dust in the corners, nothing else. She tried the chest of drawers. A stray shirt button. Why did old buttons cling so determinedly to abandoned furniture? It was always a button you found. She picked it up and rubbed it between her fingers. Then, as if someone had nudged her, she turned back to the wardrobe. She had assumed the top shelf was empty. It looked like it. She reached up and ran her hand over its dusty surface. At the back her fingers touched something hard, small, light.

It was the box.

Esther stood at the top of the stairs, listening. There was a murmur of voices and then a burst of laughter from the men. Louise made them laugh; she was easy company. They would be there for a while. Esther took the box back to her own room and

269

dusted it carefully with a baby wipe. These days even Jack didn't carry the kind of large white handkerchief her father always had in his top pocket.

She could not have said why she treated it with such reverence as she sat down on the edge of the bed, making a ceremony of opening the box at last. Why not just take it in to Margaret, who was probably still awake?

Afterwards, she was so relieved she had not, she broke out in a sweat, hot and cold at once.

Inside were a piece of paper and a man's gold watch with a black leather strap. The ring was not there. The paper was a sheet of A4 of the kind used in photocopiers, folded in four. Esther unfolded it and read, at first excited, then bewildered, hot, rigid with anxiety.

It was dated at the top, *Braeside, November 1968*. Below, in a barely legible scrawl, in writing quite different from the original list, was another.

For Esther, my mother's ring
For Louise, my mother's crystal earrings
For Esther's first son, Daniel's watch
For Esther's first daughter, my mother's pearls
In the unlikely event of Louise becoming a mother, my other jewellery can go to her
Everything else to XXXXXXXXXX
Everything else to XXXXXXXXX
Everything else to Oxfam or Save the Children or XXXXXXXXX
Including any money.

It was a few minute before Esther worked out all that was wrong with this. 1969. Caroline had given her a ring – the emerald ring given to her before her wedding and which she rarely wore. She went nowhere you could wear jewellery that might snag on a child's jersey or cause a scratch. She did not like to wear it in front of Louise or Margaret. That gift had not been repeated before their weddings. Was this the ring Caroline meant?

She looked at the first scrap of paper, at the line drawn through that original list with a red pen. Why had it been kept if Caroline had superseded it in 1969?

When did Daniel die? *1968, the year before I went to university.* When did I get the ring? *1973, the year I married.* Only months after he died, Caroline had written this, then later decided for some reason to give Esther the ring at once.

She peered at the words crossed out thickly with black pen – XXXXXX – but could not make out what was written beneath. The ink was smudged in several places as if Caroline's hand had rubbed over her words before the ink was dry, suggesting a fountain pen had been used. Which would be like her, Esther thought.

It was all wrong. It read like something a teenager might write, not a woman of – what? – twenty-seven? Esther looked again.

There was nothing for Margaret.

Her eyes blurred, trying too hard to focus, unable to believe it. No, nothing.

She sat for a long time on the edge of the bed, holding the little box in her hands, the papers and the watch inside it. The first time she had happened on this box she was thirteen, little more than a child and she had of course taken the secret to her mother, who had not thought it important at all. Now she was an adult and a mother herself. She stood up, shivering a little, realising the air had grown chilly and a stiff breeze was shaking the trees, heralding rain at last.

It was not her property. She had no right to do anything with it. It had been hidden for a reason. Who else was going to look for it there? Not Margaret, certainly. Reluctantly, Esther went to Daniel's room and put the box as far back as she could on the shelf where she had found it. Then she went to bed.

She wished Jack would come upstairs. What on earth could they be talking about, so late? *Come to bed*, she willed him, and was rewarded by the sound of voices in the hall and then his step on the stairs.

'I didn't think you'd still be awake,' he said.

'I can't sleep. I'm cold.'

'You won't be in a minute.'

He was drunk, so there was no talking to him tonight. That would give her time to think. She was glad to have his warm body the length of hers, his hands under her nightdress – *what are you wearing this thing for?* – and his winy breath in her ear as he tucked himself round her turned back, fitting them close together, his hand on her breast, tightening, ever hopeful.

'It's too late,' she murmured. 'You're drunk anyway.'

'I can try,' he said, but in a moment, his hands were still and she knew from his breathing he was falling asleep. She marvelled all over again at his wonderful ability to sleep like this, with abrupt speed.

She was warm now. With a sigh, she leaned in as close to him as she could, and shut her eyes.

Cheering Margaret up

1990

'Do you remember being the Elties?' Louise said.

'Esther turned us into an Enid Blyton adventure, didn't you?' Margaret said. 'For the children.'

'You should have written it down.'

'You don't think one writer in the family is enough?' Esther put her hand on Margaret's, smiling.

Margaret smiled back, but did not answer.

'So here you are,' Louise said, raising her glass, 'joining the ranks of the divorced and dispossessed. Though if you're more sensible than I was, you'll not be all that dispossessed. You'll make sure you get your share. More than.'

'Oh, *Lou.*' Esther tried to steer away from this, since she could see Margaret was on the verge of tears.

She raised her head, the little almost-sister, brown eyes brimming, attempting a smile.

'I'm sorry,' she said, 'I know you've been through it, you've had to deal with this stuff, but honestly, you'd hardly been married, either time, when it ended. I've been married for years, I've got a young child and there's a huge mortgage on the house, I don't see how I'm going to manage to go on living in it now – ' She

273

swallowed hard. 'The worst thing is I thought I'd be married for ever. I believed in marriage.'

Esther wanted to say 'I still do', but it didn't seem quite the moment.

Louise, becoming expansive since she had drunk her wine and not just played with the glass the way the others seemed to, disclosed her latest theory.

'I actually believe,' she said, 'that with marriage you start out by setting each other free, then in the end, you find you've taken each other prisoner.'

'Oh,' Margaret quavered, 'that's so depressing.'

'Is that in one of your romantic novels?' Esther asked. 'It's a good line.'

Louise grinned. 'No, but I think I'll use it. It's true, too. I see it all the time.' She nodded at the others. 'Drink up for God's sake, nobody's driving.'

'So what next?' Esther asked. 'Is it final, do you think, couldn't you go to a counsellor or something? Or would Mike not do that?'

'Not now he's got That Woman,' Margaret said.

'I love the way you give her mental capital letters,' Louise said. '*That Woman* – there's something impossible about saying the name of a rival, have you noticed? You don't want to grant them the ordinary courtesy of *having* a name. They don't deserve it.'

'You're *That Woman*, aren't you? Where Robin's wife is concerned.'

And Eric's too, Esther thought but did not say.

Louise shrugged. 'That's different.'

'He doesn't have *small children*,' Margaret allowed, forgiving Louise, as people did.

Esther said, 'So you think it really is over?'

Margaret did, and the tears spilled.

'Oh well done,' Louise cried, exasperated. 'I'm trying to get her drunk so she can forget it for a while, bloody cheer up, and you're trying to be some sort of *therapist.*'

Esther gave in and drank her wine, which immediately went to her head so that some guilty thing swam around in there, vaguely reminding her of the prisoner Jack, who had to be telephoned to come and get them. Prisoners or not, she thought, I still love him.

They were in a conservatory restaurant overlooking its own leafy garden. It was high summer and for once in Aberdeen, warm and sunny. They were having a rare long Saturday lunch, Louise's idea. She had arrived on the Thursday to stay with Margaret and – she said – *help her through it*. Mike had left the previous week, after hiring a van so that he could take a great many of his own belongings with him. Margaret found herself in a house with no music centre; wardrobes and drawers with empty spaces; depleted bookshelves and a gap in the corner cupboard where once there had been a sizeable collection of vinyl records and CDs. The garage now lacked golf clubs, tools and worst of all, the bigger of the two cars, that she had driven most and had thought of as the family car. Clearly, Mike thought of it as his car.

She had scarcely had time to get used to this, indeed even quite realise it, when Louise arrived in her sporty Mercedes with several suitcases and packages, and armfuls of wine, flowers and chocolates.

'The thing is, broken hearts need looking after. Tender care. Alcohol. That sort of thing.'

'You would know . . .' Esther said.

'Oh God yes, think what a disaster my love life has been. Still is. So learn from my experience. We have to spoil you.'

Margaret, surrounded by Louise's half unpacked bags and plunged into chaos of every kind, was dazed. The only person for whom Louise's arrival was an immediate success was Anna, who at seven was easily bought with the array of presents Louise showered on her: blue plastic ponies, hitherto forbidden by her parents; a manicure set with several colours of nail polish, all unsuitable; and expensive and also unsuitable (in Margaret's view) clothes.

'So,' Louise said, 'here we are together, the Elties, and it's up to us to give Margaret all the support she needs.'

Esther knew what would happen: Louise would be here for a week and when she had gone, it would be Esther giving the support, month after month, in less glamorous ways. She would be the one at the end of the phone when Margaret was struggling through empty evenings; she would be the one calling in, making sure everything was all right, babysitting Anna when Margaret could eventually be persuaded to go out and start her life again. As she must: Esther was with Louise on this at least.

They had reached dessert. Margaret didn't want any, claiming she didn't eat puddings anyway.

'For God's sake, it's the best bit. You can have something small – crème caramel or the mousse thing – but you *must* have pudding.'

Margaret gave in as it was easier, but left half her mousse. Esther, enjoying the novelty of going out to lunch, ate every morsel, rather guiltily, since it was rich and creamy. Louise talked non-stop and took twice as long as the others to finish.

'We could take our coffee into the garden if you like – I think one of the wee tables out there is free,' Esther suggested.

They gathered up handbags and coffee cups and Louise pocketed the chocolate mints to take with them. Outside there was a breeze, but the wrought iron table they found empty was in a sheltered corner.

Louise waved at a waiter. 'Could you bring us a refill of coffee and the bill? Ta.' She took out her Gauloises and lit up.

'Oh,' Margaret said, 'you're not still smoking?'

'Don't nag. Robin nags me too, though he's hardly a great example of good behaviour.'

'You'll ruin your skin and have a wrinkly old age,' Esther teased.

'You don't think I intend to be *old*, do you?'

They could not imagine it; at thirty-six she was gamine and youthful with her cap of dark hair and scarlet finger- and toenails.

Margaret was on the verge of tears again. 'That's what I'm most afraid of, I think. Being old and on my own.'

'You won't be,' Esther said. 'You'll remarry, you'll have another life after Mike.'

'Or you could be like me, and have a string of affairs as an independent woman.'

Now Esther was the only one with a husband. After three glasses of wine, she was very much in love with him and had no desire for Louise's life.

'Will you be able to give up your job?' she asked. 'Now you're writing all these romances?'

'Oh God, no. It's a nice bit of extra money but you couldn't do it all the time. Drive you mad. All these happy endings.' Louise grinned. 'I wonder if the other romantic novelists are old cynics like me!'

'I'm sure they're all blissfully married,' Margaret said. 'Nice women who *like* happy endings.'

'I like them,' Louise said. 'I just don't think they happen very often.'

She put out her cigarette stub with the high heel of her sandal, then carefully picked it up and buried it in the flower bed behind her. Esther thought, watching her, she's quite immoral in some ways, but just like Margaret and me in others. No litter, no pushing other people out of the way, please and thank you and polite to waiters and people in shops.

'What about you?' Louise asked Esther. 'Are you going to get a job now your kids are all at school?'

'I'll be much too busy for that,' Esther said. 'Jack's got a job at Drum Academy so we'll be moving house.'

Margaret looked astonished. 'You never told me!'

'Or me, but that's different,' Louise conceded. 'I don't keep in touch enough, I know. So is it a good job – what?'

'Head.'

'Wow – that's brilliant. Why didn't you *say*? I'd have got champagne.'

'We just heard this morning.' Why had she not told them right away? Mainly, Esther realised, because Margaret was so miserable. 'He's done brilliantly, everyone is saying so. They're surprised at Robert Gordon's – they didn't think they'd lose him.'

'Where will you live?' Margaret asked. She was twisting her hands in her lap, her coffee and chocolate mint untouched.

'Well . . .' Esther reddened. 'Well, actually, since the school is so near there, I spoke to Uncle Gordon about Braeside. If we could stay there for a while it would help us take our time to find the right house. Once we sell our own one, of course.'

'You will – people like that bit of the city. It's really popular now.'

Louise could see Margaret was trying hard to be pleased

for Esther. But failing. She was fed up, feeling that everyone was doing well except her. Silly woman. She put her hand on Margaret's anxious fingers, still tightly bound together.

'You wouldn't mind that, would you? It would be good for him, to have other people in that great big house.'

Esther was dismayed. 'Oh God, Margaret, were you thinking *you* might move there, now Mike's – '

'Don't you dare leave your house – he's got to give you enough money to stay in it, you know. With Anna.' Louise was adamant.

'Yes, but she might *want* to.' Esther turned to Margaret. 'Do you?'

'I don't know. I can't think. I don't seem to be living a real life, I feel as if I've got no future. As if somebody took my life and just threw it away. I have no idea what I'm going to do.' Tears welled up again and this time spilled over. She tried to stifle the sob that rose. 'Sorry, sorry. I think I'll go to the Ladies.'

'No you won't. You have a howl if you feel like it,' Louise said. 'Nobody can see us in this wee corner. Anyway, we've been having such a long lunch it's nearly time for afternoon tea – everyone else has gone.'

Margaret wiped tears away with a paper napkin. 'Oh dear, I must look awful.'

'It's terribly unfair but you look very pretty when you're crying,' Esther said. 'Like a sort of damp flower. I get piggy-eyed and blotchy – not very attractive.'

Louise lit another cigarette and they talked about nothing for a few minutes, till Margaret said, 'It's all right. I don't mind if you and Jack go to Braeside. It's not mine any more than it's yours.'

'Doesn't it belong to Uncle Gordon and Mum and Dad?'

There was silence for a moment, while they realised they had no idea. Who owned Braeside?

'Does it matter?' Margaret asked.

'Well, yes,' Louise said, 'I guess it does.'

'Did you have a nice lunch?' Janet asked when Esther called in on Monday to see her mother. She had Kirsty with her; the boys were at school.

'Lovely. It felt quite festive, strangely.'

'What do you mean?'

'Despite poor Margaret having such an awful time.'

'I don't understand it at all,' Janet said. 'What on earth is Mike thinking of? Do you want to sit in the garden? It's quite warm today.'

They took mugs of tea outside and sat on the old canvas chairs on the lawn. Janet gave Kirsty the small fork and trowel she kept for her and for a little while they were on their own. Kirsty ran off to do her weeding at the far end of the garden where Grandpa was working in his greenhouse. Harry was re-potting tomato plants and from where they sat Esther and Janet could hear Kirsty's flow of chatter and the rumble of his answers.

'How is Margaret? I've not seen her since all this happened.'

'Upset. She can't believe it's happened, I think.'

'I can't either,' Janet sighed. 'Mike has a wife and child – he can't just walk away from them.'

'Mum, he's done it already – he's completely moved out. Margaret says there's some other woman he's been seeing.'

'I wondered if that was at the bottom of it. I think it's this life they live, away for three weeks at a time on the rigs, then under their wives' feet for three. It's not a good thing, when you're married.'

'Lots of other people manage it.'

'Where on earth did he meet this woman – they're not on the rigs, are they?'

'She works in Exol's office in North Anderson Drive, I think. Mike's in the office every time he's home now he's been promoted. He was talking about taking a job onshore.'

Janet tapped her hand impatiently on the arm of her chair. These hands had not aged much. In Esther's childhood, roughened by housework and gardening, they had not been beautiful. Now that she had all the household gadgets and devices Harry could buy for her, and she had no children to care for, they were smoother, the nails better kept. Her thin gold wedding ring, that had once had a pattern chased on it, was plain and smooth.

After a moment her hand lay still, and she said, 'Well, he'll have to make sure she's properly supported, and Anna too.'

Esther, thinking of her mother's hands, her mind wandering, said, 'I was reading this article discussing what one change in the twentieth century had made the most difference to women's lives. It seemed to be about equal between the automatic washing machine and the pill.'

Janet smiled. 'Well, we didn't have the pill in my generation, but birth control certainly made a difference.'

'Is that what you'd choose?'

Janet gazed up the garden to where Harry stooped to show Kirsty something close to the ground – a plant or insect perhaps – and said, 'I'd say education. Education.'

'I think – ' Esther fell silent. She had thought her mother didn't quite get the point, but perhaps she did after all, for in terms of her own life, what she felt she had been most painfully denied was the university education she had been so insistent on her daughters having. She was right: at least Margaret would be able to earn a living, when Anna was older. She could be independent. What about me? Esther was struck with guilt. She had wasted her good degree – wee jobs in libraries, moving around with Jack, having children. These were not excuses. What would she do if Jack left her? She could not imagine such a horror on this fine afternoon in her childhood garden, her father playing with Kirsty, her mother calm and reassuring beside her.

Esther thought of Janet as the person with all the answers, someone without misgivings. She was anxious about Margaret but not distracted. She moved more slowly these days, but did everything as deftly, competently, as she ever had. On impulse, Esther stretched out her own hand and touched her mother's arm.

'At least Margaret has you and Dad, and us,' she said. 'She won't be on her own.'

'Maybe he'll come to his senses, in time,' Janet said. 'Let's hope so.' Mike had let *her* down, as well as Margaret and Anna. She had thought better of him, with his good job and breezy air of common sense.

'I know,' Esther said. 'Louise and I feel angry with him too – but I suspect he's not going to come back.'

'Well, well, we can't do anything about it. Your father is very disappointed in him, though.'

Kirsty came running down the garden to tell them about the bumble bees on Grandpa's flowers and the weeding she had done. When she had gone back up to the greenhouse with a biscuit, Janet and Esther began talking instead about Jack and his new job. They were on safe ground here, Jack now the favoured son-in-law. Less safe when they talked about Louise – could you mention Robin? Better not.

'I have some news,' Janet said. 'We had a phone call yesterday.'

Kirsty and her grandfather were coming hand in hand down the garden towards the house, Kirsty hopping like a puppet on a string, Harry treading more soberly. There was no dog now in the house, had not been for many years, but the last of Margaret's cats still lived here, and she was following them, tail in the air.

Janet raised her voice, so that Harry would hear too. 'I was just about to tell Esther our news,' she said.

'Oh aye, what's that?'

She shook her head. 'You know fine – Caroline's getting married.'

'What?'

The last thing Louise had said when they parted the day before, cheering up Margaret or reassuring herself, it might have been either – 'Well, Caroline's not married, and look at her. Hugely successful career, a super flat and as far as I can see, a great life. Holidays in exotic places, plenty of money.'

'We were surprised too,' Janet said, as Kirsty presented her with the lettuce she had pulled up for their lunch. Esther thought of that day years ago when they had come face to face with the man whose name was Martin, but about whom they had never learned much more. Louise had met him again once or twice at Caroline's old flat, before she moved.

'She's quite old to be getting married, isn't she?'

'Ancient,' teased her father.

'Well into her forties – forty-seven, -eight?' Janet was working it out.

'Who on earth is it? Have you met him?'

'Oh no, she's never brought him here. She hasn't been home for several years now. Gordon stayed with her in London at Easter for a few days. He was visiting that woman – what was her name? Mrs Ashton. She's not very well, apparently.'

'He's kept up with her all this time?'

'They were great friends.'

Esther was feeling this was a lot to take in, all at once. She had not thought Caroline even corresponded with her father. As for getting married –

'So who is it?'

'Oh, some doctor. A consultant, like her, but in another hospital. They met at a conference, she said, about five years ago. I don't know why they've waited so long.'

Or, Esther thought, why they're getting married at all. Five years. 'So it's not – he's not called Martin?'

'What did you say his name was, Janet? Not Martin. Some foreign name.'

'He's Greek,' Janet said, and seeing Esther's astonished face, added, 'He's not *foreign* – at least, he was born in England, but his family is from somewhere in Greece. Not Athens. I forget.'

'Philip,' Harry had been rooting in his memory. 'Philip Du- something.'

'Dukakis, that's it.'

'So when are they getting married?'

'No date yet,' Janet said. 'She said she'd let me know.'

Harry snorted. 'Can't think what they're waiting for at their age.'

'I wish I'd known on Saturday – we'd have had something much more exciting than horrible Mike to talk about.'

Harry frowned. 'He's behaved very poorly, in my view. As if Margaret hasn't had enough to cope with.'

Esther, still getting over the shock of Caroline's impending marriage, did not pick this up, and it was only later, going home in the car with Kirsty, that she wondered what her father had meant.

Meanwhile, the talk indoors, as Harry washed his hands in the scullery, Kirsty up on a chair with her hands in the Belfast sink also washing hers, moved back to Jack's new job.

'We did wonder,' Esther said, 'whether we could stay at Braeside for a while when we manage to sell our house. Then we could look round for somewhere to live, take our time about it.'

'You'd have to consider where the bairns are going to school. You don't want to move them twice.'

'Kitty starts Primary 1 in August, so it would be best if we could move before then – but I don't suppose that will happen.'

Janet began washing the lettuce for their salad lunch. 'Are you going to keep calling the bairn Kitty?'

'It's what she calls herself.'

'Her name's Kirsty. You need to get her used to saying that before she goes to school.'

'Maybe,' Esther said. 'Anyway, about Braeside – '

You should speak to Gordon about that.'

'We were talking about it on Saturday,' Esther said as Kirsty helped her lay out cutlery and fill glasses of water. 'Who actually owns the house? Didn't you and Uncle Gordon inherit it from Granny?'

'That's right.'

Harry sat down at the table with a grunt. 'It's Gordon's now.'

'How – '

'Just the house and garden. We sold the land after your grandmother died.'

Esther caught the look exchanged by her parents and realised there were things she did not know, that something had happened – about money – they had not discussed with Louise and her, or Margaret either.

She wanted to ask, but Kirsty was too knowing not to pick up something from their conversation, something perhaps she did not want her children in their turn to know. How we keep things from each other, she thought, and Caroline worst of all.

Lunch was much interrupted by Kirsty, nagging Grandpa to go back outside, beginning to behave badly. Esther thought it was time they left – there would be the boys to collect soon anyway.

As they gathered up their things to leave, Janet said, in a low voice not for Kirsty's ears, 'Your Dad and I will speak to you and Jack – and Louise, while she's still here. We've not really explained it and it's time you knew.'

'Knew what?' Esther raised her voice without meaning to, on the verge of being alarmed, at any rate exasperated. Kirsty, pursuing the cat to kiss it goodbye, was out of hearing.

'About Braeside, and the money. You and Louise will come by before she goes back to London?'

'Why don't you all come to us for a meal – to celebrate Jack's job? I was meaning to ask.'

'That would be lovely if you can manage it – it's not easy for you with three bairns.'

How had it been for her, Esther wondered, when one of the three was not her own? Then Daniel and Caroline too, became Janet and Harry's responsibility when they were students. A window opened on her childhood, showing it in a different light.

Kirsty ran up, howling. 'Mimi scratched me!'

A tiny red line on the back of her arm, three beads of blood. In the ensuing fuss as Esther washed this diminutive wound and Janet went to fetch a plaster, there was no further conversation.

'She's old,' Janet excused the cat. 'She's a bit grumpy these days.'

'Kitty should know not to tease her.'

'I wasn't!'

They went home. Driving away, with only half an ear for Kirsty's running commentary, Esther was unsettled and uneasy, longing to speak to Louise – Jack too. She realised something important had happened out of sight, behind the scenes. It was an uncomfortable feeling.

'*She* couldn't even say her own name,' Andrew declared. '*Kirsty,*' he pronounced, taunting his sister.

'I can so say it!'

'You couldn't when you were a baby. Kitty, Kitty, Kitty . . .'

'We could say our names,' Ross said, joining in. 'It was just you.'

Andrew turned on his brother, not recognising an ally when he saw one, Esther thought, coming into the middle of this.

'You said *Woss,*' he taunted. 'Woss, Woss, Wossy, Puss, Puss, Pussy!'

Enraged, Ross snatched up a toy truck and flung it at his brother. Andrew dodged, laughing, and it caught Esther painfully on the hip.

In the ensuing scene, the sensible discussion about where they were to live, was abandoned.

Later, she tried again, bedtime being quieter and Jack there to help. Over their meal, just before they started getting the children ready for bed, the two of them talked about Braeside.

'So you spoke to Gordon?'

'Just on the phone. He's fine about it. Said he gets lonely on his own – and I know every time we're all out there with the kids, he seems pleased to have us there.'

'An afternoon's one thing,' Jack said. 'Several months is quite another. For all of us.'

'Months! I hope it won't be that.'

'Well, we don't know how long it will take us to find a suitable house.'

'He said something else,' Esther broke in. 'Look, I've asked Mum and Dad here tomorrow night, along with Louise and Margaret. I couldn't *not* ask Margaret and anyway it makes a difference to her too. I think.'

'What does?'

Esther got up to make coffee. As she put her hand to all the things she needed, used daily, and looked round her little kitchen with its shiny work surfaces and neatly aligned cupboards, she thought of Braeside, and for the first time, did not see it entirely through the haze of nostalgia. She was realising how poorly Gordon had modernised the kitchen, what a half-baked job it was.

'D'you want a biscuit and cheese?'

'No, I'm fine. Sit down. What's going on?'

'Nothing. Well, not now. It's all done and dusted. They've sorted out Braeside, that I thought belonged to all of us.'

She put their mugs of coffee on the table and sat down to begin the explanation. She had heard enough of it from Gordon to understand what her mother was planning to tell them. The money from the land had come to her parents; Braeside was Gordon's. Hearing this, she had phoned her mother at once.

'It made sense,' Janet said. 'We didn't need the house and he did. He certainly doesn't need any capital – he told me how much he's earning with this oil company. So he must know how much Mike's earning too. Margaret should make sure he supports Anna properly.'

For a moment, Esther thought they were about to be side-tracked onto Margaret's problems again, but Janet went on with sudden briskness.

'That's how it stands. We'll tell you in more detail when we see you, but really, it doesn't affect you children. Caroline and Margaret will inherit Braeside, and you and Louise will inherit whatever Dad and I leave.'

Esther did not want to talk about anyone leaving anything. She had a fleeting vision of Caroline's 'will' in the wooden box at Braeside and shuddered. Money. She had never thought of it except as something she and Jack never had quite enough of.

Now, explaining this to Jack, she realised what upset her was that she had somehow had a foolish idea Braeside would always be there, that it belonged to all of them in perpetuity. This, he gently told her, was never going to happen anyway. It was a valuable house, worth a sum many times more than her grandparents could ever have imagined.

'Valuable!'

'All property in and around Aberdeen is valuable, Esther. You know that. Look how much our house has gone up if the solicitor's right about the asking price.'

'Ridiculous,' Esther said, but doubtfully, starting to wonder how much money the land had brought for her parents. Had they worked out what was fair, between them, her parents and Gordon?

Apart from being able to making temporary use of Braeside for his family, Jack did not feel any of this affected him. 'Come on,' he said, 'let's get those kids ready for bed and talk to them about moving house.'

Esther sat on for a few minutes in the kitchen. When you learn about one secret, she thought, all it does is make you wonder how many more there are.

Margaret realised that having Louise in the house was not disruptive, as she had feared, but distracting. She was distracted from her grief and anxiety, and briefly, able to wake in the morning without the sense of dread which had grown every day since Mike had told her he was going to leave.

Louise had said she would stay for a week. Margaret's instinctive reaction – *that's ages* – had given way to a fretful counting of the days remaining before she was on her own again. Now she wished Louise could be here longer. The house didn't echo any more, it was full of Louise. Anna, a quiet child, was equally mesmerised, so much so that she did not even complain about the garlic-imbued unfamiliar food that was appearing on the table every night.

'What's *this*?' she would ask, then, unable to understand a word of the recipe recited by her aunt, obediently ate it. Louise had brought with her some of her more innocuous romances, and read chapters to Anna as bedtime stories. 'I'll censor, don't worry,' she assured Margaret. 'I won't read any naughty bits.'

On their own, when Anna had gone to bed, Louise poured them a glass of wine each and settled down to listen.

When she said she was going to be a psychologist, Harry and Janet were sceptical. 'What on earth use is a psychology degree?' Janet had asked. 'What kind of career can you have with that?' When it had been explained to them – by Esther and Louise combining knowledge and forces, they still did not think it was suitable for Louise. Janet, dutifully, read up as much as she could about potential career options, but was not reassured.

Margaret was surprised to find herself talking so much. Afterwards, regretting it a little, she blamed the wine that she was not used to, and the way Louise kept filling her glass when she wasn't looking. Louise, for her part, knew nobody had bothered to listen to Margaret for a long time. Perhaps they never had.

'To be fair,' she told Esther later, 'Tilly never said much about herself. She was always quiet.'

Now she talked.

Keeping the box of tissues nearby, not saying much, Louise once or twice let the pauses lengthen to long silences, as she knew to do, as she knew was necessary now and then.

The tastefully, expensively furnished living room had become an empty space with nothing personal in it. It might have been a consulting room, carefully neutral. Mike had gone from it, and Anna too, her toys banished to her bedroom or the painfully mis-called 'playroom' next to the conservatory. Margaret could not surely be so negative a presence that she was represented by the blandness of marble table lamps and sheepskin rugs, silk cushions and solid beech coffee tables. Louise saw that the photograph of her wedding had disappeared, as had the one of the three of them on a beach in Corfu. Only a photograph of Anna as a toddler remained.

Louise considered she was good at keeping herself out of the listening process. She absorbed, reflected, put in a well-judged phrase or sentence, moved the topic on, not allowing the other person to get stuck. Here though it was different, this was Margaret, her almost-sister, the little one of the Elties, the one who must always be protected but who had now been left pain-fully exposed.

Only to Esther would Louise go near to admitting she felt dismayed, and if not out of her depth, at any rate less use to Margaret than she had wanted to be.

So much, she thought, so far beneath. We never even thought.

'You know that phrase about opening a can of worms?' she said to Esther later.

'Ugh.'

291

'Well, more like hissing snakes.'

Though Louise had not given much away, Esther decided to give in return what she knew – or half knew – and brought to mind again Caroline's list of bequests, and their bewildering omission.

'Well, nice to know I'm getting more stuff if I manage to have kids,' Louise said, laughing at the whole idea.

'But – '

'Yeah. I got that. Nothing for Margaret.'

'What do you think?'

'I think you're right about secrets. There are more than we know.'

Up and Down the Stairs

1990

The children had been running up and down stairs all day, exploring, shouting, dragging their toys from one room to another and squabbling. Esther and Jack, tripping over each other and their children, heaved boxes about and tried to decide where everything should go.

Gordon had retreated to the kitchen and sat in a basket chair, reading. Perhaps he had, after all, been better on his own. He had instinctively drawn his chair close to the alcove where the range had once stood. He regretted taking it out; his mother had been right.

'Uncle Gordon, which room did you sleep in when you were a wee boy?' Andrew stood in front of him, feet apart and arms folded, frowning. This was clearly an important question and Gordon considered his answer.

'Can you guess?' he said finally. He looked round the kitchen. 'Get me a writing pad from the sideboard – top drawer in the middle.' Andrew hesitated (was he going to get an answer?) then did as he was told. Gordon tore a sheet off and divided it into three strips. 'You can each have a piece of paper and write on it which room you think. Then bring them back to me and I'll see if any of you is right.'

'And does the right one get to have your room?'

Gordon was nonplussed. 'No, of course not,' he said. 'I might be sleeping in it already.'

Andrew thought of another objection. 'Kitty can't write much yet. Only her name and 'cat' and 'dog' – stuff like that.'

Tiring of this already, Gordon shrugged his shoulders. 'Oh well. Maybe one of you could write it for her?'

'We might cheat,' Andrew said. 'We won't though, honestly.'

'Good.' With relief, Gordon returned to his book as Andrew sped off and could be heard clattering upstairs.

A moment later, Esther came in and filled the kettle. 'I thought we could all do with a cup of tea. I hope the children aren't bothering you too much. '

She had a smudge across her nose and the knees of her jeans were white with dust. The house had not been cleaned much for some time. Perhaps Esther would be doing that now? He decided not to ask just yet. She seemed tired, brushing her hair away from her face with the back of her hand, sighing as she dropped tea bags into mugs.

'Oh dear,' she said. 'It's chaos, I'm sorry, we should probably just have put our furniture in store.'

'The steading's fine and dry. Nothing will come to any harm there.'

'Oh, that's all right. It's the house. An awful lot of our stuff has to be here – the kids' things and our clothes and books and. . . . Do you mind? Is it really all right?'

He was fond of Esther and Louise, having no sense of guilt about them. They were not his responsibility. Grown up, they had become charming women who were very easy on the eye, Esther even today, grubby in old clothes.

'You'll brighten up the place,' he said, duty bound to reassure her. 'I'm delighted to have you here.'

'Um. I thought you might be regretting it – the state of the place and all this rumpus.'

Upstairs, Andrew had explained the business of writing room descriptions on pieces of paper. They were finding it difficult to define clearly which room they each meant. Jack came upon them arguing over it at the top of the stairs.

'Gordon's room?' he said, misunderstanding. 'He has the big one at the front – used to be your Granny's when she was a wee girl. When he was a boy he had the one at the end – the little one looking out to the back garden.'

They stared at him in unison. 'You've spoiled it!' Andrew cried. Ross, scribbling rapidly, started heading downstairs. 'Wait!' Andrew yelled. 'That's cheating!'

Kirsty, bewildered, handed her piece of paper to her father. 'You do it Daddy,' she said.

Esther, appearing at the bottom of the stairs, was almost bowled over by Ross in his haste. Righting herself – 'Ross, look where you're *going!*' she called up to Jack,

'Did you find the box with the kitchen things?'

'No,' he said, 'but I found my CDs.'

'*That's* all right then!' She went crossly back to the kitchen, leaving Jack with Kirsty, so he drew a cat for her on the slip of paper. Puzzled, she stared at it. 'Is it a *clue?*'

'Come on,' he said, scooping her up. 'You can help me find Mummy's ladles and wooden spoons, or whatever it is she needs.'

Louise thought of calling Braeside to see how they were all getting on. She was surprised by how much her thoughts had turned to Esther during the day, knowing they were moving in. It's only temporary, she kept telling herself, and yet it did not seem like that. She could not see them moving out again to a modern house or even an old one, some former schoolhouse to do up, or a barn conversion, the kind of thing Esther was always talking about. Why bother? It was all there at Braeside, the best house you could have for growing children and family and visitors. She would go and stay herself, soon. She did not want Esther's life, but liked to picture Esther having it. My surrogate life, she thought. Their games when they were little – I'll have four children, Esther would say, and their names will be – and Margaret, interrupting complacently, would declare she meant just to have one, a beautiful little girl. Then they turned to Louise, but she had never had this vision for her life. I'm going to get a horse, she would say. A black racehorse, and I'm going to win a lot of races and be very rich. Sometimes she imagined a tiger, or a Rolls Royce or a yacht. Never a pack of children.

Esther and Margaret had got closer to their childhood plans than she had. Not even the yacht, she thought, laughing at herself. The last client had left and she was alone in the small consulting room she used in the clinic. She had only a few clients now, and took an occasional clinic for colleagues when they were sick or on leave. Soon she meant to give it up altogether, since she was making enough from romantic fiction to manage with that. A new flat first, she had decided, before prices rose any further.

She was the last to leave, so she locked up and set the alarm. Outside it was dark, but the October evening mild and dry so she hooked her jacket over her shoulder and walked to Goodge Street for the tube, glad to be alone in the crowd, thinking what she might cook for supper, since Robin was coming over. Someone running up the steps bumped violently against her. Instinctively, too long in London not to be wary, she clutched her bag. It was safe, but she was shoved against someone else going down.

Righting herself with a hasty *sorry* she almost went on, but her arm was held.

'Louise?'

It was Caroline. They stopped, commuters dividing impatiently around them.

'Let's get out of here,' Louise said. Rising to the top of the steps they moved to the inside of the pavement to find a small space where they could speak.

'How are you? I'm sorry not to have been in touch – I meant to, but – '

'It's all right – I know how it is. I'm fine. Mum says you're getting married – when's the wedding?'

'Oh. January, probably.'

'Look, have you time for a drink or something? Robin's coming round, but not till eight.'

Caroline hesitated. 'All right.' She glanced round. 'There's a place in Charlotte Street. I sometimes meet people there – '

'Sure.'

Together, they turned and walked away from the underground station.

'Were you on your way somewhere – I'm not holding you up?' Louise asked.

'No, I was at UCH to see a woman I used to work with. She wanted my advice about a job she's applying for.'

'How funny I didn't see you till we got to the tube – I came that way.'

They sat down in the corner of a wine bar, just beginning to fill at the end of the working day.

'I'll get it,' Caroline said. 'What would you like?'

Louise watched her ordering drinks at the bar. There were silver streaks in the dark hair, but she was slim and upright as ever, her skin smooth apart from tiny lines at the corners of her eyes, a deepening of the indentations on either side of her mouth. In a soft light, she might have been ten years younger or more. She had a wild thought that Caroline had a portrait in her attic not so unmarked by time.

Louise took out her cigarettes as Caroline set down their glasses of wine.

'Do you mind?'

A quirk of a smile, a shrug. 'Your lungs. Though probably mine too, if passive smoking is as bad as we hear.'

'I hate that,' Louise said, putting the cigarette back in the packet. 'People who say they don't mind and then take all the pleasure from it, making me feel guilty.'

Caroline laughed. 'Stop then. You'll ruin your skin.'

'Tell me about your wedding – I have to know all the details so I can relay them to Esther and Margaret. Mum doesn't seem to know a lot.'

'Not much to tell.' Caroline saw Louise's expression. 'Honestly. I've known Philip as a friend for years. I'm surprised you've not met him when you've been over – perhaps you have. Anyway, his marriage ended a year or so ago, and we've . . .' She hesitated.

'Got closer?' Louise suggested. 'Realised you were made for each other?'

'You write too many romances,' Caroline smiled. 'We just got into the habit of being together.'

'He's a *habit?*'

Caroline shook her head, refusing to be drawn further. 'What about you?'

'My life is less romantic than yours, if that's possible. Robin's *my* habit.'

'Is he married?'

Louise thought, she didn't get closer to him *after* his divorce. 'You want to know about it?'

Caroline flushed. 'Tell me about the family, since neither of us wants to talk about . . . ourselves.'

'Oh, I'm quite happy to talk,' Louise assured her. 'It just wouldn't be terribly interesting.' As I'm sure you know, she thought, but did not say. 'Anyhow, Margaret's divorcing Mike. Reluctantly. Well, she hates the idea of divorce, but we've all persuaded her she's better to be completely independent now.'

'I'm sure you're right. Pity, though,' Caroline said.

'Oh well,' Louise said. 'Other people's relationships . . . you can never tell.'

They fell silent as the bar filled with drinkers, the talk around them louder, the place warming up.

'Esther's moving into Braeside today,' Louise said after a few moments. 'I must ring her when I get home to see how they got on.'

'*What* did you say?' Caroline's face darkened. '*Esther* – did you say Esther's moving into Braeside?'

'Didn't Mum tell you? They're staying there while they look for a house.'

'It's temporary then?'

Louise stared. 'Of course – what did you think? It'll be your house anyway, yours and Margaret's – one day.'

'I don't think it will ever be Margaret's,' Caroline said, then bit her lip, as if sorry she'd said this. 'Anyway – that's an excellent idea. It will keep Dad happy and give him some company.'

They talked about work after that, since it was an easy subject for them. It was safe to speculate about the NHS and other lives and comment on them.

'Time I went,' Louise said eventually, gathering up her coat and bag. 'Have you a date for the wedding?'

'Look,' Caroline said, 'it's not going to be bridesmaids and flowers. That would be ridiculous. I'm nearly forty-eight, he's been married before, and we just want to have a quiet day. We've got some leave planned, so we'll go away for about three weeks. That's it, really.'

Louise smiled. 'This is your tactful way of telling me to mind my own business and I'm not getting an invitation?'

'It will just be us and about half a dozen close friends.'

Louise was taken aback. 'You really don't want any family there?'

Caroline had pulled on her coat. They both stood up. 'No,' she said. 'There's no point.'

Out in the dark street they stood for a moment in awkward silence.

'Right,' Louise said at last. 'I'd better go.'

She raised a hand in farewell, but before she could move, Caroline said, 'Look. Sorry. Come and meet Philip, come a week on Sunday when we're having people in. Not my place – his.' She dug her hands in her coat pockets and came up with a crumpled piece of paper. 'Here – this is his address. I meant to give it to Sara today and forgot. She's invited too.'

Louise put the piece of paper in her bag without looking at it. 'Ok,' she said. 'I'll see.'

Caroline sighed. 'You could come to the wedding too, since you're in London anyway. I don't – it's not – ' She stopped and Louise saw anxiety in her expression. 'You have it the wrong way round,' she said at last.

'What the wrong way round?'

'There's no reason, you know, that Esther and Jack couldn't

have Braeside eventually. I won't have children and I only go there to see Dad and of course – well, the churchyard.'

She flushed and Louise, taking pity, though she was still unsure what she was pitying, said, 'It's fine. You can have whoever you want at your own wedding. I did. Both times. Though look where that got me.' She raised her eyes, self-mocking, and Caroline's expression softened.

'Lou – it's not anything the family have done. Even Dad, though there are things we couldn't easily forgive him.' She hesitated, while Louise wondered what those things were. And did 'we' mean Daniel too?

'It's me, it's what I did,' Caroline said. 'What I made Daniel do. What he did. It was my fault.' She hitched the strap of her bag more securely on her shoulder. 'I'll see you next week.'

Before Louise had taken this in, before she had an answer, Caroline had turned and was walking away swiftly in the direction of Oxford Street, disappearing beyond a stationary group of people discussing which restaurant they were going to eat in.

Louise walked slowly back the way they had come, heading for Goodge Street station again. She was going to be late and Robin would be there before her. For the first time she did not care; she was in no hurry.

Andrew and Ross were climbing the stairs, but not in the usual way. It was an expedition: the stairhead was the mountain summit and several books were placed strategically as obstacles – glaciers, hidden snow holes, avalanche triggers. Every now and then one of them had a terrible accident and rolled all the way to the bottom with loud yells. They carried Uncle Gordon's rucksack, which they wore in turn. At the top, panting with exaggerated fatigue, they opened the rucksack and took out a bottle of water and biscuits and ate their rations. Esther had refused to give them a flask of soup and sandwiches and had insisted, most unfairly, that they eat their lunch with everyone else in the kitchen.

'You'll have to clear all that stuff away as soon as I tell you,' she said, ladling soup. 'Your Aunt Lou is coming, and she'll want to get up the stairs without breaking her neck on your rubbish.'

They gazed at each other across the table, raising their eyes theatrically. Esther, catching the look, repressed a smile.

'Watch yourself when you go up,' she told Gordon. 'I don't think you should have given them your crampons. They're going to scratch the wood and pick holes in the carpet.'

'It's an old carpet,' Gordon said, folding up his *Press & Journal* so that he could balance it on the corner of the table and carry on reading.

It was the last day of the October holidays but Jack was in Glasgow for a Head Teacher conference. Kirsty had gone to the Ritchies in the village to play with their girls; Susan Ritchie would bring her back at four. At three, Harry and Janet brought Louise out from Aberdeen, having met her at the airport the day before.

'It's only a flying visit, sorry,' she said when the boys had been greeted and the mountain on the staircase admired. ('*Now* will you tidy it away?' Esther said.)

It was evening, when their parents had gone, the children were in bed and Gordon in front of a video tape of *The World at War*, whisky in hand, before the sisters had any time together. Esther, coming out of the boys' room after a final goodnight, found Louise sitting at the top of the stairs reading one of the books Andrew had left in a pile on the landing. Esther sat down next to her with an 'ouf' of weariness. 'Thank goodness, that's them in bed and lights out.' She glanced over Louise's shoulder.

'What's that?'

'*Alice*. It must be our old copy – is it?'

Esther looked. 'Yes, we tried to keep the children's books handy but their boxes must still be in the steading. That came out of a box of our old books, all mixed up. *What Katy Did* and *Little Women,* and that awful Hans Andersen book.'

'You mean the one with the terrible story about the girl who trod on the loaf?'

'Um. I was really frightened of that story. The drawing of the poor child in hell, wreathed in snakes.'

'Her own fault,' Louise said, 'for being so vain.'

'Amy is punished too in *Little Women,* for being vain.'

'It must be the ultimate sin,' Louise mused, leafing through *Alice in Wonderland.*

Esther, by association of ideas, thinking of Caroline reading to them, said, 'Did you meet Philip, did you go to Caroline's party or whatever it was?'

'Didn't I tell you?' Louise closed the book. 'It was Sunday lunch. He has a house in Richmond, near where Gordon used to live. The garden goes down almost to a river – well, I suppose it must be the Thames. Not that it was warm enough to be in the garden or even see it properly, but there are French doors at the back. There were a lot of shrubs and trees dripping, and the river below. It poured with rain all day.'

'He's rich, then.'

'I guess.'

'What is he like?'

Louise did not answer for a moment. 'Essie, he looks like Daniel.'

'No!'

'How you'd imagine Daniel being now, at the age he would

303

be. If you see what I mean. This Philip does look quite young – I suspect younger than Caroline. Maybe forty?'

'He really looks like Daniel? Do you remember him that well? You were only sixteen when he died.'

'I know. It was a shock, he was familiar right away.'

Esther tried to conjure Daniel. Where would their grandmother's photograph album be now? They should look for that.

'I feel a bit sick, thinking about it,' Louise said. 'I keep remembering what Caroline said.'

'Said – when? At this party?'

'No, when we met that night. It was so strange. She said something about what Daniel did. No, let me think.'

Esther waited.

'What I made Daniel do,' she said. 'What he did. I don't know, it didn't make any sense. I assume it was about when he came back and he didn't tell anyone and she didn't either. Mum was so upset about that and the upset was all the worse because of the accident.'

'Because he was dead and it was all Caroline's fault we didn't know he was even back?' Esther's voice rose, indignant. 'I always thought they were so unfair to Caroline. It was awful for her. And maybe Daniel wouldn't *let* her tell anyone? He seemed to have come back different, unlike himself.'

'I can't get over it,' Louise said. 'How like Daniel this guy seemed. Not all the time, not even after a while. It was the first look, when we met, when she introduced him.'

The telephone rang downstairs in the hall.

'Jack,' Esther said, scrambling to her feet. 'I'd better get it.'

Louise went on sitting on the top stair, *Alice* open in her hands, thinking about Daniel.

She was still there when Esther reappeared. 'Lou, did you say anything to Caroline?'

Louise, deep in *Through the Looking Glass* by this time, looked up bewildered. 'What? What about?'

Esther sat on a lower stair, and catching a loose thread in the carpet, torn out by an enthusiastic crampon earlier in the day, tried to tuck it back in. 'I told Jack about Caroline marrying someone who looks like Dan, and he said, what did *she* say about that? Did you ask her?'

Louise closed *Alice*. 'To tell the truth, I drank a bit too much. I'm not good with wine early in the day and I don't usually, but I'd had a row with Robin. I'd gone on my own after all and it was a bit of a relief really, since he's always worrying we'll meet somebody he knows – '

Esther gave up trying to re-stitch the carpet. She had heard all this stuff about Robin already. She had met him once and thought him a flirt, attractive but not someone to get involved with. He's a lightweight, Jack had said and that throwaway comment had stuck.

'So what does that mean?' she interrupted. 'You did or didn't say anything?'

Louise was apologetic. 'Sorry. Don't remember. I think I did. Just casually, you know.'

'There's nothing casual about – '

'No, no, I know, but my God, Essie, it's more than twenty years since he died, surely we can speak about him without a major drama?'

'We don't though. Mum and Dad don't. Gordon doesn't. And Caroline doesn't. Not at *all*, never mind dramatically.'

Louise said, 'I think Caroline went through the looking glass a long time ago, and stayed there. She's like somebody on the other side. Another world.'

It was Daniel, though, who was in the other world, if he was anywhere, Esther thought. More likely Caroline was trying to get through and the glass wouldn't go all gauzy for her, let her into that mirror life. All she said was, 'Do you think she really will marry him?'

Louise considered. 'Maybe not.'

From the living room came the crashing chords at the end of Gordon's video, abruptly cut off and followed by the theme tune of the nine o'clock news.

'He'll want a cup of tea,' Esther said. 'Do you? I'll go and put the kettle on.'

They've been here five minutes, Louise thought as she followed Esther downstairs, and already she knows all Gordon's habits. Worse, she's looking after him. No reason, Caroline had said, Esther and her family couldn't stay on at Braeside. But Gordon might live another twenty years. Surely Esther – and especially Jack – would want their own place?

This was why she had not married. The quirks and comforts of family life amused her, drew her in, but two days with other people in this claustrophobia and she wanted out again.

Monday was full of the drama of family life Louise enjoyed when it belonged to other people: the children starting school, Jack heading to his job from this new base for the first time, worrying about staff problems, worrying that he had not made enough of an impact in his first two months up to the October break. Louise distracted Kirsty from her terror of going to a school where she knew nobody except the Ritchie children, found Jack's briefcase which had disappeared behind the sofa, and finally made coffee for Esther and herself when at last the house was silent and empty. Gordon had gone out early, having reclaimed his rucksack for a hill walk.

'I hope he's all right,' Esther said, as she cleared away the breakfast dishes. 'He's going on his own today, and I keep saying he should always go with other people now. He's not as fit as he used to be and he's awfully slow coming down.'

'Don't fuss. He's been going up hills for donkey's years,' Louise said.

'Mostly since he retired – there's not a lot of hill walking in London or Egypt or all those other places he worked.'

'He's not your responsibility. If he's anyone's, it's Margaret or Caroline who should be telling him off, not you.'

Esther wiped over the table, not answering this. 'I thought – as it's such a beautiful morning – we might have a walk ourselves. You're flying home tomorrow, aren't you?'

'Ok. Where will we go?'

Esther had thought of this.

It was years since Louise had been in the Drumoak churchyard. She could not remember being there since her grandmother's funeral, and that was brief, hurried, in the driving snow, everyone glad to get back to the newly warm Braeside.

They walked along the banks of the Dee for a couple of miles, and on their way back came through the village to the church-yard. The local names on many of the headstones were familiar, and their great-grandparents, as well as Andrew and Celia Livingstone, were buried here. Daniel's grave was next to theirs.

'We should have brought flowers, maybe,' Louise said.

'Oh no, I hate to see dead flowers on graves – and they do die, very quickly. Nobody comes so regularly they can keep renewing the flowers.'

'I suppose not.'

They stood in silence for a moment but Daniel eluded them.

Ghostly, he had departed. They could not even picture his face. Esther was thinking she should bring Margaret with her next time, then as the thought appeared, it vanished, unsatisfactory. She ought instead to be keeping Margaret cheerful. She sighed; that was going to be hard.

As they turned away, she asked Louise, 'Have you spoken to Margaret this time, seen her?'

'No, there's been no time. How is she?'

'Miserable. Never mind, now the kids are back at school and we're sort of moved in, I'll give her a call.'

All those people Esther felt obliged to look after – it was exhausting, Louise thought, since she found it more than enough just to look after herself.

As they got into the car to make the short drive back to Braeside, she finally told Esther what she had meant to say all weekend.

'I know you don't like me talking about it. I know you disapprove, you and Margaret. So you'll be pleased to hear I've broken off with Robin.'

Esther's hand fell from the ignition, where she had just pushed in the key. 'Lou, you should have *said*. I didn't like the fact that he's married, of course not, but I know *you* loved him and – '

'Love!'

'Well – ' Esther stopped. Could she be honest and say *good, about time*? Instead, she turned to her sister and, awkwardly, since they were not people who touched each other much, she hugged her.

'Hey – it's ok.' But Louise hugged her back, grateful.

'Right. Let's go.' Still she did not start the car. 'You know,' she added eventually, 'I did like Eric. I'm sorry about *him*. I think you really suited each other.'

Louise said nothing, but as Esther started the car and they drove off, she turned to look out of the window, so that she could blink away the stupid tears threatening to fall.

Time she went back to London. Coming home was always awful, in the end.

The House

1991

Esther wasn't with him when Gordon had his heart attack. She was at Braeside, changing beds, while he was in a pull-in at the foot of Mount Keen, intending to climb the hill on his own. When some other hill walkers drew their vehicle in alongside his, they found him lying back in the driver's seat, his flask on the ground next to the open door, a pool of spilled tea already seeped away.

Esther was in the boys' room, bundling sheets and duvet covers together in her arms, ready to take them downstairs, when the telephone rang. Gordon had put an extension in his bedroom so she did not have far to go to pick it up.

The day before the funeral (*another* funeral at Braeside, she could not help thinking), Esther found herself wandering through the house, touching the doors, the chest on the landing, the curve of banister at the stairhead, and trying to persuade herself that somehow it would be possible to stay. It's not, she thought, as if we've found another house we like. Not really like, and can afford. In the weeks they had been here, this house had become infiltrated by the Murrays, especially the children. They left toys in the hall or along the landing; their drawings were pinned up on the kitchen wall that needed a fresh coat of paint; their shoes in a heap by the kitchen door and she was always kicking them as she went in and out. Their coats and waterproofs were piled on the pegs in the hall. Their bedding, which she smoothed and stripped off and washed and replaced, was bright with primary colours, Disney characters or – in Andrew's case – Transformers, currently his favourite toy. They treated the house as a familiar, loved and neglected home, Kirsty making 'houses' in odd corners, the boys coming downstairs by leaning over the banister and sliding, feet held up, all the way.

At first, she had worried they were invading Gordon's property, or perhaps, still, her grandmother's house. Now the Murrays were in residence and it was almost wholly theirs.

Only, it was not.

'I guess,' Jack had said the day after Gordon died, 'this place belongs to Caroline and Margaret now. We'd better get a move on – find a house. They might want to sell.'

This was what had shocked her into the new longing. Could they not buy it from them, could they not just stay, after all? When she tentatively put this to Jack, he laughed.

'Not a hope,' he said. 'I know it needs loads of work but it's a seven bedroom house, it's huge, it has an acre of land. We could never afford it in a million years. And since Caroline's in London, and Margaret is on her own now – they're going to want to sell.'

Esther sat down at the top of the stairs, Andrew's favourite vantage point, and laid her head against the wall. The faded cream wallpaper had once had roses, she thought, pink roses. She put out a hand and traced the outline of a possible rose. The sun that reached here briefly in the afternoon, had whitened the patch she leaned on.

Soon it would be time to fetch the children from school, one disadvantage, as Jack had reminded her, of living so far out in the country. They would never be able to walk home. It made no sense. They had to find their own place. Stubbornly, she thought, this *is* our own place.

Inheriting

1991

Caroline stayed on at Braeside for a few days, partly to see John Chalmers, now their family solicitor at Cowie's but also, she said, for a rest. She did look tired.

'It's wonderfully quiet here,' she said to Esther at breakfast after the children had left for the school bus. She stood by the kitchen window looking across the yard to the steading, mug of coffee held in two hands, close to her chest. 'You forget, in London, how quiet the country is, and how dark. So dark last night, and the stars dazzling.'

'I bet London's warmer,' Esther grumbled, 'and your flat must be much easier to heat.'

'I know. Dad's central heating isn't terribly good, is it?' She glanced round the kitchen. 'He should never have got rid of the range.'

'It did keep it nice and cosy – it was more homely,' Esther admitted.

'Have you found a house yet?'

Esther turned to the sink to wash up breakfast dishes, so that Caroline would not see her face. She was so inclined to *cry* when she thought about leaving Braeside, it was ridiculous. It was Caroline's house now. Surely. Or did it belong to Margaret too?

313

She thought fleetingly of wills, of Caroline's wills, those scraps of betraying paper tucked away. *For Esther, my ring.*

'No,' she said. 'We need to get on with it.'

'Can we have some more coffee, Esther – will you join me? Leave the dishes alone. They'll keep.'

Surprised, Esther turned, heart thudding. What was this? How soon did they have to leave? She dried her hands on the damp towel on a hook by the sink, and moved aside to let Caroline fill the kettle and wash out the cafetière.

They sat down at the table with mugs of fresh coffee, the scent of it soothing despite Esther's fears.

'I don't usually drink coffee so early in the day,' she said.

'Always a first time.' Caroline smiled and Esther – touched and alarmed – bit back betraying tears. Oh, if she was going to be *nice* –

'You wouldn't want to stay here, I take it?' Caroline said. 'Jack was saying you were trying to find something in the village, so the children could walk to school, somewhere less isolated.'

'That's the sensible thing, of course. It's a pain, getting them to the school bus, and there's all the toing and froing with their friends – and the boys' football after school . . .' She trailed off. 'Well, that sort of stuff. You know.' She blushed. Caroline could not know.

'I can understand all that,' Caroline said. 'Though, obviously, I've never had kids.' She smiled again, disarming. 'Never will now.'

'You're getting married?'

'Never mind that – what I want to talk to you about is Braeside. And you.'

'Me?'

'You must be thinking about what's next. The children are all at school, you're still young. What are you going to do? Write romances, like Louise? Start a market garden? Teach?'

Why would you care, Esther wanted to say. You're never here, you're barely part of this family, you only come for funerals. But she could not say any of that with Caroline sitting opposite, being so friendly, and the coffee (much stronger than she ever made) zinging through her veins.

'The children are very young,' she said. 'And there's a house to buy, all the palaver of getting settled in that, and Jack works so hard, he needs to be able to relax when he comes home, so I have to make sure – '

Caroline held up her hands, fending off this litany. 'Stop! No more. Look, I'm not going to go on, but that's not enough. Not for someone with your good brain, that as far as I can see you've never used to the full, except maybe in your final year at Aberdeen, you worked *then*, didn't you?'

'I don't see – '

'You think it's not my business.'

'Well – '

'If – just supposing – you could stay at Braeside. Live in this house, if it was *your* house – would you want to? Never mind schools and football and Jack – just you. Would you?'

Silenced, Esther stared at her cousin, this mysterious woman who was once their dear Caroline, reading from *Alice*, doing the voices with such realism you laughed and wondered and believed in it all. Lost to them years ago, long before Daniel died. When he left, she left too, in her head, she left them. Was this Caroline back again, and anyway, what was she *talking about*? Into the space she had made for Caroline, for thinking about her, came her grandmother, and the weeks she had spent here as a child, helping in the garden and with the hens, sleeping in the big feather bed – long disposed of by Gordon – waking to the wood pigeons in the trees outside, the sun streaming in the bedroom window, Granny downstairs already and the smell of oatcakes on the griddle.

'Yes,' she said. 'I love this house.'

Caroline heaved a sigh. 'Well then,' she said, 'that's what you must do.'

'But – you mean, rent it from you? Or you and Margaret – isn't it up to both of you – I mean – whose house is it?'

Caroline's mouth tightened. 'Mine,' she said. 'The house is mine. Dad told me years ago. He's left money to Margaret from the sale of his house in Richmond. She'll be fine now without that awful Mike. Why on earth did she marry him? Women are such fools.'

Esther laughed. 'Oh, Caroline, *why* have you stayed away so long? You're good for us, you should have said that to *her*, she still thinks she did something wrong.'

'She did. She married him. Oh well – ' They were both laughing. 'Sorry,' Caroline said. 'Getting off the point altogether. What I'm saying is, you can have Braeside.'

'What do you mean – *have it?*'

'I'm giving it to you. For your lifetime. If you want it.' She looked round the kitchen. 'I'd put an Aga in here, or a Rayburn. And the wood in the doors is drying out – you need to oil it regularly if you're not going to paint it and I guess you won't.'

'But – oh, I don't know what Jack will say.'

Caroline shrugged. 'I'm not giving it to Jack. I'm giving it to you.' She leaned back, tipping the kitchen chair on its hind legs. 'I have plenty of money, I don't need to sell the place. And I want it to – stay. I grew up here too, Esther. We both did.'

Esther was about to say – and Louise and Margaret too, when she realised with a jolt that 'both' meant Caroline and Daniel.

Caroline righted her chair. 'That's decided then. I'm going in to see John Chalmers today – he's dealing with Dad's estate. I'd better find the files I need to take with me. I'll ask him to draw up something. I thought I'd put the house in trust for your children, and you and Jack have the right to stay in it – something like that. I'll take his advice, sort it out.'

When she had left the kitchen, Esther went on sitting at the table, unsure whether the giddy feeling was because of the coffee or the conversation. Was that it – had Caroline just given her Braeside? Surely not, surely it must be temporary – for the meantime? *In trust for your children.* That sounded permanent.

What are you going to do? Caroline had asked. It seemed she was going to inherit Braeside, and look after the house. Was there more to it than that? She knew what Jack would say: 'it's your house, you decide' but he would also point out how expensive the house would be to maintain. What a millstone round their necks, a great place like this, had a surveyor ever inspected it, was there damp, what was the roof like now, and what about redecoration? An Aga? How could they afford that?

I have to have answers, she thought, I have to be prepared. She got up and went to find Caroline, who might know some of them already. She was on her way upstairs when it occurred to her that what Caroline was doing was immensely unfair – if not to them, then certainly to Louise. And what about Margaret?

She paused halfway up and bent to pick up a toy truck left wedged between banisters, and a single pink sock. She would speak to her parents. Wasn't this something the whole family should discuss?

Below, she heard the postman's van rattling along the lane and

into the yard. She turned and went back down to open the door
to him.

'Cauld the day,' he said. 'Winter's on the wey, eh?'

'Probably,' Esther agreed.

There was the electricity bill and two other letters for Gordon.
She supposed she should just hand them to Caroline. But who
should pay the electricity bills now? She opened it, just to see
how much – oh God, terrifying. They couldn't possibly afford to
stay here.

She stood by the door listening to the van rattle away down
the lane. There had to be a way. She had to make it work.

Caroline was coming downstairs with an armful of files.

'Thank goodness Dad was organised. He had it all in the
bottom drawer of the big chest in his room. He told me where to
look last time we spoke.'

'The postie's been – there are letters for him. I suppose – '

'I'll take them. When I've gone home, just open everything
and pass it to John Chalmers – unless it's something you can deal
with yourself.'

'And the Hydro Electric people – the bill's come.'

'He'll sort that out. Give it to me.'

'We should pay some of it – '

'Don't worry, you'll have the next one to deal with all by
yourself.' She smiled, mocking, as if giving them Braeside wasn't
so generous after all. Look what you're landing me with, Esther
thought.

'I do need to discuss it with Jack,' she said. 'I mean – I can't
believe how generous – '

'I'm not.' She was not smiling now. 'Don't go on about it. The
only thing you should be thinking about now is your own career.
I mean it.'

Career! When had she ever come close to having such a thing?

'I don't know – '

'Make the house pay then, that's the other way to do it.'

'The house?'

'Think about it.' She was putting the files into a large cardboard box. 'Now, call me a taxi – I can't take this lot on a bus all the way to Aberdeen.'

'I'll take you.'

'Have you time?'

'Oh yes. Kirsty doesn't come out till quarter to three.'

'Fine. Get your coat then.'

As they drove to the city the sun came out, lighting the fields and distant hills with the deceptive appearance of warmth. Caroline was silent, watching the familiar landscape, but whether she was noticing, caring about it, Esther did not know.

'I'll go and see Mum,' she said, 'while you're at the lawyer's.'

'Good idea. I'll get a taxi up to Harrowden Place when I'm done at Cowie's.'

Janet was pleased to see her, so unexpectedly.

'Your father went out to the Golf Club,' she said, taking Esther into the den, where the gas fire was on and the room warm. 'He's usually there on a Tuesday.'

'Caroline is coming here when she's finished at the lawyers.'

'I've lentil soup on, you can get a bowl of that and some bread and cheese before you go home.'

'That's lovely. You've always got soup, Mum, it's very comforting.'

Janet laughed. 'Oh well, I'm glad you're pleased.'

'How are you?'

319

'Would you like coffee? I can make the stuff you like, in that cafetière Louise gave us.'

'I'll do it.' Esther knew she would make it strong enough, if she did it herself. Even stronger now, thinking of Caroline's heady brew.

'I'll heat up some milk.'

Companionably, in the kitchen, they got the coffee ready and Janet took out some of her own shortbread.

'I suppose she's handing it all over to John Chalmers,' Janet said, when they had made themselves comfortable in the den. 'Gordon's estate.'

'Well, yes. I thought maybe Margaret, but – I don't know.'

'Margaret will be glad enough to leave it all to them, I'm sure.'

Esther thought her mother looked tired. She did not touch the shortbread.

'Are you all right?'

'Me? I'm fine, dear. Just – it's not easy to take in. I can't get used to it. That he's gone.'

'I know. Braeside seems strange without him.'

'I'm glad he took it on – your Dad and I don't have to deal with that now. Caroline can put it on the market, or get the solicitor to do it. Since she's in London.'

'She says it's hers. Not Margaret's. She said he left Margaret money instead from the Richmond house – is that right?'

'Oh yes. He did tell me, some time ago. Not that it's any of our business, I said, but it's important you make your children equal.' She put more hot milk in her coffee and drank some. 'That's better. You young ones like it awful strong.'

'Sorry.'

'No, no, it's fine now.' After a moment, she said, 'Esther, your Dad and I have made everything quite clear. In our wills

– everything will go to Louise and you, equally. You'll make sure Margaret gets whatever things she wants though, from the house.'

'Of course we will! Don't talk about it, it's years away.'

Still, they did have to think about money, and inheritance. Because of Caroline, and Braeside.

Eventually, Esther managed to tell Louise. On the other end of the line, there was a stunned silence, then Louise began to laugh.

'Bloody hell,' she said. 'I was miffed about the emerald ring – but a fucking house! And *our* house, Granny's house – that's unbelievable.'

'I'm sorry,' Esther said, 'I'm sorry, I said to her, what about Louise, and she said, *is Louise going to have children now? Who would she leave it to? I'll put it in your joint names, you and Lou and Jack, if it makes you feel better.'*

'What did you say?'

'I said I'd speak to you.'

There was a long pause.

'Lou? Lou, I'm *sorry*. I hate this.'

'Did Mum say "Trust Caroline to cause trouble"?'

'Something like that.'

'She's right, that's the worst of it. I'm not going to have kids, you and Margaret are the only ones to provide the next generation. Daniel, Caroline, me – we're end-stopped. We go no further down the ages. But you do. You and Jack.'

'But it's worth a lot of money, Jack says, even though it's falling to bits – '

'It's not, well it is worth money, and it's not falling to bits, but that's not what matters. If she gives it to you in trust for the kids, you have to live in it, you can't just sell it.'

'No, well that's the point, isn't it? To keep it in the family.'

Another long pause. 'I always felt we held on to too much, in our family. Stuff. Property. The past, the bad stuff. Now Caroline's hanging it round your neck like a – what? Millstone? Who would put a real millstone round their neck? What's that about? There must be a better metaphor.'

'It's an anchor,' Esther said, realising this was what she believed.

'Ah, well done. But you do know that as long as you're anchored, you can't sail away?'

She did not want to sail away, she wanted to stay and bring up their children, work the garden, keep hens, be rooted in the same place. And yet, hearing Louise's light voice, her mocking laugh, for an instant she was afraid, and pictured Louise herself, in her little craft, sailing away from them all, as Daniel had done.

V

The Golden Key
2011–2012

Once more she found herself in the long hall, and close to the little glass table. 'Now, I'll manage better this time,' she said to herself, and began by taking the little golden key and unlocking the door that led to the garden.

Alice's Adventures in Wonderland, Lewis Carroll

The Cottage near Ullapool

2011

A year before he died, Esther and Jack took a cottage in West Sutherland for a week. They rarely went away in the summer because of the business, but this time she had taken no bookings for the first week in October, and in the second half of September they had only one which they were able to pass to a friend in the village. It had not been a good season for anyone. Esther blamed the weather, Jack the recession. The children had visited at various times over the summer, but they had all gone home now. Esther packed clothes and food in the car, Jack put up the 'No Vacancies' sign at the end of the lane in to Braeside, and they left.

The cottage was on the edge of a loch ten miles north of Lochinver, white-washed and remote, the garden area invaded by sheep undeterred by the gate. They had jumped the stone walls so often their favourite breaches had crumbled. Facing the house were the great hills of West Sutherland Jack had climbed in his forties and fifties: Canisp, Suilven, Cul Mhor and Cul Beag. They loomed on the horizon, perhaps never to be attempted again. That was a relief but it was also, for Jack, a frustration. Gordon had died at the foot of Mount Keen; Robin Cook had died on Ben Stack. The suddenness of those deaths, one private and the other public, had shocked them both. Then after Jack's heart attack Esther was even more afraid of his going out on the hills on his own. What if that happened to them?

It was nearly a year since that seizure, and he had had a stent fitted in an artery, but even now fear kept her anxious about him and – mostly – tolerant.

They had, they told each other afterwards, a perfect week. It was glorious Indian summer weather: crisp mornings warming to fine blue-skied days, hot enough when they were walking to shed their fleece tops, once even for shorts. Closer than the great hills was a rolling landscape of rock and heather, easy ascents taking twenty minutes or so, one leading on to the next, each topped by a small cairn they touched with superstitious care every time they reached a summit. At their feet the latest of the year's wild flowers faded, moss in places made the going springy and soft and below them lochans shimmered in sunshine. The water lilies were over but their flat leaves spread across the surface near the banks. In several fenced conservation enclosures there was vigorous regrowth of alder, rowan and Scots pine, beneath which the bracken was dense and tall grasses waved.

She should have been perfectly happy.

Rising late, they began the morning with Bach soaring from the I Pod speakers they'd brought with them, and the smell of coffee, then after breakfast boots on and a tramp up the hill behind the cottage or a walk to the farm for eggs. That was all they needed, that and their stack of books, bottle of malt whisky and the plain easy meals she cooked on holiday.

Foolish to be hurt that Jack was no different from the way he was at home: still arrogant and annoying as usual, she decided, stumping after him. He always managed to be five or ten yards ahead of her, however they had begun.

'I thought we were supposed to be walking *together*,' she complained at one point, catching up when he raised his field glasses to stare at a speck in the sky that might be a buzzard or just possibly –

'Yes – I think it is – look at the wing shape. That's an eagle.' He turned to her, pleased, holding out the glasses, but she shrugged.

'If you say so.'

'What's up?'

'Can't we walk side by side? We're supposed to be on *holiday*.'

He only laughed. 'We do,' he said, 'then you lag behind.'

She took a swipe at him, half playful, half angry. 'It's not that way at all.'

They stopped in a sheltered spot by a lochan to have a flask of tea and slabs of fruit cake. Afterwards, lying back on their waterproofs, his rucksack for a pillow, they dozed for ten minutes in sunny warmth, soothed by a stillness lifted from silence only by the lap of water and bird calls.

Esther stirred, realising Jack had gone. She sat up with a leap of the heart but scolding herself. He was fine, he had wandered off as usual, too restless to lie still for long. Getting up, she saw him clambering over the hill behind them. There he goes, she thought, not a word to me, off on his own. She packed up the rucksack, left it by a large boulder at the side of the path and began to follow. She was resentful, guilty about being sullen, but unable to shake off her mood. I should be happy, she thought, why am I not happy? She often asked herself this pointless question. Better to let it go.

He turned to wave and smile as she breasted the hill and joined him. She too touched the crooked pile of stones doing duty as a cairn.

'Judy would have loved this,' he said, as he had said a dozen times this week. The dog had died six months before, grieved over but somehow, for the first time in their marriage, not replaced.

'Yes,' she said, 'maybe we should think about another dog now.' She had given this answer a dozen times too. They agreed, but still did nothing.

'Look at this,' he told her, encompassing the view with his arm. 'Isn't it wonderful?'

I wish he'd just let me enjoy it, I don't have to be told, why do we always have to be saying how great it is. A moment passed, long in the silence. Then, without warning, his hand, large and hard and warm, reached out and grasped hers tightly.

'Esther,' he said.

The lump rose in her throat like remorse and she went into his arms with a sigh, resting there.

It was always like this. Marriage was full of unspoken irritations and all you could do was make sure they mostly stayed unspoken. She had decided that, over and over, and yet the resentment rose, unquelled by rational thought. We stayed the course, anyway, she thought, despite – well, despite everything. Her mind, now, sheered away from the bad times, when Kirsty was such a difficult teenager and Jack had hardly been at home, his job consuming everything, his closest friends at work, not home. Then every summer, when Braeside was full and she hadn't a minute to herself, he went off hill walking, all through his summer holiday. He made her angry and no wonder. Sometimes she wondered if she had been right to see it through.

For now, though, they stood as if on the pinnacle of the world, the bare and beautiful landscape unpeopled, entirely their own.

They drove back by way of Ullapool.

'We should call on Caroline,' Esther said as they packed up the car.

Jack threw in their boots on top of the box of unused kitchen supplies. 'Who?'

Esther retrieved the boots and found a plastic carrier bag for them. 'Honestly, Jack, these are still muddy – '

'Och, you do it, you pack the bloody car. You just undo everything I've done anyway.'

She sighed. 'You're so impatient these days.'

He turned and looked at her and their eyes caught, held.

'Yes,' he said.

Fear leapt up, burning for a few painful seconds. 'It's all right,' she said. 'We can just go straight home.'

He went into the cottage to bring out the last of their belongings for her to stow away. Even with the back seats down, the car seemed very full, as if they were taking home more than they had brought.

'Remind me – where's this place of Caroline's?'

This was as near as she would get to an apology, so she accepted it as such. 'Very near Ullapool, I think. Braes? I've never been there, but we can ask in the village.'

'Fine.'

Caroline lived up a steep hill behind Ullapool. They went slowly past several houses, checking names on gates and pillars, but hers was beyond them by a mile. It was a renovated croft house set back from the road, so they had to open its five bar gate and go slowly up the unmade drive, bumping over potholes, Jack cursing about the car's suspension.

To the left of the open front door, obscuring the living room window, sat a taxi, its engine humming, but empty, driverless. As Jack pulled into the space on the other side of the house, a man came to the door, carrying a suitcase. He opened the boot of the taxi and stowed it away.

'Bad timing,' Jack said. 'Looks as if she's going away.'

'Maybe a visitor's leaving,' Esther said.

Jack shook his head with a smile. 'So she has visitors now?'

By the time they got out of their own car, the taxi driver was in his seat and Caroline had appeared. She was formally dressed, like someone going to a meeting, Esther thought. Surely she had retired, years ago?

'Hi,' Esther said. 'We're on our way home – we've been in Lochinver, so I thought we'd just call in – but – '

Caroline shut her door firmly behind her. 'Oh dear,' she said. 'I'm leaving – and I can't wait. I've a train to catch.' She bent to the open passenger window of the taxi. 'Two minutes, Roddy, ok?'

She came round the taxi and held Esther by the shoulders. Esther almost did not move her head in time for the kiss on either cheek. When did she start doing *that?* she thought.

'It *is* lovely to see you – I'm sorry I can't stay.' She turned to Jack. 'How are you?'

'Fine.'

'Hill walking again?'

He grinned. 'Hillocks. She won't even let me near a Corbett.' He and Caroline hugged briefly. 'You look fit – are you ticking off the West Sutherland hills yourself?'

She smiled. 'I go out with some friends here. Now and again.'

'Right,' he said. 'We'd better let you get on.'

'Help yourself if you want to make coffee or anything. It's not locked.'

'No,' Esther said, 'we'll just head home.'

Caroline opened the passenger door of the taxi. 'Is everyone ok? Give them my love.'

When the taxi had gone slowly down the drive and they heard

it on the road, fainter and fainter, Jack turned their car and followed. When Esther got in after closing Caroline's gate she said, 'She does look well.'

'How old is she?'

'Nine years older than me, so – help, sixty-seven or -eight, I suppose.'

'Pretty good for that.'

'Where on earth can she be off to, all dressed up as if she's going to a meeting?'

'You should have asked her.'

Esther did not answer. After a moment she scrabbled in her handbag for a tissue and blew her nose.

'Esther?' She could not speak. 'What is it? Are you all right?' He drew the car into a passing place and cutting the engine, swung round to look at her.

'Sorry,' she said.

'What's this about? Caroline was fine, she was leaving for a train, what on earth are you crying for?'

'I don't know,' she said, still crying, searching for another tissue. Her father, she thought with a spurt of angry loss, would have shaken out his big white handkerchief and given it to her. Jack just sat there, accusing.

He leaned over and pulled her close, patting her back, stroking her hair. Her face pressed against his woollen jersey, the tears soaking in. She breathed him in with a hiccup and a sigh.

'It's all right, sweetheart,' he said. 'It's all right.'

Though what was all right, neither of them could have said.

331

Louise's visit

2012

Esther had sometimes been surprised to see Jack next to her when she woke, surprised to find them still married, together and companionable. After all their difficulties, here he still was. Here was his familiar beaky profile, head flung back on the pillow, a tiny snore escaping, and his hand warm and present, clasping her thigh. *We're still married, he's here.* She had what she wanted then: she was a married woman with children.

After she was widowed she woke with dismay, suffering all over again that hollow falling away of loss, but she was never surprised, as people are said to be, remembering that someone has died. It was as if she had always expected it. He was bound, one way or another, to vanish from their life. Though she knew it must be endured, she could not resign herself to being alone, probably for ever. Perhaps if the children had still been at home it would have seemed more normal and the pattern of everyday habits would have been re-established, to comfort her. Quite soon after the funeral the children had gone back to their grown-up separate lives, the lives of course she wanted them to have. Full of grief, yes, they suffered too, but they had more to take them forward, while she seemed only to have memories and habits that pulled her back.

On a grey Monday morning in February, standing at the kitchen sink washing up one plate and one mug, she was thinking how terrible it must be when the person who has died was young. That must seem as if a cliff edge has broken off at your feet and tumbled into the sea, far below. This dramatic image had come to her because she had heard on the radio news at eight and nine and ten o'clock the report of the mysterious death of a teenage girl in the South of England, missing for days, her body discovered on a lonely beach. At the same moment, she was gripped by a new emotion – more thrilling than nostalgia or loss – which took her thoughts with a rush of blood to Daniel. Recently, it seemed she had almost caught sight of him, his shadowed figure, the turn of his head, as if he stood in the room beside her. This had happened several times since Jack's death and she was sure it had some meaning.

What had it been like for Caroline? Daniel had no wife or lover, but he had Caroline and she had him. Then she had not.

They had been close in a way that was beyond Esther's experience of being with Louise or Margaret, or the ordinary togetherness of her own children. Fifty years later she could remember the fusion of understanding between them that excluded everyone else. She had been almost jealous of it. It was what she thought, on the verge of her wedding, marriage would bring: a bond no one else could breach.

For a while, perhaps. Then again, after Kirsty went to Edinburgh as a student. Oh dear, she mustn't worry. Kirsty would be all right, of course she would.

Outside, rain had evaporated to dampness and a mist had crept in, making it impossible to see as far as the old steading, now a garage and storerooms. The mist condensed on the tiny clustered leaves of the cotoneaster that touched the edge of the kitchen window and dripped down the glass. On an afternoon like this, out of season and with no possibility of gardening, she was thrown on her own too slender resources.

She could sort the photographs; she could make a start. There was going to come a time – soon probably – when there would be everything in her mother's house to deal with. So far, this was too grim to contemplate, but she could tackle the photographs.

They were in a box in the long space under the eaves at the west gable end of the house, on the top floor. She knew exactly where to find it, having stored it there carefully after she had taken it from her mother's house, with a promise to put them in albums.

It was dusty from lying a long time in the box room at Harrowden Place, and now here. She blew off the remaining dust, triggering a sneeze, then took it up in her arms with some difficulty, the cardboard splitting at the corner, an awkward weight. On the landing she rested it on the banister for a moment, shifting the balance, conscious of silence and the large empty house around her. It seemed to be waiting to be filled again, perhaps by all the people about to be released from the box she carried down to the kitchen, the box that was full of the past.

She would get them all in order and docket them for the new albums she had bought. Her idea was that she could then go through them with Janet. It was difficult to know what to talk about these days, the conversation so often caught in a surreal loop, the same thing repeated over and over. Perhaps her mother would remember better with photographs to talk about. It was warmer here in the kitchen, the gentle heat of the Rayburn keeping from it the chill that lay over the rest of the house on this bleak winter day. She began to spread out the yellow Kodak envelopes on the kitchen table. She would sort the loose photographs

334

later, since it was easier to date the packs, related as they were to some occasion or holiday, or at any rate defined periods in their family life. There was one last envelope, a large brown one, tucked down the side of the box.

She slid the single photograph out and saw Daniel for the first time for many years. This was not the Daniel of the portraits on the sideboard in Harrowden Place. Here he was in his twenties she guessed, still a medical student. Behind him, half concealed, stepping out from the shadows of an unknown doorway, was Caroline.

He was such a beautiful young man, slender and dark, with that half fringe falling almost over one eye, the humorous twist of his mouth and the easy grace of the way he stood. She held it up to the weak February light, not sure now he was as young as all that. In a flash, she saw something different. This was not Aberdeen, it was not when he and Caroline were students. She looked again. This was after he came back. This was the time they knew nothing about, that Caroline said lasted only a few days, when he had first contacted her and she said to everyone, after he died, we were about to tell you all, I had just seen him again. And yet, here they were in front of a strange doorway coming out as if they belonged there. There was something familiar about it. She saw enough of the sandstone frontage to recognise a building like the one Ross had stayed in when he was a student. It was Glasgow. It was a tenement building in Glasgow.

How long had he been living there before Caroline told them he was back? How *long* had Caroline known? Even more mysterious, how had the photograph come to be in this box?

Esther traced her finger lightly across the face, the shoulders, of the long dead boy, and he went on gazing at her, sharing the truth, relieved she knew at last, yet conspiratorial.

The telephone rang, making her jump. She rushed into the hall since it cut to the answer machine too quickly. Her foot caught on the matting in the passage. Righting herself she snatched up the receiver with a gasp – 'Hello?'

'Esther?'

'Yes, it's me – Lou?'

On a breath, two syllables, you know each other's voices, know even how the other is, the mood, whether something has happened. Louise sounded fine, breezy as usual.

'Yeah – are you ok?'

'Fine, tripped on the rug – where are you?' Since Louise might be anywhere. This time there was an echo and much noise in the background.

'Here. Back. I mean Scotland, I'm at Waverley.'

'What – I can't hear you very well – *Waverley?*'

'I'm getting on a *train* – can you meet me?'

'Aberdeen?'

'Of course Aberdeen – I think it's – ' more hissing, Louise saying something Esther guessed to be 'I'll text you' and the line went dead.

Esther straightened the rug and went back to the kitchen. She swept up the Kodak packets and thrust them into the box. The past had lost its appeal, Louise bringing a blast of the contemporary world, its language and ideas. You had to wake up to cope with that. She dreaded being seen as a pathetic widow, however kindly, and however loved. She would get rid of these for now, put them in a cupboard for the next low day (which was bound to come, about a week after Louise's departure). She had done that, washed her hands and made coffee, before she realised the faded picture of Daniel and Caroline had fallen onto the seat of a rush-bottomed chair and was still here in the kitchen.

She propped it up on the dresser, lodged between an Indian Tree plate and a pewter mug, both legacies from her grandparents' life. Seeing it again, she decided she couldn't really be sure. It might be anywhere. It told you nothing, this brief moment in a dark doorway, the amused look on his face, Caroline stepping out as if to protect him, or perhaps to keep him from saying the one thing he had really better not say.

Louise brought with her a sharper air, like a clean breeze through leaves that have hung in damp mist for too long. The real mist had cleared and they could see the River Dee, gleaming in fitful sunshine, as they drove out past Drumoak towards Braeside. Louise was dressed casually in jeans and a fleece, but her silver earrings were pretty, her hair cut sleeker and shorter than usual, the grey more noticeable among the black. She had a carpet bag (when had anyone last seen one of those, Esther wondered?) and a large suitcase on wheels.

'How long are you planning to stay?' Esther had asked as she heaved them into the boot (she was stronger than Louise, gardening requiring better muscle than writing). 'Are you moving in on me?'

'I'm having a rest,' Louise said. 'We do have to talk about Mum, don't we, but can I stay for a bit longer? I won't overdo it, you won't get sick of me. Or no sicker than usual.' She grinned.

What Esther felt now was relief. Someone else. She wouldn't be alone any longer. Louise would be no help in any practical sense. She would leave used coffee cups all over the house, feel the cold and need the stove on all day and heating in her bedroom, and hang about getting in Esther's way while she cooked, washed up, fed the hens, worked in the house. She would repaint her nails in an appalling stink of acetone, complain about her figure, drink

337

wine and be indiscreet about famous people. At the thought of all this disruption, Esther's spirits rose mile after mile of the road. She would be company.

By the time she left, Esther would have had more than enough and be longing for peace and the house to herself. Or, this time, maybe not. In the meantime, there would be someone else to make the days more real and give her purpose, someone who would make her laugh and not feel guilty for laughing.

Louise strewed her room with unpacked clothes then went to run a bath. She sang out of tune, filled the bathroom with steam and used all the hot water. Esther did not care.

By seven o'clock they were in the kitchen. Soothed by the familiar tasks of preparing and cooking food, Esther made their meal while Louise drank a large glass from one of the bottles of wine bought when they had stopped at Sainsbury in the city to stock up.

'You'll be so proud of me,' she said. 'I still drink buckets, but I've stopped smoking.'

'Well, thank God for that. About time.'

'Not that you ever let me smoke here anyway – even though I've got a stake in the place too . . .'

'You? You're a wandering minstrel. You don't have a house. Only your current flat. Not one you really care about.'

'How would you know?' Louise mocked. 'I might have a wee cottage tucked away, or an apartment in Paris.'

'Have you?'

'No. But . . . some other people have had them. Quite nice places. Quite nice people too.'

'Not home though.'

'No. This is home.'

Esther did not believe her: Louise would have sickened – again
– of home in a week or so. She never stayed long.

'Have more wine,' Louise said, topping up Esther's glass from
which she had taken two or three quick gulps, enough to put the
careful cooking of the risotto at risk. She took a small sip and
went on stirring, seasoning.

'Tell me then.' Louise leaned back in the basket chair that was
usually occupied by the cat. Her jeans would be covered in ginger
and white hairs. Warmed by alcohol, Esther did not mention
this. 'How is everybody? My favourite niece?'

'You mustn't say that.'

'Why not? She is. My wee sparkler – just wait – she's the one
who'll be famous.'

'As if I care about that! She'll be fine if she gets rid of – oh well,
never mind.' Too much wine – somehow the glass was almost
empty. Shut up, Esther.

Louise was shrewder, always, than you remembered. 'She'll
come to her senses, don't you fret about her.' She poured more
wine into her own glass. 'And the boys? And Laura? They're all so
grown up now.'

'Andrew and Laura are planning a baby next year.'

'Oh help. Then you'll be a granny and I'll be that grim old
thing a great-aunt.' Louise laughed. 'I suppose we'd better get
used to it. I think of us always being young, don't you? Elsie,
Lacey and Tilly, the three little girls.'

'Sometimes, yes.'

'Time we three little girls were together again.'

'Why? You're the last person to be nostalgic.'

'I actually re-read *Alice* from time to time. No more fantastic
than the truth, some days.' She tipped her chair back, balancing.

'You know the bit I liked best?' Esther asked.

'The tea party with the Dormouse – '

'No. Not that at all. What I liked was when Alice eventually managed to be the right size to use the Golden Key and go through the wee door into the beautiful garden.' She sighed. 'I used to think, I wish I could find that key, and the little door. I wish I could get in there.'

'Don't we all!' Louise smiled. 'I guess it wasn't all that great in the beautiful garden – the Queen ordering people's heads off . . .'

'Still,' Esther said, 'I like the *idea*. If only I could find my golden key.'

Louise, bored by whimsy, changed the subject. 'What about Mum – how's she doing?'

'Coping. Just. I don't think for much longer. I get weird calls sometimes, she asks me where Dad is, when he's coming home.'

'Oh God, no?'

'The carers are good, but they can't be there all day and half the time she doesn't remember who they are anyway.'

'So we have to see about a place for her, sort out what's best.'

'That's why you came?'

'Well, yes, to look at places with you. What's that one you mentioned like? Is it nice?'

'What do you think? It's a nursing home.'

'They sit in a circle of chairs and the TV blares out but nobody's watching it?'

'It's the nicest one I've seen. By far. I just feel too guilty to do anything about it. She could always come here, but I think it would be harder to get the support, out of the city.' Esther banged her wooden spoon against the edge of the pan to knock off some rice sticking to it, but perhaps more violently than necessary.

'Sorry, yes, I know,' Louise said. 'But a nursing home's best, honestly. She'll get worse, she'll need full-time care. You can't take that on. As long as they're kind, as long as the food is decent and – sorry.'

Esther sighed as she put warmed plates on the table and began to serve up. 'Anyway, you'll see for yourself.'

Silence, as they began to eat.

'This is lovely, what a good cook you always are,' Louise said after a moment.

'Don't butter me up,' Esther said. 'I feel cross now.'

'I know. I'm useless. Never mind.' Louise reached across the table and covered Esther's trembling hand with her own one, warm and strong. Esther blinked away tears.

'Look,' she said, bracing up, 'since you're here, maybe we should contact Caroline and ask her what she thinks. I did email her about Mum, but she was a bit abrupt. Said what you've said, I suppose. Get as good a place as you can.'

'And you've spoken to Margaret.'

'Yes, of course. We talk about it endlessly. She offered to have her, but I don't think that would be a good idea. Anyway, I have more space.'

Esther did not manage to eat much, but she watched Louise with at least the satisfaction of seeing her food appreciated by someone else. As she cleared away the plates she caught sight of the photograph on the dresser.

'Look – there – see what I found today.' She began stacking the dish washer.

'That's nice,' Louise said after a moment, bored. Turning, Esther saw she was reading a postcard Margaret had sent from Florence where she had gone with a friend at New Year to cheer herself up. Margaret often needed cheering up. 'Nice, but not interesting.'

'Not *that*.' Esther pointed. 'That.'

Louise took down the photograph. 'Who – '

'You must know. It's Daniel and Caroline.'

Louise had become quite still, gazing at them. 'Yes,' she said. 'Now when was that taken? Not in Aberdeen. So . . .'

Relieved, Esther took another swig from her rapidly emptying glass and sat down on a chair with a thud. 'You see it too. I thought I might be imagining things. I think it's Glasgow, and I think it's after he came back from his travelling about. Before – anyway, I think he was there for a while, don't you?'

Louise held the photograph up to get a better light on it. 'It looks like a Glasgow tenement. So Caroline knew for some time that he was back. I wonder how long. You know, it's a bloody good shot. It's a bit faded but whoever took it knew about judging the light, framing it . . . Caroline – is she coming to join him, or to stop him from – what?'

'Saying something?'

'Yeah. Could be.'

They looked at each other.

'Right,' Louise said, changing tack, propping the photograph back on the shelf, 'now tell me how you are.'

'Me?' Was that it, was that all they were going to say about Daniel and Caroline? And yet, she was grateful to Louise for acknowledging it then letting it go, and for wanting to know how *she* was. Nobody asked now except in the safest, most perfunctory way. Death still hung around, spoiling the party. 'I'm all right.'

'Oh rubbish. Of course you're not. You adored Jack. Here.' She topped up the glass again. 'Hm, better get another bottle, this one seems to be nearly empty.' She got up to get another from the fridge. 'Tell you what, make some coffee and we can get comfortable. Then you can talk about Jack all night if you like.'

Esther's throat closed, choking. 'I can't,' she said.

'Of course you can. What you mean is no one else wants to.'

This was true. Esther swallowed hard, and obediently, made coffee.

Allowed to talk about Jack, she found that perversely, she did not want to. He and Louise had been tolerant of each other (for Esther's sake) but not close. He had disapproved of smoking, bad language and drinking too much – at least in women. Louise, guilty of all of those, increasingly thought him arrogant and narrow-minded. She seemed anyway to have forgotten her offer to listen. She talked on, as they took up residence on a sofa each in the sitting room and the second bottle of Chablis emptied, unwound long stories about herself and the people she knew. She referred to them as if Esther must know them too; it was all first names with Louise. 'So Rory decided we'd had enough for the day and got this little man to take us out in his boat. It was mad, the wind had got up and Sam was desperately seasick and – '

Louise's life was full of these adventures. Esther grew sleepy, no longer taking it in.

'Anyway,' Louise said sharply, 'you're to listen to this bit. Are you awake?'

'Of course I am,' Esther lied, sitting up with an effort.

'I've been in touch with Eric.'

'Eric who?' A pause. 'Oh – *that Eric?*'

'Yes, that Eric. After all this time.'

'Is he still in – where did he go – Exeter?'

'Bristol. He's retired, or semi, at any rate. He still has some PhD students, but he doesn't go in every day.'

'So . . . what made you – '

'I saw a review he did, in the *Guardian*, and I'd loved the book too, so I took a guess at his email address, that he'd still have a uni one, and he did. He replied right away.'

'Well . . . that's nice. But – '

'Pam left him. More than a year ago.'

'She left *him?*'

'She stayed while he had the position and the salary. Then she left. Moved in, it seems, with a former colleague of Eric's. He didn't say anything bad about her, but he never did. I couldn't work out if he was hurt or relieved, but he was very glad to hear from me. Said he would have been in touch, but he didn't think it was fair. Poor old Eric, he always got it wrong.'

'Have you seen him? It's been years, Lou, he must be quite old now.'

Louise laughed. 'We're all older!' She refilled her cup with cooling coffee and sat down again, but since she didn't drink the coffee, Esther thought this was to give her time to think what to say next. For once she seemed less sure of herself.

'Yes, I've seen him. We've been emailing, I went to Bristol, he's come to London. I think I'm going to spend a bit of time with him in Bristol, maybe several days a week. Then we'll see.'

'Wow. Mind, I always thought he was the only one you really – '

'Really loved? Well, he was a pal, he was my greatest pal, of all the men I've known, he was the only one I missed afterwards. He got me writing, he gave me ideas, he made me feel I could do anything. I owe him a lot, though I know nobody in my family would think so.'

'Oh, Louise – don't. I'm glad you've seen him, I'm glad if it's going to work out after all – '

'I've not told you all of it.'

Esther waited. So much for being able to talk about Jack, she thought wryly, but not minding.

Louise took a gulp of wine, and began.

'He's ok, I don't want you to think I'm going to be some sort of carer, I'm not, but he's been diagnosed with the early symptoms of Parkinson's. And since Pam's not interested, in fact that's when she left, when they found out, well, I thought I'd go there.'

'But he has children, doesn't he? What about them?'

'Jeremy's in New Zealand and Ruth's in Canada. They left the country as soon as they could, basically. Unable to bear the fridge their parents' marriage inhabited, I guess.'

'For goodness sake – ' Esther said. 'Parkinson's – that's degenerative, isn't?'

'I know – don't say it. There's Mum and if I'm going to look after anybody it should be my mother. I don't know if I'll stay the course. Not sure I would cope if he really got ill. But they have amazing new drugs now and he could be fine for years.'

'Right.'

'I find I've missed him. A lot.'

'You couldn't look after Mum. I know that. If it's anyone, it's me, and maybe Margaret. Not you or Caroline.'

'Sorry.'

'Poor Eric. Getting older is horrible. It's all horrible.'

'I know.'

Esther got up to put another log in the stove. Louise filled her own wine glass again, but set it down full on the low table beside her. After a few moments, she said,

'Is Caroline still in that cottage in the Highlands – Ullapool or somewhere?'

'I suppose so. An email address doesn't give you that sort of information. But she didn't say she had moved. I've not seen her since Jack's funeral.'

'She comes to funerals, not weddings. Nothing's changed there.'

'I did think she'd come to Andrew and Laura's. But no. Sent a big cheque, apologies. No reason this time, as if there's no point lying any more.'

'I think I want another coffee,' Louise said. 'You?'

'No . . . maybe a cup of tea. I'll get it.' Esther stirred herself.

'Don't you move. I can find everything – I bet it's all in exactly the same place as last time.'

Esther gave in, too tired to care. She never stayed up as late as this. Went to bed at ten, fell into a deep sleep, woke at three, didn't sleep again till half past five or six. That was the pattern since Jack's death and there was no use fighting it. At least she didn't have to go to work, be out of the house by eight, functioning like an intelligent being. That was beyond her.

She got up and went to the window that overlooked the garden. If she went behind the heavy curtains, she could, after a few moments, fancy she saw faintly the lawn Jack had sown, the shrubbery he had planted in front of the stone wall. Beyond was the lane leading to the main road. At this time on a winter night there was only an occasional vehicle, the headlights briefly glimmering in the distance as it passed. Esther leaned on the side of the window, the curtain wrapped round her, listening to her sister clatter about in the kitchen, the chink of crockery, the kettle hissing. For the first time since Jack had died, she had a sense of some new thing, a change coming, in what might now be acknowledged as the future.

What it means to get old

2012

What Margaret wanted to do most was retire. It was monstrously unfair that whenever she considered this, however cautiously she approached it, the Government then changed the rules and women her age had even longer to wait. There were indignant features in serious newspapers and on the radio, but the poor middle-aged women affected did not march on Downing Street with placards and petitions or go on strike or even (speaking for herself) write to their MP. Perhaps she should – she could start with that. There was always something you could do to make a difference, start the ball rolling. But the ball remained obstinately in the same place. She never did a thing about it, except complain.

They all complained, in the staffroom of the primary school where she had taught for ten years, generations of infants passing through her classroom and her life. All of them except Emma the probationer and Tony the Head Teacher, wanted to retire. They had had career breaks (though they called it 'bringing up the kids'); they had worked part-time and been on the supply list. Their pensions, they often said, were pathetic.

In earlier years, it had not occurred to Margaret that she need even think about pensions. She was a married woman and her husband a high-earner in the oil industry. It all looked different now. She was divorced, Mike had married again and he was anyway in a much less secure job with a construction company, having changed career at the request of his new wife, who didn't like him going offshore. Margaret took a certain grim satisfaction in that, wickedly not hoping for an upturn in the industry, since it wasn't going to help *her* any more.

What she most looked forward to when she finally retired (aged about 90 at this rate), was throwing out every single lesson plan and reading scheme, every piece of paper which mentioned *5-14* or *Curriculum for Excellence*. It was all going on Mr Thompson's annual bonfire. She would enjoy watching it burn and she would regain her third small bedroom. It would no longer be cluttered with school boxes and files, a room which gave her a throb of apprehension every time she went into it.

She seemed to live in a state of constant anxiety, unfocused and so unable to be dispelled. Even now, she woke each day with a sense of dread. It had been like that since Mike left. She told herself that she could not have gone on after she found out about Sara; she could never have forgiven him. At the time she had been desolate, unable to believe he would not come back, full of remorse. It was hard to come to terms with the feeling that she wouldn't want him back now, didn't even like him much. Perhaps that had been the trouble all along.

It was all right for Esther: widowhood was a protected state and anyway, she had Braeside. They must have made a lot of money out of turning it into a guest house nearly six months of the year. Louise had had a successful career, and now she had her novels. As far as Margaret could see, she just wrote more or less the same story, with different names and settings, over and over. You could go on doing that quite peacefully all your life. It couldn't possibly *exhaust* you, as twenty-nine five- and six-year-olds did. She was tired all the time.

The one thing Mike had done for her was pay off the remaining mortgage of their house in Aberdeen and leave Margaret in sole possession. Very soon she had sold it and moved to her neat bungalow on the edge of Westhill, close to the school where she taught, and more or less on the way to Braeside. She was of course not going to be destitute. She had inherited money from her father that Harry had helped her invest. A good deal had been put in trust for Anna. So she had her house and savings though her pension would be meagre. And yet, she still worried about being poor and alone; she worried about old age. What she wanted most was to be married again, but that was never going to happen. Primary teachers don't meet suitable men.

'What about internet dating?' Louise had said to her the last time she was here. She usually stayed at Braeside, but sometimes she spent a night or two with Margaret at the beginning or end of her visit. 'I always end up with a headache after Louise has been here,' she complained to Esther. 'That's the wine,' Esther said. 'I'm the same. We're not used to it.'

Alcohol betrayed, it made you say things you'd rather not reveal. That was how they had got onto meeting men.

'Goodness no,' Margaret said. 'I couldn't possibly do that. You don't know who you're contacting. And it seems so – blatant. Here I am, come and try before you buy.'

Louise laughed. 'You make it sound as if it's one step up from going on the game!'

'Maybe I think it is.'

'Rubbish – everyone does it nowadays, it's very respectable.'

'I don't. And I've no intention of it.'

349

'Then don't complain. If you don't make an effort, how can you expect to meet anyone?'

'Oh stop it,' Margaret said wearily. Louise tired her out. She had an answer for everything.

Then, just before February half-term, one of the women she taught with confided at morning break that she was seeing someone she had met on the internet.

'We just had a coffee the first time,' she told the others. 'Somewhere safe, you know, in town. In public.'

'Loads of my friends meet people that way,' Emma said, Emma who was long-legged and pretty and looked as if she should still be in school herself.

Now, on this sunny Friday morning at the start of the half-term break, Margaret had wakened with the thought that she might after all change her mind. If Sue could do it, Sue who was quite plain really, and older than she was, why shouldn't she? She thought she would call Esther to see if she'd like to meet for lunch. She could talk it over with her. First she'd get the house straight and hang out the washing.

Mr Thompson was in his garden behind hers, pruning something. She didn't go beyond pansies and bedding plants in her little patch, and keeping the grass cut. His was bountiful and loved, a different kind of garden, a different kind of life. He worked there daily, his gnarled hands never still, pipe clenched between his teeth. The tobacco scent drifted over the fence towards her. Fiercely against smoking, Margaret nevertheless did not mind Mr Thompson's pipe in the open air. He was too kind and Mrs Thompson too shrewish, for her to feel anything but fondness for him.

He nodded a good morning. Margaret waved, 'Lovely day!'

'Aye,' he said, 'it is that.'

She was pegging out a towel when she heard the telephone ringing through the open back door.

It was Esther.

'I was going to call you later,' Margaret began. 'I wondered if you'd – '

'It's Mum. She's had a stroke, she's in hospital.'

'*No* – oh God, how bad is it?'

'I don't know, I'm heading there now. Lou's driving me, she arrived yesterday.'

'What happened?'

'It seems she fell in the kitchen and one of those Social Services people found her. Do you have a phone number for Caroline? Lou tried the mobile number but it doesn't seem to be switched on – or maybe not working, I don't know – we're not even sure she has a landline in Ullapool and I don't have time to look – so – '

'I might have it. Which ward? I'll get there as soon as I can.'

'Yes, come. If you can't track Caroline down, we'll do it later, I'm sure she'll be all right, it's just we don't know yet – '

Margaret heard Louise's voice in the background and Esther said, 'I'm coming.'

'Off you go – I'll see you there.'

Hastily, Esther told her the ward number, and hung up.

For a moment Margaret stood by the telephone, not moving. Here was a new fear. They knew they were losing Janet, she was less herself every time, every visit and phone call. But not this, not *this*. She would look for Caroline's phone number, then go straight to the hospital.

Margaret knew where everything was in her tidy house. In the hall as she passed it she touched Anna's photograph on the small beechwood bookcase, Anna captured by a friend when they were in Greece, aged eighteen. A fair vivacious Anna in cut-off jeans and yellow vest top was looking over her shoulder, behind her the Aegean and a low white building dazzling in sunlight against blue sky and sea.

The bungalow with its deep roof cavity had a floored attic with a skylight window and a loft ladder she could easily pull down. From time to time, having gone up there to fetch something – Christmas decorations, spare blankets – Margaret would find herself sitting on in a kind of dream in the hush and coolness of the roof space, listening to a drip of water in the tank or a seagull thudding about on the tiles. This time she went straight to the box with last year's Christmas cards and The List. She updated The List in November every year, checking it off against last year's cards, incorporating new addresses, scoring off old ones and sometime scoring off people who had died during the year or simply gone so far out of her life she could see no point in sending them another card. There was the sad card that was signed, for the first time for many years, 'Love Esther'. She's like me now, Margaret had thought, opening it, she sends cards on no one else's behalf.

Here was The List, and here was Caroline's name: Dr Caroline Livingstone, Garve Cottage, near Ullapool. No telephone number. She scrambled down the ladder with the list in her hand, and went straight to the laptop set up on her dining table to switch it on. It was an elderly computer, so while it went through its lengthy warm-up she washed the dust from her hands. When she tapped in the name, it occurred to her that it would be just like Caroline to be ex-directory.

The number was there. That was her, it had to be. She was shaking when she called it, shaking not just because of Janet, but because she never called Caroline, and Caroline never called her. They did not speak. There had been no quarrel or misunderstanding.

352

Caroline had withdrawn from them all, but from Margaret most completely. She knew why, or thought she did, but it was another thing she did not allow herself to think about.

The ringing went on in Caroline's empty cottage until the electronic voice cut in and told her there was no one available. Briefly, so that she would not sound as if she were trembling, though she was, she left a message and her mobile number.

Then she went to get her coat.

It was Sunday evening when Caroline appeared in the ward. They were all three by Janet's bed, and though she had been awake for a while, knowing they were there, even trying to smile and speak, she had just fallen into a doze. She was in a single room, but was to be moved to the ward next morning.

'She's doing very well,' a young doctor had told them that afternoon. 'It's not a major stroke, but she is having some difficulty with speech and there's a definite weakness on the right side.'

'What does that mean?' Louise had asked. 'What sort of recovery – '

'Too soon to tell,' the doctor said, smiling as if to soften this.

Caroline pushed the door open and said, 'How is she?'

They looked up in unison.

'Oh,' Esther breathed, 'I'm so glad you're here.'

'I'll find another chair,' Louise said, going out. Margaret sat still, holding Janet's hand.

'Thank you.' Caroline came in pulling a small suitcase on wheels. She tucked this behind the door and took the chair Louise had been in, next to Margaret. 'I got home quite late last night so I didn't pick up your message till morning, I'm so sorry. I set off as soon as I could, but with trains as they are, it's taken me all day.'

353

'She was trying to talk to us earlier – she's not long fallen asleep,' Esther said.

'I suppose it's too soon to tell what the damage is?'

'That's what they say,' Louise agreed, coming in with another grey plastic chair. She set it down next to Esther. Caroline opened her black coat and shook it off her shoulders.

'How hot hospitals are,' she said. 'I ought to know that, but you forget.' She leaned forward to look at Janet. 'She's going to be ninety this year, isn't she?'

'I'm surprised you remember,' Margaret said.

'I'm not good at birthdays, but I always remember Janet's.'

'We were thinking we'd have a wee party, but lately I've wondered if she would even like it,' Esther said.

'That's a nice idea. We'll just have to wait and see.'

Margaret, resenting the 'we', shifted her chair a fraction closer to the bed.

Louise glanced at her watch. 'They'll be throwing us out soon.'

'Where are you going to stay?' Esther asked. 'Do you want to come out to Braeside? Lou's staying with me. Or – ' she glanced at Margaret, suddenly doubtful but unable not to say, 'or maybe Margaret could put you up?'

Margaret, flushing, said, 'If you like.'

Caroline shook her head. 'I thought I'd go up to Harrowden Place and stay there, if it's all right with you? I don't want to put anyone to any trouble, and I'll be able to get to the hospital easily.'

'Good idea,' Louise said. 'Then there will be someone in the house. How long can you stay?'

'As long as I need to. I've no animals or small children – or men – to miss me.' She smiled. 'I'm free.'

'You were away,' Margaret said.

'It's all right, I've no more trips or commitments till the spring.'

Janet made a small sound and moved her head on the pillow, but she did not wake.

'I think we should go,' Esther murmured. 'It would be a shame to disturb her now, when we have to leave anyway.'

As they got up and moved the chairs away from the bed, Caroline went closer to it, leaned down and put a gentle hand on Janet's arm. 'See you tomorrow,' she said softly. Janet moved her head again, muttered something, but went on sleeping.

They said goodnight, touched her tenderly, and left as quietly as they could.

At the hospital entrance, Caroline said, 'Will you all be here tomorrow afternoon? What about coming to Harrowden Place afterwards for something to eat? There's such a short gap between afternoon and evening visiting, and you can hardly go back to Braeside. Even Westhill – are you still there, Margaret? Anyway, I'd like to see you all.'

What could they say but thank you, yes, that would be fine? They were all exhausted, and Caroline must be too, having travelled from Ullapool. They stood around for another moment or two, unable to think how to part.

'What about a key?' Louise asked. 'For the house.'

'I still have one. Unless – you've had the locks changed?'

'Definitely not!'

'Ok. Fine. See you here tomorrow?' Caroline turned to Margaret. 'Will you give me a lift? It's not out of your way, is it?'

'You don't have a car?'

'No. As I said, I had to rely on Scotrail to get here today. And taxis.'

Has Margaret forgotten, Esther wondered, that Caroline never drives, never has?

Margaret indicated her car, aimed the key at it to unlock the doors, and got into the driving seat, saying only, 'Yes, ok.'

'Wait,' Louise said. 'Let's check we've got the right mobile number for you – we couldn't get through on the number I had. We can text, if anything changes – '

She and Caroline, heads bent over smartphones, keyed in numbers. Esther thought, we're in touch now, that's it, for good, and tried to smile at Margaret, but she turned her head away.

As Margaret and Caroline drove away Louise unlocked her own car. 'Poor Tilly, left with no choice. You never know, do you?'

'About what?'

'Cousin Caroline. She looks pretty good, I must say, for her age.'

Esther would have laughed at that, if she had not been so upset about her mother. That took over everything. How white she was, and that dragging at the corner of her mouth, the limp arm.

'Granny died of a stroke,' she said. 'If she has another one – '

Louise opened the passenger door for her. 'Come on, you're shattered, let's go home.'

As they drove away from the hospital in silence Margaret seemed to give herself a shake, making an effort.

'Are you sure about going back to Harrowden Place on your own? I don't even know what sort of state the place is in. We were going to go in tomorrow to get more things for Janet, maybe tidy up if it needs it.'

'It doesn't matter. As I said, it's near the hospital – I can get there without being dependent on anyone else.'

'Why didn't you bring your car?'

'I don't have one.'

'You still don't drive? All those years?' It was out before she could stop herself. Glancing sideways, she saw that Caroline, however elegant, was an old woman. It wasn't just years – it was a lifetime.

'No, I never have. In London it scarcely mattered.'

'But you're living in Ullapool!'

Caroline almost laughed. 'Yes, I admit that's more of a challenge. But I'm not going to start now.'

'How do you manage?'

'Taxis, public transport . . . I walk a lot.'

As Margaret drew up outside the familiar house, all in darkness, they fell into silence, the engine switched off, the street empty and quiet.

'Better go in, I suppose.' Caroline put her hand on the door. 'Do you want to come in for a cup of tea or something?'

I have been rude to her, Margaret thought, guiltily. It was churlish, it's all so long ago, and she's had her separate life, I've had mine. It doesn't matter now, does it? For all that, it was difficult to say, 'Yes, thank you. Just for a wee while, before I head home.'

'Good.'

Margaret had her key out first and opened the front door, switching on lights as she went through the hall. The house smelled stale. A film of dust coated the mirror on the hallstand, the parquet was dull, unpolished, and there was the sound, from the kitchen or scullery, of a tap dripping. Except that the central heating had been left on twice a day and it was not quite cold, the house might have been empty for weeks.

'You put the kettle on,' Margaret said, determined not to comment, however much this change upset her, that she had been aware of for months, but not felt so strongly till now, with

Caroline beside her. 'I'll just nip upstairs to the loo, and I'll see if the bed's made up in the spare – in your old room.'

The bed was stripped and bare. Janet did not have visitors now who stayed overnight. Margaret was relieved to find the linen cupboard still faintly warm and sweet smelling. She made up the bed quickly and put out fresh towels.

Downstairs, Caroline had put the central heating back on and the boiler was humming loudly in the scullery, the kettle switching itself off in the kitchen.

'Tea?' she said as Margaret came in.

'Yes, that's fine. I wonder if the milk's ok.'

'Does she still manage by herself?' Caroline asked as they took their mugs through to the den.

Margaret, leaning down to switch on the gas fire, which was old-fashioned and troublesome, pressed the starter switch several times. 'Damn. Right, that's it, I think. Why on earth did they never get a new fire? This one's quite dangerous.'

She sat on the Windsor chair next to the fireplace. Caroline, poised on the edge of the sofa, said, 'But Janet copes with it?'

'I suppose so. She has people coming in now, twice a day, but we've been wondering how much longer . . . We're worried she'll leave something on the cooker, or gas herself with this blooming fire.'

'Has she had a diagnosis?'

'Some kind of dementia.'

'She's been assessed?'

'Ask Esther. She knows more.'

A pause. They drank tea they did not want.

The room was warming up now and they had taken off their coats. Caroline leaned back on the sofa, not the same one she and Daniel had lazed on, reading and planning and talking, but another, moved out of the sitting room when it was replaced there. Still, it was quite like the old sofa, comfortable and sagging. She could imagine it was the same.

'I sometimes think,' she said, 'now I'm in the cottage most of the time, am I going to be one of those old women you read about in the newspapers: *former distinguished consultant, specialist in neurological disorders . . . found bludgeoned to death in a remote cottage.*' Seeing Margaret's startled expression, she laughed. 'Maybe not as dramatic as that. *Found dead . . . had lain there for weeks . . .*'

'Someone would – I mean, you have friends who – '

'I was only joking,' Caroline said. 'But the point is, Janet has you and Esther close by, Louise in regular contact. She has people calling in daily. So she didn't lie for a week before she was found and taken to hospital.'

'Why are you living in such a remote place?'

'I still have a flat in London. I should probably sell it.'

'You don't live there any more?'

'I'm usually in London most of the winter. Ullapool's for finer weather. But I spent Christmas and New Year at the cottage, so I just stayed on. Then I had a meeting in London, but I thought I'd come back and close up the place properly, till May or June. I don't know, maybe I just felt I wanted to go north again. When you can do anything you like you dither more, become less organised.'

'Why are you still going to meetings? You've retired, haven't you?'

'Years ago, but I'm still involved in various things. Committees, panels . . .' She sighed. 'You know, I think I might just go to bed.'

Margaret had put on the overhead light, when perhaps lamp-light would have been better. In this harsher glow, Caroline did look old, the lines round her eyes etched more deeply, her skin, though skilfully made up, not as fine as it had been. Her hair was white, but cut in the same way, that sharp bob, jaw length.

'I'll go now,' Margaret said, but neither of them moved.

We are two old women, Margaret thought, at least, one old and the other middle-aged, who have nothing in common except that they grew up in the same family, a family who were the closest relatives of neither. What else do we have in common?

Daniel.

They had once loved Daniel more than any other person, Daniel their brother. Not that this had made them close. They had moved away from each other steadily throughout their lives, Caroline moving faster and more surely. The old doubt that shifted uneasily under her ribs, had returned. If anyone knew in this world, anyone you could safely ask (not Janet any more) it was Caroline. If she was ever going to find out, it was now.

'Janet,' she said, 'was my mother, is my mother, more than Diana ever was. That's why I worry so much about her, feel responsible.'

'She and Harry thought of themselves as your parents,' Caroline said. 'Janet said once to me, "Margaret's special to us."'

'Special!' She did not want to be special, included, taken in to the fold. She wanted to be there already, integral.

'I'd better put my things upstairs.' Caroline had laid her coat on the sofa next to her, and she began to gather it up.

'Is there something I don't know?' Margaret asked, her heart thumping. Now or never, if I don't ask now, I never will.

'About?'

'Our family. Dad. Diana – any of it. Or about Daniel.'

There, she had said his name, he was brought into it at last.

Caroline smiled her remote, reassuring, consultant's smile.

'No,' she said. 'Nothing at all. You were loved, we all were. Any breach is my fault, not Dan's, not Dad's. Mine.' She got up. 'Now, I'm not chasing you away but you have a drive yet, don't you?'

Outside, sitting in her car, the house door closed against her with a wave from Caroline, Margaret sat burning with anger. *Chasing me away* – from my own home, my safe place, where I grew up and was loved and looked after and that *you* abandoned and betrayed.

She should have said more, whatever the risk. She had started the car engine. Now she switched it off and got out again, shaking. If I don't say it now, I never will. And what is there to lose? She doesn't care about me.

'Are you all right – did you forget something?' Caroline asked as Margaret opened the door and stepped into the hall.

'Just to say. To say – I've never said it before and not even to Esther, though I think she knows and Louise has an idea, she's much better than you would think, at listening.'

'So am I,' Caroline said. 'Come in, come through to the den, I'll put the fire back on, tell me what it is.'

Seduced, she almost went.

'No, there's no need, it won't take long. It's just – did you never care, never once even think how it was for me? I don't want to complain, I don't, but it's held me back, all this time, and now I think I might just be happy. But I don't want it to happen again. Why does everyone leave me? Is it just chance, an accident, or is there something about me?'

'Leave you?'

'My mother, my father, Daniel, then you. And then Mike. They all left.'

There were tears pouring down her face and she could not stop shaking.

'Not Janet and Harry, they were so kind, but that was it, they were kind, I wasn't their daughter, I was nobody's. Was I? Tell me the truth, tell me the truth for once.'

'Wait – wait – ' Caroline put out her hands and clasped Margaret's between them, warm and firm.

'I don't know why I'm saying this, what's the point? You're not going to make it any different now. Don't tell me – I don't want to know now. Whose daughter I really am.' She stopped with a gasp, appalled. What on earth had got into her? She should just have gone home.

'No, listen – ' Caroline held her hands tighter, not letting go. 'I never left you. Daniel didn't leave you. I can't say a thing about your bloody mother, she let you down, of course she did, and Dad, but he let *us* down as well, you know that.'

'But – '

'No. Daniel left me. *Me.* And I left because of him. Believe that. Truly.'

'I don't understand.'

'You don't need to.' The hands still gripped hers, painfully, painfully. 'I never left you. And I'm sorry.'

Margaret, weakening, pulled her hands away and stepped back.

'I've made a fool of myself. I'm fifty-five, I'm a middle-aged woman, and I feel as stupid as a teenager.'

'That's how it is,' Caroline said. 'For all of us.' She put her arms round Margaret and hugged her close. Her scent, the soft brush of her hair against Margaret's cheek as she bent to her, so much taller, bent to cradle her. Margaret moved away, but gently, patting Caroline's arm.

'All this with Janet – it's upset me.'

'Will you be able to drive home?'

'Yes of course.'

'I'll see you tomorrow.'

At Braeside, Esther and Louise sat up talking for a while, but it was colder there, even in the kitchen. It was getting late and they were tired.

The minutes ticked by on the noisy old wall clock, but they did not go to bed.

'I don't think she's going to be able to go home,' Esther said. 'That's what I'm afraid of. We're up against it now, we have to decide.'

'Let's make appointments to go and see some places then,' Louise suggested. 'We'll speak to the doctor, see how long they're going to keep her in, what plans they've got for rehab, convalescence. They'll have specialist units where she can go while they assess her, we won't have to do this all on our own.'

'I wish I had your confidence in the NHS and Social Services,' Esther said.

Louise smiled. 'Yeah, maybe I'm being a bit optimistic. We'll see.'

'What did you think about Caroline?'

'We did ask her to come.'

'Yes, but – how did you think she looked?'

'The same, but dead tired. How old is she? She must be nearly seventy.'

'Yes.'

'White hair suits her.'

'It's still impossible to get past the barrier, the front she puts up.'

'Poor old Tilly, you could see she didn't want to offer her a bed – or even a lift!'

'You can hardly blame her,' Esther said. 'After all, they're sisters but Caroline doesn't treat her like one.'

'For Caroline,' Louise said, 'the world stopped when Daniel died. Even when he went away, you could see her change, pull herself away from us all. Even Mum.'

'It was the accident,' Esther said, thinking back. 'It changed them both, brother and sister.'

Sitting there in the ticking quiet, there occurred to both of them the same idea: that there was more than they knew, that there were things Caroline could tell them, but had chosen not to. After so many years, it was hard to go back in memory to that time, to what they had known, never mind all they had not.

They sat on in silence, wondering.

In her old room, Caroline slipped between cold sheets and switched off the bedside lamp. She lay in shadows made grey by the street light outside, listening to silence with its faint backing music of traffic on Queen's Road in the distance.

I'm old, she thought, you cannot pretend seventy is not old. At first she thought what she felt was a thrill of fear, and perhaps it was, but it was blurred by relief. She was actually relieved. Nearly over, she thought, unless I live till I'm ninety like Janet. Even then, I don't have to think about this any more, I don't have to bother. There must come a time, and I think it should be now.

If she kept it all to herself, though, as she had done for so many years, what difference did her decision make? Only in my head, she thought, unconvinced, knowing that a commitment becomes real only if you share it in some way. There was no one now to share it with, no one but the Elties, and they were the people she should probably not tell. Besides, all lies become a kind of truth if they last long enough, and everyone else believes them. She thought of Margaret, screwing up her courage to say all that. No question now, of undoing Diana's lie. Daniel was right about that.

There were other things she could say. If not now, never.

Sleep crept in, bringing images of strange creatures, unrecognisable places, the precursors of her dreams, and she turned over, giving way to them, unable to think any longer.

The Photograph

2013

i

For months, Esther had been obsessed with ageing – not just her own but the ageing process generally, if process was what it was. She was irritated by its recent commercialisation – *60 is the new 40!*

She thought about ageing a lot because of Janet.

Every Friday, the supermarket shop completed, she drove to the care home in Culter where Janet now lived, a large Victorian house, converted and made convenient with all the ugly apparatus of social care. It was not her home. That was the Harrowden Place house, soon to be on the market. None of them could keep it on; it had to go. Because she had Braeside, Esther had become philosophical about this.

She signed in, exchanged a few words with the girl who greeted her, and went upstairs to Janet's room, along the narrow landing and into the rear wing of the house, a modern extension with a dozen new bedrooms. On the way she paused to let a woman in a blue overall go by with a wheelchair, the occupant huddled in a glower of ill temper, ignoring Esther's attempt at a friendly smile. A very old man, toothless, hairless, as so accurately predicted by the much younger Shakespeare, staggered past, clutching – and pursuing – a three-wheeled trolley, the next model up from a Zimmer frame, Esther supposed. His cardigan had food stains down the front and was buttoned wrongly, but at least he smiled back, seeming quite cheerful.

It was all horrible and she ached with guilt.

Janet's room was like a single bedroom in a good but not luxurious hotel: clean, pleasant enough but no more. Janet sat in a velour-covered upright chair, an unread book in her lap. Esther knew it was unread; it had been the same book for weeks. Not like the old days when she often had a book propped up behind the taps on the sink or on her lap as she mended clothes or plaited a child's hair or fastened awkward buttons on a frock. She had taken them to the library once a fortnight, coming out with four new books for herself each time.

When Janet looked up she smiled, and Esther thought thank goodness, she knows me, it's all right. Esther often tried to bring some small gift with her, this time a tube of rose-scented hand cream. Janet's hands, once rough with housework and gardening, were soft and freckled, a large brown stain spreading over the back of one, the veins knotted cord beneath thin skin.

'How are you?' Esther bent to kiss her mother's cheek, the skin here delicate as silk crumpled and then smoothed out.

'Ach, I'm fine. Just the same.'

Today seemed to be a good day, but you could never be sure. Sometimes, dismayingly, Janet asked about Jack – *I never see him these days* – and Esther had to decide whether to remind her mother about his death, and risk upsetting her. Most of the time, Janet wasn't upset or even put out by this. 'You'll miss him,' she might say, or 'I still miss your father', and they could move on to reminiscence. Janet's memory flickered. Sometimes she seemed to remember everything and be as sharp as ever, but you could not rely on it. Esther told herself that even if she could have coped with the physical effort of looking after her mother since the stroke, she could not cope with this. It would get worse. Already, no conversation was reliable.

She had never managed to get all the photographs into albums, but she brought in a few each time to show Janet, some very old, others of her own children, taken recently. When she thought of the imminent great-grandchild, she realised unhappily that Janet would not celebrate the birth, or enjoy seeing the baby.

'Look,' she said, 'Andrew sent me this nice snap of him and Laura in Morocco on holiday last year.'

Janet held up the snap and peered at the two young people in shorts and vest tops, arms round each other, in front of a hard blue sky and white buildings. Then she looked at Esther.

'How's your boy?' she asked.

Esther's heart skipped. *Here we go again.* 'That's Andrew and his wife. You remember he's married now? I told you they're going to have a baby at the beginning of August?'

She saw the shift in Janet's expression, from surprise to resignation. Something else she did not know. She had moved in a few weeks to this new state of not knowing things, from simply not remembering. With a pang of pity, Esther added,

'You meant Ross, didn't you, when you asked about my boy?'

'Ross?'

She sifted through the photographs – surely there was one of Ross? 'Here. In the garden at Braeside. It's quite an old one, he can only be about fourteen.' She gave it to Janet, who held it, wavering, in her hand.

'I have the two boys,' Esther prompted, 'and Kirsty. Kitty.'

Janet put the photograph down. 'I know that,' she said. 'I'm not daft.'

'Sorry, of course you're not – '

'He's very like,' Janet interrupted, handing the photograph back to Esther.

'Very like?'

'I think so.'

Who did she mean? 'Andrew takes after Jack's side, of course, but Ross – '

'Like Daniel,' Janet said. 'A real look of Daniel about him.'

Esther thought of the photograph still propped up on the kitchen dresser, the boy with his face half turned away, and Caroline, coming out of the shadows.

'I found an old photo of Daniel,' she said on impulse. 'Would you like to see it?'

'Oh I don't know.' Janet looked away, losing interest, restless. 'I wonder they're not here with our tea and biscuit. What time is it?'

'They always come and see you, when they're home,' Esther said, desperate, guilty all over again. 'The children – it's just they're not often here these days.'

Her mother looked surprised at this non sequitur, as well she might. I'm as bad as she is, Esther thought, jumping about from one thing to another.

'I like to see them.' Janet leaned forward, patting Esther's arm. 'Don't you worry, I'm fine here. I'm all right.'

'I wish – '

'Can you leave me this one – ?' It was not the old likeness of Ross she had picked up, nor Andrew and Laura, happy in a hot country. It was Jack and Esther, taken years ago by one of the children, in the garden at home. They posed for the child (Andrew? Kirsty?), their smiles a little rigid by the time the shutter closed.

369

'Of course I can. You can have any of them.'

'It's fish tonight. Cod. I'm not that keen.'

'Maybe they'd give you something else, if you asked?' You could do nothing but go along with these disconcerting changes of subject. They did at least provide a new topic of conversation. In a little while, the smell of cooking would drift along the corridor and Esther would get up to go, full of relief and anxiety, to drive away thinking about her mother, and whether after all, she could manage to look after her.

On the way home, to break this pointless cycle of self-reproach, she thought about what Janet had said about Ross. *Very like Daniel.* Was he? Photographs are deceptive; Janet was thinking of Daniel for some reason, that's all. She makes mistakes all the time, mis-remembers and forgets. Every week there's another fragment of memory gone, her mind a completed jigsaw someone is piece by piece dismantling. Sometimes you can put the pieces back for her, but they soon disappear again, or others do.

Esther did not think Ross looked like Daniel; she did not want him to *be* like Daniel. How could anyone tell anyway – Daniel had died when he was younger than Ross was now, when she was a teenager. Her father was dead and Janet's memory not to be relied on. There was no one now who could tell her what Daniel was like, no one recalled him with the perfect clarity of love or friendship and no one, in any case, had talked about him for a very long time. It was all so long ago and clouded by the years between, the lives of those other people – friends and teachers – who had known him, filling up with the complex layers of work, family and desires, success and failure, their own losses looming far greater than the distant tragedy of a dead boy. Only Daniel remained the

370

same, young, that half-smile as he turned away, keeping his secrets.

There was Caroline, of course.

Louise was using her laptop when Esther came through the hall from the kitchen where she had left the bags of shopping. She was at the top of the stairs, where it was easier to access the wireless signal. She looked down at Esther over half-moon glasses.

'How is she?'

'All right.' Esther hung her jacket over the newel post. 'Are you wearing my socks?'

Louise looked down at the red hiking socks. 'My feet were cold.'

'It's *May* – nearly summer. You've gone soft, in the South.'

'My clothes are all wrong for here. I always underestimate how cold it will be.'

'You should have come with me.'

'I'll go tomorrow. Then she'll get two visits.'

'Mm.'

Esther went into the kitchen to unpack the shopping. A moment later she heard the thud of stockinged feet on the stairs and Louise came in.

'I tried to work in here,' she said, 'but I couldn't get online.'

'Signal's best upstairs or at the front of the house.'

'So much for broadband and rural Scotland being connected to the rest of the world.'

'Who says?'

'Will I make coffee?'

'I'll have tea. Didn't get any with Mum. They must have missed her out when they went round. She mentioned it, then seemed to forget again, but I told the girl on reception when I left.'

371

Louise was unpacking bags but since she never remembered where anything was kept, dumped it all on the table. Esther, sighing, decided not to complain.

'You make tea – coffee – whatever,' she said. 'I'll put the stuff away.'

Eventually they sat down on either side of the table (Louise nearest the stove) and opened a packet of chocolate biscuits.

'You've still got that photo of Daniel on the dresser,' Louise said. Scanning the familiar bits and pieces added to over the years by children bearing gifts, a precious pottery bowl or wooden carving made at school, she had snagged on the image of Daniel. She kept coming back to it, uneasily.

Esther twisted round in her chair and reaching up, caught the photograph between her fingertips. She laid it on the table between them so that Louise saw it the right way up.

'Do you think he looks like anyone – I mean anyone *now*? Not Caroline.'

Louise studied it. 'No.'

'Sure? Not either of my boys?'

'Your boys?' Louise looked again. 'I don't think so. Why?'

'Mum said Ross reminded her of Daniel. Had a look of him, is how she put it.'

'When did she last see Ross?'

Esther explained.

'That's a good idea – taking old photos in. Have you shown her this one?'

'It's been up there since I found it. I thought I might, next time.'

From the top of the stairs the shrill singing of Louise's mobile interrupted them. She got up. 'Sorry.'

The noise stopped before Louise reached it, lying on the

landing next to the laptop, but there was silence as she called back, then Esther heard her voice muttering – *Hmm – sure – I don't know – ok then . . .'* – monosyllables which could only make sense when joined to the inaudible other half of the conversation.

When she came down, Esther was on the landline, speaking to Margaret. She said, 'Here's Lou now, I'll ask her.'

'What?'

'Margaret is saying, would Saturday be all right for going through the house, at least making a start?'

'Sure, I'm here till Tuesday. Have you spoken to Caroline? She should probably be there too. There might even be some of her things in the house.'

'I doubt it. Did you hear that, Tilly – yeah? Right, I'll do that. Ok.'

'What are we having for supper?' Louise asked, hopefully raising a saucepan lid.

'It's just a tomato sauce, I'll do some pasta.'

'What was that about Caroline? Have you heard much from her since Mum got out of hospital?'

'What do you think? She's gone back into her hideaway, I suppose, that cottage.'

'No, she's in London.'

'How do you know?'

'I met her for a drink. Three or four weeks ago, me and Eric. She asked for you all, for Mum, and she said she was selling the cottage.'

'Really?'

'I guess taking taxis from Ullapool was getting a bit pricy. Or ridiculous.'

'So she's staying in London?'

Louise shrugged. 'To be honest, she didn't seem sure. She said she might put the flat on the market as well. She said a funny thing about the cottage – something about it not being the same one, and she should have known that would be no good.'

'The same as what?'

'I said, what do you mean, and she said she'd wanted another one, but it wasn't for sale. She sort of shrugged and laughed and said, well, that probably wouldn't have been a good idea anyway.'

'The *same* cottage.' Esther thought about this. 'I wonder if she meant – do you remember George?'

'George who?'

'He worked with Dad, and he was a great hill walker, went all over the Alps as well.'

'What,' Louise said, trying to be patient, 'has that got to do with Caroline?'

'He had a cottage near Ullapool, I'm sure it was there. And Caroline and Daniel stayed in it one summer. I'm trying to remember when that would have been.'

'How strange,' Louise said. 'But that would fit. She seemed rather vague and distant, but not – I don't know, I can't quite explain. She seemed softer.'

'*Softer?*'

Louise sat down at the table and laid her phone in front of her. 'It's been easer since Mum's stroke, somehow. She even answers texts. Will I give her a call?'

'If you like. Do you think she could come here on Saturday – it's quite short notice.'

'I told her that now the power of attorney was in place, the house was on the market and we'd be going through it soon. She offered to come – said just let her know.'

'You had quite a conversation then.'

Louise had the phone at her ear, and Esther, moving to the other end of the kitchen to start getting dishes out, could not hear it ringing, but she gathered no one answered. Cheerfully, Louise gave her name and cut the call.

'Left a message,' she said.

'Yes, I heard.'

Louise glanced round the tidy kitchen. 'I meant to ask, but we've hardly seen each other since I got here this morning. Don't you usually have B&Bs by now?'

'I've cancelled them.'

'You shouldn't have done that for me – I wouldn't mind giving you a hand.'

'No, I've cancelled them all.'

Louise took this in. 'Just for May or – '

'For good.'

'You've wound up the business?'

'Not quite. There's all the accounts and the tax and stuff, but I've taken it off all the websites, and taken our own one down. At least, Ross did it for me.'

'When did you decide this?'

'I started thinking about it as soon as Mum went into the nursing home. What with visiting her there, and now the baby coming in August, I don't want to be so tied. Anyway, I've had enough.'

'And Tilly says she's retiring next year?'

'She's had enough too.'

'Right.'

Esther sat opposite Louise. 'Don't you get fed up with the same thing, year after year? You get to a point when you think, if I don't please myself now, when on earth am I going to? But you probably don't look at it like that, you're a writer.'

Louise, for once, was silenced. She felt – what? Outflanked, perhaps.

'I don't know,' she said. 'It's not high art, it's just blah. . . . I churn it out, I don't even think about it much now. That's not quite true, I do try to make it fresh and at least amusing. The chick lit wave has been excellent news for me. It's just, my heroines are getting older, and I've started persuading my publisher that hen-lit is the way to go. I'm not around young women any more, not the way I was when I was in employment full time. You always have to make things up, but I've been wondering lately if I'm making up the wrong things.'

Esther laughed. 'I still think it's funny, the way you write romance when you have no faith in it at all.'

'Who says?' But she grinned, accepting this.

'How is Eric?'

'Fine. Pretty good.'

Esther thought, she is going pink, almost blushing. *Louise!*

'Getting older, it doesn't really change how you feel, does it?' she said, and got up to boil water for pasta.

Louise rested her elbows on the table, leaning her chin on cupped hands. 'No, but maybe it changes what you *think* about what you feel.'

Esther looked at Louise's mobile phone and her own, lying face up on the table, waiting for the beeps that would interrupt their conversation, draw them away to something else – a friend, publisher or agent, one of the children, perhaps the nursing home.

'It's different now, we're much more connected to the world. It wasn't until I started the B&Bs that I felt truly connected to anyone or anything beyond Jack and my family. Well, beyond the school playground, the PTA, the village . . . you know what I mean.'

'It was good for you.'

'Oh yes.'

As if to reinforce Esther's point, Louise's phone starting ringing. It was Caroline. Yes, she would come north, there was nothing to keep her just now. She would fly up on Friday. Louise arranged to meet her at Dyce airport.

'What about Tilly,' Louise asked. 'Will I try her now?'

But Margaret said she couldn't join them – she would see them on Saturday at the house.

'She didn't actually say what she's doing tomorrow. She was very coy about it,' said Louise.

'Oh, it will be one of her internet dates.'

'*What?*'

'Yes, I forgot to say. She's been meeting people for a while. In fact, I think the last one was a bit of a success. This must be the second date.'

Louise started to laugh. 'My God, she's come round after all. She was appalled when *I* suggested it.' She looked at Esther. 'What about you – haven't you fancied trying it?'

Esther flushed. 'That's not funny. There was only ever Jack, you know that. Even when I was furious with him, even when I longed to leave, or kick him out, or whatever. And there *were* moments – weeks even. Ages ago. But – no, I couldn't imagine it.'

'Give it time.'

Esther shook her head. 'It's different for Margaret. She just wants to be married again. I feel I've done that, I would never want another marriage.'

Louise, for a moment, forgot she had had two marriages in the past. She thought of herself as single, always single. Like Caroline, who had never gone through with that marriage to – what was his name? Perhaps they could ask her why not. The old barriers seemed to be breaking down, the boundaries they had set shifting and dissolving.

'Anything is possible,' she said aloud. 'Even now.'

There was a hiss from the saucepan, which must have had a wet patch on its base, as Esther put it on the hotplate.

'I think she will find another man – now that she's made up her mind.' She sat down at the table again with Louise. 'I meant what I said. I really don't want to marry again. But since Mum went into hospital – in fact really since the poor old cat died – I've been so *restless.*'

'The cat?'

'Flossie, my tortoiseshell and white cat. I *told* you.'

'Yes, but – '

'Anyway – apart from half a dozen hens, I don't have any animals now. No children at home, no animals to look after.'

'And no B&Bs?' Louise smiled. 'You'll have to find somebody else to look after now.'

'Right,' Esther said. 'Since apparently that's all I ever do.'

'Sorry, no, I really didn't mean Mum – honestly.'

Esther had reddened. 'Look at me,' she said. 'I finally managed to get something for myself – a career of sorts – a business. But what did I choose?'

'It was successful, wasn't it?'

'Oh yes. But if you examine it from the outside, and I've been trying to do that – all it meant was I cooked and cleaned for a whole lot of other people, not just Jack and the kids. It kept me here, kept me *tethered.*'

Startled, Louise said, 'I thought you liked it, I thought this was the kind of life you wanted? The house, the garden, chickens . . .'

Esther laughed. 'Chickens! I've had a life very like Mum's, even

378

– if you include the chickens – like Granny's. I don't seem to have moved into the modern world the way you did, Caroline did, and *she's* older than all of us. Even Margaret, though she often said she'd rather stay at home, has actually had a proper job for years, teaching. She could have been a head teacher if she'd had the – well, courage maybe, though I don't like to imply anything by that. She said she just liked being with children and other jobs in education are about a lot more than that.'

'She only went on teaching because Mike left,' Louise said. 'She resented him for that more than anything.'

Esther sat down at the table again, picking up her mobile phone and turning it over, upending it, balancing it on its edge.

'I think she had a hard time, don't you? Her mother, Uncle Gordon, and then being just left with us, as if she was a parcel. Not that Mum thought so. She loves her, I sometimes think . . . oh well.'

'We've been over this, we agree,' Louise said. 'But sometimes she's so *passive* you can't help being impatient. If what she wanted so much was having a man, why hasn't she done something about it all these years? Instead of waiting till she's in her fifties?' Louise shrugged. 'Oh well, you know her better than I do, you've always been close.'

'Yes, we have, but it doesn't mean I don't think she's got her faults. Margaret and I sort of fell out only once, a stupid argument, when Jack was made Assistant Director. I said it was unusual for a head teacher to get that sort of job when they'd not been out of teaching, in management already, but he'd done so much to develop the new curriculum, he was the obvious choice. I was really proud of Jack, I could see everyone thought highly of him. But Margaret said, "Oh the *curriculum* – I could see all those changes far enough, the amount of paperwork they generate and all for what? I'm still teaching the way I always have, I can't see it's made any difference to me." And I said – it was a mistake, the moment the words were out I regretted them – I said, surely it *should* have made a difference, didn't she want to change the way she did things, improve all the time? You know Margaret, she didn't shout back at me, as you might have done, or say something cutting, as Caroline might – even Jack, he wouldn't tolerate criticism either. She just closed up like one of those shellfish when you touch them, snapped herself shut and said she'd better be going, she had so much preparation to do for the next day. Just when she'd got her coat on and I was trying to think of something to say that would defuse it, make everything ok again, she said, "If you'd ever had a job, Esther, you would understand." Touché, right enough.'

'That was a bit unfair.'

Esther ignored this, unstoppable now. 'What was *wrong* with me? I followed Jack around, supported him. Once the kids were at school I tried writing wee stories but they weren't very good – I'm no rival, you needn't worry. I was no good at sewing, making things. I decorated, but even that Jack often had to do again. Hopeless. Then one day it came to me, when I was cleaning this place for the umpteenth time, sick of it, sick of myself, I thought, it's big enough for a bloody hotel this house, what on earth made me think living in it all my life would be a good idea? And yet, I *love* Braeside, I can't imagine being anywhere else.

'Then I remembered what Caroline had said when she gave it to us, I hadn't taken it in then, I was so overwhelmed by what was happening, by the whole idea of living here. Make the house pay, she said to me, quite sternly. So there was another voice in my head suddenly, quite a cross voice, saying 'get on with it'. I don't know where that came from. I'd been watching something on TV about women starting their own businesses, maybe it was that. Or maybe it was Kirsty, she said to me when she was choosing her third year subjects, no offence Mum, but I don't want to be like you. I want my own career. That's when I thought, I'm just like my mother, and that was ok in her day, but I'm missing the boat, I have to do something. So I started to research running a guest house, then I went to a *Start Your Own Business Day* for women, in the Treetops Hotel, and that was the best thing of all. Not the workshops, not the stuff they gave you about cash flow and VAT. That was gobbledegook. No, it was the other women. So many of them were like me, kids growing up and feeling redundant and stupid. We all wanted to *do* something, to prove we could.'

'And you did,' Louise said, marvelling at this tirade, that she wouldn't have interrupted even if it had been possible. 'You made a huge success of it.'

'Saved me. Saved my marriage,' Esther said.

Another pause. Louise said, 'Really?' This had not seemed to be a joke.

'Oh yes. I got confident, I wasn't so dependent, and I didn't care so much what he was doing all the time. I thought, if he left me, I'd be ok.'

'*Left?* You and Jack had a really good marriage.'

'I suppose we did. But there was a spell – when it sort of fell apart. Or I did.'

Louise said, 'I wish you'd said. I thought – once, when I was up and you were a bit distant – I wondered. If I hadn't been so preoccupied with my own dreary love life, I might have been more use to you.'

'If you'd been living here, I'd have told you,' Esther admitted. 'I wanted to. I did talk to Margaret, but with Mike . . . oh you know. It was quite difficult. Anyway, it was hard enough keeping it from the kids. They knew of course. Not the details, but they knew their parents were unhappy. With each other.'

'But you got through?'

'Oh yes,' Esther said, tired of talking about it. 'We got through.'

ii

They had eaten Esther's apple crumble and she was making coffee when Caroline noticed the photograph. Esther had forgotten it again, tucked behind the Indian Tree plate, or she might have put it away in a drawer.

Caroline had been sitting with her back to it, but when she put the pudding plates on the draining board and turned to the table, she checked.

'That photograph – ' she said.

'It's you, isn't it?' said Louise, reaching up and taking it down. 'You and Daniel. Esther and I were trying to work out where it was taken.'

Caroline took it from Louise and stood gazing. She was pale anyway, but seemed paler. 'You mean *when*,' she said. 'You must have wondered when it was taken.'

'Well, yes.'

Esther had put the coffee things on a tray. 'I thought we'd go through to the sitting room.'

Caroline brought the photograph with her. When they were sitting down, Esther pouring coffee, she said, 'I've never seen this.'

'How do you mean? You're in it.'

'I know. I've been trying to think. Where did you find it?'

'Among Mum's photographs, in the box room at Harrowden Place.'

Caroline looked stunned. 'I just can't think how it *got* there.' She realised the others were poised, waiting. 'I'd better tell you.'

'Is it Glasgow?'

'Yes, after Daniel came home. He was living in a flat there with two students. One of them – was it Kenny or Joe? One of them was a photography student and one day he caught us just as we were coming out of the door. It must have been shortly before Daniel was killed, because I was never shown it. The only thing I can think is that one of the boys put it amongst his things and when I collected them I didn't see it. I left some of that stuff with Janet when I went to London. Somewhere in her house there must be, unless she threw them out, and I can't see she would, a box of letters she started writing to me when I left Aberdeen for my first job away from here. I stored them in a shoebox, and I gave it to Daniel because he wanted to read them all.'

'How long – how long was he home before – before *we* knew about it?' Esther asked.

'He was in Glasgow a month before he even got in touch with me.'

'Why – '

Caroline leaned forward, the mug of coffee held tightly in both hands. 'It's difficult to explain now – and it's so long ago. But he wasn't the same, at first. He was damaged in some way that I didn't really understand, though in my career, later, I saw people who were like him. He was very fragile. I was terrified he'd leave again, *terrified*. So when he said he didn't want anyone else to know yet, I went along with him. I did try – ' She stopped.

'It must have been awful,' Esther said. 'And yet, were you happy, to have him back?'

'Happy! It's not so simple. I felt – ' She stopped, her colour coming back, her face, they saw, *glowing*. 'I felt complete again.'

More than we realised, Esther thought, and more intense, though I knew they were close. I wonder how much Mum knew – or guessed. This photo was in her box. She must have seen it.

'So his death,' Louise said, 'was the worst possible thing that could happen. Even worse because of *when* it happened.'

Caroline set her mug down on the low table, but she did not answer. What answer could she give, that was not just cliché, what words could she use but those so commonly flung across newspaper reports they had become cheap and devalued – *horror, tragedy, I was devastated* . . .

'Did he go away because of the accident?' Louise asked. 'I was so young at the time, and nobody talked about it. Essie and I did, and Tilly, but secretly. We had the feeling we weren't supposed to. We talked, but we had nothing to go on, no information.'

'It's strange,' Caroline said, 'I've been thinking of this a lot recently. I'm not sure why. Such a series of events now, today, might be so different they wouldn't even happen. I mean, the accident, ok, but if he did go away after, it would be with a mobile phone. He wouldn't send postcards, he would text, and we'd have texted back, and maybe used skype. He wouldn't be cut off from us. He would have come home sooner, because he could never have made himself so isolated.'

'And then,' Louise said, grasping this, 'when he did come home, you'd have known in advance and been keeping in constant touch with texts at least.'

'All the time he was in Glasgow and I was working long shifts in the hospital we had to rely on phone calls and letters. He sent me these little notes. I didn't leave *them* with Janet, I still have them.'

She passed the back of her hand under her eyes, as if – astonishingly – there were tears to brush away.

'Oh Caroline,' Esther sighed, 'what an awful thing. Why haven't you told us before?'

'I'm more interested in why you're able to talk about it now,' Louise said, smiling, pouring more coffee. 'Here, you need this.'

Caroline could only say something trite about Janet's stroke, the passing years, getting older. Since, after all, she had not told them the one thing that really mattered.

'So,' she said, 'we're going to the house tomorrow.'

'Yes, we just have to brace ourselves,' Esther said, 'for a major throw-out.'

'Have you had any offers?'

'Three notes of interest, so they're going to put a closing date on. I said we'd agree that with them on Monday,' Esther said. She picked up the photograph of Daniel and looked at it again. Then she handed it to Caroline.

'It's yours,' she said. 'I was going to show it to Mum, but that doesn't really matter now. You should keep it.'

Esther could not sleep. Usually she managed to fall asleep, and it was staying that way was the problem. She had developed a number of strategies for dealing with this, most of which resulted in her being awake for hours, but occupied in some way by reading, listening to the radio, or counting to five hundred without losing concentration once – the rule was you had to start again if you did. This was more difficult than it sounded.

It had been a clear day and the sky cloudless at night. Darkness seemed slow in coming, even though it was not yet June. Perhaps that was what was wrong. Her mind, clouded by anxiety about finally tackling her parents' house, something she had simply put off worrying about, was now on fire with the day's conversations, with the change in Caroline and the implications of what she had told them.

Why am I bothering, she scolded herself, since it makes no difference now? She swung between pity and annoyance, the irritation felt on behalf of her mother and father, who had been so distressed by Daniel's abandonment and his silence. Janet did not speak about the postcards when they arrived, simply put them in an envelope and sent them on to Caroline. Harry had been watchful, kind, knowing how much she was affected by these unpredictable and random messages, too enigmatic to tell them anything they needed to know. Janet was always looking out for them, and always taken unawares when one came.

Who was there to blame now? Not Daniel, surely, coming home ill and strange; not Caroline, coping with her loss and fear. *He was very fragile. I was terrified he would leave again.* Besides, Caroline was on the verge of old age, so what was the point in blaming her for a young woman's mistake, made more than forty years ago.

We will soon *all* be old, Esther thought. Getting older seemed a kind of disappearing act. Look at her mother, her real life vanishing as she lost her memories and her understanding. Esther was disappearing too; she was not the same girl, the same young woman. When she thought of the Elties, of her childhood, all that seemed to have gone, gradually, year by year, whittled away by all that happens, responsibility and work, and fitting in with others and childbearing and rearing and marriage and compromise and of course illness and death. Worst of all was old age itself, which takes away with ruthless cruelty, so that by the time Esther was her mother's age, there would be nothing left of the little girl who slipped out by the back gate and found Caroline's ring in the lane.

Daniel's Gloves

2013

The first thing they did was open windows. The house was clean, since Esther had arranged for her mother's cleaner to go in once more. It was dusted, the floors had been washed and the kitchen and bathroom gleamed as freshly as they could, given the age of everything in the house, nothing renewed since some time before Harry's death in 1998.

On this mild May morning it smelled of disinfectant and cleaning creams and the kind of aerosol polish Janet would not have allowed near her furniture in the past. Opening windows helped.

Margaret was there first and had put the kettle on.

'How are we going to do this?' she asked as they sat round the kitchen table.

'We could do the easy stuff first,' Esther said. 'If everyone marks what they want to take, and you let me know if you're organising that yourself or if you want me to get a van or something. Andrew and Ross said they'd come and help with heavy stuff if we want them to. I just need to give them a bit of notice.'

'It seems very final. Ruthless,' Margaret protested.

'What else can we do?' Louise took out a pack of coloured sticky-backed notepads. 'We can use these. Just put your name on.'

'What about your children?' Caroline asked. 'Don't they want to choose – ?'

'Anna said she'd like some china, if nobody else wants it, and the good cutlery. For her new house. And the chair in Mum's bedroom, the little velvet-covered one.'

'I've got a list from my lot,' Esther added. 'But I think we four should choose first.'

With a sense of unreality, and then of daring (this was Janet and Harry's house!) they began, faltered, gathered themselves and began again. Caroline was not much use. She didn't want anything, she said, only the letters from Janet if the shoebox turned up. She was found by Margaret reading in the den, a little pile of books beside her that she thought she might just take, if no one else wanted them.

Esther sorted Janet's clothes: a pile for charity, one to throw out, and some good things to keep at Braeside since Janet didn't have much space in the home.

'Oh my God,' Louise exclaimed, coming up from the bottom of what had been Harry's gentleman's wardrobe, that they had thought long since emptied. 'Look what I've found!'

It was Granny's fox furs, tired and balding, but when Louise held them up, their little black eyes gleamed as sardonically as ever.

'Well?' she asked Esther.

'Oh, charity. . . . Goodness. No one's going to *wear* them.'

'The tip, then?'

'I don't think I can bear to do that.'

'I'll do it,' said Louise, not having the same sentimentality about a set of fur rags that had once been animals but so long dead you could hardly care, surely.

Esther went hurriedly next door, finding Margaret in the room she and Louise had once shared. 'How did it go? Did you have a nice evening?'

Margaret looked round, pink with exertion or perhaps excitement. 'Fine. He's a terribly nice man. He's just as embarrassed as I am, about the internet thing.'

'What's his name? Are you seeing him again?'

'Alistair. He's quite old-fashioned in some ways, but I like that. He's been widowed for five years.'

'Is he retired?'

'Not yet. He's a deputy head teacher, so maybe Jack would have known him. I haven't asked yet.'

'How lovely,' Esther said, meaning it, but thinking, thank God I didn't try this, I would absolutely hate to meet anyone Jack knew.

Downstairs, Louise had abandoned any kind of method and was randomly going through drawers and making unhelpful piles of stuff on the floor. She was taking a box of books out into the hall for herself when she thought of the hallstand. She could surely clear that, at least. She wondered what might be in the drawer. Old gloves and scarves, easy to put out to charity or the rubbish bin.

In the den, Caroline looked up with a start when Louise called, 'What lovely gloves. I'll give these to Eric, he feels the cold so much.'

Caroline went into the hall. Louise was wearing black fur-lined gloves, as good as new, like bear paws on her small hands as she held them up.

Caroline went white in a second, drained, swaying on her feet, grasping the newel post at the bottom of the stairs.

Louise was there, holding her. 'Are you all right? What is it?' She put her arm round Caroline. 'Sit down on the stairs for a minute. I thought you were going to faint.'

389

'So did I.'

They sat down side by side, Louise holding Caroline's cold hands in her own, still with the gloves on. Caroline drew one hand out and stroked the gloves.

'They were Daniel's,' she said.

'What's wrong?'

Esther and Margaret were at the top of the stairs.

'Time to stop for coffee – where's that stuff you brought?' Louise said, getting up but shedding the gloves, leaving them in Caroline's lap.

They took coffee and biscuits into the den, where the sun had not yet reached and it was cool. Esther struggled with the gas fire, since Caroline looked so white and ill, and her hands were icy.

'I'm sorry,' she said. 'I can't believe how – very stupid of me. It must be being back in this house, with all of you. It's as if the years just telescoped.'

Louise said, 'They were Daniel's gloves.'

'You gave them to him,' Esther said, remembering, 'when he passed his driving test. Oh.'

'It's not what you think,' Caroline said. She looked from one to the other.

'It wasn't his fault, though,' Margaret said. 'The police were quite clear about that. Didn't the man just walk out in front of you? He was drunk, wasn't he?' She sighed. 'I could never understand why Daniel took it so hard. I mean, at the time, I was young, I didn't understand any of it. But thinking it over – and I often have – why did he have to go away?'

'Because of me.'

'How do you mean?'

This is it, Louise realised. There was always more than we knew. She waited, and for once neither of the others said a word.

Even now, more than forty years later, Caroline hardly knew
how to tell them. If I do, she wondered, will it all go away, will I
be absolved at last? No guarantee. Perhaps even if they couldn't,
she might forgive herself now. If she told them.

'That night,' she said. 'The accident. He wasn't driving. I was.'

They took this in, or tried to. Louise was there first.

'I thought you couldn't drive?'

'I can't. Couldn't. I hadn't even got my provisional licence. The
idea was, Daniel would pass his test, I could practise with him,
get some lessons . . . I hadn't bothered, I'd done nothing about
it. Lazy, I suppose, or just preoccupied with other things. Work,
friends, our new flat, our social life. It was all so good. So *good*.'

'But,' Esther said, 'how could you be driving?'

Caroline stroked the gloves in her lap. 'We came here to collect
my sandals, and he left his gloves behind. It was so cold in that
car – the heater didn't work. His hands – he got those frozen
fingers, dead fingers, it was terribly painful. He wouldn't even try
my gloves. He could be really stubborn about pointless things.'

'So you drove?'

'We swopped over when we were away from the city centre.
I *could* drive, I mean Harry and Daniel had taken me out at
Braeside, on Grandpa's land, several times. I wasn't incapable.
Just – illegal.'

'So were you driving when – ?' Esther was working out the
implications.

'He said, "we'll tell them I was driving, we won't tell them
it was you." We were in enough trouble you see, and though
we knew it hadn't actually been my fault, the police might have
taken a different view if they knew a girl with no driving licence,
no L plates, was driving. He took it on himself, and he never
once, not *once*, reproached or blamed me. Never. But I blamed

myself. When he wanted to go away, how could I stop him? I'm not reliable, I should never have let you drive, he said. I'm not fit to be a doctor. That sort of thing. I couldn't stop him, and I couldn't tell the truth without going against him. I had to let him go.'

She laughed shakily, gripping the gloves.

'How mad it is. I'm seventy, I'm an old woman, and yet when I talk about it, it seems to come back and I'm young again and frightened, and don't know what to do.'

She looked at Margaret, at her cousins, gauging their reaction, seeing only shocked and bewildered and pitying faces.

'Oh poor you,' Louise said. 'Why didn't you tell *us?*'

'We wouldn't have *blamed* you,' Esther said. 'You were young, we all do stupid things when we're young, just mostly we get away with it.'

I didn't, thought Margaret, sorry she had no foolish things in her past, though not this, this was awful.

'So there you are,' Caroline said. 'Better late than never, perhaps, to tell you. Now you know.'

'Did you really think we would blame you – and when Daniel died, blame you for that too?'

'Yes.'

'But we'd *never* – '

'I had promised Daniel I would never tell anyone. I suppose I felt it was my guilty secret we were keeping, so I had no choice. He was doing that for me, so I let him go away on his own. After that – it was so hard to keep anything from Janet, she had an instinct for the truth. The only way was to leave Aberdeen altogether. I tried not to be here more than I had to.'

'So it cut you off from all of us as well,' Esther said.

'You didn't give us the chance to understand,' Margaret said.

'Or forgive,' Louise added.

'It wasn't easy,' Caroline said, though at the time, it had not been as hard as all that. Better to be away, better to create a separate life. It was what she'd wanted all along. Though not without Daniel. She took a deep breath. 'So,' she finished, 'I became a doctor, and work had to be everything. I was glad of it, in the end.'

Her bargain with Daniel, kept all her life, had been driven by guilt, and always guilty, she had stayed alone. That was the punishment. Should she say that to them too? It would sound melodramatic, and as if she had suffered. Well, she had. But guilt works its way into your bones, so you could no longer separate yourself from it if you tried.

They sat on in the den, surrounded by the furniture, books and photographs they had grown up with, in Janet and Harry's familiar space: the worn Turkish rug in front of the fire, the china horses on the mantelpiece, the big blue vase that used always to have flowers in it. Here was the truth at last. Perhaps it had come too late, since it made the past an uncertain picture, blurred and changing by the minute.

'You're back though,' Esther said. 'You're with us now.'

Caroline smiled. 'I suppose so.'

She looked from one to the other. None of the faces judged or censured; there was no accusation. The three little girls sat waiting for the end of the story, and if the end was told already, they did not mind, they were content to wait with her for the next one. Something shifted in her like a stone moving. I'm sorry Dan, she thought, I've told them now, but you don't mind anyway. Perhaps you'd never have minded.

'Don't cry,' Esther said softly. She put her hands over both of Caroline's holding Daniel's gloves tight on her lap.

'Here,' Margaret said, taking a clean folded handkerchief with daisies embroidered in the corner from the pocket of her cardigan. She shook it out, and tenderly, patted the tears away.

'Good grief,' Louise said, 'you've got a proper hanky!'

Margaret flushed. 'I found them on that little shelf at the back of the linen cupboard. 'We got so many from Eileen, a pack every year, and there they were, all the packs that you two never used. I always thought they were pretty, so I decided to take them, or they'd be thrown out.' Offended, she protested, 'I don't know what you're laughing at – you could all have a pack if you wanted them.'

'You keep them,' Louise said. 'We were so ungrateful – poor Eileen, she meant well.'

'At least Caroline's not crying any more,' Esther said. 'Are you?'

'No. No, I'm not. Ridiculous old woman, sorry.'

'You're all right? What a burden to carry.'

They did not really think so, she saw. For them, it was sad, it was a pity, it explained a lot, perhaps, but all they felt was sorrow that she'd cut herself off from them. With a surge of gratitude that was not wholly free from exasperation, she said,

'I thought, if it helped, I might buy the house.'

'*This* house?' Esther said, astonished.

'If you didn't mind waiting till the London flat's sold. I know it seems stupid, I don't need a big place, but it would make things much easier for you. In time, if I sell it, we won't have to throw everything out in such a rush. We can deal with it bit by bit. What do you think?'

'You *are* back,' Esther said again.

'You'd really come here, to Aberdeen, to this house?' Louise asked.

'I might.'

'So we'd be together again,' Margaret said. 'In a way.'

They were silent, and in that silence, for a moment or two, they were not four women on the verge of old age, but three little girls in the sunny garden at Braeside, listening to Caroline, seventeen and adored, reading to them all the long summer afternoon.

The other people stayed in that big room with the noise that went on all the time. Music, loud voices, more music, braying laughter. Where did it come from – oh yes, that thing on the wall. Not cinema. Like that, but smaller. When had she last been to a cinema?

Janet preferred to come back to this room, where her bed was. A bed, anyway. The girl with the blue overall had wheeled her along the corridor, pushing the door open: 'Here we are, Janet, sure you want to be on your own?'

She had a label on her overall that said 'Shona'. 'Thank you, Shona,' Janet said. 'I'm going to read my book.'

Shona had left her in the wheelchair, but the book was on the table on the other side of the pink chair. She'd rather have been in that because it had a nice firm back, upright. She could imagine the soft velvet of the arms beneath her hands, a feeling she liked. She could of course move out of the wheelchair on her own, she wasn't helpless; she could still do things for herself, still walk.

She was tired. Maybe in a wee while. She felt round her neck for the cord with the oval button at the end of it. She was supposed to press it if she needed anything, but they didn't really like you to do that. So she would just wait and in a minute, move by herself, and get her book.

Sometimes she wondered what was keeping Harry, why he didn't come and get her. She missed him, missed the girls, though one of them had been in today, the bonny fair one with the wavy hair, Esther. Good. Esther. She wasn't daft, she knew her own girls. She had loved them equally, never understood those women with favourites among their children. She and Harry agreed about that. Treat them all equally, he said. Of course they weren't all hers, though after a while, Margaret was almost as much their daughter as the others. She was a quiet wee thing, sickly, you had to watch her all the time. That old story of Diana's – Harry had said it might not even be true, she wasn't a woman you could trust. He loved Margaret too, and she had no one else.

Then there were the twins and she had to care for them as if they were her children too, though they never were. She and Harry had called them 'the cuckoos' but only to each other, never of course to anyone else, even her mother, though she wondered if *she* had thought of them like that sometimes. Only, these cuckoos did not edge anyone else out of the nest, they were the ones who flew off, so they should have had a better name for them. Flew off and never came back. There was a reason, but she couldn't think of it right now, it eluded her as so much did if she tried too hard to grasp it. Daniel, she thought, oh poor Daniel. Daniel had died, their bonny boy, and Caroline so lost without him.

Her head nodded forward, uncomfortably. You couldn't rest in this wheelchair, you kept jerking awake. In a while she supposed Shona or the other one – what was she called? – would come and help her get into bed and she could lie there more easily, dreaming.

Soon, the dreams began to appear anyway, would come closer if she kept still and waited, the pictures of the girls on the sideboard, the graduation pictures, the wedding ones, and in the hallway their outdoor shoes flung off when they came in, so that she had to remind them to put them away neatly at the front door. Through the hall and into the big front sitting room that only got warm in summer or at Christmas with a fire on all day, so she came out of that again when she'd looked at the Japanese vases at either end of the mantelshelf, wondering which one had the crack in it, left or right?

Where was everyone? The house was very quiet. Sometimes she went all the way through it without finding any of them, and that was frightening, she didn't like that. Somehow this time she knew somebody was upstairs, though she avoided going up there yet, not wanting to test this, just in case. If she stayed down here, in the kitchen, she could believe they would all come rattling downstairs soon, ready for their tea.

A sound in the corridor broke into the dream – where was she, what on earth was she doing in this little room? She closed her eyes, tight, too tight for the tears to come, because if she waited long enough, she would be back in her house, her real house, and the girls would be there, and Caroline and Daniel home and then at last, his key in the door, his step in the hall, Harry, calling her, as he always did. Janet? I'm home.

Into the Future

1964

'Damn,' Daniel said. 'I've left my gloves in the house.'

They were turning into Queen's Road, joining traffic heading towards the city centre. He took first one long-fingered hand, then the other, off the steering wheel, opening and closing them.

'On the hallstand I think.'

'We're *late*,' Caroline said. 'We're late already – Alison will think we've forgotten.'

'It's ok, the car will warm up in a minute.'

On the steering wheel, his hands were already white with cold.

'I'll turn the fan up, will I?'

A blast of icy air chilled their faces, Daniel's hands.

'That's not a lot of help!' He reached over and turned the fan off. 'I thought there was something wrong with the heater – it's been making wheezy noises.'

'So much for Harry's friend and his bargain car.' Caroline stretched out her own hands in their pink striped woollen gloves. 'Do you want to put mine on? They might stretch enough.'

'Then you'd have freezing hands.'

'It doesn't bother me so much – I don't get dead fingers the way you do. Anyway, I can fold my arms and tuck my hands under, like this.' She demonstrated.

'They'd be too small. It's fine, don't worry.'

'It's because they're pink, isn't it?'

'Of course not.' His cheekbones, despite the cold, turned a little pink themselves, and Caroline smiled to herself.

The car was not heating up. 'It's like sitting in a bloody freezer,' Caroline grumbled, rubbing her nose with one gloved hand. She glanced at Daniel. He couldn't bear cold, and his fingers, that he was flexing again, one hand at a time, were stiff already.

'I could drive for a bit,' Caroline said. 'We keep saying I should get some practice but I never do.'

'You haven't got your provisional licence, even, lazy woman,' Daniel said.

'Och, who would know? We're going out to the Bridge of Don, it's not an area the police are likely to be patrolling, is it? There's nothing there.'

'I'm not stopping in freezing cold to try and put L plates on.'

'Don't then, just pull over. Let me drive. I've got gloves. They wouldn't be much good to you now, you've let your hands get too cold.'

'When we get out the road a bit, ok?'

He stopped as soon as they were clear of the city centre, drawing in to the wide driveway of a house on the suddenly empty road. Caroline hopped out so that they could change places.

'Right,' she said, 'mirror, signal, manoeuvre.'

Daniel stamped up and down on the pavement outside, his arms folded, hands tucked into armpits, then began running on the spot. Caroline leaned across the passenger seat. 'Get *in!*' she shouted. He got in.

'Are you sure you're ok? Do you remember what to do?'

'I'm fine,' she said. She wiggled the gear stick. 'Your teeth are chattering.'

'Never mind that. Put your foot down.'

'What?'

'Clutch.'

'I *know*.'

With a couple of jerks, they were off. After a few moments, having managed to change up the gears without trouble, Caroline began to increase speed.

'This is ok, isn't it?'

'Fine. Just take it easy.' He leaned back. 'You'll be a good driver,' he said. 'You should start practising properly. Get those lessons sorted out.'

'I will.'

'Promise?'

'You and your promises.'

'We don't break them, that's the point.'

'You don't.'

He didn't. If Daniel said, 'I promise,' she believed him.

Successfully, she got them through the last traffic lights before the country road began. 'I'm doing very well, I think.'

'Terrific. Soon as you pass your test, you can do all the driving.'

'Good. You wouldn't mind? I thought men always wanted to be the ones to drive.' She kept her hands firmly on the steering wheel, trying not to grip it too hard. She was quite good at this really. 'Look at Harry and Janet. He always drives, though in my opinion, Janet's actually a better driver.'

'She has more patience,' Daniel said, and she sensed he was grinning, but did not want to turn her head, since the car might not keep going straight ahead if she did.

'It's ridiculous. Even when she takes him to the station or whatever – he drives there and parks, then she has to move over and drive home. There's no discussion about it, no *decision* made.'

They were beyond street lights now and the road stretched unmarked in front of them.

'Put the full beam on – look.' He did it for her. 'If a car comes, you have to dip them.'

'You do it,' Caroline said. 'I can't do that as well as drive.'

'Maybe I take it back about you being a good driver . . .'

'I will eventually. Obviously,' she conceded. 'Sorry. Concentrating. You'd better look out for the sign as well.'

'Where do we turn off for Alison's?'

'It's on the left – something like Cullen, Cullearn. . . . Cullernie, that's it.'

'How far now?'

'I don't know really, she said to look out for a garage on the left. It's about two miles after that.'

'Ok, I'll keep an eye out.'

They drove in silence for a moment, then Caroline, growing confident (it was easy, you just held the steering wheel and kept going), said, 'You remember the book the girls always wanted me to read, *Alice in Wonderland?*'

'Well, you were the one who read it. I tried them with *Treasure Island*, but Margaret was frightened of Long John Silver.'

'She was frightened of everything,' Caroline scoffed. 'She didn't like it when we got to the Queen wanting to cut off everyone's head in *Alice*.'

'What about it, anyway?'

'It's where they got the Elties from, the names they used, Elsie, Lacey and Tilly. The Dormouse's story, though only Tilly really stuck. You know the little girls in the story were supposed to live in a well – a Treacle Well?'

'I don't remember.'

'I often think about the Treacle Well. I mean, it's nonsense, but it's also quite a good metaphor. You're stuck in it, you can't get out, and it seems you never will. It's such an effort – and it makes me think how everything about living in a family is so . . . *sticky.'*

Daniel laughed. 'That's true enough!'

The more Caroline thought about this, the better the analogy. Now that she and Daniel had left home, had their flat, the car, it was as if they were clear at last of the Treacle Well. Already it was the dream, their new life the real one. It occurred to her that this interlude, driving on the dark road, was also dreamlike. It was hard to keep concentrating.

'Is that snow?' Daniel said, peering. A few flakes floated towards the windscreen, landing like wet stars, dissolving slowly.

'It's not much,' Caroline said. 'We can't be far from the turning now.'

'Remind me why we're going to this party?'

'I thought you wanted to!'

'Oh sure. It just seems . . . such a long way to get there. I hope it's worth it.'

'It's all worth it,' Caroline said. 'It's where we're going.'

'To a party?'

'To our future. Our lovely, unknown, brilliant careers, the travelling we'll do, the places we'll see, the people we'll meet.'

'Our lives to come.'

'Yes.'

They were passing houses again, set back from the road in a new estate, a knot of people on a corner, the garage they were looking out for, still open and lit up, a pub with people standing outside, then the road dark again. The snow was falling faster, thickening.

'Put the wipers on.'

'What – where are they?' They fumbled, hands together, his cool but no longer icy, and the wipers came on fast, but made no difference, the snow clouding the air in front of them, so that Caroline could see nothing but snow.

'I can't see,' she said. 'I'd better slow down, eh?'

'It might be icy – don't brake for God's sake. Just ease up a bit with your foot, let the car slow itself.'

'I wish I could see the road better,' she said, leaning forward, peering, her foot resting more heavily on the accelerator than she meant it to, than Daniel had told her to, but she couldn't see, and the car seemed to have a will of its own, she wasn't really in control after all, so when it happened, when the blow came, she was almost prepared for it, though hardly ready, hardly capable of thought at all.

All through her life, in dreams, she drove that dark road again with Daniel by her side, peering through the windscreen at the secret life to come, and longing for it.